SHE WAS A HALF-BREED,
BUT ALL WOMAN . . .

He drew her into his arms, kissed her long
and hard, removed her negligee from her
shoulders, and let it slip to the floor.

"Did you miss me?" he asked.

In the soft lamplight her skin glowed with
a satin sheen. They began caressing one another slowly, softly, until they were both
trembling with passion.

"Take me with you, Hernando," Felicia
murmured.

Hernando laughed. Sounds of the music outside the brothel drifted into the room. Felicia
smiled sadly. She would never be able to spend
her life with Hernando—he was the son of a
wealthy and noble family, and she was hardly
a lady!

THE
TRADERS

Marjel De Lauer

A DELL BOOK

Published by
Dell Publishing Co., Inc.
1 Dag Hammarskjold Plaza
New York, New York 10017

Dell ® TM 681510, Dell Publishing Co., Inc.

ISBN: 0-440-18586-6

Printed in the United States of America
First printing—December 1981

Dedication:
Joe Stacey of *Arizona Highways* magazine;
Two Hawks; Harold Moskovitz of the Associates;
and Kathy Sagan of Dell

THE
TRADERS

CHAPTER ONE

Junior Officer Carlin Napier checked the date in his log. November 28, 1884. It was his twentieth birthday. His second birthday at sea and the second year that there would be no celebration. He closed the log and then, unintentionally, caught a glimpse of his reflection in the glass that housed the charts. He hardly recognized himself—he looked years older. His thin, austere face was bronzed from the wind and the sun; his blond hair was bleached almost white; the scowl on his brow seemed permanent and gave him the look of an older man; and his blue eyes mirrored the disillusionment of a sensitive young man who had not known tenderness or affection for more than two years.

Carlin made his way to the deck and leaned against the railing. The once brightly shined brass oozed green scum and oil, and when he glanced skyward he noticed the rigging hung slack as if to reflect his mood. The English ship, *Vesteen*, had been in the port of Shanghai for more than two weeks, laying off and taking on cargo. Carlin knew that the tall, once gallant, square-rigged, three-masted ship had seen her prime. The Union Jack was still flying from her mizzen-peak, but her wide decks now showed stains and scars of neglect. He no longer loved her, and so he dismissed the thoughts of her deterioration and turned to look at the alluring bay.

November was a beautiful time of year in Shanghai. White clouds billowed on the horizon against a perfect blue sky, and a light breeze rocked the ship with the gentleness of a mother's hand. Ships from many nations filled the harbor. Their colors jolted Carlin's senses and his mind filled with the visions of other ships he had seen in other ports.

For a few moments he longed for his home in Glasgow. In spite of himself, he damned Captain Waldren. Waldren had been his father's friend and a welcomed guest in their home in Glasgow. As a child Carlin had been an avid reader, and after years of listening to the tales of Captain Jonathan Waldren, he longed to visit the mosques of Persia, the Taj Mahal of India, and the Buddhist temples of China. Young Carlin had spent hours sitting on the rocks above the harbor of Glasgow watching the ships sail in and out of the bay and dreaming of what was beyond his visible sea. Waldren had stimulated his imagination with stories of the adventurous and romantic life of a sailor—and he had lied!

At the age of fourteen Carlin persuaded his family to allow him to enter the British Maritime Academy in London. Four years later, when he had been graduated among the top ten in his class, he immediately signed aboard Waldren's ship, the *Vesteen,* as a junior officer.

He remembered that in spite of his expectations and excitement over his prospective adventure at sea, he had been reluctant to leave his family. He would never forget the forlorn expression on his mother's face as she kissed him good-bye; his father had seemed more approving as he extended a firm handshake to his only son. But it was Megan, his eleven-year-old sister, who had really torn his heart. She had wept openly. "I'll never see you again," she sobbed. "I know that you'll never come home if you leave us now!"

"What nonsense, I'll be home before you know it," he had promised, sweeping the child up into his arms. "I'll be gone for two, maybe three, years, but I'll come home. And I'll bring you presents from every port in the world."

The thought of exotic presents quieted the child somewhat. "Promise on my life?" she asked soberly, still unconvinced.

"Promise on your life," Carlin answered, as he kissed away her tears. "You'll be a beautiful young lady when I return, and I'll be horribly jealous because you'll have so many beaux."

"No! I'll never have a boyfriend. You're my only love!"

She had been so serious, so sincere, that Carlin was unable to answer. He gave Megan over to his father's waiting arms, then turned abruptly and walked up the gangplank. It wouldn't do for his family to see him cry. He didn't turn back when he reached the railing— the thought of Megan's sweet, tear-stained face made the parting too difficult.

And so the voyage was begun. Carlin respected Captain Waldren immensely during the first few weeks at sea. Within a very short time, however, his respect turned to disgust. He found out that regardless of how noble a man might seem on shore, once that same man was at sea and the captain of his ship, maritime law gave him total, unquestioning, and absolute power over his subordinates. Unless a man were made of steel and had the morality of a saint, the title of captain could turn him into a despot and a tyrant.

Jonathan Waldren was not made of steel—but of flesh and blood—and if there had ever been any trace of sainthood in his character, Carlin was sure it had been washed out of him years before and had been replaced with the grossest of human failings.

Carlin's thoughts were interrupted by Watkins, the bosun. "Well, are ye feeling any better?"

Carlin acknowledged that he was.

Watkins stood back, hands in his pockets, admiring the young blond giant. The boy was tall, nearly six foot two, and nary an ounce of fat on his strong, lean body. His blue eyes were honest and direct, and his finely chiseled features put Watkins in mind of the statue of David he had seen in the square in Rome years before. "I'm tellin' ye right now, son, I ain't gettin' ye out o' no more fights—nor no more jails. Ye kin git that fine face tore to pieces, 'n I won't lift a finger to help ye. Yer supposed to be an officer 'n a gentleman, 'n that's the way it be!"

Carlin laughed at his friend's seriousness. He had heard the same story a dozen times before. "I'm always a gentleman. It's the others who don't mind their manners."

"Nay—it's that bloody Scottish temper. One day it'll git ye into serious trouble, 'n I won't be thar to help ye."

"Well, I'm not going ashore this afternoon. So that's one day less you'll have to worry about me." Carlin turned his gaze to the sea. "How much longer do you think we'll be in Shanghai?"

"It might be awhile," Watkins replied thoughtfully. "The Chinee hate the British. They don't want to give us none o' their valuable trade goods. Don't blame 'em none neither."

"Why?"

"Mostly I suppose it's because o' the opium we bring in. It's one of Britain's biggest exports to this part o' the world, ye know. The Chinee high 'n mighty muckie-mucks don't like us ruinin' their people," the old salt cackled and lighted his pipe. "Then it don't help none either that the Crown pushes the sale o' India 'n Ceylonese tea 'stead o' Chinee tea!"

Carlin shook his head. The old man had a brilliant mind and was a constant source of knowledge. He, rather than Waldren, should have been the captain of the *Vesteen*. "What if we can't ever find a cargo? Will we stay in this port forever?"

Watkins nodded. "That's an interestin' possibility!"

The men became silent, each lost for a moment in his own thoughts. "Well, I'll be goin' ashore," Watkins said finally. "Is thar anything I can bring back for ye?"

"Bring me back a woman!" Carlin quipped, trying to keep a straight face.

Watkins's response was immediate. "Don't you fun me 'bout such things! Damn ye, Carlin, I'll not be tellin' ye agin—stay away from whores!" the old man stormed. "Ye know bloody well that I would 'ave quit the sea years ago if I hadn't got a dose of the syphilis

13

from a whore. Ye'll never be able to marry a decent woman if ye go to the whores!"

Carlin laughed as the first mate stomped down the gangway mumbling to himself. As curious as he was about having a woman, Watkins had counseled him well on the dangers involved. There had been a time, earlier on in the voyage, when he had accompanied some of the sailors into the dark, smoke-filled whorehouses of France, but he had not found the women appealing. Perhaps the other men had been right when they accused him of being too romantic. Perhaps it was because he was looking for the same beauty and innocence he knew Megan would possess when she became of marriageable age.

There had been one time when he almost lost his virginity. In Bombay the bosun had taken him to an elegant brothel of international acclaim, the Palace d'Amour. The women were young, clean, beautifully gowned—brought and bought from every nation. They were trained to speak in several languages as well as trained in the true art of lovemaking. Carlin, after listening to the stories of the other officers, could hardly contain his passion.

A beautiful Oriental with dark, almond-shaped eyes and a boyish figure caught his attention. She was small and shy, dressed in a sheer white kimono of the finest silk. In the seclusion of her small cubicle she undressed him, washed him, and caressed him until he could hardly contain himself. Then, for some reason, he asked the girl her age. The doll-like creature's eyes widened with surprise, and she replied in singsong English, "I am eleven years, sir."

14

His passion was gone in an instant. "My God! How long have you been here?"

The girl was thoughtful. "Four, perhaps five, years, sir."

"You're the same age as my sister!" Carlin was almost dumbstruck. "You should be playing with dolls!"

"I don't please you, sir?" The girl's lower lip began to quiver.

Carlin pressed a twenty-dollar gold piece into her small hand. "You please me very much—it's this place that doesn't please me!"

He dressed quickly and went downstairs. The thought of an eleven-year-old prostitute, the same age as his dear Megan, made him shudder with disgust. What kind of perverse savagery could induce a man to lay with a child, he wondered? By the time he reached the bar he was blind with rage. It was the first of many brawls in bars and brothels—and the first of many times when Watkins would come to his rescue. He never mentioned the cause of his anger, nor did he ever again join the other men when they went in search of women. Carlin found his physical release in drinking and brawling.

Now, on his twentieth birthday, once again he wondered where the adventures and romance of his boyhood dreams had disappeared. Instead of finding beauty his visions were clouded with memories of slave markets, disease, violence, greed, filth, and every other form of human suffering that tends to make life miserable. It seemed that they were hated by almost everyone in each foreign port.

The two weeks in Shanghai had done nothing to improve his outlook. He felt more despised in China than he had ever felt before, yet he felt a great love for the people. They were, he believed, remembering the young prostitute in India, the most beautiful race of people he had ever seen.

He reached into his pocket and found his well-worn copy of Dana's *Two Years before the Mast*. Lately, Carlin had found his escape from reality in books, and Dana's chronicle had become his favorite. It angered him when he realized how little had really changed in the British merchantman's life since the book had been written. Perhaps one day he would write a book that inspired men to respect one another. The thought of him becoming a crusader amused him for a moment, then he began to read.

The captain appeared suddenly from out of nowhere and stood beside him. "Nothing better to do, Mr. Napier?"

It was a stupid question on a Sunday afternoon when the men were on free time. "No, sir," Carlin replied. "Is there something I can do for you, sir?"

"Yes, Mr. Napier, you can find me some jade or pearls or silk." Waldren spat the words out. "Mr. Napier, you might devise a plan whereby I could send all of these slant-eyed bastards straight to hell!" He turned on his heel and left Carlin standing awkwardly at the rail.

Carlin shook his head in disbelief of the captain's tirade. He would never understand Waldren's attitude that all non-Englishmen, and particularly nonwhites, were "inferior bastards." It was more definite than ever that Waldren had no intentions of sailing for the

New World until he had a full manifest, and that he took the attitude of the Chinese as a personal attack.

Carlin was interrupted by the arrival of a captain from an American frigate anchored starboard of the *Vesteen*. He noted that the man was taller than average with aquiline features and looked well in his uniform. He saluted as the American approached.

"Is your captain aboard?" the American asked.

"Aye, aye, sir. This way, sir." Carlin led him below decks to the captain's quarters. Waldren was annoyed by the interruption, but introductions were made and Carlin returned topside. He didn't feel like reading or writing letters home, so instead he just wandered lazily around the decks enjoying the scenery and the balminess of the weather.

It was more than an hour before Waldren and the American finally appeared. Carlin was surprised to find his captain in an almost jovial mood. The older men shook hands and gave hearty farewells.

That evening when the full crew had returned to the ship Carlin learned that the balance of cargo had been arranged and would be loaded from the small China port of Hwei-Ho three days hence. Before dawn of the next morning the crew was ordered to make preparations to be under sail by the next outgoing tide, and the ship began to spring to life.

Just before the sun cracked up over the horizon, when the sea and sky merged into vivid shades of pinks and blues, the head pump was rigged; the top decks, steerage, and fo'c'sle were washed and scrubbed in a slovenly manner; gear was made fast; the anchor catted and weighed; and the yards

17

trimmed and light sails set. The *Vesteen* was on her way. It was at times like these on the voyage that Carlin trembled with anticipation, as if a voice deep in his heart cried out that perhaps there *was* something better yet to come!

The feeling passed quickly when Carlin overheard scuttlebutt passed between two of the older officers. Hwei-Ho was not a common port for British vessels, and there were no inspection officers there. He overheard words like "coolie labor" and "price-per-head" and suddenly had an uneasy idea of what cargo had been arranged.

In the darkness of the evening of the third day his suspicions were confirmed. Several Chinese junks pulled alongside of the *Vesteen* and Jacob's ladders were thrown over the side. More than a hundred opium-drugged Chinese coolies were carried aboard the ship and thrown roughly into a cargo hold where there was barely enough space to hold twenty men. In the dim lantern light Carlin recognized the American captain. He saw him hand Waldren a large sum of money and then disburse some silver coins among the Chinese pirates who had carried their brothers aboard!

Carlin felt ill. For all Waldren's faults, he had never before stooped to carrying human contraband. Carlin knew very well that when the coolies awakened from their opium-induced dreams of paradise, they would find themselves in a living hell. They were on their way to the New World, not to find a new life of freedom, but to be sold as slave labor for the railroads and the mines.

The first few days of the journey from the China

mainland to the United States were, for the most part, uneventful. The captain changed course for the Hawaiian Islands, instead of the coast of Alaska, and Carlin tried to perform his duties as he had for the past two years. His conversations with Waldren and the other officers were brief and respectful, and he was fair in his dealings with the crew. He tried to ignore the human stench that seeped up from the hold, but it was a losing battle.

By the time they reached the island paradise, Carlin found that he couldn't deafen himself to the cries of agony, or blind himself to the injustice that surrounded him. He was determined to make life more bearable for the Chinese.

While the rest of the crew were enjoying the Hawaiian women, Carlin ventured down into the black hold. He bribed the steward and the cook in order to get extra rations of rice and tea for the starving men, and soon, instead of being just chattel, he began to recognize the coolies as individuals and friends. He discovered that several of them had been educated in missionary schools and spoke English quite well. Carlin was surprised at their bright minds, and the fact that they knew the trap into which they had fallen. Instead of being anxious or resentful, they believed their roles in life had been predestined. In some ways Carlin found himself envying their blind acceptance of life. He wondered if his life had been preordained also.

As they continued on the voyage, Carlin spent as much time as he dared with the Chinese, trying to improve their lot and give them some hope for the future. From the Chinese he learned the teachings of

Confucius, the philosophy of Buddha, and some words of their language. In spite of his fondness for them it was always a relief when one of the coolies died. It meant that he had been released from a living death, and there would be more room and rations for those who survived.

At times, during the solitude of his watch, Carlin prayed that he, too, would somehow be delivered from a world where such cruelty was tolerated and into a land where justice might prevail. He didn't have much hope that his prayers would be answered.

The southern route of the *Vesteen* provided unusually fair weather and fresh winds, and by early April the ship was just a few miles off the coast of California. Carlin noted its beautiful coastline—rugged and clean. Even the ocean water, in contrast to the water off the China coast, was pristine. This New World was still surprisingly untainted by humankind. It reminded him of the clean, uncluttered shores of Scotland. Just one more year, Carlin was relieved to remember, and he would see that beloved shoreline. He would be home surrounded and protected by the love of his family.

One morning, when Carlin came topside to stand his watch, he found the ship becalmed in heavy fog. It gave the *Vesteen* a ghostly attitude, and he felt uneasy. When he was finally able to visit the Chinese, he found them more quiet than usual. Even the tea and biscuits he had arranged to have smuggled to them did not lift the oppressing feeling of impending doom.

"I would like to know more about the Great Teacher, Chang Li," Carlin stated simply, hoping to relieve the tension in the air.

"Not this morning, dear friend," Chang Li answered. "There is a feeling among us that our journey is almost completed."

Carlin stared intently into the face of the old coolie. He sensed that Chang Li spoke the truth, and there was nothing more to be said. He left the hold to continue his watch. It was of little relief when it ended.

At breakfast the crew, overworked and underfed, seemed more restless than usual. Later in the morning, after the fog had burned off, Captain Waldren examined the charts and altered the course of the ship. Nothing seemed to be going according to plan, and Carlin's uneasiness persisted. In the late afternoon they anchored within sight of a small island about two miles from the mainland. Then they waited. Up on deck Carlin watched as two gulls turned on one of their own and began to attack. Within minutes the small victim fell into the sea.

Waldren's attitude seemed the antithesis of Carlin's. He strode over to where the young man was standing and said, "It's good to get rid of the weak! Keeps the species strong!" The captain was relaxed and smiled broadly. "When we've unloaded our cargo, we'll pull into the Santa Barbara harbor for fresh supplies, and then we sail north to San Francisco."

After dinner the captain asked the officers to his quarters for a snifter of brandy. The invitation was totally out of character for Waldren, but Carlin was even more surprised when it was extended to him. It was the first time he had been asked to the captain's quarters socially since the voyage was begun.

The warmth of the room, brightly lighted with lamps, surprised Carlin, as did the cordiality and camaraderie among the men. It was as if, by closing the door, he had entered another world. Armor and masks were removed, and human beings emerged from their hideous disguises.

"You'll enjoy San Francisco," Waldren exclaimed, as he patted Carlin on the shoulder in a sudden burst of affection. "The finest women in the world—outside of London—are berthed in San Francisco. Isn't the sea all I told you it was, son?"

It was the first time in more than two years that the captain had acknowledged him as anything more than a junior officer, and the term *son* caught Carlin completely off guard.

"Aye, aye, sir," he replied haltingly. "Being at sea is an experience I will never forget!"

Totally unaware of the sarcasm in Carlin's reply, Waldren continued, "It'll be your life now. You were a mere boy when we started out, but now you're a man! I'll have some fine things to tell your father when we return home to God's country."

Carlin felt a twinge of bitterness when Waldren mentioned God and bit his tongue to keep from answering. He, too, would have some things to tell his father when he returned home. But they would certainly conflict with anything Waldren might impart. And God willing, Carlin thought, he would never have to leave Glasgow again. The sea—and all those who chose its way of life—could be damned! He took a long drink of brandy and forced a smile onto his face.

After what seemed an eternity, the ship's bell rang, signaling the change of watch. Carlin put his glass down, took proper leave, and walked through the narrow, damp passageway up onto the deck. He breathed deeply of the cold Pacific air, glad to be free of the charade he had been forced to play with the captain.

Early the next afternoon, Carlin watched through his telescope, as a small brigantine approached the *Vesteen*. He informed the captain that she was not flying her colors, and he couldn't identify her. Waldren took the glass and smiled. He had been expecting the brig and ordered a longboat lowered. When the brig had anchored twenty to thirty yards from the *Vesteen*, several of the crewmen rowed Waldren to the ship where he spent the best part of an hour and then returned to the *Vesteen*. He ordered the coolies brought up on deck ten at a time and the task of unloading them was begun. There were only sixty Chinese still left alive.

They offered no resistance. In spite of the extra rations Carlin had been able to secure, they had become cadaverlike creatures. One by one they were brought forward to be lashed together. They were silent and hopeless, almost blinded by the light of day. Carlin recognized Lin 'Tang, Kee Shang, Tien K'Wang—he knew them all by name. He swallowed and tried to keep his revulsion to himself. Occasionally one of the Chinese would give him a sign of recognition—a slight smile or a weak gesture of his hand—and Carlin, in shame, would turn away.

They were loaded like bales of cotton into the cargo net. The net was lowered into the longboat and then the *Vesteen*'s sailors rowed them the short distance to the brigantine, where the net was attached to a boom and the pitiful cargo was taken aboard.

The ghoulish procedure continued until there were

just ten coolies left to be transferred. The venerable Chang Li, who had become Carlin's teacher as well as friend, was among the last group to be brought up on deck. Carlin stood just a few feet from where Chang Li and the rest had been herded. He stared straight ahead past the old man, trying desperately to avoid Chang Li's eyes. He felt that somehow he had betrayed his friend; perhaps he had betrayed the whole human race.

The brigantine experienced difficulties with their boom, and the longboat was delayed in its return to the *Vesteen.* Suddenly there were frantic signals from the nearby ship. Waldren called for the telescope and pointed it toward the southern horizon. Within seconds he recognized the silhouette of an American coast guard vessel. To be boarded by the coast guard and have the human contraband discovered would bring ruin and disgrace to Jonathan Waldren—and he was not about to let that happen. He ordered that the remaining coolies be loaded into the cargo net, and disappeared into the main cabin. Carlin noticed that the longboat was still some distance from the *Vesteen.* Waldren returned almost immediately carrying a fireax and ordered that the net be raised and positioned to drop load. Before anyone realized what he was about to do, with the net swinging wildly above the water, Jonathan Waldren suddenly raised the ax high in the air and chopped free the heavy hawser rope that held the net of human cargo. Ten Chinese, screaming pitifully and clawing the air, dropped into the ocean and sank from sight in a matter of seconds.

It was as if time suddenly stopped aboard the *Ves-*

teen. Even the most hardened of sailors stood in stunned silence. The captain waited calmly until the longboat was alongside and ordered it raised. He then called for the crew to prepare the ship to be under way. As the men began to recover their wits, something snapped in Carlin's mind. Blinded with rage, he attacked the captain. All the cruelty and injustice he had seen and experienced in his term aboard the ship were culminated in that last senseless act of murder. If insanity gave a man strength, Carlin Napier had the strength of a dozen men—and it took that many to restrain him.

Waldren recovered his footing and wiped the blood from his face with his handkerchief.

"Mr. Watkins," he ordered in a trembling voice, "lash Mr. Napier to the railing and bare his back!"

Watkins hesitated for a moment, not able to believe the tragic events that had occurred within the last quarter hour.

"*Now,* Mr. Watkins!" Waldren was more in control and his voice echoed out over the water. Watkins stepped forward and lashed Carlin securely. Then, with his knife, he slashed Carlin's jacket and shirt cleanly down the center and exposed the young officer's back to the captain. Waldren ordered the first mate to bring him his whip.

In a futile attempt to stop the flogging the bosun pointed once again to the horizon. "But, sir," he said, "the American vessel hasn't changed her course! She hasn't seen us! This isn't necessary!"

"One more word, Mr. Watkins, and you'll be alongside Mr. Napier! *Give me my whip!*"

The captain seemed to grow stronger as he lashed Carlin. The young man fell into unconsciousness and still the beating continued. Finally, appearing greatly refreshed, Waldren put the whip aside and called for Watkins to get his log.

"Gentlemen, you will kindly witness this entry into the ship's log," he wrote with great flourish. "On this day, 26 April 1885, Junior Officer Carlin Napier fell overboard. All attempts at resue failed!"

He noticed the sullenness of the men and continued, "May I remind you, gentlemen, that laying hands upon the captain of any ship is mutiny and punishable by death. Mr. Napier's father is one of my best friends, and I feel the need of charity in sparing his feelings. He shall never know of his son's cowardice. Now cut him loose and throw him over the side!"

Carlin regained consciousness in time to hear Waldren's eloquent and vitriolic speech to the crew. He didn't have the strength to move or lift his head. He was barely aware of being unshackled, but he heard Watkins's voice whispering—pleading—for him to swim for his life! Then he felt himself being lifted up and over the railing. He hit the water as if he had been a sack of stones, and his wind was knocked out of him for a few moments. Deeper and deeper into the clear green brine he sank, until he felt his lungs would burst—then the icy water revived him and his sanity returned. He forced himself to the surface and began swimming.

The salt water in his open wounds was agonizing. After a time he rested. The face of the child prostitute and his sister Megan's face kept interchanging in his mind. Somewhere in the distance he imagined that he heard Chang Li calling him to swim on, to meet his destiny. As if some indestructible survival mechanism had been locked into place, Carlin kept swimming toward the shore. The *Vesteen* vanished from sight, darkness fell, and the bare thread of coastline disappeared from his view. Black sea merged into the black night, and still he kept swimming.

Carlin had no idea how long he was in the water, only that he endured long past the time when his human strength gave out. Somehow he reached the shore. The cold water of the Pacific numbed the pain in his body, but he didn't have the strength to drag himself completely out of the surf and onto the dry land. Muscle spasms in his arms and legs kept him awake until dawn. Finally, when the sun was in the midheavens, the heat began to restore him and he was able to crawl up onto the beach above the waterline, where he collapsed into a deep sleep.

It was hours later before Carlin awakened, and still later before the exhaustion passed and he was able to think. One thing he realized for sure was that by some miracle he was still alive. That awareness dimmed when he remembered the captain's words—he had committed mutiny. Regardless of the circumstances, he had attacked his captain, and the punishment for that crime—death—was universal among all the civilized nations of the world. It had been the law in Dana's time and would be the law forever. As far as Carlin was concerned, he was a living dead man—a man without a country. If he were ever recognized, he would be arrested and hung. He could never go home again!

He remembered his last words to his sister. "I promise on your life I will come home!" He could imagine his family's heartbreak when they were told that all attempts at rescue failed. One thing Waldren was right about—better his family believe he had died an honorable death than see him hung as a mutineer. And Megan would survive. She was young and full of heart. She would survive.

Perhaps his Chinese friends had been right and there was such a thing as destiny. Perhaps, he thought, his destiny was here in the New World. The United States.

He pulled himself up and looked around. He didn't know where he was or where he was going, but he did know that he would never go to sea again. Perhaps the tragic events he had witnessed were a blessing in disguise—at least he had been delivered. Carlin was not a man with a great sense of humor, but he laughed in spite of himself. Where had he been delivered to?

A sand hill sloped sharply upward from the beach in an easterly direction. The only vegetation was salt grass and scrub brush. If he were to survive, he reasoned—and it seemed that a power greater than himself wanted him to—he would have to find water.

Carlin had lost his boots and what was left of his shirt and jacket during the long swim. He was clad only in his socks and breeches; a fact he was made keenly aware of as the hot sun beat down upon his pale body. He forced himself to stand erect and explore the area. Each step caused him excruciating pain. Just over the top of the dune he found a higher hill with more vegetation. The most encouraging sight he saw was a ribbonlike cut running north and south just below the horizon. When he reached the spot he was pleased to find that it wasn't just an animal trail, but rather had the look of a well-traveled road. People traveled on roads, and if his luck continued, he might find a stream meandering across the road on its way to the sea. He had no doubt that it would be just a matter of time before he found help.

After some deliberation he decided to walk north. He knew that somewhere to the north lay the city of San Francisco. Had he decided to walk south, instead, he would have found himself in the pueblo of Santa Barbara in less than a hour. But Carlin Napier did have a destiny—one that could only be fulfilled if he traveled north.

By nightfall he had still not found water. Nor had he seen any living creatures, except for birds that flew over the land in grand abundance. He shivered with the coldness of the night, and when he could walk no further, lay down in some brush beside the road in order to sleep. He was sure he would be stronger after he rested for a time.

He did not stir at dawn. Instead, in the heat of the morning he was awakened by a lizard crawling up his bare arm. The beast stared curiously into his face and then jumped to the ground and disappeared into the brush. Carlin tried to rise, but the effort was too much. Dehydration had set in, the world began spinning, and he collapsed.

CHAPTER TWO

As the heavy, mule-drawn freight wagons of Andrew Dundee Fast Freight, Ltd. reached the crest of the ridge, Andrew's son, Hernando, signaled for a rest stop.

"Gawd, Jake," Hernando said, wiping his face with his bandana. "This road gets worse every year. My head feels like it's goin' to fall off my body. We gotta stop for a while!"

Jake Anderson smiled at his tall, dark, good-looking young boss and shook his head. "It ain't the road that's bothering yer head—it's the whiskey ya drank in San Francisco. We'll pull over for a while."

Jake remembered how many times he had had to pull over to the side of the road when Hernando's red-headed father, Andy, had been suffering from the same ailment. The two, father and son, were cut from the same mold. Hernando had his father's build—tall, broad-shouldered, and slim of hip. Liked the ladies, too—just like his old man. But the young man had his Mexican mother's good looks—dark hair, dark eyes and complexion—almost too handsome, Jake thought.

The two friends laughed as they swung down to the ground from the high-seated wagon. They watched as the other drivers drove their wagons off the road and, following the lead of Hernando and Jake, jumped down from their perches to stretch and relax.

The drivers joked about the fact that the journey back from San Francisco always seemed to take a few days longer than the journey up from Santa Fe. They, too, agreed that Hernando was just like his father—business was business—until you got to 'Frisco. That was the city that separated the men from the boys. That city had the best whiskey and the best women in the world. And, if you were man enough to handle the action, you could spend a whole week without neglecting the business—or the whiskey—or the women! Of course it might take a few days to recover, but there was no doubt it was well worth it.

"Jake, did you ever see such soft white thighs on a woman in your life like that Russian woman had?"

It embarrassed the older man that they had shared the same woman. He ignored Hernando's question and walked over to the edge of the bluff. Hernando followed him and sat down on a large flat gray boulder to explore the view. Sensing Jake's mood, Hernando remained quiet for a few minutes. Then, following Jake's gaze, he noticed buzzards circling high in the sky.

"Something dead down there," he stated matter-of-factly.

"Dead or dying," Jake answered.

Circling buzzards were not an uncommon sight to either man, and it was not curiosity, but rather boredom, that led them to investigate further. Jake went back to the wagon and found a pair of army-issue binoculars. He fastened the strap around his neck and scanned the area below, looking this way and that way until something held his attention.

"What is it?" Hernando asked.

"Damned if it don't look like a man! Right down there where the road curves below us."

Hernando took the glasses and adjusted the lenses. "It is a man! Or leastwise it's a body. Why don't you get the wagons moving? I can make better time if I go straight down the hill."

He walked back to the wagon with Jake and signaled for the men to mount up. Then he picked up a canteen from the floorboard and started leisurely down the bluff. If the man were dead, time wouldn't be important, Hernando reasoned, and if he were still alive, he would last for a few minutes more.

The direct route down the hill was much steeper than it looked, and Hernando fell several times before he reached the prostrate form of Carlin Napier. He swore under his breath about the inconvenience and the fact that the jog down the mountain had made his headache worse. Why did Jake have to find the damned body anyway?

Hernando had seen men killed with guns and knives, and he'd seen them meet their maker in barroom brawls, but he was not prepared to see the angry, red, festering whip marks on Carlin's back. The man was still alive but was burning with fever and very close to death. Hernando was not a Good Samaritan; nonetheless, he took off his shirt, dampened it with water from the canteen, and laid it gently over Carlin's unconscious form.

"Good Gawd a'mighty," he murmured. "What a mess!"

It took Jake almost fifteen minutes to guide the freight caravan down the steep winding grade to the spot where Hernando stood waiting.

"Is he alive?" Jake asked.

"Just barely. Better give me some whiskey to clean out the wounds." Hernando raised his shirt so that Jake could see how brutally the man had been beaten. "Then give me some more water—we gotta cool down his fever."

"I've seen men beat worse than that," the old Indian fighter grumbled—but he couldn't recall when he'd seen worse—" 'n they all survived!"

Jake reached under the seat and pulled out a small keg of whiskey and another canteen, then returned to Hernando and pushed him out of the way. "I done this sort o' thing before," he acknowledged, forcing some water down the man's throat. The other teamsters grumbled as they watched Jake pour the whiskey over Carlin's raw flesh.

"Waste o' good drinkin' stock if yah ask me," one of the drivers commented.

"He's beat near to death," another observed quietly. "Wonder what a man would have to do to be cut up like that?"

Hernando silenced them with a glance. "Better cover those wounds with some clean axle grease. It'll help keep down the infection," he instructed Jake, "and see if one of the men has a clean shirt while I make room in the back of the wagon. We'll find someone to take care of him in Santa Barbara."

After a few minutes Jake returned leading one of the drivers. "Piggy's got a clean shirt, but he won't give it to me."

"It's brand new—I bought it in 'Frisco," Piggy protested.

"Get the damned shirt!" Hernando commanded, trying to remain cool. "I'll give you two shirts when we get to Santa Fe."

"New ones?" bargained Piggy.

"New ones," Hernando agreed.

Jake helped Hernando make space in the wagon, then dressed the wounds with axle grease the best way he could. It took both men to get Carlin into Piggy's new shirt, then they lifted him as gently as possible into the makeshift bed. They forced more water through his parched lips, dampened his clothes to try to cool him down, and then continued on the last leg of their journey to the pueblo of Santa Barbara.

The caravan usually stayed over in the picturesque village for a few days in order to rest the mules and men—in that order—before they began the long journey inland across the great desert into Arizona Territory, then on into New Mexico Territory, and finally to headquarters in Santa Fe.

The lush greenery of the pueblo, and the splashes of bright red-tiled roofs which capped the glistening white adobe homes, was a sharp contrast from the colorless, desolate wasteland that surrounded the small coastal settlement.

Although it couldn't compare with the excitement and glamour of San Francisco, the stop in Santa Barbara would be a fiesta time for the drivers—with friends, whiskey, and women. For Hernando there was something more special. Dolores and Felicia awaited him in Santa Barbara.

As usual it was the children who spread the news

that the freighters were on their way to the pueblo. The townspeople, always anxious to see the free-spending teamsters, began to prepare a welcome for them an hour before the wagons arrived.

There were no customers in the cantina when Manuel Garcia heard the news. He quickly locked the door, pushed back one of the tables, rolled up the well-worn rug, lit a coal-oil lantern, and opened the hidden trapdoor that led to the deep, dark cellar below. He climbed down the rickety ladder and, holding the lantern high over his head in order to see, quickly found four treasured bottles of Amerella Espanole, a sour cherry brandy imported from Spain. It was a favorite of Hernando Dundee. Manuel had paid a small ransom for the entire case, and these precious four bottles were all that was left. Hernando would, and could, afford to pay any price Manuel asked for the rare liquor. He managed, with great difficulty, to get the Amerella, the lantern, and himself back up the ladder; closed the trapdoor; replaced the carpet; pushed the table back into position; and, once again ready for business, unlocked the door. After he had carefully washed and dried the dusty bottles, he pulled himself up to his entire height of five feet two inches and waited for his customers.

The widow Castiaga was in town shopping when she heard the news. She paid her bill, found her driver, and ordered him to deliver her to the hacienda as quickly as possible.

Bonnet askew, skirts flying, Maria Castiaga raced from room to room, calling her daughter. "Dolores! Hernando is coming!"

"Mother, you're screaming," Dolores scolded from

her reclining position on a lounge in the patio. "It's not good for your heart to be so excited."

"But Hernando is coming! I want you to be beautiful. You must wash your hair."

Dolores lowered her eyes and stared at Maria through half-closed lids, "I'm always beautiful, and Fresia washed my hair this morning."

"But Dolores, it would please me so if you and Hernando could be married. I won't be around forever, you know," Maria protested, as she tried to catch her breath. Then she smiled and said, "Your father and I talked of this when you were first born. We had no better friends in the world than Andrew and Isabella Dundee. And Hernando was just as handsome when he was a small boy as he is today. When you were born—such a beautiful baby girl—we knew that when you became of age you and Hernando were destined to be married. To combine the great families of Ernesto Castiaga and Andrew Dundee has always been my dream."

"Oh, Mama, you're such a romantic!"

"Who will take care of you when I'm gone if you don't marry Hernando?" Maria cried in anguish.

"But I will marry Hernando. He just doesn't realize it yet." Dolores tried to reassure her distressed mother. "And we will live here in Santa Barbara, in this house, and I will be very, very rich and give parties every night!"

Maria shook her head sadly. While it was true that Dolores was one of the most beautiful women in California, it was also true that she was selfish beyond reason. "When you marry, you will live in a place of your husband's choosing. Hernando would never be happy here, nor would he tolerate such extravagance as a party every night!"

Dolores laughed. "My husband will do everything in the world to please me. I will not tolerate anything less!"

Maria felt a sharp pain run down her arm and sat very still until it passed. Then she walked slowly into the cool adobe hacienda. She knew better than to try to argue with Dolores.

Felicia Montez was seated at the bar having a drink with the banker, Hedrick Norton, when her black maid brought news of Hernando's expected arrival. She clapped her hands together. "Oh, Clissa!" she cried. "How wonderful! Start heating the water for my bath!"

Norton stared at Felicia's reflection in the mirror behind the bar. Her long raven-black hair fell loosely over her shoulders, framing her small heart-shaped face and emphasizing her pale skin. She belonged in another, less complicated time. Had she lived in Spain, she might have married a nobleman. He could dress her in the finest gowns, but she would still have the look of a savage. Her obvious pleasure at seeing Hernando again annoyed him even more than her constant refusal to wear her hair up off her neck in a more civilized fashion. "I suppose you'll 'service' him yourself?" he asked, sarcastically.

"No, Hedrick," she replied, gently. "I don't service anyone anymore—I have girls for that. I make love to Hernando. There's a difference." She touched his face softly and spoke with tenderness. "I'm grateful to you—but I adore him. He's the greatest lover in the world!"

Norton flushed with embarrassment. "When are you going to realize that you're a very beautiful woman?" he asked. "You're also a very wealthy woman, thanks to me, and you're still young enough to leave this place and start a new life."

Touched by his genuine concern, Felicia leaned over and put her arms around his neck. "But, Hedrick, when are you going to realize that I like my way of life? Now run along and let me get ready."

The banker tried to regain his composure, realizing that he had much to learn about women. He kissed Felicia tenderly on the forehead, placed some coins on the bar, picked up his hat and cane, and left the brothel by the rear exit.

Felicia sighed as she watched him leave. She did owe him a great deal—and perhaps one day she would be able to repay him—but now Hernando was coming. She directed Clissa to fill her tub. "And don't forget to use the lilac bath salts," she reminded the girl.

In the leisure of her perfumed bath Felicia thought about what Norton had said. Although she would never admit it to him, nor to any other living soul, she had always hated her profession as prostitute and madam. But what else could she do? She knew no other way of life. Even if it were possible for her to assume another identity in another town—just what could she do? And where could she go where she wouldn't eventually be recognized?

When she finished bathing, Clissa rubbed her dry with a large, soft linen towel, then massaged her pale body with warm almond oil. "You don't seem happy, missy. Why you not happy when yo' man's a-comin'?"

"I wish I knew, Clissa," Felicia answered in her soft husky voice. "Sometimes I just don't understand myself." Then she arose, slipped into a sheer chiffon negligee, and reminded Clissa to scrub the tub meticulously. Hernando would want to bathe before they made love. She pulled a small chair up next to the window in order to watch for her lover. Clissa could begin heating more water when she saw Hernando enter Manuel's cantina just across the way.

How strange, Felicia thought, that she loved *this* man. She knew him so well that she could sense his moods and know what he was thinking even before he knew himself. She was aware of exactly how long it would take him to drink and joke with the men, then join her, just by the quickness of his stride. Perhaps it was not so strange, she smiled. After all, they had been lovers for more than five years!

Mama Ignacia began to grow impatient as she waited on the only two customers in her bazaar—a British sea captain and his first officer. In spite of her age and immense size, Mama Ignacia usually enjoyed flirting with strangers, but she didn't like these arrogant Englishmen. From their conversation she knew that they were annoyed with the delays in getting supplies they needed; and the captain made it quite clear that he didn't like the tiny pueblo nor the dark-skinned inhabitants.

He inquired about the sudden activity in the streets. "That's the fastest I've seen anyone move in this town since we arrived. What's going on?"

"Freight wagons returning from San Francisco, senor," she informed him politely. "The wagons of my friends Andrew Dundee and his son Hernando. There will be a grand fiesta tonight—and tomorrow—and tomorrow night!"

"I trust this will not interfere with us getting our ship supplies?" The captain was obviously annoyed.

Mama Ignacia didn't like being intimidated by anyone, and especially by this cold-eyed gringo. "I'm afraid it may well interfere, senor. If you will excuse me, I cannot take up any more of your valuable time nor can I take any more of your rudeness. I must close the bazaar so that I can go home and rest, and prepare myself for the fiesta tonight!"

With no more explanation Mama escorted the irate captain and his embarrassed first officer to the door and out onto the cobbled street. "You may give me the rest of your instructions the day after tomorrow, or you can pick up more supplies when you reach San Francisco. Until then I suggest you try to enjoy yourselves at the cantina—it's right down the street."

She bolted the door, drew the blinds, and locked her money in the safe. When she was sure that the Englishmen had left, she let herself out the front door; and although she weighed more than 200 pounds, marched down the street with the grace and dignity of the grande dame that she was.

It took her almost an hour to walk home, and when she arrived in front of her *casita*, Hernando was just

40

pulling up in his wagon. He reined the mules to a halt, waved his hat, and bowed low in an exaggerated salute. "Mama Ignacia! How is the most beautiful woman in Santa Barbara?"

Mama flushed with pleasure. "To what or to whom do I owe this honor, Hernando? I usually don't see that handsome face until it is thoroughly unrecognizable from too much wine at the cantina. You look completely sober. Are you well?"

"Yes, Mamacita, but I have a very good friend of mine in the back of the wagon who is not so well." He didn't like lying to her, but it saved the time of an explanation. He would tell her the truth once they had attended to the stranger.

"As a matter of fact, he may be too ill to continue the journey—but I would be pleased to pay you for your time and board if you could care for him for a few days—or until he is well enough to be on his way."

Mama Ignacia stared at Hernando suspiciously—she was always a little wary when he was so charming. But she opened her heart as easily as she opened her door, and when she saw the unconscious Carlin in the back of the wagon, demanded that Hernando and Jake carry him into the house immediately. She called for her Indian servant girl to heat some water while she made sure the young stranger was comfortable.

"*Dios mío*, he doesn't look well at all! What has happened to him?" she demanded. Then before either of the men could answer, she noticed that the young man had no boots and that his breeches were the same as the English seamen's who had been in her

41

bazaar. "Hernando, I think there is more to this story than you are telling me. Who is this man who is your very good friend?"

Hernando glanced nervously at Jake. "We will tell you the entire story later, Mamacita. Right now we must tend to the mules."

They rushed from the house before she could question them further and headed the wagon down the street toward the freight dock. In their haste they almost ran down the British captain and his officer. Waldren grabbed the halter of the lead mule and abruptly brought the team to a halt, lashing out at Hernando's stupidity.

"You damned greaser! If I had my whip, I'd flog you to death," Waldren screamed, totally out of control.

Hernando grabbed the whip from Jake's hand. "Let go of that mule or I'll skin you alive!"

For the first time in many years, Waldren knew he had been bested and released his grip on the halter. He spat on the ground, then turned quickly, and followed by his young officer—who had paled considerably during the altercation—proceeded rapidly down the street.

"Did you notice their trousers?" Hernando asked, still shaking with anger. "I think I know now what happened to our friend. He's a sailor and he's been flogged!"

"Prob'ly a cat-o'-nine-tails," Jake agreed knowingly. "Bet he jumped ship—Lord knows how he got to where we found 'im!"

"It's none of our concern. He can stay at Mama Ignacia's until he's well, then he can do as he damned pleases."

Jake knew from the tone of Hernando's voice that the subject was closed. They drove on to the dock where they tended to the manifests and animals, then headed for Manuel's cantina.

Most of the other drivers were already at the bar and made room for Hernando and Jake. Manuel, anticipating their arrival, had the Amerella waiting. After a few drinks, Jake nudged Hernando and motioned toward one of the tables. Hernando turned and stared directly into the eyes of Captain Jonathan Waldren, the man he had almost run down, but the Englishman appeared drunk and apparently didn't recognize him. The brandy seemed to turn bitter in Hernando's mouth. He didn't like the man. He took some gold coins from his pouch, put them on the bar to pay for the drinks, and took his leave.

It was late afternoon and Hernando was glad to be by himself at last. Something was bothering him, and he wasn't sure what it was. His headache was gone. He decided to take a walk rather than go directly to Felicia as he usually did. He wanted time to think. It had to do with the young man they had found. Had he jumped ship? Why had he been so brutally flogged? There were too many questions, Hernando thought, and too much responsibility in saving another man's life.

Ah! That was it! That was what was bothering him. He suddenly remembered the stories his father had told him when he was a boy. When his father was a young man living with the Indians in the great Rock-

43

ies, he saved the life of a young brave. The Indians believed that if you saved another man's life, you had to assume the responsibility for that life. The story had made a tremendous impression on Hernando, because that brave, Carlos, was still with the Dundee household!

Responsibility was fine, Hernando mused, as long as it didn't belong to him. Oh, it was all right to be responsible to one's immediate family—or to one's business—or in a limited way to the men one employed. That's where you drew the line. Hernando gloried in being free and unemcumbered. That was why, at the age of twenty-six and in spite of his mother's pleading, he had not married. And if he didn't want the responsibility of his own wife and family, he certainly had no intentions of becoming responsible for a perfect stranger.

He would pay Mama Ignacia to care for the sailor until he was well enough to be on his own—and that would be the end of it.

Without realizing it, Hernando had walked to the beach at the edge of the pueblo. The sun was just beginning to set and the sky was ablaze with gold, orange, and lavender. The high, steep mountains, which cupped the village to the east, reflected the colors of the sunset and added deep purples and dozens of shades of violet. To anyone but Hernando it would have been a magnificent sight, but he was more impressed with the full breast or well-shaped ankle of a passionate woman than with the beauty of nature.

He thought of Felicia. It was stupid to stand here in the damp sand when he could be resting in a comfortable bed with the irresistible half-breed. He stopped by the loading dock and rummaged through the goods at the back of his wagon to find the gift he had bought for her in San Francisco. Then, feeling better than he had felt since he had begun his journey home, he walked quickly up the street toward the small adobe house of pleasure.

Felicia had watched Hernando leave the cantina and was surprised when, instead of crossing the street to join her as he always had before, he walked briskly in the opposite direction. By the time he finally arrived at the brothel she was frantic with worry. At the most they saw each other a dozen times a year, but that short time with him meant everything in the world to her. Even those few times when he was too tired to make love, she was content to lay next to him and watch him while he slept. There was magic between them—something she found with no other man.

She recognized the sound of his footsteps in the hallway and rushed to the door. They stared at one another for a moment, then he drew her into his arms, kissed her long and hard, removed her negligee from her shoulders, and let it slip to the floor. He lifted her up and carried her to the bed.

"Did you miss me?" he asked, as he placed her gift on the dresser.

"Only if you've brought me something wonderful!" she replied in a coquettish tone of voice as she watched him undress and step into the tub at the far end of the room.

"I brought you a box of toads—they can swim around in this ice water when I'm finished," he teased, sloshing some of the water out of the small vessel as he washed. In less than a minute he was through and drying himself. He walked over to her and pulled the sheet away so that he could enjoy the pleasure of seeing her naked body. In the soft lamplight her skin glowed with a satinlike sheen—her figure was flawless. It pleased him that she had the face of a Madonna and the soul of a whore; it also pleased him that she enjoyed their lovemaking as much as he did. There was no pretended climax with Felicia!

She cupped her full breasts in her hands, pushing them upward toward him as an offering, totally and shamelessly delighting in his lust.

He accepted, kissing her dark nipples tenderly, eagerly, as a thirsty man accepts water. They began caressing one another slowly, softly—until they were both trembling with passion. Their climax came quickly—spontaneously—and in harmony. They clung together afterward, each knowing that they had been completely fulfilled, and knowing they were more than lovers.

"Take me with you, Hernando," Felicia murmured, finally breaking the silence.

Hernando laughed. Sounds of the music from the mariachis outside the brothel drifted into the room through the open window, signaling that the crowd had already begun to gather for the fiesta. Felicia rolled a cigarette and lighted it for Hernando, then stood up and stretched like a cat. "You'll be going to the fiesta?"

"Of course."

"Why don't you stay here?"

"Why don't you come with me? If you'd run off with me, surely you could come with me to the fiesta."

Felicia smiled sadly, once again aware of the reality of her situation. She would never be able to spend her life with Hernando—she was a prostitute, and he was the son of a wealthy and noble family. She crawled back into the bed and began to nuzzle his neck.

With other women, Hernando made love, paid them, and was on his way. With Felicia, aware of her adoration for him, he preferred to linger. He told her about the stranger he found, and his suspicions that the young man was a British seaman who had probably jumped ship. Then, abruptly, he changed the subject. "You know," he whispered, feeling himself aroused once more by her tangy smell, "in all these years—I've never seen you in a dress! Why don't you open your present before I make love to you again and find myself too weak to enjoy the dancing?"

Her face lighted up like a child's face, and she sprang from the bed to fetch her gift. She untied the ribbon carefully and opened the box. She gasped with pleasure as she withdrew a stunning blue silk gown. "It's the most beautiful dress I've ever seen!" she exclaimed, holding it up and dancing around the room.

"Then come over here and thank me properly!" He pulled her down on the bed and they made love again.

And then, reluctantly, he washed himself off and dressed. He placed a twenty-dollar gold piece on the dresser, blew Felicia a kiss, and left the room.

Hernando made his way through the gala crowd to the stables where he hired a buggy and directed the driver to take him to the Hacienda de Castiaga.

Maria Castiaga could hardly contain her pleasure when the handsome freighter finally arrived. He was more than an hour late, and their dinner was probably ruined—but she could forgive him anything. Maria and Hernando's mother, Isabella, had been friends since childhood, and had secretly planned for years that their families would become united through the marriage of Hernando to Dolores. She hoped she would live long enough to see their dreams come true. "Dolores," the widow called cheerfully up the stairs, "come down immediately. It's not proper to keep a gentleman waiting!"

"Why not?" Dolores called back. "He's kept me waiting—he should have been here hours ago! Besides, he's no gentleman."

Hernando laughed, realizing that part of Dolores's rage was because she had been unable to seduce him. He watched with amusement as she glided regally down the broad stairway—head and shoulders set at a haughty and appealing angle. She would make some man an exquisite-looking wife, he thought. If only she had Felicia's sense of humor and light touch, and her mother's generous heart, he might find her enchanting. "Dolores, you're even more attractive when you're angry!"

The petulant girl ignored his flattery and, taking his arm, fairly pulled him into the dining room. "I'm starving—let's have dinner before the food rots on the table!"

It was past midnight, and the fiesta was well under way, before Hernando and the Castiagas joined the merry Santa Barbarans. They drank wine, sang songs, and danced until dawn. Finally exhausted, Hernando hired a group of mariachi players to serenade them on the way home.

The carriage rocked slowly and gently over the cobblestones while the musicians followed, singing their plaintive love songs. When she was sure her mother was asleep, Dolores moved closer to Hernando and proceeded to kiss him passionately. At the same time she took his hands and cupped them over her firm, full breasts. "Hernando—*Querido!* Make love to me!" she whispered, breathlessly.

He clasped her hands firmly in his and laughed. "You've had too much to drink, my pretty senorita. Now just lay your head on my shoulder and behave yourself—we'll be at the hacienda soon."

She pulled herself free and slapped him with as much fury as she could muster. "I hate you!"

"No, little one, you don't hate me. But you don't love me either. Now take care or you'll wake your mother; and if you do that, I'll turn you over my knee and you won't be able to sit down for a week." It surprised Hernando that he found his passion for this woman so easy to contain. Most men would be bowing at her feet. And under other circumstances he was sure that she would be marvelous to have. But she was still a virgin, and if they did make love he would have a responsibility toward her. In spite of his family's wishes, he wasn't ready for a total commitment.

One day soon the railroads would eliminate the need for the Dundee's freight lines to San Francisco and that would be the end of his visits to Santa Barbara. Dolores would eventually grow tired of waiting for him and marry someone else. She was ripe for the picking—and not every man would be so gallant. He wondered for a moment about his reluctance to marry and then they were home.

After he had seen the women to their door and had given the mariachi players a bonus, he instructed the driver to take him back to Felicia. In spite of himself he found that Dolores had aroused his passion, and there was no sense in letting it go to waste.

Mama Ignacia missed the fiesta. She had been up most of the night tending to the misery of young Carlin, and she was waiting on the porch when Hernando finally arrived.

"Good morning, Hernando," she said, almost too sweetly. "I've been waiting breakfast for you. Let's go into the dining room."

Hernando knew her well enough to know that whenever Mama Ignacia was really angry, she spoke sweetly and always prepared her victim by serving delicious food. He followed her into the room, sat down to be served, and waited for the ax to fall. When he had finished his second cup of coffee, she came directly to the point.

"I want to know exactly what your plans are for Carlin Napier."

"Who is Carlin Napier?"

"Don't you remember?" she replied, sarcastically. "Your very good friend—whom I've been nursing all night—is Carlin Napier! Now tell me your plans."

Hernando grinned sheepishly. He knew by the slow, deep tone of her voice that she expected an honest answer. He also knew that he was in trouble. After a few minutes he explained the circumstances under which they had found the young man.

Mama Ignacia was thoughtful for a few moments,

then replied, "And what do you intend to do with him now?"

"I don't intend to do anything with him," Hernando stated, quite impatiently. "I was hoping that you might take care of him until he's on his feet, then let him go on his way. I'll pay you well for your trouble."

"No, Hernando," Mama Ignacia now spoke even more slowly and softly. "This is a situation you cannot buy your way out of. Mr. Napier was conscious for several hours last night and was able to tell me everything that has happened to him for the past two years. Believe me, it was not a pleasant story to hear. At this moment, less than a mile from our shore, there is a British ship anchored." She paused to moisten her throat with a large swallow of red wine. "Your friend is from that ship—and if he is discovered, he will be hung."

"He is a mutineer?"

"In a manner of speaking, yes. But I'm sure that in the eyes of God, he is an innocent victim," Mama Ignacia lowered her eyes. "He witnessed a terrible murder and attacked his captain. The beast of an Englishman had him flogged, then thrown overboard to become food for the sharks."

Hernando recalled the British captain's words of the day before when he had grabbed the mules' halter. *If I had my whip, I'd flog you to death!* There was no doubt in his mind that Mama Ignacia was right—the man was a beast and capable of murder with very little provocation.

"What do you want me to do?"

"I think that for some reason God has spared this

51

man's life and placed him in your hands. I know he isn't safe here; this is a small community and people gossip. If the men from the ship hear rumors about a dying man found on the beach—a man who's been flogged—they'll know he's alive and will search for him."

"And?" Hernando asked, thinking of Carlos, his father's Indian ward.

"And so, you must take him with you to Santa Fe. I think it would be wise for you to leave quickly. After all, you have saved his life. Now you must care for him. He might be safe if he's far enough away from the sea."

"Damn it!" Hernando muttered under his breath. He knew she would not accept his protest. The teamsters would not be happy about having to leave so soon, but he realized that Mama Ignacia was right. At least, for the time being, this man had become his responsibility.

Mama Ignacia patted his arm. "Do you know that he is from the same town your father was born in?"

"Glasgow?"

"Yes, Glasgow. Until now I thought your father was teasing me about that name. Who in the world would give a town such an ugly-sounding name? A town should have a beautiful name—like Sevilla or Granada or San Diego! But Glasgow—what a terrible sound!"

She was happier now, and Hernando knew the decision had been made.

Mama sensed his gloom. "Cheer up, *muchacho*! He may even be a relative of yours!"

CHAPTER THREE

The journey from Santa Barbara to Tucson, in Arizona Territory, was more than 800 miles through the torturous and barren wasteland of the Great Sonoran Desert. This year, following a seven-year drought, there had been an overabundance of rain throughout the winter months, and the desert bloomed as it had not bloomed for a hundred years. The May weather was still cool enough for travel during the day, although the freighters made their best time in the early morning or at dusk.

Carlin's introduction to the Territory was visually spectacular. Nature had dipped her brushes into a cosmic paint-pot and splashed the usually dreary landscape with a myriad of color. Golden poppies and fuchsia verbena covered the gray-white sand dunes like delicately embroidered Indian beads. There were vast expanses of ocotillo cactus—their spiny tendrils filled with brilliant red blossoms—and almost every arroyo gave birth to yellow-blooming palo verde trees and white-belled yucca. Jake pointed out barrel cactus and cholla, bursting forth with flowers in shades of orange and pink.

"It's like a garden of Eden!" Carlin exclaimed, awe-struck by the beauty of the lush vegetation.

Hernando wiped the perspiration from his brow and stared at the naive young Scotsman. "Well, my friend, that garden can turn into a hellhole! In the summer temperatures can reach 120 degrees. A man can die of thirst in a matter of hours. Most of the water in this stinking desert is contaminated, and the rattle-snakes get so big they can jump ten feet to bite a man."

"Still, it's clean and free," Carlin protested, remembering the filthy and overcrowded cities of Europe, India, and China. "And if it could be irrigated properly, men could probably produce enough food to feed the poor and hungry of the entire world."

"The way I see it," Hernando replied, not bothering to hide the sarcasm in his voice, "is that the Lord made two kinds of people—rich ones and poor ones. And I ain't about to interfere with the Lord's plan. Let the hungry ones feed themselves—that's what life's all about." He rolled a cigarette thoughtfully, then continued as if to make his point. "Look at you. You got to admit you were a damned fool to stick yer neck out fer some low-life Chinamen. Now you got no place to go, and if you want the truth, them damned slant-eyes would end up bein' murdered or workin' themselves to death on the railroads or in the mines. You went against the Lord's plan."

Carlin realized it was useless for him to try to explain his feelings. He remained silent, trying to enjoy the scenery and thankful to be alive.

Jake listened to the conversations between the two men with amusement. They were as different in philosophy as they were in looks. Both liked to drink and fight—but there the similarity ended. Carlin was a poet and a dreamer, a romantic in the true sense of the word; Hernando was a skeptic and a realist; and neither aware of nor concerned with what happened to his fellow man. He spat a stream of black tobacco juice out of the side of his mouth. "Sometimes I wonder where ye came from, Hernando," Jake ventured. "Yah ought to look at the sunsets once in a while!"

Hernando missed the point but Carlin smiled. It was nice to know that in this strange land he had the acceptance of at least one man.

In spite of the fact that Mama Ignacia had carefully packed crocks of poultice and packages of herbs to be used to nurse Carlin along the way, by the time they reached Tucson he was weak and feverish.

The grueling sixteen-day journey ended long past sundown, and when the dusty, mule-drawn wagons pulled into the frontier town, the streets were practically deserted.

Tucson, in the mid-1880s, was a crude, ugly settlement of adobe-and-stone structures, populated with miners, speculators, cattlemen, gamblers, dancehall girls, and renegades. It flourished only because it had become a crossroads for trade in the Southwest, and during the daylight hours the streets were crowded with wagons of every description.

The drivers and animals of Andrew Dundee Fast Freight, Ltd. were covered with alkali dust that had caked with sweat, giving them the appearance of a ghost train. They pulled up to the deserted freight docks and the men stepped slowly from the wagons.

The tortured movement of their bodies and lack of conversation indicated how tired they were.

Jake watched Hernando with admiration. As exhausted as the young man was, he walked straight and tall. Jake could barely straighten his legs. He leaned heavily against the wagon as Hernando shook the dust from his hat, dipped his bandana in the watering trough, and began slowly and methodically to wash the dust from his handsome face. "Shore could go fer a drink 'fore we unload," he called out, knowing Hernando would ignore the suggestion.

"We'll unload first," Hernando replied, finishing his impromptu toilet. Then, ignoring the moans of the drivers who stood tiredly around rolling cigarettes, Hernando moved to the rear of his wagon, climbed inside, lighted a lamp, and looked anxiously at the crumpled figure of Carlin resting uncomfortably on the makeshift bed.

"How are you feeling?"

Carlin managed a half-grin. "Jake's got the right idea. I could do with a drink."

"Let's see if you can walk. Then we'll get you a drink."

"I think I could do with a bath, if we have the time. These clothes feel as if they're glued to my body."

Jake pulled back the wagon flap. "How's he doin'? Need some help?"

"Yeah, climb aboard."

The two men lifted Carlin to his feet. In the dim lamplight they could see where the infection had oozed through his shirt, making the lash marks underneath plainly visible.

"Well, old-timer," Hernando murmured to Jake,

"look's like yer goin' to get out of unloading after all. Better help me get him over to the inn."

They eased Carlin out of the wagon, holding him up between them, and, half-dragging and half-carrying the young Scot, started down the dusty street. Within the two blocks they had to travel to reach their destination, they passed seven saloons. Sounds of laughter, the calls of faro-bank dealers, and the off-key music of rinky-tink pianos and tinny banjos emanated from each set of swinging doors.

"Ain't you thirsty?" Jake asked, glancing nervously at Hernando.

"Hell, yes, I'm thirsty! So's the kid. He's also hotter than a whore's breath—in case you hadn't noticed!" Hernando strained to move faster. "After we get a room, you go find Sandy and tell him to start up the fires and get us some hot water for tubs!"

"He ain't goin' to like bein' waked up this time o' night!"

"That's too damned bad—he'll like the money."

Jake nodded. Everybody liked Hernando's money.

Sam Branson, the night clerk at the Tucson Inn, rushed over to give the two men a hand with their burden. "Packin' quite a load," he laughed, assuming that Carlin was drunk; then he got a closer look. "My Gawd! He's sick! Ain't got nothin' that's catchin', has he?"

"No. Jest got beat up some," Jake answered as they laid the prostrate body down on the overstuffed sofa next to the registration desk behind which Branson had taken refuge.

"He'll need a room to himself, Sam," Hernando informed the timid clerk. "Then after we've signed in,

I'd take it as a personal favor if you'd see if you can find us a doctor."

"No—and—no!" Sam Branson replied in a patronizing tone of voice.

"What do you mean no-and-no?" Hernando demanded.

"Mr. Dundee, we got no rooms. Leastwise none that a man can have by hisself!" Branson became apologetic. "And worse than that—we got *no* doctor in town! There was an accident out at the Pima Mine a couple o' days ago. Doc had to cut off one of the mucker's legs—and the damned fool was so mad, he ended up payin' the doctor off by shootin' 'im in the back!"

"Shit!" Hernando felt his stomach turn. He needed a drink. "Any rooms anywhere in town?"

"No. The town's full up—never seen anything like it! Even raised the rates—nobody cares. Everybody's got plenty of money. I can put you in a room with four beds—five other men in it." Branson went behind the counter to get the register. "That's the best I can do, Mr. Dundee, and about the best you'll find anywhere in town."

Hernando knew the man was speaking the truth. It had happened occasionally before. Lately it seemed to happen more and more. He would talk to his father about the possibility of building another hotel in the area.

"Jake, you go wake up Sandy. Sam can help me with the kid."

Jake didn't need any encouragement. Carlin was heavy, and the thought of carrying the dead weight up the narrow wooden stairway didn't much appeal to him. "Be right back. Or should I meet you at Nellie's?"

"Nellie's? Yeah, I guess we'll have time for a drink while the water's getting hot . . . I want to get the kid into a tub as soon as possible. Tell Sandy to fire up the stove and don't save on the kindling."

Carlin regained consciousness by the time they reached the top of the stairs. He was very weak, but managed to get to the room under his own power. Sam unlocked the door with his pass key, and they entered the room. There were two beds on one side of the room—side by side—and two beds on the other side of the room—side by side—with barely enough room to walk between them.

All of the beds were occupied, and the tenants didn't take kindly to being disturbed. "Close the damned door!" one of the men yelled.

Hernando struck a match and lighted the wall lamp.

"Put out the damned lamp or I'll shoot it out!" screamed another one of the irate roomers.

"Hold your water, amigo," Hernando replied. "I got a double eagle for each one of you for disturbing your sleep, and an extra one for the man who gives up his bed for my friend."

As he knew it would, the money salved the wounded feelings. The men grumbled, but they agreed to the arrangement and made room.

"Carlin, you just rest here for a little while. Jake's gone to make arrangements for us to get a bath. Sam here will bring you some water, and Jake n' me'll be back for you in about an hour."

* * *

Jake was already at Nellie's Saloon by the time Hernando arrived. He had a bottle of whiskey waiting at the bar.

"Did you find Sandy?"

"Yeah, he was asleep in the back of the barbershop. Didn't take too kindly to bein' waked up, neither. He'll have three tubs ready before we finish this bottle, but it's goin' to cost ya plenty."

"Don't it always?" Hernando grumbled.

They couldn't remove Carlin's shirt without taking the blistering and abscessed flesh with it, so Hernando and Jake took off the rest of his clothes and lowered him, shirt intact, into the large wooden tub.

The water was so hot it turned his flesh bright pink. Sandy, who was general overseer of the baths, as well as the barber, dentist, and horse doctor, shook his head with disapproval. "Ought to let me throw in a handful of creosote! That'd fix 'im right up!"

"Well, do then," Hernando ordered.

"We don't have any left!" Sandy replied, sheepishly.

Hernando was tired and exasperated. "Sandy, just shut up and go and get us some more hot water. If we fall asleep, wait ten minutes or so, then wake us up. And keep an eye on the kid—make sure he don't drown!"

Hernando and Jake wrestled out of their clothes and got into their tubs. They were asleep before their proprietor left the room. True to his word, Sandy kept bringing buckets of hot water until the embers of the fire cooled down, at least a half hour later; then he wakened Hernando and Jake.

The three men lifted Carlin from his tub and peeled off his shirt. Then they dried him as if he were a baby. Sandy opened a new keg of axle grease and bandaged the wounds with strips of clean sheeting. They dressed him using some secondhand clothing that had been left behind by other cowboys and miners and that Sandy had laundered and had for sale. The faded pants and shirt hung on his frail body like rags on a scarecrow; the secondhand boots were well-worn but a pretty good fit.

Carlin managed a smile. "Well, let's get on to the party!"

"No party tonight," Hernando laughed, admiring the boy's humor when he was in such obvious pain. "We want to get an early start in the morning. We can have a party after we get up to Santa Fe!"

All the beds were again occupied by the time Hernando and Jake got Carlin back to the room. It took Hernando a boot in the back of one of the surprised sleepers to clear the bed for Carlin. The man grumbled for a moment, then picked himself up off the floor and climbed into the next bed without ever coming fully awake.

"Gawd a' mighty, I ain't goin' to have much trouble sleepin' tonight!" Jake told Hernando as he started, fully clothed, to crawl into another of the occupied beds.

"Hold it. I'll be damned if I'm going to stay in a room with a bunch of snoring jackasses. You sleep with the kid. I'm going down to the Palace. Come wake me up in the morning!"

* * *

The bartender recognized Hernando as he came through the door and reached for the special stock. Hernando glanced around the room. The bar was empty except for a few regulars he recognized who were too drunk to fall down. A game was still in progress at one of the poker tables with some nearly broke miners who were trying to recoup their losses. At a table at the end of the bar a few of the less attractive whores sat waiting to see if they would end up with one of the stragglers and be able to make their quotas for the night. Hernando didn't recognize any of the women, but that was not unusual. Ladies who worked the Palace didn't usually stay too long.

He talked with the bartender for a few minutes, then picked up the bottle. "Bring some glasses for the girls," he said, as he ambled down the bar to their table.

He didn't choose the prettiest or the youngest. He decided on the one who remained quiet. Armed with the bottle of his special stock, he put his arm around the girl and led her up the stairs.

Her room was small and dark. Heavy draperies covered the one window, and the room smelled of dust and kerosene. It was still better than the room at the Inn which smelled of perspiration, dirty socks, and sour breath. He placed the whiskey on the dresser, turned up the lamp, and took a long hard look at the woman. He guessed her to be about eighteen, though she looked much older. Her gray eyes were dull and her ash-blond hair fell limply over her shoulders as she took out the pins. She didn't look clean. Hernando shook his head sadly thinking of the contrast between this poor wench and Felicia.

"What are you shakin' for, honey? You sure as hell can't be cold."

"No, I'm not cold," she answered in a small voice.

"Hell, you must have bedded down with a hundred or more men." Hernando sat on the bed and began pulling off his boots. "So you can't be scared."

The woman turned away from him and began to unbutton her bodice. "I could have been to bed with a thousand men, mister," she spoke so softly he could hardly hear what she was saying. "It don't make no difference. Each time is like the first time—I still get scared."

Hernando finished undressing and sprawled out on the bed. "Well, honey, don't worry too much about it!" He was asleep before he finished the sentence.

Dawn came too early for Jake. The journey had taken its toll on his aging body, and his joints ached to a point that he was seldom without pain. Sleeping next to Carlin had given him little relief—the Scotsman had been restless and feverish, and when Jake had been able to sleep, he dreamed of sitting on hot rocks in the eternal fires of hell. That, combined with the noise of the other men snoring or waking or dressing and leaving the room at uneven intervals left Jake tired and cranky. He hadn't signed on as a baby sitter, and as much as Jake liked the kid, he determined that Carlin would have to make it on his own from now on.

Jake sat up on the edge of the bed and pulled on his boots. He found the makings in his pocket and rolled a cigarette. It always took him a few puffs of tobacco to get his thoughts together and get the blood circulating.

"Hey, kid," he said, shaking Carlin. "Time to rise and shine!"

It took Jake a few moments to realize that Carlin was not going to awaken. The Scotsman was still breathing, but his breath was shallow and labored. Jake found himself more concerned than he cared to be. "Damn!" he swore under his breath. Anxiety set his head pounding as he rushed from the room, bounded down the stairs, and headed for the Palace.

Hernando was already eating breakfast by the time he arrived. Jake sat down and ordered steak, eggs, and a pot of black coffee. "I'll tell you true, Hernando. I don't think the kid is goin' to make it!"

Hernando continued eating. Jake took a big swallow of coffee and went on. "He's goin' to die fer sure less we get some real help fer 'im."

"What do you mean by real help?"

"Well," Jake's eyes narrowed and he lowered his voice. "I was thinkin' 'bout me and you goin' north with him, an' meetin' with Ole Sorebelly . . ."

"Ole Sorebelly!" Hernando could scarcely believe what Jake was suggesting. "That snaky old Navajo would kill him for sure! 'Sides—we got a schedule to keep."

"Snaky or not—that old medicine man done a lot fer yer father 'n me. I 'member one time when the 'Paches got us trapped up in the hills, 'n we took a dozen or more arrows a'tween us 'fore they give us up fer daid! We made it into the Naveeland, 'n that Ole Sorebelly had us 'live 'n on our feet 'fore sundown the next day!"

Hernando laughed. He'd heard the story over and

over again from Jake, since he'd been a child, but his father had never confirmed it. "Relax, Jake. He ain't goin' to die. He's too tough." Hernando wiped his mouth and pushed his chair back from the table. " 'Sides—that would mean goin' over the Apache trail—damned near suicide. You goin' to take him?"

The old man smiled craftily. "Seems to me yer the one who's been chawin' so much over him being yer responsibility. If we take him through El Paso, he'll never make it to Santa Fe. If you go north it'll shave a week or more off the trip."

Hernando shook his head in disgust. The next man they found dying by the side of the road could damned well stay there for buzzard bait. Talking of the Navajo medicine man recalled thoughts of Shell Woman, the Apache witch. Even his mother, Isabella, believed in her magic. He thought of the times when he had been younger when he had walked up the long, steep trail behind his hacienda with Phoebe to visit the old woman in her cave. Then he recalled his grandfather Ramon's words: "The only good Indian is a dead Indian!"

"Shit!" Hernando spat into a spitoon. "Reload one of the wagons. Lighten it up so that I can make some time, and be sure I have enough coffee, flour, sugar, and bacon to trade with the Indians."

"I'll finish my breakfast, then send some of the boys 'round to the hotel to git Carlin." Jake spoke quickly, hoping that Hernando would not change his mind. "I'll have everythin' ready by the time you get back to the docks." Then, as if to reassure himself, he said, "Hernando, yer doin' the right thing!"

It wasn't yet seven o'clock, but the adobe mud

streets of Tucson were already beginning to reflect the heat of the sun. It was going to be a scorching day, and Hernando was anxious to be on the trail. First he had to attend to business. There were bills of lading and manifests to be taken care of, cargo to be unloaded, and new cargo to be taken on for El Paso and points north.

It didn't take him long to finish his duties with the warehousemen and the bankers; then he headed for the freight docks. Jake, true to his word, had the wagon loaded by the time Hernando arrived.

"Managed to git some coffee into Carlin, but nothin' else. He's asleep in the back," Jake informed him.

Hernando climbed up onto the seat and took the reins. "See you in Santa Fe, old-timer," he called down to the teamster. Then he straightened his Stetson, pulled his bandana up over his face in order to keep out the dust, and released the brake. "Say hello to my gals in El Paso!"

"I'll do that," Jake yelled after him. "An' you watch out fer the hostiles!"

CHAPTER FOUR

As Hernando and Carlin proceeded north over the infamous Apache trail, Hernando's father, Andrew Dundee, sat warming himself in the sun on the veranda
of his rambling adobe Hacienda de la Villanova
Dundee, a few miles outside of Santa Fe in the foothills of the Sangre de Cristo Mountains. From his vantage point on the veranda he could see the cottonwood trees along the streams beginning to turn green
with the coming of the spring. Blue lupine and various shades of Indian paint brush pushed their way up
through the remaining patches of snow that dotted
the pale gray hills.

In the past the coming of spring always triggered
his wandering spirit—his desire to see what was on the
other side of the mountain. Now, in his sixty-fifth
year, the adventurous urge came less frequently. His
capacity for alcohol had decreased, too. He knew he
was not the man he once had been! Andrew wished
that Hernando would return; he missed the boy. He
found that recently, more and more, he was living his
life vicariously through his son.

Thoughts of his son triggered thoughts of his own

youth and of his own father. It gave him great pleasure to recall his father and his heritage.

"Ha!" he thought aloud. "Damn the English!" Then he laughed at the memory. Although the thrones of Scotland and England had been united with the death of Queen Elizabeth in 1603—when James VI, son of Mary and Lord Darnley, became king of England—the Dundee family, more than 200 years later, had still refused to accept the fact that they were subjects of King George III.

The Dundees could trace their lineage back to 846 A.D. when Kenneth I. MacAlpin became the first Scot to rule both the Scots and the Picts.

"Andrew," his father used to tell him, "always remember that you are a Scot! First—last—and always! All the British can be damned—and that goes for the King himself!"

It was statements like this—and worse—that finally forced the elder Dundee, with his wife and eight-year-old son, Andrew, to flee to the New World. Andrew's mother had been as frail as she had been beautiful, and she had not survived the voyage. When they arrived in the New World, Andrew's father was a broken man, a shadow of his former self.

"Andrew, there is just one thing in the world I love more than I loved your mother and that is a good hunt. And there is just one thing I hate more than I hate the English and that is living in the city! If I am to survive to an old age and help to rear you to manhood, we will have to travel into the wilderness of this great land. We will have to journey to the West."

And they did. They traveled to the great Rocky Mountains, where they lived and hunted with the Indians. This wild and wonderful life enabled Andrew's father to live for ten more years.

Andrew, true to his heritage, was a Scotsman in every sense of the word, with shaggy red hair, bright blue eyes, broad shoulders, and a lean six-foot-four frame, which should have been clothed in tartans rather than buckskins. He was a Scotsman, too, in his frugality. He was not a miser, nor was he selfish or unkind; but he was frugal. This trait, learned well at an early age from his father, enabled him to amass a small fortune from fur trade and trading with the Indians. By the time he was twenty-five he owned more than a dozen freight wagons that journeyed over the Sante Fe trail from Missouri to the Southwest; and over the Butterfield trail from the Southwest to San Francisco.

During the time of his youth, Andrew remembered, he had been with more beautiful women, had drunk more whiskey—both good and bad—and had seen more virgin country than any other man he knew. He hadn't married Isabella until late in life—he had been thirty-nine. Probably would have never settled down if he hadn't won that card match and amusingly agreed to consider the loser's daughter as partial payment. But since that time he had never been unfaithful to her. For him it had truly been a love match. He wondered if it had been the same for Isabella.

The marriage had been arranged by her father when she was just seventeen. Andrew had seen the Spanish beauty at a distance several times while he was trading in Santa Fe—and remembering back, it seemed to him that he had fallen in love with the innocent Isabella at first sight. Andrew's eyes flooded with tears at the thought of what a beautiful bride she had been. Once again he spoke aloud, "My God, Isabella—how much I loved you then—and how much more I love you now! Has a man ever been so blessed?"

Outside the hacienda, in her small chapel at the rear of her garden, Dona Isabella Villanova Dundee sat quietly as Padre Francisco Dominquez served a Special Mass for the Dead. It was May 6, 1885, the twenty-eighth anniversary of her mother's death. Isabella lighted candles and listened, without really hearing, as the padre chanted the prayers to the dead. "Strange," Isabella murmured to herself. "Today I mourn the death of my mother, and tomorrow I will celebrate the Fiesta of the 335th birthday of Santa Fe." True, there were those who insisted that Santa Fe had been founded in 1610—but all the native Spaniards knew that the true date was 1550. She wondered how, after all these years, anyone knew the true date. Isabella was sure because her mother had recounted the history of the Spanish immigrants to her many times. Her mother had been a brilliant and well-read woman—most unusual for the truly aristocratic women of the time. But then her mother had been exceptional in almost everything she did. Isabella sighed, remembering the gentle and patient companion she had lost so many years before. Uncontrollably, her thoughts turned to memories of her father and how cruel he had been to both Isabella and her mother. Indeed, she remembered bitterly, her father had been directly responsible for her mother's premature death! Evil thoughts! She chastized herself, but the vivid recollections returned.

Don Ramon Garcia Villanova, Isabella's father, was known throughout New Mexico Territory as a pompous, arrogant, and sadistic man. At one time he owned the largest Spanish land grant in the area, deeded to him for service to King Philip III. That was before Ramon's best friend, Governor Manuel Armijo, betrayed the people of Santa Fe to the forces of the American general, Stephen Kearney, in 1846 and most of the Spanish families were ruined.

Isabella also remembered the governor. He was enormously fat, and the people called him "His Obesity" behind his back. When she had been just a child, he had held her in his lap and tried to touch her private parts. The only thing that saved her from his rude advances was her mother's entrance into the room. Her mother had snatched her from the vile-smelling man and was in the process of berating him for his conduct when Isabella's father entered the room. She recalled bitterly that he had been furious and accused her mother of insulting his best friend. When the distraught woman tried to explain what had happened, Ramon slapped her hard enough to leave a bruise that lasted for several weeks, and then he locked both of them in a rear bedroom for the rest of the day.

It was not uncommon for her father to punish both Isabella and her mother with severe beatings, and she was sure that it was from the results of one such beating that her mother had finally died.

The Villanova women were blessed with a silent revenge a short time later when His Obesity, Governor Armijo, fled Santa Fe taking as much of his own wealth as he could carry and allowing the pueblo to be captured by the American army. He had not warned his "dear friend," her father, and Ramon, in addition to being humiliated, lost most of his fortune. As if to emphasize His Obesity's brutality, the Villanova family was told by a servant that when General Kearney entered the governor's office, he found five pairs of ears that the governor had ordered nailed up on his wall. They were the ears of five Texans the governor had ordered shot after they had honorably surrendered. This final bestial gesture by the governor did nothing to endear the citizens of Santa Fe to the Americans, and most of them paid dearly for the outrage.

With the signing of the Treaty of Guadalupe Hidalgo in 1848, the lives of the Spanish New Mexicans were changed drastically. Ten short years later, in 1858, most of Isabella's father's enormous holdings had been sold or confiscated. Unable to face ultimate poverty and consumed with shame, Don Ramon Villanova began drinking and gambling heavily. Isabella never knew from one day to the next whether there would be a roof over her head.

One night, shortly after her mother's sudden death, she was awakened from a sound sleep by her father's drunken screams. "Isabella! Isabella! Come down here at once! I want to introduce you to the man you are going to marry!"

Isabella remembered that she felt paralyzed with fear and overcome by nausea. However, she was more afraid of her father's temper, so she lit the candle next to her bed, slipped into a robe, and tiptoed shakily down the stairs and into the large foyer where her father waited.

Standing next to Don Ramon was the biggest, tallest man she had ever seen. He towered above her! He had wild red hair, a shaggy red beard, and piercing blue eyes. She was sure that it was the devil himself who had come to claim her.

"Let the girl go to bed," the giant protested, awed by his first real contact with Isabella and overwhelmed by her beauty. "I'll not marry her unless she herself agrees to it!"

"She'll do as she's told," her father bellowed. And then Isabella fainted.

Two nuns and Padre Dominguez were at her bedside when she awakened. The padre had been a young man then, she remembered. What were his exact words? Oh, yes, he had said, "you should offer prayers of thanks, child! Your father's hacienda has been saved from his debtors, and you are to be married to one of the wealthiest men in the Territory! Senor Andrew Dundee!"

"But, padre," she had protested. "He cannot be a Spaniard with a name like Dundee, and if he's the man I saw last night, he looks like a monster! Is he Catholic?"

"No, he is not Spanish—and I can assure you that he is no monster. He's not Catholic either; however, he is a dear friend of Monsignor Lamy, and I'm sure we can get him special dispensation from Rome. He has given the Church a most generous contribution!"

Then she knew the truth. She had been sold to this devil by her father in order to save what was left of his estate—and she had been forsaken by the Church in exchange for a generous contribution.

She smiled as she remembered how Andrew had insisted that he be allowed to court her properly. In the months that followed, while they awaited permission from the Church in Rome, he did just that. First, because Isabella had objected to it, he shaved off his beard. She was delighted to find that underneath the mass of red hair was an extremely handsome face. She was very deliberate in not letting Andrew know how attracted to him she was. She was also pleased that he didn't seem to object that they were well chaperoned at all times. Every day he sent her gifts—marvelous gifts! Lovely filigreed silver bracelets and earrings; a magnificent gold tiara; an ermine cape made by the Indians from the north; and a silver hand mirror with her initials on it! Even today Isabella treasured them all.

She couldn't remember ever receiving a gift from her father. Not on her birthday or at Christmastime or any other time! Until Andrew came into her life, she hadn't had a present from anyone except her mother. Andrew made it seem that every day was her birthday, and she loved him for it.

And she adored Andrew's voice—it was deep and resonant, with a trace of Scottish brogue. Often, in the evenings, he would strum his Spanish guitar and sing her love songs. She had been taught that it was unladylike to show emotion, so Andrew was never aware, before they were married, how much she loved him.

During the period of their courtship, Andrew took complete charge of the hacienda. He went to great expense to refurbish the hundred-year-old structure—enlarging the windows and whitewashing the adobe inside and out. He designed and had new furniture built, purchased potted plants and books, and made each room a showplace. Isabella was consulted on the changes, but always deferred to Andrew's wishes. His taste, it seemed to her, was impeccable—and for Isabella the transformation was a dream come true. She was even more grateful when, after one of her father's drunken and abusive tirades, Andrew purchased a small *casita* for him in Santa Fe and forbade him to visit Isabella without an invitation.

In spite of Andrew's generosity and in spite of her love for him, after the wedding ceremony when they were finally alone and he led her upstairs to their bedroom, Isabella was terrified.

The remembrance made her flush. How foolish she had been. That first night when Andrew made love to her it was everything she had dreamed it would be—and more! Although she would never admit it to her priest, she was very grateful to those many women Andrew had slept with before they became engaged. They had trained him well in the art of pleasing a woman. She knew this was true because of all the tales the older matrons had told her about how painful "it" was—and how "degrading"! It was neither painful nor degrading when Andrew made love to her. "It" was heavenly!

* * *

Suddenly Isabella became aware that the Mass was finished. She shook her head to clear away thoughts of the past and forced herself back to the present. Padre Dominguez gave her communion, blessed her, then walked with her through the garden.

"Isabella, I have never seen anything like it! Every year you become more beautiful. You are the only woman I know who seems truly contented. God has smiled on you!"

"Yes, Padre." *After all,* she thought, *He has given me Andrew and Hernando.* Yes, she was sure, it was God's will. But how strange it should all have come about because her father had lost in a poker game in Dona Tula's Poker Club!

When they finished their refreshments and the priest had taken his leave, Isabella entered the hacienda and strode leisurely up the polished stairway to their bedroom to join her husband on the veranda. She felt a chill in the air as she entered the room, and stopped to get a lap robe out of the highboy so she could cover Andrew's legs. He was sitting in the wicker rocker with his eyes closed, and for a moment she thought he was asleep. She placed the robe over him and knelt to kiss his cheek. His face felt cold to her lips, and she noticed he was covered with perspiration. It was as if an alarm went off in her head.

"Andrew! Andrew! Are you all right?" She was trying to keep the panic out of her voice.

He opened his eyes and tried to smile. "It's very hard for me to breathe. I have a sharp pain in my chest."

She barely waited for him to finish the sentence before she rushed downstairs calling for her servants.

"Juanito! Carlos! Go as quickly as you can into town and get the doctor! Pronto! Pronto!"

Phoebe, her Apache housekeeper, heard the commotion and rushed from the kitchen.

Isabella was so upset her voice quivered. "Come upstairs with me at once—Senor Andrew is ill!"

The two women raced upstairs to the helpless man. Isabella kissed him tenderly. "Juanito and Carlos have gone for Dr. Vargas. It shouldn't take them too long."

"You mustn't be frightened, my darling," he tried to reassure her. "I'll be fine. I have too many things to do—and too many things to tell you—to leave you just yet!"

Her kisses silenced him, and with Phoebe's help she got him to the bed and undressed him. After they had made him as comfortable as possible, Phoebe went downstairs to brew some special herb tea. It was a remedy she had learned to make from the medicine men of her mother's tribe.

It took Dr. Vargas more than an hour to reach the hacienda from Santa Fe. Phoebe was waiting at the door when he arrived and took him directly upstairs. He examined Andrew thoroughly and signaled Isabella to join him in the parlor where they could speak privately.

"It's very serious. When will Hernando be home?" he asked.

"I don't know—perhaps not for several weeks! What do you mean it's serious?"

"Andrew's had a stroke. There's not much I can do for him. You must keep him in bed and keep him quiet. No heavy foods and no alcohol."

"Will he live?"

"I don't know. But I think you should send for Hernando to come home as quickly as possible."

Isabella sat quietly for a few moments, trying to regain her composure, then she summoned Phoebe. "Please ask Juanito to come to me."

She went to the desk and wrote out a message which she directed Juanito to take to the telegraph office in Santa Fe. "I want this message sent to the loading docks in Santa Barbara, Tucson, and El Paso!"

She noticed the young Mexican trembling. "Juanito, get control of yourself! After you have sent the messages, I want you to follow the trail southward and see if you can intercept Hernando! He could be anywhere! When you find him you are to tell him to come home the fastest way possible. His father is ill."

Isabella instructed Phoebe to serve some refreshments to the doctor before he began his journey back to town, and then, with very special meaning, she whispered to the Apache woman, "And, Phoebe, after you have served the doctor and shown him out, I want you to go *directly* to your mother and tell her what has happened."

Isabella looked into the eyes of her dear friend and servant to be assured that Phoebe understood. Then she thanked the doctor, excused herself, and slowly climbed the stairs to be with her beloved husband.

Phoebe was gracious but stoic as she served Dr. Vargas his tea and fresh corn cakes. He was hurried, not by her manner, but rather by her cool gaze. When he finished, she fetched his hat and showed him to the door.

Realizing that she would not return from her mother's until after dark, Phoebe lit the lamps in several of the rooms and went to find Rosa. "Stay near the mistress until I return," she instructed the servant. Then she went back upstairs and opened the bedroom door quietly in order not to disturb Isabella. The bedroom, which faced the east, was already dark in the late afternoon, and Isabella sat in the shadows weeping softly.

Phoebe felt great affection for the gentle Spanish lady, and, although she was much younger than her mistress, felt very maternal. "Senora, I am about to leave. Rosa is downstairs, and the dinner is already prepared. Is there anything else you will need?"

"No, Phoebe. Thank you. Your mother will know what to do." Almost as an afterthought, Isabella arose and walked to the large ornate hand-carved chiffonier and found a red plaid woolen scarf of Andrew's. "Please give this to your mother as a gift."

CHAPTER FIVE

Her Apache name was Yii Bitoo, Laughing Spring, but she preferred to be called Phoebe, the name given her by her adopted family, the Dundees. Phoebe was the only living child of Shell Woman and Spread Moustache. She was twenty-eight, almost middle-aged for an Apache, but her delicate features and serene nature made it difficult to guess her age. She had a childlike innocence that gave her the look of a maiden in her teens, and the only hint that she might be older was seen in the premature gray streaks in her waist-long jet-black hair.

With her head held high and her shoulders back, she walked with the poise and grace natural to most Apache women. Her attitude was not that of a servant, nor did the Dundees consider her one. She was a person who received much pleasure from serving those she loved, and she loved her adopted family dearly. She had been with the Dundees for more than twelve years and by now considered them as her own family.

Years before Andrew had built Phoebe her own *casita* a short distance from the rear of Isabella's chapel.

It was small and utilitarian, but private, and Phoebe liked it. In the Indian custom the entrance faced the east and there were no windows. She kept her belongings neatly folded in various-sized willow-and-grass baskets; and although Isabella had provided her with a lovely brass bed, Phoebe preferred, even after all these years, to sleep on a fur-covered grass mat on the floor.

She dressed in warm Spanish-style clothing—a very heavy velvet full skirt over which she wore a long, loose velvet blouse. In the privacy of her *casita* Phoebe went barefoot, but in the hacienda, or when she traveled to town, she wore soft leather Apache boots that she had made and beaded herself.

Within a few years after she had come to accept the hacienda as her home, Phoebe converted to Catholicism. She found, however, her early religious training in tribal ritual was too deeply ingrained for her to forsake it; and so, in her mind's eye, she combined her belief in the Apache Gahns—spirits—with the Holy Saints and allowed them to work hand in hand.

In order to keep away evil spirits Phoebe always carried a small leather pouch, sewn into the lining of her skirt, filled with bits of turquoise, coral, abalone shell, white clay, and pollen. And to be doubly sure she was protected, around her neck, under her beaded choker, she wore a Saint Christopher's medal.

In her *casita*, next to her sacred eagle's feathers and her burden basket, was her most treasured possession—a small statue of the Virgin Mary. The white alabaster reproduction stood upright in a miniature artificial garden arranged in an ornate wooden box she had painted and decorated with semiprecious stones. It stood next to her mat and was often the last thing she saw before falling asleep.

Although she never confessed it, part of her love for the Virgin Mary was because the features of the Lady reminded her so much of her mother, Shell Woman, before the tragedy. Phoebe would often pick up the statue and trace the delicate nose and chin line with her finger—remembering how lovely her mother had looked when Phoebe was a child.

Satisfied that her mistress would be well tended in her absence, Phoebe left the hacienda and hurried to her *casita*. A cold wind was blowing down from the canyon and she was anxious to be on her way. She carried a basket of food and a lantern to light the way on her journey home. Inside the *casita* she found her heavy Apache blanket and draped it over her shoulders, then she knelt down for a moment in front of the Virgin Mary and said a silent prayer. When she finished, she was on her way with the speed of a frightened deer.

The spring warmth had opened the buds of the flowers and fruit trees, and their sweet aroma made her feel heady. Surely, she thought, at this time of the year when the Gahns and the saints had called forth the flowers and all new creatures, they would not call Don Andrew into the underworld!

The sun was sinking steadily in the western sky and she quickened her step. She wound her way through the orchard, climbed over the fence, and made her way up the narrow foot trail which led up the steep face of the canyon wall to the hidden area where her mother lived.

She was more than halfway to her destination by the time the sun dropped below the horizon. There was no moon, but with her lantern she had little trouble finding her way. After all, she had made the journey back and forth at least once a week for almost twelve years. Each turn and twist in the trail was indelibly etched in Phoebe's mind.

It had not always been so. She remembered how difficult it had been for her to find her way on the first journey to visit Shell Woman.

When had it all begun? For so many years she had blocked out the past; she could hardly remember how traumatic it had been. The realization that her benefactor, Andrew Dundee, might well be dying brought the memories flooding back.

It seemed to her that it had all begun shortly after *nah-ih-eh,* the puberty ceremony that celebrated the initiation into womanhood of her cousin Standing Doe. She and her mother had been godmothers to the girl, and the ceremony had been in progress for four days. She remembered how the medicine men and the singers had purified themselves in the sweat lodges; she could almost hear the rhythmic beat of the drums and the excitement of the chanting. There had been an abundance of food and many gifts for Standing Doe. What a happy and carefree time that had been for her!

At the time Phoebe was married to Nanquito and expecting their first child. Love was good—life was good! But everything began to change on the fourth night of the ceremony. Her father, Spread Moustache, just released from jail in Gallup, had made it back to the camp in time for the ritual, but on that fourth night he became ill. He burned with fever and ugly red spots covered his body. By morning he was dead. Then Nanquito became ill. He suffered from the same fever and his body was covered with the same red spots that had appeared on her father's body. Phoebe moaned with pain as the medicine men chanted and danced and tried to work their magic in order to heal her husband. But the magic had not been strong enough, and within a few days, Nanquito was also dead.

The medicine men directed the fear of the tribe toward Shell Woman. They said she must have looked directly into the eyes of her son-in-law. The worst of the tribal taboos! And in doing so she had angered the spirits! In order to punish her, the medicine men claimed, the Gahns had taken the lives of Spread Moustache and Nanquito. They proclaimed her a witch! After the proclamation, other women of the tribe came forward to tell of strange things that had happened to them in the presence of Shell Woman. When Phoebe miscarried her child, the medicine men had their proof. Shell Woman must die!

As was the custom of the tribe when dealing with witchcraft, Shell Woman was beaten and stoned and dragged out of the camp to an open field where a single tree stood. Phoebe would never forget the twisted and gnarled look of that tree. She screamed and pleaded in an attempt to save her mother's life. No one would listen. They ordered her to be silent or she, too, might be considered a witch! Some of the braves tied her half-conscious mother to the tree, gathered wood faggots and bound them together in

84

bundles, then piled them around the feet of Shell Woman. When they lit the fire Phoebe tore herself free from the women who were holding her and ran to try to save her mother.

Andrew Dundee and some of his cowboys had been looking for stray cattle when they came upon the grisly scene. They rode into the clearing, firing their guns in the air, and sent the Apaches running. Phoebe, who was already trying to pull the burning bundles away from her mother's body, was in such a frenzy that she didn't realize that her clothing, too, was on fire.

Andrew smothered the flames with his serape while the cowboys stamped out the fire around the tree and scattered the burning embers. Then they cut Shell Woman loose from her bonds. The lower part of her body was already badly burned as was her arm and a portion of her face. The smell of burning flesh was sickening.

Andrew instructed the men to carry both women to a nearby stream, where he submerged them in the freezing water. He kept them there until some of his men returned from the hacienda with clean sheets, blankets, and two litters.

Isabella insisted the women be brought into the house instead of the barn and, along with the doctor and two nuns from Santa Fe, helped nurse them as best she could. During this period of time, most of the Indian help at the hacienda left the Dundees— only the faithful Carlos remained. He felt that if the Dundees and his squaw didn't mind having the witch and her daughter in their house, he didn't mind either.

Phoebe healed quickly. Her hands had been burned, but her fingers were intact, and the body burns were superficial. Shell Woman, on the other hand, was almost beyond help. Her once beautiful face was badly scarred; the tissue on one arm had burned away and the arm had to be amputated; and her legs were so hideously charred that the doctor informed the Dundees that although the Apache woman might recover, she would never walk again.

In an embarrassed confession to her priest, Isabella asked to be forgiven because she believed the woman would be better off dead. Yet by some miracle, Shell Woman survived. She was bedridden and helpless, but she was alive. One morning, when Phoebe entered her room to bring her some sweet coffee and fruit, she found the bed empty. It was as if Shell Woman had vanished into thin air. Andrew and his men searched for the squaw for days, before they finally gave up. Phoebe contained her grief in silence. She moved out of the hacienda immediately and set up a small camp in the orchard. At night, when there was no one around to hear, she cried for her mother. She was sure that the Gahns had taken her away.

It was during this time, at Isabella's insistence, that Andrew built the small *casita*. Slowly, with Isabella's gentle persuasion, Phoebe began to return to the living.

Almost a year passed, Phoebe remembered, and she and Hernando were in the garden. It was just a few days past his fifteenth birthday when, just as suddenly as she had vanished, Shell Woman reappeared. She was dressed in a crude buckskin dress with long fringe hanging from the shoulders and the hem. Her hair, which had been burned away, stood up in white patches all over her head, giving her the appearance of a porcupine. The skin on her once-lovely face was scarred and tightly twisted over her skull, leaving her mouth in a permanent grin. Shell Woman walked slowly with the stub of her arm over a stout willow branch, and dragged one leg painfully behind her as she moved out of the light and became partially hidden behind one of the trees.

Phoebe stood paralyzed, too frightened to breathe. But Hernando, curious about the awesome sight, ran up to help Shell Woman. She couldn't speak above a whisper and spoke no Spanish or English, but Hernando understood enough of the guttural Apache to know what she was saying.

"It's your mother, Phoebe!" Hernando shouted, not understanding Phoebe's reluctance to come forward. "She wants to see you!"

Phoebe still couldn't move. It was as if she were looking at a specter. Hernando ran to her and began pulling her toward Shell Woman. "She wants us to follow her. Don't be afraid! I'll protect you!"

It was the first of many visits Shell Woman made to the hacienda, but she always remained hidden from everyone except her daughter and Hernando. When it became too strenuous for her to make the long journey from her hidden place to the garden, Phoebe and Hernando began taking bits and pieces of food and clothing to her. At first Hernando loved keeping their secret, but later, when he began wearing her amulets and carrying her bags of shell and pollen in order to

guarantee his protection, he confided his experiences
with the witch to his mother.

She was shocked when Hernando told her of Shell
Woman's miraculous healing and reappearance. But
having been born and raised in the Territory, she knew
much of the ways and superstitions of the Indians.
There had been times, Isabella admitted to her son,
she believed in their powers herself. And so, in order
to keep Shell Woman from casting any evil spells over
them, she sent food and gifts to the old woman at
least once a week with Phoebe. She made it clear,
however, that she didn't want Hernando to be influenced in any way by Indian witchcraft—and he was
forbidden ever to accompany Phoebe on the journey
or to see Shell Woman again. It had all happened so
long ago that Phoebe had almost forgotten.

Andrew's illness finally forced Isabella to realize
how much faith she actually had in the mystical
power of the Apache witch. Phoebe was equally sure
that her mother's magic would not fail them. She
stood at the mouth of the cave that had been her
mother's home for so many years in order to catch her
breath. The last part of the trail had been very difficult,
and her basket was heavy.

The fire, which her mother had laid for the evening
warmth, was set in such a way that Phoebe could
barely see the reflection from where she stood. She
walked deeper into the cave and found her mother sitting on a bearskin rug next to the fire pit. Shell
Woman was naked from the waist up and her body
and hair were covered with clay and pollen. The frail
woman rocked back and forth chanting a spell.

Phoebe remained quiet until her mother acknowledged her presence.

"Good evening, daughter," she whispered in Apache.

"Good evening, Mother," Phoebe replied in her native tongue.

"I have been expecting you. What have you brought for me?"

Phoebe put the basket down close to her mother and began to unpack the contents. There was a small crock of honey, corn cakes, dried fruit, salted pork, and marmalade.

"Hmm—it is good," her mother purred, looking over the gifts. "And what else have you brought for me?"

Phoebe unfolded the soft woolen scarf. Shell Woman touched the material and held it to her cheek. Her eyes brightened and she began, once again, to rock back and forth and chant. After a time she stopped and groped under the bearskin to find a large leather pouch and a carved amulet on a slender buckskin strap.

"I already know of your master's sickness. Take these herbs and brew a strong tea for him. Be sure he drinks it in the morning and in the evening," Shell Woman instructed. "And place this amulet around his neck." She closed her eyes. "Go now—I am tired and I must rest."

There were no further explanations necessary. Phoebe would never understand the witch's mystical power. She took the pouch and the amulet and gently kissed her mother's cheek. It felt soft and warm. Oh, that things could be the way they were when she was young! But they were not—and never would be again.

She placed the pouch in her basket, slipped the amulet around her neck so that she would be sure not to lose it, relighted her lantern with a taper from the fire, and bade her mother good-bye.

CHAPTER SIX

It wasn't until Tucson had disappeared from view that Hernando allowed himself to enjoy the freedom of being on the trail. He pulled the bandana from his face and breathed in the fresh, clean air. The mules clipped along at a steady pace, heads down and tails whipping to and fro with relief of carrying the lighter load.

Unconsciously, Hernando checked the knife and the pistol he carried in holsters strapped to his belt. Then he raised the poncho from the floor of the wagon to check the two loaded rifles hidden beneath his feet. He knew the weapons would be of little use if they were attacked—but at least he'd take a few Apaches with him when and if the time came.

Arizona was a land of magnificent contrasts: panoramic vistas of lush deserts, high rim country with lofty forests, flat-topped mesas and deep canyons, sandstone monuments so gigantic that they dwarfed a man standing next to them, and shadows and sounds so eerie that even Hernando felt uneasy.

The Apache trail cut through the heart of some of Arizona Territory's most beautiful country. It was also a trail that was to be avoided except in cases of extreme emergency, or unless one was accompanied by military escort. Hernando slowed the mules to cross a flooded arroyo. "I must be out of my mind," he said sarcastically to the beasts.

From a distance, with the dust trailing behind and the white canvas top billowing—and seen through the distortion of mirage-causing heat waves—the freight wagon could have been mistaken for a ship riding on the gentle waves of a calm sea. In his delirium inside the swaying wagon, the sounds of the creaking boards started Carlin dreaming. The wagon became his ship. He was at sea again. He could almost smell the fresh salt air and hear thunder of the waves as they smashed against the hull. In the dream he and Hernando were on the deck hanging onto the railing. Looking in one direction, he could see the China coast—in the other direction, the sharp rugged coastline of California. The continents were slowly drifting apart, and Carlin felt frantic—as if, for some reason, he was personally responsible for the rift. He was screaming for Hernando to help him but couldn't make himself heard over the roar of the waves. Somewhere he heard Captain Waldren laughing—and then, because he had no control of his dream, he saw the faces of his Chinese friends. The captain was chasing them with an ax and they screamed for Carlin to help them! When he tried to move he found that his feet were tied to the deck, so once again he screamed for Hernando to free him!

Hernando drew the wagon to a halt by the side of the trail and quickly climbed into the back. He lifted the canteen to Carlin's parched lips and gently awakened the young seaman from his nightmare.

"Take it easy—you were just dreaming!"

"I thought we were at sea. I saw Waldren chasing the Chinese," he tried to explain but he was too weak. Hernando forced some more water into his mouth, then sponged his forehead.

"Dehydration can kill a man out here as fast as a fever." He opened a small keg of water and propped it up next to Carlin so that it wouldn't spill. Then he tore up some sheeting and fashioned it into a rope, putting one end in the keg and the other end in Carlin's mouth. "Yell out if you think you're getting dry. We won't stop to make camp 'til sundown."

It was midafternoon of the second day when Hernando heard a sound that made the hair on the back of his neck stand on end. Horses! He could tell by the sound that it was a big herd—running hard. He pulled the mules off the trail into the brush, untied his bandana, and wiped his face. They were close. He picked up a rifle and stood up on the wagon seat in order to get a better view. And then in the next moment he saw them, a dozen Apache warriors wearing paint! They were driving more than thirty horses at a full gallop. Maybe the horses were stolen—maybe just a wild herd—Hernando didn't much care. He cocked the rifle and raised it to draw a bead on the Indian nearest to him, but he held his fire. They were moving fast.

He hoped they would pass leaving the wagon undiscovered, and then before he could catch his breath, he was aware of a young brave to his left. He glanced over his shoulder to look straight down the shaft of an arrow pointed directly at him. The warrior hesitated for a moment, and the men stared at each other. High above the wagon, the Apache shot the arrow into the air and looked arrogantly at Hernando as if to say, "I don't have time to kill you, now!"—and then rode off after his brothers.

Hernando's legs were shaking. His fear angered him. He sat down on the seat and once more wiped the perspiration from his brow. Damn the bastards, he thought. You never could predict what an Indian would do. It had been close! One thing he knew for sure: if he had had the bead drawn on the Apache— and if he hadn't been afraid of attracting the bucks with the noise—he would have shot the bastard right through the head!

When he regained his composure, he started the mules back up the trail. With a little luck they would be in Navajoland by nightfall.

Juanito, changing horses at every way station, reached El Paso in record time. There he found out that the Dundee wagons were en route from Tucson. He slept for a few hours, exchanged his horse for a fresh one, and started out to intercept Hernando. After a three-hour ride out of El Paso, he met the wagons.

Jake understood Spanish as well as he understood English, but Juanito was talking so fast that Jake had to slow him down. Finally, he understood the urgency.

"Son-of-a-bitch!" Jake stared at Juanito. "I don't know whether or not you'll be able to find him. He's somewhere on the 'Pache trail on his way north to Naveeland!"

"But, Senor—the Senora says he must come home pronto—*el patron* plenty bad sick!"

"Shit!" Jake cried in exasperation. "Yer just goin' to have to go after him. He cain't make too good time with that wagon." He jumped down from the wagon, knelt in the dirt, and began drawing a crude map with his finger. "If you head northwest through Silver City—an' cut across the pass at Alpine—you'd hit the trail about here. If you keep goin' north yer bound to catch up to him!"

Jake caught the look of desperation in Juanito's eyes. He knew there was little love lost between Mexicans and Apaches. "There's no other choice, man. I'll go on with the wagons and pick up a horse at the Dawson Ranch, then I'll git on up to Santa Fe. There's got to be something I kin do for Andy!"

Although he was torn between his fear of the Apaches and his love of the Dundees, Juanito didn't hesitate. He swung up onto his saddle and spurred his horse to a full gallop northward toward the Apache trail. Juanito and his father had cowboyed all through the Territory—but neither had ever ventured into the Indian country. Now the young Mexican was alert, not to the wondrous beauty of the land, but to the hidden dangers that he knew were there. He slowed his pace only long enough to refresh his horse and study the trail. Whenever hunger pains began to gnaw at his stomach, he reached down into his saddlebag for a slab of venison jerky or a dry tortilla.

Phoebe was the only Apache he'd ever trusted—and at times he was afraid of her. Of course Carlos was an Indian, too, but he was from the north where tribes were more civilized, and he had been with the family

so long he even spoke with a brogue! Juanito felt better thinking of Carlos. They were almost friends.

Juanito made record time to Silver City, rested
briefly, once again changed horses, then forged ahead
northward. It took almost an hour to find a shallow
crossing at the Gila River, but after he crossed, the
elevation was higher and Juanito and his horse began
to cool down.

If he hadn't met an old prospector, he would have
missed the trail, which turned off for Alpine. The
road, seldom used except for wild horses and renegades, was overgrown with cheet grass and mesquite.

By nightfall he reached Alpine Pass, the last rem-
nant of civilization, and an hour before sunrise he was
on the move again. Juanito knew instinctively when
he entered the land of the Apache. It was as if an in-
visible curtain had dropped behind him. It was a silent world without a living creature stirring.

He fingered the cross that hung loosely from a
chain around his neck and murmured a silent prayer.
His throat felt dry, but he knew he must go on. He
paused at the top of a ridge and studied the small valley below. No movement. Embarrassed by his fear,
once again he spurred his horse into a fast gallop. By
noon he noticed that his horse was covered with a
sweaty foam. If he didn't rest the gelding, the horse
would drop dead under him. He brought the steed
down to a fast trot in order to cool him slowly. Glancing around the area, he noticed lime-green threads,
obviously mountain streams, zigzagging down the
hills below him. He slowed the horse to a fast walk
and unloosened the catch on his gun holster. For some
reason his mount drew his ears back and shuddered

under the weight of his rider. Juanito knew the horse sensed danger, but try as he would he could see nothing to make him alter his course.

Two Apache braves followed the young Mexican on their unshod ponies just out of sight behind him.

In the shade of a Spanish oak Juanito stopped a short distance from one of the swirling streams. He looked around cautiously, then slowly circled the area where he had decided to rest. Instinctively, he looked this way and that, checking for signs of Indians or their ponies. Finally, confident there was no immediate danger, he dismounted. As a precaution he eased his gun from its holster as he loosened the cinch on his saddle. Gun in hand he walked the horse slowly to the water and allowed him to drink.

The braves, camouflaged in the brush above him, watched as Juanito watered and hobbled the gelding, and knelt down to sip water from the cool fresh stream. Then, with the speed of the wind, shrieking at the top of their lungs and riding at full gallop, the Apaches ran the trespasser down!

Juanito was fully conscious when they staked him out and scalped him. It took almost six hours for him to die. His last thoughts were of his mother, Maria; and his last words were to the Virgin of Guadalupe, "Pray for us sinners now and at the hour of our death!"

CHAPTER SEVEN

Hernando scarcely noticed the contrast of the barren plateau country as he descended from the high, forested, rim territory of the Apaches into the vast monolith-studded land of the Navajo. He was even too tired to notice the peacock-colored sunset that painted the sandstone monuments in gold and brown and lavender. His only thought was finding a place where they could bed down with some degree of safety.

In the distance his hawklike eyes noticed movement and he reined the mules to a stop. Then he realized that the white dots on the horizon were sheep. A Navajo herder was taking them home for the evening. Somewhere, not too far distant, would be a hogan, a fire pit with hot stew, and Navajo bread. His mouth watered at the thought.

Hernando checked on Carlin and realized immediately the young Scotsman was dying. Only a miracle would save him, and the Navajo medicine man was his only hope. In spite of his skepticism, he realized he would have to find Ole Sorebelly!

Although it was dark, the desert was illuminated with moonlight, and luckily he had no trouble locat-

ing the shepherd's hogan. On the way he tried to remember what his father had taught him about Navajo
custom. Hernando knew it was considered bad manners to ask anyone his name. If you wanted to know
who someone was, you had to ask a friend. It was also
considered rude to look directly into anyone's eyes;
rather, you looked at a person's mouth when he was
speaking.

The Navajos were reserved with strangers but were
always hospitable and were delighted if a stranger
shared a few gifts with them. It was their custom to
feed all strangers. If the stranger arrived while they
were eating, it was never necessary for them to extend
an invitation. It was simply taken for granted that he
would share their food.

Hernando drove his wagon cautiously up to the
camp. He wished suddenly that he had listened to his
father's advice and learned more of the Navajo language. But at least he knew a few words. He greeted
the Indians and then placed a bag of beans next to his
host.

The family ignored him as he sat down. He could
smell the frying bread and mutton stew, and his stomach growled. He felt as if he hadn't eaten in a week.
Without looking at him, the woman handed him a portion of the meal, and after a time he was able to make
her understand that he had a friend in his wagon who
was also hungry. She looked frightened for a moment,
wondering why the friend hadn't joined them. As best
as he could, Hernando explained that his friend was
suffering from a bad stomach and that he was taking
him to Ole Sorebelly. At the mention of the medicine
man's name, the Navajos became more friendly, and

the husband motioned for his wife to bring another portion. The woman filled a bowl with stew and vegetables and placed it on the ground so that she would have no contact with the white man, then disappeared inside the hogan.

Hernando awakened Carlin and spoon-fed him some of the nourishing broth. When he had tended to Carlin's needs, he joined the Navajos around the campfire and finished his own meal. Knowing it would be considered rude to leave his host immediately, Hernando pulled a sack of tobacco and some papers out of his pocket and offered the Navajo the makings for a smoke. They sat together quietly, enjoying the tobacco and the stillness of the desert. After a decent time, Hernando bid them good night, checked on Carlin, opened his bedroll, and spread it down on the sand next to the wagon. Relaxed for the first time in days, he fell into a sound sleep.

In the morning the strong pungent smell of Indian coffee, boiled with the sugar in it, awakened him. He lay still for a few minutes, watching a small scorpion, tail arched high over its pearl-white body, dancing back and forth in the sand next to his arm. He could have smashed it; instead, he watched until the poisonous insect tired of its attack and scurried away. Then he arose, and after shaking his boots carefully, pulled them on. Carlin was still asleep, so he joined the Navajos for breakfast. The sweet coffee and corn mush cooked with cedar ashes was pleasing to his taste, and the Indians seemed less reserved. When they finished eating, Hernando found some gifts for the family, and once again, after an appropriate length of time, questioned the brave about the location of Ole Sorebelly's hogan. The Navajo drew a map in the sand with a pointed stick, directing Hernando with the utmost accuracy to where he might find the medicine man. It was still some distance away.

Hernando was amazed as he found himself recognizing landmarks that he had not seen since he was a child and had made the journey to visit Ole Sorebelly with his father. The Inscription Rocks, the Teapot Dome, and the Mittens triggered his memory as if he were reading a surveyor's map. He had no trouble following the sandstone monoliths that directed him across the trackless desert as if they were road signs, and he arrived at the hogan by midafternoon.

It took some time for Ole Sorebelly to recognize the young man as the son of his great friend Chee Dundee. Then a wide toothless grin spread across his face and he welcomed Hernando by his Navajo name, Nez Tsoh Chee Dundee Begay, Son of Big Red Dundee! After the proper greetings had been exchanged, and Hernando had presented the family with gifts of coffee, sugar, flour, bacon, and bolts of colorful material, he pulled back the flap on the wagon and motioned for the old man to come and see his friend. It didn't take long for Ole Sorebelly to realize that Hernando wished his help in curing the man.

The Navajos believe that rather than trying to control nature, man must live in harmony with it. They know nothing of germs or infection, but believe rather that illness is caused because man has fallen out of harmony with nature. In order to cure sickness, the Navajos believe that it is necessary to bring the body together with the spirit and back into the balance of nature's forces. This is accomplished by any one of a hundred ritualistic ceremonies, each very complex and elaborate. These ceremonies, or "sings" as they are called by the Indians, are passed down from father to son and guarded with great propriety.

Ole Sorebelly was one of the powerful of the Navajo religious leaders, and his sings were very strong medicine! Because of his warm friendship with Andrew Dundee, Ole Sorebelly had great patience with Hernando. In his best Pidgin English he explained that there were two classes of personal forces for the Navajo: the Earth Surface People, living and dead, and the Holy People. He gestured to emphasize his point. "Holy People—Spirits—travel on the sunbeams," he told Hernando. "And they travel on the rainbows and on the lightning!" He waited until he was sure that Hernando understood his meaning. "They have given the *Diné*—the Navajo—a strict set of rules by which we must live or suffer the consequences. Your friend has broken the rules; therefore, the Spirits punish him with his sickness!"

Hernando nodded his head in agreement with Ole Sorebelly and waited for him to continue.

"There are two sicknesses: *naalniih*—white man say small pox, diphtheria, or influenza—and *tah honeesgai*—this means body fever or body ache or more better say sick all over! Your friend is suffering from *tah honeesgai*," the medicine man diagnosed, with great authority.

Hernando indicated that he agreed and rolled the old man a smoke.

Finally Ole Sorebelly conceded that if he could appease the proper Spirits for whatever violation Carlin had committed against the Holy People, he might be able to cure him.

Hernando looked at the medicine man's mouth and believed—or at least he wanted to believe! He hoped that it wouldn't take too long.

Ole Sorebelly began to make preparations for the curing ceremony. It would be an elaborate sing because Dundee had given him many fine gifts. First the singers must be called. He would have to study and plan the proper chants and sand paintings that would be used in the ritual. Carlin was carried gently to the medicine hut. There were vessels for administering herbs; minerals ground powder-fine to be used in the sand paintings; various aromatic substances to be burned for incense or fumigants; bowls of pollen; sacks of precious and semiprecious stones; and bits of shell to be used as offerings to the supernatural.

Hernando had learned from his father that the Navajos never used smoke signals nor drums, but rather had some other mysterious method of communication that no white man had ever been able to understand. Now he was able to witness the phenomenon firsthand. Within hours of his arrival the singers began to arrive at the camp from all directions!

First Carlin was placed in a sweat bath and given an emetic. Then he was bathed in a ceremonial bath of yucca suds. Rattles decorated with turquoise and tortoiseshell were shaken over his body. The chants of the singers and the throbbing beat of the ceremonial dancer's feet pounding against the earth echoed in Hernando's head. He had never seen such a ceremony and was impressed in spite of himself. The melodious voices of the chanters, the colorful costumes, the

103

beauty and sincerity of the people stirred feelings in Hernando that he had never been aware he possessed. It was like a dream.

Later that night, when the ceremonial had been going on for hours, Hernando finally sat down near the fire in front of the hogan and wondered if Carlin would live. He was not a religious man in the Catholic sense, although he often attended services with his mother in order to please her, but he found himself uttering a silent prayer. It was out of keeping with his nature, and he suddenly felt foolish. He was interrupted when there appeared, within the small circle of light, one of the dirtiest, scrubbiest old Indian traders he had ever seen. The man was so small he almost looked like a gnarled elf. He made himself at home next to the fire, greeted some of the Indians in Navajo, pulled a tin mug from his pack, and poured himself a cup of coffee.

"The name's Mulie Turner! Heard the Navees were havin' a healin' 'n heard that you was here—so I figure I'd come over 'n eyeball the son of my good friend Chee Dundee!" Before Hernando could answer him, he continued, "Please ta meet ya—knew yer daddy well. What happened to yer friend?"

Dundee smiled in spite of himself. The man had a pixie quality, and in spite of his age there was a twinkle in his eye. Hernando recalled the name of the famous old trader immediately. Mulie had been one of his boyhood heroes—although until that very moment, Hernando had never laid eyes on the man.

"I've heard my father speak of you many times, Mulie. It's a pleasure to finally meet you!" Hernando stared at the man in disbelief. He must be in his nineties, he thought, amazed at how spry the old man was.

"What happened to yer friend?" Mulie persisted.

"I'd like to tell you the story, but it would take some time to tell."

Mulie motioned to the crowd of Navajo children who had gathered around the fire to greet him as he sat down. "Nothin' the Navees like better than a good story—and the longer the better. It might also help them to understand what's wrong with yer friend, 'n they'd know fer sure what medicine to use. They could git the right spirits workin'. 'Sides, we got plenty o' time. This shindig should last for a couple o' days!"

Hernando, pressed for an explanation, began the story slowly, wondering how much of it he should tell. "Carlin Napier was born far across the great water in a land called Scotland. The town was called Glasgow, and it is the same town my father was born in . . ." He decided it would be best if he started at the beginning.

"Nez ytsii con tsah wai a pe Skóótlaaii a biin nachi nazzie tsoh nes aquí ii," Mulie Turner translated for the Navajos.

The Indians were greatly impressed. They waited for the story to continue.

"My Gawd, Mulie," Hernando complained, "at this rate it's goin' to be a long night!"

"Yah got somethin' better to do?"

Hernando acknowledged that he did not and continued the best he could. Mulie interrupted every few minutes so that he could translate for his ever-increasing audience. Hernando told of how the young man, who had been searching for a dream, had found instead misery and suffering, filth and disease, and cruelty and neglect. Hernando doubted that Mulie understood much more than the Indians, but everyone seemed to be enjoying the story, so he continued. Repeating the story in his own words seemed to give Hernando a better understanding of his young companion, but he still didn't agree with Carlin's philosophy.

Every so often he heard a sob from one of the Navajo women who was overcome with sadness by the young man's misfortune. When he was exhausted and his voice was hoarse, he stood up, excused himself, and wandered over to the wagon. He could hardly summon the strength to climb inside, but when he did he found that he was too tired to sleep.

Inside the medicine hogan, Carlin, delirious, relived his nightmare. He once again felt the horror he had experienced as Waldren chopped away at the hawser rope and heard the agonizing screams of the coolies as they plunged to their death in the Pacific; he felt the excruciating pain of the whip against his back and relived the struggle of his swim to the shore. The medicine man understood his anguish and fought to drive the demons from his body.

Ole Sorebelly sang hundreds of his magical chants, each one repeated just as his father and grandfather had sung them, without changing a word. He honored the six cardinal points—east, south, west, north, upward and downward—all represented by their personal colors. He and his assistants worked all day, every day, making beautiful symbolic sand paintings on the floor of the hogan. Every detail of each picture was perfect and done from memory. Then, each night, according to custom, the picture was erased and the colored sands were scattered before the sunset.

At last, five days after the sing had begun, the magic began to take effect. Carlin's fever subsided, his color and strength returned, and his nightmares ceased. Hernando was assured by Ole Sorebelly that his friend would be well enough to continue his journey to Santa Fe within the next few days.

Before this sojourn into Navajo country, Hernando had never acknowledged an Indian with more than a passing nod. He even ignored those Indians whom his father considered close friends. With the exception of Phoebe, he didn't try to conceal his contempt of the redskins. Even Carlos was suspect at times. The Indians were there; they were to be tolerated, but he could never understand his father's attitude of treating them with equality or respect.

Now, however, during the days of the ceremony, and with Mulie Turner's help, he had come to know them as human beings. He recognized them as individuals. He had seen a glimpse of their culture, had walked through their gardens, shared their food, and slept under the warm wool blankets they had woven on their looms.

With the help of Mulie's interpreting, he listened to their problems and shared in their triumphs. He would never again think of them as shadowy figures wrapped in blankets who would slit your throat if they had a chance. Living with them, even for that short period of time, he began to realize what they meant when they called themselves the *Diné,* the "People." It was an interesting sensation. He recalled what his father had said to him years before. "They're an honorable people if they're given a chance. If the Indians prosper, we will prosper. If the Indian dies out, or if the white man kills 'em off, it's just a matter of time before a part of us dies, too! And we will never be able to recover!"

Yet, even with this new understanding, he could not forget the words of his grandfather, Ramon Villanova, "The only good Indian is a dead Indian!"

Hernando sat silently on the top of a sand dune a short distance from the camp, watching the singers pack up their wagons and prepare for their journeys home back to isolated and lonely hogans spread out over a hundred-mile radius—and it occurred to him that his grandfather Don Villanova might have been wrong.

Hernando and Carlin said good-bye to Ole Sorebelly and his family, and Carlin promised to return. He was still in a state of awe over his miraculous recovery. The red lines that had begun to form around the wounds, indicating blood-poisoning, had disappeared completely and his eyes were clear and bright. He found that he had an enormous appetite and that the Navajo food was to his liking.

There were many things Carlin still found difficult to reconcile in his mind. One mystery was the uncanny physical resemblance of the Navajos to the Chinese. Even the designs on their baskets and woven into their rugs and blankets were similar to designs he had seen on ancient Chinese pottery.

"I wonder if Chang Li was right when he said that people were born again," Carlin asked Hernando. "Perhaps when the Chinese die, they're born again as Navajos!"

Hernando stared at the young Scotsman as if he were out of his mind. "Carlin, you're full of shit! Or else the fever weakened your brain!"

Mulie, who had overheard the conversation, came to Carlin's rescue. "Lissen here, Hernando. I'm an old man—but I seed 'n hee'rd things that there ain't no accountin' fer! Mebee, people is borned agin! I don't know—'n you don't know neither!"

Carlin and Hernando laughed at the old man's sincerity. "One thing I do know for sure"—Carlin was emphatic—"I'll never go to sea again! I've had enough of the fog and dampness—I wish I could stay here forever!"

"Yer goin' to have to stay. If ye ever go back they'll hang ya!" Mulie replied.

Hernando winked at Mulie. He knew Mulie, too, was a fugitive. If Mulie ever left the reservation or was caught by the authorities, he would be hung.

They stopped for lunch at the foot of the Chuska Mountains. There was no urgency in their travel now, and they took more than an hour to finish the cold mutton and corn grits the Navajos had given them to take along on their journey.

Finally, sadly, Mulie decided that it was time for them to part company. Hernando promised to say hello to his father for the old man and they shook hands. They watched until Mulie and his pack mules became small specks in the distance, and the tinkling of the Indian bells draped around the animals' necks were no longer audible, then cleaned up their camp and were on their way.

Hernando wondered if he would ever see Mulie Turner again.

He had been born and raised in this country, but until now Hernando had never really seen it. He began to see it through Carlin's eyes. Yes, it was beautiful. Yes, it was vast and untamed. Yes, it was clean. Funny, he had never thought of the earth being clean or dirty. And Carlin was right about the similarity between the sea and the desert. Both could be deadly unless they were treated with respect.

When Hernando and Carlin left the Chuskas and started up the narrow, winding trail that led to the rim of the Lukachukai Mountains, 8,000 feet above the valley, they were halfway home. In the distance, to the east, they could see Shiprock, the gigantic monolith that the Navajo believed was the center of their beginning and their creation. It was so magnificent that neither of the men spoke. For some reason, which he didn't understand, Hernando was anxious to get home. It had been almost three months since he had seen his family.

CHAPTER EIGHT

During the ride from Shiprock to Santa Fe, Hernando learned from Carlin that the handsome young Scot had never been with a woman. It was an unthinkable situation, to Hernando, that a twenty-year-old man might still be a virgin. "My Gawd, what kind of an upbringin' did you have?" he asked with genuine concern. "Hell, my grandfather fixed me up with my first whore when I was thirteen years old!" They rode on in silence for a few minutes, then Hernando continued, "Course my folks didn't know anything about it."

The mention of Hernando's parents brought a sharp pain to Carlin's heart. It was the first time since he had swum ashore on the deserted beach that he had felt the pangs of homesickness. He realized it would be a feeling he would have to learn to live with. Someday, the Lord willing, he'd have a family of his own.

Hernando, mistaking Carlin's silence for curiosity, studied his friend. "You know, it ain't healthy for a man to go without a woman—ain't natural either."

"I'd just as soon wait 'til I get married," Carlin assured him. "I've seen sailors so crippled with syphilis that they went mad. Seems more natural for a man to want to be clean when he takes a wife."

Hernando stared at Carlin with amusement. "*All* my whores are clean! Only trouble I've found is that the marryin' kind of woman bores the hell out of me. Tell you what I'm goin' to do—I got a little ol' gal in Santa Fe that will fix you up just right! Her name's Lydia. Now there's one hell of a lady! She's got breasts that remind you of buttercups—enormous buttercups—and the biggest, roundest butt you ever saw! Carlin, I envy you—wish I could have it for the first time again!"

"Don't go to any trouble on my account," Carlin protested.

"Trouble! It'll be my pleasure. That gal can teach you how to please a wife. That little lady is a real toe-turner—'n she opens up for a man like a lily about to bloom!"

Carlin felt a sudden, uncontrollable passion begin in his legs and spread up through his loins. He wanted to change the subject. "I haven't seen grass like this since I left Scotland."

Hernando guffawed and whipped the mules to a faster pace. It was good country! The break in the drought had opened the heavens and let go of the precious rain—almost seven years worth—in a single season. Entire villages along the river had been destroyed, and hundreds of families had been left homeless; but in return for the destruction, the grass grew belly-high and the sheep and cattle grew fat.

Hernando admitted that he had never seen the hills so green. It looked as if a giant mantle of velvet had been laid over the land. Finally, in the distance, they could see Santa Fe. Twenty years before it had looked like a stark brown mushroom perched on top of the hill. In those days, before the arrival of Father Lamy, now the first Archbishop of the province, there had not been a single tree in the town. But since the arrival of that dedicated and holy man, the landscape had changed dramatically. Single-handed, Lemy had planted hundreds of trees, and now in these later years Santa Fe exploded with color.

Blossoms of apple, peach, pear, lemon, orange, lime, and plum trees blended together in shades of pastel beauty—elm, maple, cottonwood, locust, weeping-and-osier willow trees burst forth in the spring warmth with new leaves of every conceivable shade of green.

Carlin breathed deeply and stared in wonder as they rode through the town. They passed the new St. Francis Cathedral, as magnificent as any Carlin had ever seen in Europe. Hernando explained that volunteer citizens from all over the area had come day after day in order to build the new church right on top of the old—and when their work was completed they had painstakingly taken down the original structure brick by brick, timber by timber.

They rode on past the plaza and through the heart of the town. Carlin questioned everything, and Hernando, who now had come to enjoy thoroughly the companionship of the young man, delighted in expounding upon the history of the area.

Hernando guided the mules over the cobbled streets to a more commercial section of the town, and finally reined them to a halt in front of a large, impressive adobe building. The sign on the front of the structure was in keeping with its extraordinary size, and read: ANDREW DUNDEE AND SON, LTD. Several coverall-clad men came out to greet them.

"Welcome home! We weren't sure whether you were dead or alive!"

"Wasn't sure myself—a time or two," Hernando joked.

" 'Magine yer anxious to get out to the hacienda. Charlie's gone to saddle up a couple of horses for you . . ."

"Much obliged, Tom," Hernando replied, as he and Carlin jumped down from the wagon onto the dock and Hernando introduced the younger man to the group. Within a few minutes a cowboy brought two beautiful bay mares from around the back of the building. The horses carried heavy Mexican hand-tooled saddles trimmed with silver, and their coats shone like brushed satin.

Hernando and Carlin swung wearily up onto the saddles, anxious to be on their way.

"Give my best to your mother—and tell Jake his vacation should be about over!" Tom called after them. Hernando turned and waved, wondering what the hell Tom was talking about.

"We have two stops to make—no, three—then we'll head on home," he announced to Carlin.

"Three?" Carlin asked. He was well aware of one stop Hernando seemed determined to make and was beginning to feel nervous.

"First we stop at Spiegelberg's General Store 'n buy you some clothes and boots of your own. And some kind of a good-lookin' hat. You look like hell in those hand-me-downs. I'm embarrassed to be seen with you!"

Carlin knew he was joking, but Hernando had

114

pricked his Scottish pride. "But I have no money—and no job. I have no idea when I'll be able to repay you."

"Don't worry about it. I'll take it out of yer hide if I have to. Or better yet, if it floods again next year, I'll get you a job as first officer on the ark."

Carlin smiled. "And the second stop?"

"For Ceerist sake—you really ain't had no education! You ain't goin' to wear new duds without a bath are you? We're goin' to Antonio's barbership and bathhouse 'n get rid of some of this dirt. I always keep a change of clothes there. Can't go a-courtin' them gals lookin' like this!"

There was no need for Carlin to ask about the third stop.

Aaron Spiegelberg seemed surprised to see Hernando in such a jovial mood. "Thank God, you're home, Hernando. At a time like this it's good to have the family together."

"Yes, it's good to be home," Hernando answered patiently. Although Spiegelberg was one of his father's best friends, and they played chess regularly, the man's sentimentality annoyed him. "And how is your family, Mr. Spiegelberg?" Hernando asked politely.

"Quite well. And how is your dear mother bearing up?"

Hernando wondered whether the old man was getting senile. "Everything is just fine—but right now we're rather in a hurry. I'd appreciate it if you could outfit my friend, Mr. Napier," Hernando replied hurridly, pushing Carlin between himself and the shopkeeper. "Put everything on my bill, and you might see if you have a pair of lizard boots that fit him." Hernando hastened to the door to avoid any further conversation with Mr. Spiegelberg. "When he's finished tell him how he can find Antonio's," he called back over his shoulder.

Aaron Spiegelberg shook his head in amazement. That the young man was so happy, and going to Antonio's, when his father lay dying was beyond his comprehension. The goys! He would never understand them! He continued muttering in Yiddish as he fitted Carlin's new wardrobe.

By the time Carlin arrived at the barbershop Hernando was already bathed and shaved. He instructed the Mexican attendant to burn Carlin's old clothes and to make sure that his back was treated gently. Then he retrieved a bottle of bourbon and two glasses from his locker and poured a healthy shot. "You know, kid," he said slowly as he handed Carlin his drink, "I never had a brother. My mother had two girls stillborn, but I never had a brother. Always felt kind o' cheated—most of the families 'round here have six or seven kids." He poured himself another stiff drink, then pulled up a stool next to the tub and sat down. "Tell you what I'm goin' to do. I'm goin' to adopt you as my brother."

Carlin laughed, then swallowed his drink straight down just before the attendant soaked his head with a bucket of water. "You're a kind and generous man, Hernando," Carlin sputtered, "and I'd be honored to be your brother. Do I also get to share the wealth?"

"No, just the women!"

Within a half an hour Carlin had finished his bath, and was clean-shaven and dressed in his new outfit.

"My Gawd, yer a good-lookin' fella. Just don't give

me too much competition." Hernando was half-serious. "Now let's get on over to Maria's 'n get you fixed up with Lydia!"

Carlin had passed the stage of trying to argue with his friend. He swung his leg up over the saddle and they were off.

"Do you think that with your blue eyes and blond hair people would really believe we were brothers?" Hernando questioned.

"Not really."

"Well, they would be wrong. Brotherhood, true brotherhood, is a matter of the heart—not the sperm!"

It was the first time in all the weeks they had known each other that Carlin had ever heard tenderness in Hernando's voice. There was something else, too, Carlin became aware of. This tough, brawling, hard-hitting, two-fisted cowboy was lonely.

In spite of all his good intentions Carlin found, when they entered the brothel, that he was filled with anticipation. Hernando's graphic descriptions of the women had excited him, and now, finally, he was eager to experience the act of love. The room was surprisingly small and seemed more like an ordinary bar until his eyes became accustomed to the dim light. It only took a moment for Carlin to realize that it was not an ordinary bar. There were a dozen or more women—girls—dressed, or rather half-dressed, in short, brightly colored dresses, bare-legged, bare-armed, and bare-breasted! Carlin gasped. He had never, in his short lifetime, seen women so exposed.

Maria spotted Hernando almost immediately. Short, plump, with a mass of red hair piled high, she practi-

117

cally leapt from her seat at the bar, threw her arms around his neck, and kissed him full on the mouth. Gushing with pleasure, Maria spoke rapidly in Spanish. "Darling boy—heart of my hearts—you've been away too long!" She held Hernando at arm's length then turned to stare at Carlin. "What a handsome lamb you've brought me," she murmered in a husky voice, not bothering to mask her admiration.

"Maria, this is Carlin Napier," Hernando announced, "and if you keep staring at him like that, you'll make me jealous. I want him to meet Lydia."

"Lydia?" Marie was surprised, then her eyes lit up with pleasure. "You mean he's still a virgin? How wonderful!" She spoke to Carlin in English. "Lydia is very skilled and most gentle with inexperienced lovers." She started to lead them to the bar when her expression suddenly changed. "Hernando, you've just arrived—yes?"

"Of course. You know this is always my first stop when I've been away."

"You haven't been to the hacienda? No one has told you the news?"

"What news?"

She sat the men down at the bar and ordered three snifters of brandy. When they had been served, she explained as gently as she could. "Dear boy, your father is very ill. He has had a stroke."

Everything became clear to Hernando at once. The anxiety in Tom's voice—Mr. Spiegelberg's questions—and the uneasy feeling in the pit of his stomach. "Carlin—brother—you will have to see Lydia another time. We must leave now for my home."

* * *

They rode fast and hard for more than an hour, slowing the mares to a fast trot just long enough to cool them. When they entered the mouth of the valley, and were in view of the Hacienda de Villanova Dundee, Hernando brought his horse to an abrupt halt. The thought of his robust father being stricken was almost impossible for him to believe. They had not gotten along well in the past. But the last year or so Hernando had tried, for his mother's sake, to be patient with the old man. "You two are so much alike," his mother had told him, but he doubted the truth of her statement. Andrew Dundee was, in Hernando's opinion, a stubborn and dominating man. His positive nature made it impossible for him to relinquish control of any situation, and he was not susceptible to change. Andrew Dundee, by his own standards, was generous, kind, and reasonable. In Hernando's eyes he was heavy-handed—and either unwilling or unable to understand any points of view that conflicted with his own. He was not fond of his father. Perhaps his opinion was colored by his grandfather's unadulterated hatred of the giant, red-headed, mountain man. All this was now beside the point. His father was ill— perhaps even dying.

Carlin sensed his friend's agony and remained respectfully silent. In the distance he could see the hacienda situated on a high bluff on the eastern slope of a long narrow valley in the foothills of a majestic mountain range Hernando called Sangre de Cristo. Hernando explained that the original land grant had contained hundreds of thousands of acres deeded to his grandfather by the king of Spain. Much of the territory had been lost after the Treaty of Guadalupe Hidalgo, but it was still the largest privately owned ranch in the Southwest. The Dundees had vast holdings of grazing land, timber reserves, and mineral rights—enough so that it would continue to be used and developed for generations.

Hernando spurred his horse into a slow lope, and with Carlin by his side soon arrived at the heavy iron gates that led to the entrance of his home. Alerted to their arrival by the yelping and barking of the ranch dogs, the vaqueros, as excited as the animals, had the gates open wide and led the riders quickly to the main house.

Isabella and Phoebe stood waiting on the terrace. The two men dismounted and Carlin stood awkwardly in the background as Hernando embraced his mother. Her joy at seeing him was so overwhelming that she could not speak for a few minutes. Finally she broke free and held him at arm's length. "Juanito is not with you?" she asked quietly in Spanish.

"No. I've not seen him. Why do you ask?"

"I sent him to try to find you over three weeks ago. He found Jake near El Paso, and Jake sent him up the Apache trail to try to intercept you." Her eyes filled with tears and she looked downward. Both she and Hernando knew that they would never see the young vaquero again.

"How is my father?"

Isabella smiled. "He grows stronger every day. He's sitting up in the patio with Jake. Go and see him." Then she turned graciously to Carlin. "I know all about this young man. I'm pleased to see that you

120

have been completely healed of your illness." She turned and led the way into the hacienda. "Phoebe, please show Senor Napier to the guest room and make sure he has everything he needs. After he has rested you may bring him outdoors to join us. I'm sure Don Andrew will have a thousand questions to ask him about Scotland."

Carlin looked after Isabella as she followed Hernando out of the room. He could see where Hernando had inherited his good looks. The woman was lovely. The hacienda, too, was exquisite: a two-storied dwelling of thick adobe block, stone, and glass with giant timbers, which the Mexicans called *vegas*, as support beams. It had been built in the Spanish tradition with a central courtyard. Unlike those of other haciendas the rooms were large and open and filled with pots of rare plants that seemed to thrive in the grandiose setting. Each of the major rooms contained a fireplace large enough for a man to stand up in, and the umber-colored floor tiles were polished to such a sheen they reflected his image.

Carlin suddenly became aware of Phoebe waiting stoically at the foot of the stairs. She was much taller than the Navajo women he had met on the reservation—almost as tall as he was—with high cheekbones and almond-shaped eyes. Her light, copper-colored skin was clear and radiant, and her features were as perfectly proportioned as any woman's he'd ever seen. She possessed a primitive, exotic beauty of which he was sure she was completely unaware; and which reminded him of native women in paintings by an obscure artist named Gauguin, whose work had haunted him since he had first noticed it in a small shop in Marseille.

Carlin followed her upstairs to a large sunny room with a small veranda from which he had a view of the entire valley. He was impressed by the luxury. Logs had been laid in the fireplace ready to be lighted when the room was filled with the evening chill. A soft white mink-pelt robe covered the massive walnut four-poster bed; and one entire wall was lined with books. If his food was brought to him, he thought wistfully, he could spend the rest of his life in this room and still not have time to read them all!

Phoebe interrupted his reverie. "I will bring you a pitcher of water so you can bathe. Would you also like some tea?" She spoke perfect English. Her voice was low and pleasing to his ear.

"Perhaps you are hungry?" she suggested, embarrassed by his silence and the way he was staring at her.

"No, thank you. I'm not hungry—but I would enjoy some tea. It's been a long while."

She excused herself and went downstairs. Carlin walked around the room touching the polished wood and soft fur robe. Then he began to examine the books. Dickens, Shakespeare, Voltaire, and other authors whose names he didn't recognize. He had never seen such a library. He wondered if the rough, raw-boned Hernando had read any of them. Obviously there were many facets in his benefactor's personality.

Phoebe reentered the room so quietly that he wasn't aware of her presence until he heard her pouring water into the basin that had been placed on the marble-topped dresser.

"I will bring your tea in a few minutes," she informed him. "Then perhaps you should rest. Dinner will be served at eight o'clock. I will call you."

Carlin washed his hands and face, then removed his new boots. He admired the craftsmanship of the footwear for a moment, then, although he felt uncomfortable sitting on the bed, succumbed to the weariness of his body and fell into a deep sleep.

Andrew Dundee and Jake Anderson sat in the shade of a large Spanish oak playing chess. It was obvious from their comradeship that they had been friends for many years. Their movements were easy and conversation was unnecessary. Hernando stood in the shadow of a flowering bougainvillea, watching them with a feeling akin to envy. They had shared experiences in the wilderness that were no longer possible to experience. They had walked the land together before it was civilized—and had been the first white men to leave footprints in many areas of the Rockies. Hernando wondered briefly what it would be like to be first in anything when it came to comparing his life with his father's. Then he became painfully aware that beneath the crocheted shawl which covered his father's massive shoulders, one arm hung limply by his side. It was only when his father laughed and threw his head back that Hernando noticed the half-closed eyelid and the uncontrollable sag of his father's lower lip. Hernando wavered; he was totally unprepared for the rude shock of finding the old man half-paralyzed. For a moment he was unsure of what to do, then Isabella put her hand gently on his shoulder and urged him forward.

"It's about time you got home!" Andrew's voice was gruff, but the warmth in his expression revealed his pleasure at seeing his son. "How are things on the reservation? Did Ole Sorebelly cure your friend?"

It was just as if Hernando had returned from a short trip into town. The stroke hadn't mellowed his father too much.

"He worked his magic. Carlin is upstairs resting. He'll join us later if you feel up to it."

"Up to it? I've been bored to death listening to your mother and Jake. A fresh young face will do wonders for me." Andrew paused to catch his breath. "Did Juanito come home with you?"

"No."

Andrew looked away and was thoughtful for a moment. "Too bad. I liked the boy very much. He was a good worker. Jake, you'd better ask the boy's parents to the house. We'll have to tell them."

Isabella interrupted, "Perhaps it would be better to send Carlos into town to find Father Vieja. I'd like him to be here with us so that he can comfort Maria and Juan. We can invite him for dinner and he can spend the night."

"Yes, of course," Andrew agreed, then motioned to Jake that he wanted to be alone with his family. Jake gave Hernando a strong bear hug, then excused himself. He knew the Dundees had much to talk about.

It tired Andrew to speak, so he rested for a few minutes and then chose his words carefully. "Were you able to stop at Po'Se'Da'?"

The question surprised Hernando. He had expected his father to ask about Ole Sorebelly and was anxiously anticipating telling him about his experience with the Navajos and his first meeting with Mulie Turner. Hernando and Andrew never spoke of Po'Se'Da'. It was one of their Indian trading posts, and a portion of their business in which Hernando took no interest. He hadn't visited Po'Se'Da' in years and was mystified by his father's question.

"Why would I stop there? It's miles out of the way," he answered sharply.

Andrew half-rose from his chair, his face flushed with anger at Hernando's acid tone. "Just like your grandfather!" he exclaimed. "No use for the Indians! Well, let me tell you something. They're an honorable people—at least they show respect for their parents."

Hernando caught sight of his mother's anguished expression and his manner immediately softened. "I meant no disrespect, Father. I was only surprised at your question. I'm much more interested in knowing how you're feeling."

Andrew leaned back once more and tried to collect his thoughts. His breathing was labored but he continued, "The railroad will be completed just south of the reservation in a matter of months. Not too long after that the freighting business—our business—is going to come to a rude ending."

"But we've known about the railroad for quite some time—we'll still have routes north and south."

"It will only be a matter of time before those routes will have no value. Hernando, I had word a few weeks ago, before I became ill, that a band of drunken renegades shot old Fred Myers at Po'Se'Da'. I had no choice but to send Peaches McGraph up there to run things until I could find someone else—

someone more suitable. I wasn't prepared for this damned attack, and I'm a little behind schedule . . ."

"What has Peaches got to do with the railroad?" Hernando asked with controlled patience.

"I'll get to that. Peaches is running the post, but he's also running the Indians away! It's a bad situation. He's got no use for the Navees and they've got less for him."

"What's that to do with me?"

"The lambs will be ready for sale in the fall, and they'll bring a good price. Especially when we'll only have to drive them as far as Holbrook!"

"Holbrook?" Hernando asked, trying to make sense out of his father's seemingly disjointed thoughts.

Andrew's eyes sparkled slyly. "We're goin' to put them lambs on the railroad! Our enemy don't know it yet, but they're goin' to end up being our best friend!"

Hernando smiled. He recalled his father's favorite expression: *Whenever they toss you a lemon, make lemonade!* For as long as he could remember, there had never been a time when his father hadn't managed to turn defeat into success. "And what do you want me to do?"

Isabella straightened the comforter around Andrew's shoulders. "Must we talk business?" she said. "I'm afraid it will be too much for you."

Andrew smiled and patted her hand. "It would be too much for me if business was *not* taken care of. Now let me be." He waited until he felt stronger and then he continued. "Trouble is we might not have any lambs. When you have a bad manager in one trading post, and the Indians won't trade with you, word'll spread to the other posts, and before you know it none of the Navees trust you and you're out of business. Then some bastard from Washington gets his hands on the trading permits, comes in, and steals the Indians blind—and they rebel. You got a hell of a war on your hands. It's that simple. One rotten apple spoils the whole barrell"

"It can't be that bad . . ."

"It is that bad!" the old Scot insisted, his voice shaking. "I've thought it over and decided that you're the only one I can trust to do a proper job. You're going to have to return to the reservation and run Po'Se'Da' until I feel stronger and can find the right man to replace you."

Hernando looked suddenly stricken. He was about to explode with anger when he caught the horrified expression on his mother's face. She stifled a cry of anguish, tears glistening in her eyes. Hernando regained control of his temper immediately. "Of course. I'll go as soon as necessary."

With great effort Andrew smiled and signaled his son to come closer. He hugged Hernando with his one good arm and said with great affection, "I knew I could count on you."

"Enough!" Isabella cried out. "You must rest before dinner, or I won't allow you to come to the table. Hernando, call the men to carry your father to his room."

Hernando stayed alone in the courtyard, trying to examine the new turn of events. It was as if his father had sentenced him to prison. He knew that it took a very special breed of man to become a successful Indian trader and to manage one of the isolated posts. At least that was something that he and his father agreed on. He felt he could remember enough of the language to get by—and he had a fair understanding and respect for the Indian's religion and traditional beliefs. A trader must act as mortician, advisor, confidant, and diplomat, and—more important—he must believe in what he is doing with his whole heart. Hernando knew he could never be that special person.

He paced back and forth across the worn-brick courtyard, trying to think of some way out of his commitment. He recalled the summer he had spent at the post with his father many years earlier. With temperatures reaching well over 100 degrees in the shade, it had been like living in the ashpit of a stove. He'd been told the winters were worse. It was not uncommon to hear stories of men who had been lost in snowstorms and whose bodies were not found until the spring thaw. Being on the reservation for a few days—and being up there for six months at a time—were two different stories. It would be worse than being in jail—it was like a death sentence. But then he realized, ironically, that his father needed him—really needed him—for the first time in his life. If he were ever going to be able to prove his worth, this would be the time.

With the problem as resolved as it would ever be, Hernando suddenly felt hungry and remembered that he hadn't had a chance to speak to Phoebe since his return. He headed for the kitchen. His relationship with Phoebe was very special to him. Long ago he had ceased to think of the handsome woman as an Apache. She was gentle and understanding, and next to his mother he loved and respected Phoebe more than any other woman he had ever known. Although she was only two years older than Hernando, she seemed to him years older and wiser.

As usual Phoebe had anticipated his needs and had a steaming bowl of cornmeal mush and hot coffee waiting for him when he entered the room. "Why don't you marry me?" he teased, as he sat down to enjoy his meal.

Phoebe poured herself a cup of coffee and sat down to join him. "Tell me about your adventures on the trip."

Hernando beamed with pleasure—it was good to be home and good to be sitting with Phoebe. She was the one person in the world he felt truly cared about him and what he did. His mother adored him, but with Isabella her husband always came first. Hernando began with stories of San Francisco, and an hour later reached the part of his tale that dealt with his encounter with the Apache braves on the infamous trail. "The bastard could have killed me, but I would have gotten off one shot and sent him straight to hell!"

Phoebe listened in rapt attention, never taking her eyes from his face, never interrupting. Once she refilled his bowl, and twice she filled his cup. Hernando left out no detail, including how he had first heard of his father's illness from Maria, the madam. When he had finished, he was unabashedly candid. "If I ever found a woman like you, I'd marry her! Trouble is you're one of a kind."

Phoebe, knowing he was joking, took his hand. She had heard him say the same words a hundred or more times before. "You will marry when the right woman finds you. When that happens you will have nothing to say about the matter."

Hernando smiled. Perhaps she was right. Perhaps he had never met a woman who cared enough about him to pursue him in the proper way. Certainly *he* had never actively pursued a woman! Once, when he had been in his teens, he had been intrigued by Phoebe. Firmly, but gently, she had refused to sleep with him. It had been quite an affront to his ego, and, in order to soothe his wounded pride, he had convinced himself that he didn't want to bed the damned Apache anyhow! Yet in his heart he knew this wasn't true. If he could ever find anyone as loyal and loving as Phoebe, he would bed her and marry her in that order. He recalled the many times she had nursed him through his hangovers, laughed at his jokes, bolstered his ego, and acted as his priest when he was too ashamed of his actions to go to confession. Regardless of what he had done, Phoebe always gave him her full support and approval—and never asked anything in return.

Felicia was like Phoebe in many respects, but he could never forget that she was a whore. He had known many men in the West who had married prostitutes, and without exception those unions had turned out well. Hernando and Phoebe had discussed these marriages at great length, and although Phoebe could see no reason why these relationships shouldn't work out, the thought of a whore as the mother of his children was repugnant to Hernando.

* * *

Andrew didn't feel up to joining the others for dinner. Instead, Isabella took him a tray, then returned to the dining room where she acted as hostess for her son, Carlin, Father Vieja, and Jake. After the sadness of the discussion of Juanito's probable fate, Hernando amused the guests with his account of Ole Sorebelly, the Navajo medicine man, and his impressions of the notorious Mulie Turner. "He's a dwarf! And one of the kindest and gentlest men I've ever met. Yet he's accused of murdering four men. I just can't believe it!"

"I'm not sure it's true," Jake spoke up. " 'Sides—that was more than thirty years ago. Seems they'd-a pardoned him long ago."

"I was just a young man then," Father Vieja added, "but it was different with the Mormons. They were a bitter and secretive people. I understand that although these men were emissaries from Washington, they insulted the Mormon women and abused some of the children. The rumor was that Mulie Turner was acting upon direct orders from Brigham Young. No one ever knew for sure, of course, but the Indians respected him as a trader and have given him refuge on the reservation for all these years."

The group was thoughtful, then Hernando became serious. "I'll be leaving for the reservation in a few days. Father has asked me to manage Po'Se'Da'."

Jake almost choked on his coffee. "Now I've heard everything!"

Carlin became enthusiastic and wanted to know all the details. Hernando tried to explain the difficulties involved and the importance of the position. "Pay day comes just twice a year—once in the fall when we buy

131

the lambs, and once in the spring when we buy the wool. It's lonely out there! No one speaks your language—you have to speak theirs. A trader might not see another white man for months on end. It takes a very special breed of man to survive out there."

"I might be that very sort," Carlin mused. "Not every man can survive at sea. It's lonely out there, too. You must allow me to go with you. If I could learn the language, I might make a very good trader. And it would give me a job and a reason for being here."

It soon became apparent that Carlin was not going to take no for an answer; and Hernando was secretly delighted at the prospect of having his company. He continued explaining the importance of their mission. "Each year we need wool and sheep to fulfill government contracts, not to say anything about satisfying the demand for lamb in the East. Using the railroads to ship the livestock will cut down on loss and make the business more profitable. More important, the Navajos need us and we can't let them down!"

It astounded Hernando, as much as his mother, to hear how much like his father he sounded. Impressed with himself, he continued, "If a trader steals from the Indians or doesn't take proper care of his business, the entire Navajo nation could suffer." He paused to let the entire group digest his thoughts, then directed his attention to Carlin. "There will be times when you'll find that you would rather be in jail—or even back at sea! It would be safer."

When Phoebe was sure they had finished their dinner, she served brandy and informed Isabella that Don Andrew had requested that Mr. Napier join him in his room with his after-dinner drink, so that they could discuss Scotland, Isabella nodded, indicating that the idea met with her approval, and excused the young guest.

Andrew Dundee was not at all the man Carlin had pictured based upon Hernando's description. It was to be expected that the stroke would have diminished the elder Dundee somewhat in size and strength, but his robust curiosity and the sparkle of life in his vivid blue eyes was still very much apparent. Carlin liked the old man immediately—and the admiration was mutual.

"Sit here next to me on the bed where I can have a better look at you," Andrew insisted. "Carlin Napier? Sounds more like a British name than a Scot's! If it weren't for the look o' you, I'd wonder."

"My mother's grandfather was Welsh. Carlin Atkins. I was named for him. However, Napier is a true Scot's name, and that I am from my heart!"

The men laughed. Jake had already informed Andrew of Carlin's experiences, and how he had been accused of mutiny and presumed dead in the sea. "I'll bet the captain of your vessel was a son-of-a-whore of London!"

"He was English."

"I knew it!" Andrew exclaimed. "Those followers of the Queen are not to be trusted. Think they're better than the Lord almighty! But one thing you'll find out about the West is that no decent man will ever ask you about your past. It's considered a breach of ethics. Every man in the West is judged for himself. Oh, we have our share of outlaws and renegades, but if a man wants to forget his trespasses, he'll get a second chance out here." Andrew drew a flask of brandy from under the mattress and took a healthy swig. He winked at Carlin. "What the ladies don't know won't hurt 'em, eh? Now tell me what you think of my son."

"He's a fine man. He saved my life."

"He's got the blood to be a fine man. Handsome, smart, strong as an ox—but no discipline! Too good-looking and too much money!" Andrew flushed, then apologized, "I don't mean he's not a good worker or that he's not dependable—he is—but he's arrogant. His Spanish blood! Won't settle down and marry some good woman. I want grandchildren, and I may not live to see them if he doesn't find someone soon!"

Their conversation lasted for almost a half hour before Isabella entered the room and suggested it was time for Andrew to get some rest. Carlin was sure the old man was pleased he was accompanying Hernando to the reservation; and he had also been given some insight on the relationship between father and son. They were very much alike, but both too proud and stubborn to admit it. And Hernando would marry only when he found a woman like his mother.

Carlin found Jake and Father Vieja snoozing in front of the fireplace in the living room. He wandered to the rear of the hacienda and finally found Hernando in the kitchen, watching Phoebe cleaning up after the sumptuous dinner. She welcomed him into her private domain, poured him some coffee, and served him a generous slice of raisin pie; then she continued her work. Everything she did, it seemed to Carlin, was done without effort. She moved as quietly and gracefully as a gazelle.

Although Hernando was tired, he was also restless.

"As long as we are about to be exiled into the wilderness, I suggest we ride back into Santa Fe and join Maria and Lydia for a drink!"

Carlin was embarrassed when Hernando mentioned the whores in front of Phoebe. He glanced quickly at the woman but couldn't tell from the expression on her face whether or not she understood what he was talking about. "You go, my friend, I'm too tired," he said. "I think I'll get a good night's rest. Perhaps I'll join you another time."

Hernando laughed at Carlin's reluctance but didn't pursue the subject. He kissed Phoebe on the cheek, bid them both good night, and went hastily to the stable to saddle his horse.

As much as Carlin wanted to talk with Phoebe, wanted to know everything there was to know about her, when they were finally alone he found it difficult to speak. The silence was awkward; it was the first time in years that he had been alone with a woman. And the fact that he found himself physically attracted to her made conversation even more difficult.

"Hernando tells me that you're an Apache," he finally said.

"Yes. But I have been away from my people for quite some time," she stated simply.

Carlin put more sugar into his cup. "Do you ever get homesick?"

"No. I see my mother quite often, and I have no other ties to my tribe." She finished the dishes. "May I get you something else?" she asked.

"No, thank you. I suppose I should get some sleep."

"Rest well. I'll see you in the morning," she said and

smiled, as she slipped her blanket around her shoulders. "Until then . . ."

He sat at the table for a few moments after she had gone, then lowered the lamp and went upstairs. Phoebe had lighted the fire in his room while they were at dinner, and now the dying embers filled the room with a rosy glow. He undressed, placing his clothes carefully over the leather chair, found a book, turned up his lamp, and began to read. Images of the beautiful Indian woman clouded his vision. He was asleep before he had finished the first page.

In his dreams he accompanied Hernando into town. The painted faces of the whores leered at him as he moved slowly to the bar. In the distance he heard coarse, loud laughter, and when he turned to see where it was coming from, he recognized Hernando leading a faceless woman in his direction. She had enormous breasts, and he was embarrassed to see that she was completely naked! After what seemed like an eternity, he was able to flee from the brothel. Outside, waiting for him, was the Apache woman, Phoebe.

It seemed to Carlin that it only took moments for them to reach the pine forest. He could smell the sweet aroma of the branches. Phoebe moved away from him silently, removed her blanket, and spread it down over soft pine boughs. Then she beckoned him to join her. He looked down on her naked body. It was thin but strong and supple and bronze in the light of the sunrise. He began to caress her. Her skin was tender, sensuous at his touch, and emitted a delicate perfume. He felt the fullness of her breasts against his chest as he lowered himself to mount her. Phoebe led him gently into his first climax—and then they made love again and again. For the first time he understood the mysteries of love; he would love her forever. He heard her calling him, sweetly, softly.

"Senor Napier, it's morning. Time for breakfast."

Reluctantly, Carlin opened his eyes. He watched as Phoebe set a tray down on the dresser, then retired from the room. He rolled over in the bed and stared at the ceiling. "Oh, God!" he murmured under his breath.

He washed the bed as well as he was able, then dressed and sank down in the great leather chair. He was mortified! The dream had seemed so real he was almost reluctant to face Phoebe for fear she would be able to read his thoughts. He forced himself to have a second cup of tea, replaced the cup and saucer on the tray, and, summoning all of his courage, proceeded downstairs.

"It's about time you joined us." Andrew's tone was gruff, but there was a twinkle of pleasure in his blue eyes. "Sit here next to me."

"Sorry to be late. I'm usually an early riser." He bowed his head to Isabella and greeted Father Vieja and Jake but noticed that Hernando, too, was late for breakfast.

Isabella rang the small silver bell next to her plate and a moment later Phoebe entered the room bringing more trays of food. Carlin smiled shly at the Apache, noting how Oriental she looked, and hoped she could not hear the pounding of his heart. He wondered how a dream could seem so real. She returned his smile,

137

and too quickly for the smitten young Scotsman disappeared into the kitchen. Carlin, feeling suddenly flushed, tried to recover his wits and join in the conversation. But it was almost an impossible task—his head was completely filled with thoughts of Phoebe.

They were finishing their final cup of coffee when Hernando, obviously suffering from a horrible hangover and looking as if he had had little or no sleep, staggered into the room.

Andrew bristled, and Carlin noticed that this time there was no twinkle in his eyes. "If you're going to spend your time in Santa Fe wasting yourself instead of staying home with your family where you belong, you might as well start for Po'Se'Da' today!"

The older Dundee's outburst was so sudden and vehement that Carlin was surprised. But from the dark scowl on Hernando's face and the sadness in Isabella's eyes, he began to suspect that this might be a common occurrence in the Dundee household. He took advantage of the moment to excuse himself. "I think I'll go to the kitchen and get another cup of coffee." He could hear the argument continuing as he retreated down the hallway.

Carlin hesitated a moment before he entered the kitchen, wondering what he was going to say to Phoebe. Somehow, he knew, he must talk to her and really get to know her. But, if old Andrew were serious, they would be leaving for the reservation that very day. There was so little time! Such precious little time to make his feelings known to Phoebe. He pushed the door open and entered the room. A Mexican woman was scrubbing the woodwork and glanced up as he entered. "*Buenos días*, senor," she said.

"Is Phoebe here?" he asked anxiously.

"*No habla inglés* . . ." the woman replied.

Carlin suddenly felt foolish. After all, it had just been a dream. It would take time to get to know Phoebe, gain her confidence, and court her properly. And if he were to become a trader, he had plenty of time.

Hernando came through the door looking very pale. "I need some strong black coffee. Rosa, *por favor, café negro.*"

Carlin joined him at the table.

"Well, *mi hermano,* I've cooked our goose. The vacation was short but sweet, and now it's over. My father wants us to start for the reservation as soon as we can get a wagon packed. But—it was worth it! Maria has a new girl from the East. Marietta! She's beautiful and very accomplished. I should have insisted you join me last night."

Carlin just smiled.

Within an hour they were packed and the wagon outfitted. Andrew had prepared a list of everything they would have to pick up at the headquarters to take with them to Po'Se'Da'. Isabella instructed Rosa to include a choice side of beef, packed in salt to prevent it from spoiling, and fruits and vegetables canned the previous fall. Carlin was grateful when she had one of the vaqueros bring a box of books she had packed for them to take. "So that you won't die of boredom . . ." They made their parting brief. Isabella knew it would be quite some time before she saw her son again and didn't want him to see her tears. Andrew, knowing that once again he had been too hasty in sending Hernando away, clasped his son to his breast and wished him "Godspeed!"

By midafternoon they had picked up the additional supplies at the warehouse in Santa Fe and were on their way out of town. They had been at the hacienda less than two days, and yet in that short period of time Carlin knew that his life had changed. He felt that finally there was a reason for him to be alive—something for him to look forward to. He had found a woman he might love and a new profession. He was to become an Indian trader.

CHAPTER NINE

A few days out on the trail Hernando and Carlin began to feel the full heat of the summer and looked forward to reaching the cool, sweet air in the high mountains of the Lukachukais. In just a short time the grass had begun to turn brown, and the warm wind carried the odor of parched earth.

Most of their conversation dealt with what would be expected of the men once they assumed the responsibility of the post. Hernando repeated himself so many times that Carlin began to suspect he had an ulterior motive, but when Carlin mentioned his suspicions, Hernando laughed. "Guess it's sort of like when yer a little kid 'n yah hear ghost stories, 'n yer really scared to death, but you want to hear them over and over again. By the tenth time you've heard the story, yah ain't scared no more! Truth is I'm scared to death that I won't do a good job—'n *I have to prove that I can.* Not only for my father but for me. I haven't spoken Navajo for years, never did speak it well." He glanced at Carlin and realized that once again he was repeating himself. "No more talk about Po'Se'Da'—at least for today. You have something on yer mind?"

They had reached a fork in the road, and in a leisurely manner Hernando reined the animals to the right and to the north. Then he stared closely at his friend. "You do have something on your mind. You've been quiet as hell for the last few days. Let's get to it."

After what seemed an extraordinary length of time, Carlin asked, "How does a man know whether or not he's in love?"

Hernando jerked the reins and brought the mules to an abrupt halt. "You can't be serious?"

"Quite serious," he replied simply. "When I was aboard ship one of the sailors talked about being in love. When I questioned him about it and reminded him that he had only seen the woman twice in his life, he said, 'Ah, yes, but I've met her in my dreams more times than I care to mention—and I never stop thinking about her.' He was sure that he was in love. Is that possible?"

"Now how the hell would I know? I've never been in love. As a matter of fact, if it weren't for the way my mother and father feel about each other, I wouldn't even believe there's such a thing." Hernando removed the makings of a cigarette from his breast pocket. "What happened to the sailor?"

"He jumped ship at the next port and no one ever saw him again."

"Well, you just stay clear of that sort of tangle. I don't want you jumpin' my ship."

Carlin seemed content to let the subject drop, and it wasn't until the next day that he found the courage to question Hernando about Phoebe. Regardless of how hard he tried he couldn't stop thinking about her, and he felt an uncontrollable need to know more about the woman of his vivid dream. Where had she lived when she was with her tribe? Had she ever been married? Was she a full-blooded Apache? How had she come to be with the Dundees?

Hernando, never dreaming that Carlin's conversation had the remotest connection with his conversation of the day before, was amused by the Scot's interest in Phoebe. He elaborated on Andrew's rescue of the two women and painted a clear and accurate picture of Shell Woman and her witchcraft. His statements about the cruelty of the Apache way of life were not exaggerated, and his voice was edged with bitterness. "With the exception of Phoebe and Shell Woman I never met an Indian I'd turn my back on—'n the Apache is the worst of 'em all."

Carlin remained silent for a moment, wondering whether or not to admit his true feelings to Hernando. Finally he could contain himself no longer. "I sincerely believe that all men are brothers. Guess I was born color-blind—I never saw a white man or a black man or a yellow man or a red man—I only saw a man who was good or was evil, kind or cruel, honorable or dishonorable."

The seriousness of the conversation made Hernando uncomfortable. "What about the women?" He laughed. "That's sort of the way I judge the women—pretty or prettier, passionate or more passionate, and firery or more firery!" He slapped Carlin on the back and shoved the reins into his hands. "I'm going to rest awhile in the back of the wagon. It's time you learned to handle these long-eared brothers of ours. Just head straight west, you should see Shiprock before too long. We'll camp at sundown."

Carlin had never driven a team of eight mules, but he positioned the leather reins between his fingers and soon felt comfortable. Hernando had instructed him to let the mules take care of themselves. "They're a hell of a lot smarter than we are," he said, and now that he was in charge Carlin was sure he was right.

Perched high up on the seat and alone with his thoughts with just the sounds of the wind in the grass and the steady beat of the mules hooves on the sun-baked trail, Carlin felt it difficult to stay awake himself. What kept him awake was the wonder of his new life. He couldn't seem to drink his fill of the beauty of the land and the magnificence of the endless space. Despite the intense heat of the sun that boiled up from the ground like dry fire, discouraging even the lizards from making any unnecessary moves, Carlin breathed deeply and felt exhilarated in his new surroundings. He was free, really free, of the past. One day perhaps he would find a way to see his family once more, but for the time being they were better off thinking he was dead.

By the time Carlin identified the huge volcanic plug known as Shiprock it was late afternoon and he noticed a sudden, unexpected buildup of thunderheads on the horizon. The winds picked up and he felt a nervous strain on the reins as the animals lowered their heads and quickened their pace. He sensed the need to get the wagon off the trail and onto higher ground, but before he could translate his feelings into actions, a squall sent torrents of rain to the earth in a matter of minutes. Lightning shot down from the black clouds dangerously close to the wagon, and the deafening clap of thunder awakened Hernando. He was out of the wagon and onto the seat within seconds taking the reins roughly from his companion. "Hee-aw!" he screamed at the mules as he cracked the leather whip over their heads. They barely made it to the high ground before the arroyos were turned into raging rivers, destroying everything in their paths. New channels in the sand and clay were cut where channels had never been before. The trail they had been following just a few minutes earlier completely disappeared; it was transformed into a muddy, churning river. Carlin was too excited to be frightened, and the violence of the storm seemed to bring Hernando back to his carefree self. It was over almost as quickly as it had begun.

"I wouldn't have believed it if I hadn't seen it," Carlin exclaimed.

"Get used to it—that was just an ordinary desert storm!" Hernando assured him. "We might as well see if the water damaged any of the supplies. It won't take long for everything to dry out, then we'll set up camp right here. How are you at cookin' over a campfire? I feel half-starved."

Both men awakened at sunrise the next morning feeling rested, refreshed, and anxious to be on their way. Carlin heated coffee and biscuits while Hernando repacked the wagon. If there had been any hesitation about returning to the reservation the previous day, all traces of it were washed away with the summer storm and a good night's rest. Both men felt the spirit of adventure ahead of them.

Much of the time there was little need of conversation. Other times Hernando continued to explain more about what would be expected of them in their new roles; and still other times they would burst into song at the top of their lungs. They were good companions.

The coolness of the air in the mountains and high plateaus was a welcome relief from the heat of the valley. In the land of the Navajo Carlin experienced the strange sensation of "coming home." The country was familiar—yet unfamiliar. Instinctively, he also realized that the land was to be respected. If you didn't know exactly where you were going, it would be an easy matter to get lost; and because the area was so sparsely populated, you might never be found. Hernando was certain he knew the country—at least most of the time.

The route they traveled took them in a northwesterly direction from Santa Fe, past the landmark of Shiprock, then sixty miles in a more northerly direction over the Lukachukai Mountains. When they reached the Canyon Jeddito, Hernando assured Carlin they would be less than ten miles from Po'Se'Da'.

As heavily as the wagon was loaded, they managed to average forty to fifty miles a day, and barring any unforeseen accident would reach the post in six or seven days.

"My father, Jake Anderson, and Mulie Turner were the first white men to come into this area," Hernando told Carlin. "More than forty years ago. The Indians didn't raise sheep or cattle in those days—didn't make any silver jewelry either. I've been told that it was

146

nothing to buy and sell squaws just like you'd buy or sell cows. My father never had to buy his women, or so Jake tells me. Always had two or three that traveled with him. If the truth were known, I'm probably related to half the Navajos on the reservation!"

Carlin looked shocked. "Your father doesn't seem the kind of man who needs more than one woman!"

"Hell, Indians often have two or three wives. In those days I guess he wasn't much better than an Indian. 'Course that was way before he married my mother. She civilized him. I'd have to be pretty hard up or pretty drunk 'fore I'd sleep with a squaw."

Carlin thought of Phoebe. The word *squaw*—at least the way the word emanated from Hernando's mouth—seemed derogatory. He wondered if he would ever be able to convince his friend that there was no difference between Indian women, white women, or Chinese women. The only thing that made them different was the way you felt about one woman! And God knows what caused that particular feeling. He began to think about his dream of making love to the Apache. At times he fantasized that it hadn't been a dream at all and that he had really caressed her smooth body and kissed her full, sweet lips. If he wasn't in love with Phoebe, Carlin thought, it was the closest thing to love he could imagine.

They were right on schedule when they descended the steep, switch-back, curved trail down the west side of the Lukachukais and found themselves in an area of the reservation where torrents of water had gouged out the arroyos and changed the terrain. The washouts left Hernando confused about which route to take, and he was unable to recapture his sense of direction. A toss of a coin decided them to bear to the right. When they rounded a sharp bend in the wash, they found a small band of sheep blocking their path. Carlin jumped down from the wagon and herded the animals to one side.

A few minutes later there were more sheep, then more, and then more.

"They're pretty scattered," Hernando noted. "Strange we haven't seen a shepherd."

At the top of the next rise he stopped and looked the area over with his spyglass. There was no shepherd to be seen. "I wouldn't worry about it except there are no dogs around either. Just doesn't seem right for some reason."

With Carlin following along behind, Hernando stepped down from the wagon and climbed to the top of a hill where he scanned the area with greater concern. "Looks like a hogan over there in the distance. I think we ought to mosey over and see what's going on."

The hogan had been so constructed that it blended in perfectly with the landscape, and Carlin couldn't see the dwelling until they were almost on top of it. "What's that hole in the back?"

Hernando walked around to the rear of the crude structure and stared at the hole that had been broken through the north wall. The muscles in his face tightened as he explained. "It's *chindee*. A ghost hogan. Means that someone died here, and they poked that hole in the wall so's the spirit could get out."

Carlin was impressed. "Doesn't look like it happened too long ago." They left the wagon to explore the area. Carlin was the first to find the body of a handsome young Navajo. It was inside the hogan just below the hole.

"Looks as if his woman couldn't get the body out." Hernando scowled and shook his head. "I'm surprised she didn't just burn it down. We'll have to bury him. Get the shovels out of the wagon."

Here it was—his first experience as a trader. Hernando tried to recall the ritual. If he were to bury the Navajo, he would have to do it properly. He remembered that the Brave should be dressed with his clothes on backward and his moccasins worn on opposite feet in order to confuse any evil spirits who might try to follow him into the other world. He tried to explain the custom to Carlin as he cut the clothes away from the young Navajo, washed the thin body, and redressed him for his spirit's final journey.

"But there's no one around to see how we bury him. You don't believe in these ridiculous superstitions, do you?" Carlin asked.

"Whether I believe or not has nothing to do with it. We're here to be proper traders," Hernando replied patiently. "I know that even after all these years my father don't seem to have any doubts about certain powers of the Indian beliefs."

"How's that?"

Hernando paused and looked directly at Carlin. "'Cause when I was home I noticed that he was wearing one of Shell Woman's amulets around his neck. He probably has more faith in that amulet curin' him than in Dr. Vargas's mumbo jumbo."

Carlin was surprised at Hernando's seriousness.

149

Then he remembered how Ole Sorebelly had saved his life. If a man as intelligent and respected as Andrew Dundee believed in Indian magic and lore, perhaps there was something to it. He wasn't sure, but the thought did not repulse him.

Hernando's mood changed. "Do you believe in the Bible?" he asked, with a twinkle in his eye.

"Yes, I guess I do," Carlin admitted.

"Then you must believe that Jonah lived in the belly of a whale, and that Noah marched them animals—two by two—into the ark. When you think about it, maybe the Indian's version of life and death ain't too farfetched."

Carlin laughed. "I guess there's a lot in this world I have to learn. Who knows what's possible and what isn't?"

"Now then, don't stand around like a scarecrow. You wanted to be a trader. See if you can find a blanket, and let's get on with this!"

Carlin found a handwoven wool blanket folded neatly in a basket inside of the hogan and watched Hernando cut holes in it. Then he noticed that Hernando found the Indian's saddle and mutilated it also. "Seems a bloody waste to me," Carlin commented under his breath.

"I don't give a damn how you feel about it," said Hernando. "We got a job to do, 'n part of that job is respecting Navajo custom! We got to 'kill' these things so that no one else can use them. Understand?"

"Not really—but I'll try."

After they buried the man, Hernando, following the custom to the letter, broke the shovel handle in two and left it beside the burial site.

"Carlin, I can't explain everything to you just now, but it's important to me that we do a good job. Maybe I don't believe in any of this any more than you do, but if we're going to be successful, we can't take shortcuts. Everything we do has to be accepted by the Navees. And when you get right down to it, who in hell are we to tell them that their beliefs are just stupid superstitions?"

"You're right. I'll try not to be so critical from now on!"

"I remember my father explaining the custom to me when I was a kid. There's nothing a Navajo hates more than seeing something dead. Even an animal—unless it has to be killed for food. Death is an evil thing to them—and to me, too. And they have a terrible fear of ghosts." Hernando's mood lightened. "You believe in ghosts, don't you? At least you believe in the Holy Ghost! We have to play by the rules, and the greatest favor a trader can do for a Navajo is to bury their dead—and respect 'em!"

Carlin had been thoroughly chastized, and Hernando began to wind down. "Let's take a look around and see if there's anything left of this poor buck's family."

The vegetation was sparse, and it seemed to Carlin that if anyone else were around, it would be difficult for them not to be seen. But he felt as if he had behaved badly, so now he assumed a positive attitude and began the search in earnest. They looked behind every bush and in every rocky crevice within a mile of the hogan. They were about to give up when two barking sheep dogs finally led them to the woman.

It was obvious she was very ill. She lay almost unconscious among some rocks several hundred yards and then, apparently too weak to go any further, had crawled most of the distance on her hands and knees and then apparently too weak to go any further had collapsed. Hernando couldn't understand why they hadn't found her sooner. "Just like trackin' an animal!"

The men agreed that she probably had influenza, and Carlin waited with her while Hernando brought the wagon around. They loaded the woman along with the dogs into the rear of the wagon, and Carlin found a can of milk, which he opened with his knife so she could have some nourishment. The woman began to protest, but he couldn't understand what she was saying.

"*Kee! Kee!*" the woman kept repeating with what little strength she had left.

"Holy Mother of God!" exclaimed Hernando, finally recognizing the words he had learned in his youth, "*kee* means 'boy'! There must be a child out there somewhere!"

Now both men became very conscious of "tracks," and with the help of the dogs they found a handsome four-year-old boy hiding in the brush not far from where they had found the woman. "We must o' passed the kid a half-dozen times when we were looking before," Carlin said in wonderment.

"I told you—they got instincts like animals. We never would have found either one of 'em if it hadn't been for the dogs."

Hernando carried the frightened child back to the wagon and reunited him with his mother. The woman smiled and closed her eyes, while the boy sat huddled in a corner with the dogs, his face hidden in his arms.

"He's afraid she's going to die," Hernando explained, "and he doesn't want to see it."

"He may be right—she's very sick. Well, we have the family. What about the sheep?" Carlin asked.

"First we'll get to the trading post and see what we can do for the woman, then we'll try to find out who she is and send word for some of her relatives to round up the animals."

When they reached Po'Se'Da', Peaches McGraph came out of the shoddy-looking post to welcome them. Carlin thought the man's name suited him. He was rather plump with round, peach-colored cheeks and a yellow complexion. His bald head was covered with a pink fuzz and from the back looked exactly like an oversized, overripe peach. He was all smiles until he noticed the child and watched as Hernando lifted the woman from the wagon and started to carry her inside.

"Whar do yah think yer goin' with that In'jun?" he demanded.

"I'm going to take her inside and get her some broth. She's goin' to have to rest a spell, and if she don't get any better, I'll have to find a medicine man," Hernando answered in an even tone of voice.

"Yer not takin' her inside the post," proclaimed the fat little man, blocking the way. "She looks sick enough to me so's she might not make it,—then we got a *chindee* tradin' post, an' you won't see another Navee 'round here fer the next hundert years!"

Hernando ordered Peaches out of the way, but the man refused to budge. "Hernando, yah don't know these In'juns like I do! Yah ain't had no experience runnin' a post! Yah gotta listen to me. Yah cain't bring that squaw in here!"

Peaches's tone offended Carlin, but it enraged Hernando. His mere look at Peaches was enough to make the man back down, and he and Carlin proceeded into the post with the woman and her child.

"Well," Peaches mumbled sullenly, "at least the damned dogs has got to stay outside." Then, as if to make a final point, Peaches shook his finger after the men. "And I'll tell yah somethin' else, Mr. Bossman, you ain't goin' to git her to no medicine man fer some time. The trail's muddied up to a horse's belly, 'n it'll take more 'n a week fer it to dry out!"

"Peaches," Hernando yelled over his shoulder, "shut yer mouth!"

Carlin viewed the unfamiliar surroundings as he would study a navigation chart. Nothing missed his eye. The post itself was not a large structure. Much smaller, in fact, than he had imagined it would be. It was nestled in a small clearing against a high bluff just a few yards from a natural spring. There was a fair stand of cottonwood trees surrounding the main structure, insuring the building of summer shade. The post had been constucted of hand-hewn logs with heavy timbers used as support beams. Adobe clay and dirt were used as seam fill, and more than a foot of earth had been shoveled up on top of the flat roof to insulate the interior against summer heat and winter cold. Iron bars were sunk vertically into the walls in front of the small windows. A large corral containing a dozen or more horses and several roughly constructed holding pens for cattle and sheep were sadly in need of repair. Several other odd-sized buildings completed the compound.

When Carlin entered the interior of the post, he found it dark and dismal. There was no flooring, and it was obvious to the Scotsman that the unpleasant odor did not come from the earth. The main room of the post, or as Hernando called it, the "bull pen," had a long, wooden counter with crude shelves behind it; it was sloppily stacked with tins of coffee, baking powder, canned milk, and canned tomatoes. Bolts of flannel, velveteen, and calico did little to brighten the atmosphere. On the walls, hung on pegs, were crude cooking utensils, bridles, saddles, ropes, and farming gear. Sacks of flour, sugar, and salt were also stacked up at one end of the room; and barrels of pickles, pinon-nuts and honey were lined up at the other end. In the center of the bull pen was a large, round, iron stove. Three hand-carved chairs were placed around the stove and hung on the back of each chair was a crudely printed sign: INGUNS DONT SIT IN CHARS. Wood and kindling were placed behind the counter, leaving barely enough room to walk.

Attached to the bull pen was a small kitchen area and sleeping room, which Carlin found were even more of a disaster than the main room. Unwashed dishes were piled up everywhere. Flies dined on decaying food scraps, and the table balanced precariously on three legs. The straw-tick mattress on the floor in the sleeping room was so dirty that it was almost impossible to see where the tick ended and the dirt floor began.

Hernando shuddered with disgust. Carlin found it difficult not to gag because of the stench.

"Damn it, Peaches, how could you live in this pigsty? I want it cleaned up—and cleaned up pronto!" Hernando thundered, his face flushed with rage. "And get a fire going in the stove so that I can make a mustard plaster!" He turned on his heel and carried the half-conscious woman back to the wagon, "It's goin' to be all right, honey. We're goin' to take care of you and the boy!"

She didn't fully understand the words, but she understood the tone of his voice and managed a weak smile. He laid her gently down on one of the bedrolls and then found a new soft cotton blanket to cover her.

Carlin perched the half-starved boy on the wooden counter in order to feed him some cheese and hard-tack—then he found some stale biscuits which he threw to the dogs.

"Get yer ass movin', Peaches—'n I mean fast!" Hernando yelled as he picked up the filthy tick and flung it out of the room through the back door. "And when the fire's built in the stove, go outside and start a bonfire, 'cause there ain't much of this crap we can salvage!"

The mustard plaster and the broth came to a boil on the stove at the same time, and Hernando stopped working in order to care for the woman. First he took a bowl of the broth to the wagon and spoon-fed it to her. Then he made a poultice of mustard plaster and made a large bandage from a torn piece of white flannel. Hernando had been with more women than he cared to remember, yet he still felt embarrassed as he undressed the young Navajo. It made it worse for him because she smiled, indicating total trust. Her body was painfully thin but exquisitely formed. Her almost translucent skin was golden-brown, and her young breasts were small and firm with pink-brown nipples that reminded Hernando of spring rose buds. He became aroused in spite of himself. With the exception of Phoebe he had never been attracted to Indian women, although he had seen many Indian prostitutes. It often mystified him why the Indians attached no social stigma to prostitution—they simply referred to such women as "She Who Stands by the Side of the House." He wondered if the Navajos were more civilized, or less, because they didn't practice a double standard of morality. Then his thoughts returned to the woman—she blushed with modesty at his gaze, so he quickly applied the poultice and flannel, and tucked the blanket around her.

Inside the post the boy finished eating and crawled under the counter, where he immediately fell asleep. Carlin placed his jacket beneath the child's head for a pillow. "I don't think he'll wake up for a while. God knows how long he's been out there without food or sleep." And then, without further ado, the three men started to work.

Peaches was sweating and panting with exhaustion, and still Hernando would not let him rest. In a state of confusion and near panic, Peaches mumbled under his breath that all this effort was unnecessary. Hernando replied by ordering him to heat another bucket of water and to scrub down the shelves and woodwork with lye soap. The final indignity came when Hernando ordered the wretched little man to burn all of his personal clothing "It's all past ever bein' clean again. I'll give you a voucher to have it replaced in Santa Fe!"

They worked for hours before the rooms began to take on some semblance of order and the acrid smell disappeared. After a sudden, final burst of anger, Hernando burned the offensive signs that had hung on the backs of the chairs, and allowed Peaches and Carlin to be seated. "Where's all our customers, Peaches?" Hernando asked accusingly.

"Whal," Peaches replied sheepishly, "some of 'em cain't get through 'cause of the mud I tole yah about. Some of 'em don't need nothin'—'n some of 'em jest don't care to trade here no more."

"What does that mean?" Hernando persisted.

Peaches sat up stiffly in his chair. "Whal, some o' them In'juns is so high 'n mighty they say they don't like the service! So I tole 'em to go trade at Fort Defiance!"

Hernando, near his boiling point, leaned back and stared up at the ceiling. "Mighty considerate of you."

"Where's Fort Defiance?" Carlin asked.

" 'Bout a hundred or more miles from here," Hernando replied, trying to restrain his temper.

"Isn't it a hardship on the Indians to have to travel that far?" Carlin didn't blame the Indians for not liking the service. He didn't like anything about the pig-eyed little man sitting next to him.

"To hell with the hardship on the Indians! That's our business this bastard is sending away!" Hernando's eyes narrowed, and the veins in his temples became visible. He realized once again that his father's estimation of the situation had been correct. It would take Hernando time to reestablish the credibility of the Dundees' good name and build up the trade at Po'Se'Da' to a point where business was once again profitable. He had to be sure that they would have lambs from the Navajos in the fall to fulfill their contracts. He overcame his instinct to strangle the ineffectual Peaches and directed his attention to the task at hand.

"First thing we're goin' to have to do after we finish clean' up this mess is knock out a couple of walls and make this place bigger—put in some more windows and let some air in," Hernando said, directing his conversation to Carlin. "Then we'll make some 'dobe bricks and put down a proper floor."

"Let's get on with it," Carlin suggested, standing up and stretching his weary body, "It'll be dark before long, and we should have a decent place for the woman and the boy." Once again he began rearranging the supplies. "Take a look at this!" he exclaimed, uncovering a wooden box filled with silver-and-turquoise jewelry. "Some of this work is exquisite!"

Hernando took one look and exploded. It was the final straw as far as he was concerned. He looked accusingly at Peaches and stormed, "You know better than to treat pawn like this! What in hell's the matter with you?" He turned to Carlin. "This can be another lesson in what's important as far as being a trader. This is pawn. It's jewelry made by the Navajo for himself. To them jewelry is a symbol of their personal wealth—and the wealthier they are, the greater respect they demand from their peers."

Carlin held up a particularly heavy necklace and examined the workmanship. "It must have taken months to make something like this. It's really very beautiful."

"Navajos take all the time they need; they're a very patient breed and they value their jewelry highly," Hernando replied, examining the box. "Personally, I wouldn't give you a quarter for this stuff. Let me try to explain the way the Indians think. They don't give a damn about the white man's way of doing business. They think that gold or silver coins in your pocket, or a big roll of paper money hidden away in your poke, is of no value whatsoever. No one can see it. The Navajo is proud of what he has and wants everybody to know how rich he is, so he melts down the coins and makes them into buttons, bracelets, belts, or necklaces. Some of this pawn is handed down for generations."

"Why is it called pawn?"

"That's the name the traders have given it. When the lean times come, the Navajos use their jewelry for credit to buy food or whatever else they need. Same as we'd put up security for a loan—'cept they're too proud to call it a loan. They pawn their jewelry. Then after they're paid for their lambs in the spring or their wool in the fall, they settle up their accounts and redeem their property. One thing I know for sure is that stuff ought to be hung up in a special place so's the Indian who owns it can see it's safe. We got a hell of an investment tied up in that silver."

"Damn it, Hernando," Peaches protested, "you know I've been too busy to hang it anywhar! Even if yah melted it down just fer the silver, you'd never git out of it what the damned In'jun was into yah fer!"

Both Hernando and Carlin realized it was hopeless to pursue the subject. As soon as they were able, Hernando would see to it that a special room was built to house the pawn properly. Right now he was more concerned with finishing cleaning the post so that he could bring the woman inside. He found some sheepskins stacked in one of the outside storage sheds and brought them inside where he placed them on the floor of the sleeping room in order to make a bed for the woman and her child. When he had covered the skins with fresh linens and reheated the broth, he carried his patient inside and awakened the boy. The woman seemed a little better, but she was still feverish. The boy was still reluctant to look at her, but had no trouble finishing his supper. Carlin hung a blanket up between the sleeping room and the kitchen area so the Navajos could get some rest, then the men sat down to enjoy their own dinner. It had been a long day.

Just before bedtime it occurred to Hernando that he had been so busy he'd forgotten to ask Peaches the details of the murder of Ben Myers, the previous manager of the post.

"Couple o' prospectors named Denver and Garren found 'im inside here deader than a mack ll! The bull pen was all tore up, they said. If you think it was bad when you got here, yah should o' seen it when I got here!" Peaches looked at both the men to make sure he had made his point. "Anyways, those two prospectin' fellers buried ol' Ben in the back, then headed fer Santa Fe to tell the authorities! I din't know nothin' 'bout it till yer dad sent fer me to get on up here 'n run things fer a while."

"Seems funny they didn't head fer Fort Defiance. It's less than half the distance, 'n if it was renegades, seems the prospectors would want to get the Army

161

boys involved," Hernando commented thoughtfully.

"Oh, it was renegades! No doubt 'bout that!"

"Was anything stolen?"

"Now how the hell would I know that? I din't git up here fer nearly three weeks after he was daid 'n buried!"

Hernando paused to think about what Peaches had said. Something didn't make sense. "The Navajos wouldn't have stolen anything. They wouldn't even have come inside the post!"

"I don't get yah," Peaches replied.

"You said it yourself. If someone died inside Po'Se'Da' the post would be *chindee*, and everyone in the Navajo nation would have heard about it. I know you ain't had much trade, but if the post was *chindee*, you wouldn't have any."

The logic of what Hernando had said began to sink into Peaches's head. "Wal, I'll be damned!"

Carlin said, "What do you think happened?"

"I'm not sure. But I don't think it was renegades that killed old Ben. He'd been here for years, and the Navajos trusted him. Doesn't make sense that any of them would have done away with him. He was too valuable to their way of life. I'm not sayin' that they wouldn't kill a trader. They would 'n they have, but only when they had good cause. If they was bein' cheated 'r somethin' like that."

"When we know the language a little better, 'n got things fixed up the way they ought to be, I think I'll try to find out a little more about them prospectors." Hernando crushed his cigarette out on the iron stove. "Got a big day tomorrow. We'd better turn in."

* * *

Carlin and Hernando lay next to one another in their bedrolls near the stove in the bull pen. Moonlight filtered into the room through the narrow, barred windows, casting eerie shadows everywhere. Carlin lay, wide awake, reflecting on the happenings of the day. "Are you asleep?" he whispered to Hernando.

"No. Body's too tired to give up."

"It's everything I dreamed it would be—almost like being in heaven," the young Scot said softly.

Hernando was silent for a few minutes, then replied, "It's a stinking purgatory. I'll stay as long as I have to and do what has to be done. If you want to stay here, you'd better learn fast, because when I leave, I ain't never coming back!"

CHAPTER TEN

Almost immediately after they arrived, Hernando became aware that the same mysterious silent force the Navajos used for communication during Carlin's healing sing at Ole Sorebelly's was at work at Po'Se'Da'. He couldn't see the Indians, but he could feel them. Waiting. Watching. There was no way of knowing whether or not he and Carlin were going to be accepted as traders until the Navajos decided to make themselves visible. He sensed that that would not happen until they sent Peaches packing.

It took almost a week of steady interrogation before Hernando was convinced they had extracted every ounce of knowledge about Po'Se'Da' and trading from the unctuous little man. He suggested that Peaches repeat every Navajo word he knew to Carlin, so the words could be written down phonetically, and he and the Scot could practice the language.

Often it seemed to the younger men that it was more difficult to communicate with Peaches than it would be with the Navajos. From morning 'til nightfall they grilled the old trader, extracting this information and that until, exhausted, Peaches exploded with anger. "I ain't goin' to tell yah no more!" he screamed, his round face red with anger. "I'm tired, 'n I want to get out o' this hellhole. I had to larn everythin' the hard way—'n you kin, too!"

Hernando and Carlin looked at one another and smiled triumphantly. Early the next morning they helped the frustrated little man pack what few belongings he had left, saddled his horse, and wished him Godspeed. When he disappeared over the hill in the distance, the men roared with laughter. "I ain't goin' to tell yah no more!" Hernando mimicked Peaches's high-pitched voice. "Gawd a'mighty, with help like that we'd be out of business for sure—if we ain't already!"

The Navajo woman was recovering nicely. Her fever was gone, and although she was still weak, she could feed and do for herself and her son. The boy stayed within the confines of the curtained sleeping quarters with his mother, coming into the bull pen only when he was hungry. At those times, which were fairly often, he would enter the room and stare at either Carlin or Hernando until he was noticed. Then he would look away and rock back and forth on his heels until he was given something to eat.

"It'd be a hell of a lot easier if he'd learn to bark!" Hernando commented. "Do you know that we ain't heard that kid speak since we found him? Maybe he's a mute!"

Carlin wondered, too, whether or not there might be something wrong with the child. He decided to try out his new Navajo vocabulary on the stoic boy the first chance he got. He didn't have to wait long. Within an hour the boy was back at the door of the bull pen. Carlin knelt down before him and began to speak very slowly. "I-like-to-eat-a-big-breakfast! *A-bee-nee-go t'óó a-haa yói ná áshdííh!*" He repeated the phrase several times, first in English, then in Navajo. The boy stared at him, his big brown eyes expressionless.

Carlin referred to his notebook. "*Dah díníilghaazh dóó dibé bitsi nídeidííh dooládó̕ likan halchin da leh.*" He tried to speak without moving his lips, the way the Navajo spoke. "In English that means 'we eat fried bread and mutton!'" Once again he repeated the phrase, and once again there was no response from the boy.

"You speak our language very well," the woman said in a rhythmic voice. "But I think he would like some coffee with much cream and sugar."

Hernando and Carlin were startled to see the young Navajo mother standing in the doorway. She smiled sweetly. "Would you too like some coffee?"

"You speak English!" Carlin could hardly believe his ears.

"Very small English," she answered shyly. "I went to mission school when I was a child. I am Bah-Tsosie. And this is my son Atwa Kee."

Carlin searched his book for a translation of their names. "I know that bah means 'girl'—and that kee means 'boy' . . ."

"Yes. It is our tradition that every child, when it is first born, be called either girl or boy—and then, as they grow older, they are called according to either how they look or how they act. I am slim—you might say slender—and therefore I am called Bah Tsosie, Slim Girl. Since birth my son has been a very quiet child, so I call him Atwa Kee. In our language *atwa* means 'quiet.' Do you understand?"

"We understand," Hernando interrupted. "I am Hernando Dundee and this is Carlin Napier. Are you feeling well enough to be up?"

Bah Tsosie assured him that she did, then pronounced their names several times to make certain that her pronunciation was correct. Her words were formed with exploding sounds, breath checks, and final breathing—with a strong Navajo accent—but the tone was not guttural. "I think that I cook now. Not to offend, but I much better cook!"

The men readily agreed with her and Carlin asked what he might do to help.

"I don't feel clean and would like very much to bathe. You have a sweat lodge, yes?"

Hernando led her out the back door to where a small domelike structure had been built. At the opening of the hoganlike lodge was a fire pit for heating rocks, and it was near the spring so that cold water was easily accessible to pour over the rocks in order to create steam. It was customary for the Navajos, after spending some time in the hot steam, to jump into a pool of cold water. Where water was scarce, they rolled naked in the sand or in winter in the snow. Hernando's father had taken an Indian-style bath at least once a week ever since Hernando could remember. "Tones the skin and muscles. Keeps a man fit!" his father had told him.

Carlin gathered wood, while Hernando fetched two pails of water and lighted the fire. Then they left the woman in privacy for her bath.

When she had finished and dressed, she returned to the bullpen and informed the men that she would need material, thread, needles, and silver buttons in order to make new clothes. "I will need two skirts and two blouses if I am to look well." There was nothing shy in her attitude, nor was it demanding. Just a simple statement of fact. Once again she smiled sweetly, then disappeared into the kitchen to begin the noon meal. She seemed as relaxed and at home as if she had been at the trading post for years.

The first Navajo arrived at Po'Se'Da' early the next morning. Hernando and Carlin watched him ride slowly into the compound and in the Navajo custom look everything over carefully before he dismounted. He seemed wary as a fox. Even when he reached the door, he peered in cautiously before entering. Hernando waited behind the counter and motioned for the man to help himself to the tobacco and papers. After a reasonable length of time and silence, Bah Tsosie entered the room and spoke to the brave. Almost immediately he began pointing to items he needed. Hernando and Carlin stood by silently admiring the grace and ease with which Bah Tsosie adapted herself to her new role. When everything had been gathered and the business completed, the Navajo smiled broadly at the traders. He touched Hernando's hands lightly in a gesture of approval and spoke. "*Ní nahalin. Shilééchaa* Chee Dundee Begay!"

Bah Tsosie translated: "He says he is your friend and is happy to know the son of Red Dundee." Then she announced proudly, "Your father is greatly respected by my people—and now you will be called Chee Dundee Begay! Son of Red Dundee!"

Hernando nodded graciously. Even hundreds of miles from home he stood in his father's shadow. But he had been given the Navajo name and knew he had been accepted as a trader.

"What name will I be known as?" Carlin asked anxiously, not willing to be left out.

Bah Tsosie smiled and turned to speak with the Navajo. He grinned broadly and shook his head up and down, and when he had answered, both Bah Tsosie and the brave burst into laughter.

"I do not understand why you are called so, but you are already known to my people as Tall One Who Likes Yellow Faces!"

Hernando and Carlin looked at one another in amazement. They understood the meaning of the name. They also understood how quickly news traveled by Navajo telegraph throughout the entire reservation.

Still grinning, the Navajo picked up his goods and nodded farewell. Bah Tsosie turned eagerly to Carlin. "Are there really such people? People with yellow faces? They must belong to the Corn Clan! Tell me about them!"

Hernando laughed, but Carlin was embarrassed. "Another time. I'd rather hear about you and Atwa Kee."

There was no time for either story. Within a few moments the trading post was filled with curious Navajos, and it remained so until late afternoon.

The Indians didn't easily show their emotions publicly, but Hernando and Carlin couldn't help but notice the pleasure on their faces as they nudged each other and pointed with pride to their pawn, which was now properly displayed. It was almost like a celebration with the traders giving sweets and tobacco to each customer.

"I'll bet we've done more trading in one day than has been done at this post in six months!" Hernando said proudly, when they finally sat down to rest.

"We couldn't have done it without Bah Tsosie," Carlin replied, as he tried to remove his boots. "My feet feel as if they belong to someone else." He suddenly became alarmed. "I can't get my boots off!" he cried.

It took both Hernando and Bah Tsosie more than twenty minutes of tugging and twisting before they were able to free him from his torment.

Bah Tsosie's delicious supper was made even more pleasurable by the success of the day's work. When they finished eating, Hernando walked outside to be alone with his thoughts. It was a beautiful evening. A cool breeze stirred through the cottonwoods, and the clear air seemed to magnify the millions of stars in the blue-black sky. Hernando rolled a cigarette and wandered around to the back of the post. There was no moon, but the stars were bright enough for him to make his way up the path on the face of the steep bluff. Halfway up he found a rock and paused to rest. He felt a peace and contentment that comes from total relaxation at the end of a hard day of labor.

In the past week he and Carlin had mended sheds and corrals, piled and burned rubbish, and mixed and molded enough straw and adobe to tile the entire floor area of the post. Hernando couldn't remember ever working harder. Now that the Navajos had come back he would hire a few of the younger men to cut and drag timber down from the mountain country, and they could begin building additional rooms and enlarging the post. It would take time, but he would finish everything that had to be done, and when he was sure that Carlin was ready, return to Santa Fe. He inhaled deeply on his cigarette, crushed it out, and rolled another one.

Somewhere in the hills beyond he heard the plaintive wail of a coyote calling to his mate. Somehow it reminded him of Felicia—his beautiful whore in Santa Barbara. She was a full-blooded coyote! He wondered if she had told him the truth when she told him that she had not slept with anyone but Hernando since they had first met. "I'm the madam and the owner. But I'm no longer a whore!" He laughed. Once a whore, always a whore! he thought.

He let the memories of the hot-blooded Felicia slip from his mind and wondered, for a moment, how his father was progressing. Damn the old man. Chee Dundee—Red Dundee. Mountain man and squaw man. In spite of everything Hernando realized that he loved him. Suddenly, he felt no anxiety. The old man was tough, and with his mother's prayers, and Shell Woman's amulet, Hernando was sure it would only be a matter of time before Andrew Dundee recovered completely.

Hernando noticed that below him inside the post the light in the cooking area dimmed and then brightened in the bullpen. Bah Tsosie had finished the chores in the kitchen. He pictured Carlin and the Na-

vajo woman chatting and laughing together. Carlin
would probably ask her to teach him more of her language and customs. In return the Scot would be
teaching her English and explaining the circumstances
of how he had come to the Southwest and Po'Se'Da'.
Atwa Kee would be standing next to his mother,
hanging onto her long skirts, watching everything and
saying nothing. Strange little creature, Hernando
mused. Then, overwhelmed with loneliness, he lit another cigarette.

A little later Hernando saw the light in the kitchen
brighten again. Bah Tsosie and the boy were preparing for bed. "God," he murmured, thinking of her firm
young breasts. He felt the need of a drink as much as
the need of a woman. No liquor was allowed on the
reservation. He would have to bide his time before he
indulged in either of his favorite pastimes. It was getting late and he felt very tired. He slowly retraced his
steps down the bluff. Carlin would still be wide
awake and probably reading. He wondered if the
Scotsman ever felt passionate. Perhaps there were ad-
vantages when a man was twenty and still a virgin! At
least he didn't know what he was missing.

Chee Dundee Begay, Son of Red Dundee, entered
the post and began to undress. He wouldn't have any
trouble sleeping tonight. "Well, Scotsman, I guess
you're going to be a full-fledged trader!"

Bah Tsosie heard Hernando enter the bullpen and
listened as the two men joked with each other. She
waited quietly in the darkness until she heard the
shuffling of chairs as they made room for their bedrolls. After their lamp had been out for a time, she

172

heard the sounds of their deep breathing and was sure they were fast asleep.

She crept from her bed and lighted a small candle. From a cupboard in the rear of the kitchen she retrieved Carlin's boots, a piece of rawhide, and a roll of soft buckskin. How could a human being wear such stiff uncomfortable things. The thought of them being made of lizard skin disgusted her even more. Never, ever would she understand the thinking of the white ones. Then she settled down to work.

Within a few hours she had fashioned a beautiful pair of Navajo moccasins, knee-length, with four silver buttons to keep them tight to the leg. They would fit Carlin perfectly. She examined them critically, checking each stitch. Then, pleased with her workmanship, she placed them next to Carlin's chair, shoved the offensive store-bought boots in the back of the cupboard under the washbasin, and went to sleep.

CHAPTER ELEVEN

Hernando watched with a combination of envy and amusement as Carlin slipped into his new Navajo boots and strutted up and down across the room. "Maybe we should dye your hair black, then you could be Navajo from head to toe," he said without a trace of sarcasm.

"I can't believe it! They're so comfortable I can't imagine why everyone doesn't wear them," Carlin replied with great enthusiasm. "I could sell hundreds of pairs of boots like this in Scotland. They're just like slippers."

"Spoken like a true trader. You were born for the job," Hernando said and laughed. Then he suddenly became serious. "As for me, if I don't get out of here soon, you're going to have to lock me up."

"If business is as good today as it was yesterday, we'll need more supplies before you know it. Why don't you take the wagon into Santa Fe? I could handle the post until you returned."

Hernando rolled a cigarette and thought about the suggestion. His father would never believe that they had accomplished so much and had done so well in such a short time. Nor would he believe that the young Scotsman had adapted to the new way of life so quickly. If Hernando went home, even with the legitimate excuse of needing supplies, his father would be upset. Besides, they really had enough on hand to last for a few more weeks. It would not do to upset his father at this time.

But there was another reason why Hernando was hesitant about returning to Santa Fe. He had become more curious about Ben Myers's death and about Denver and Garren, the two so-called prospectors who had found and buried the old man. First of all, Hernando had known old Ben all of his life and had been quite fond of him. Second, the government didn't allow prospecting on Indian land. If, and Hernando reasoned that there might be a possibility, the two white men had murdered Myers, Hernando wanted to know about it and make sure that they paid the price. Perhaps he could kill two birds with one stone.

"I might take a ride north, up around the San Juan country," Hernando ventured, "if you're sure you can handle the post alone. I wouldn't be gone more than a few days—a week at the most."

Carlin spoke in Navajo in order to make his point, "With the help of Bah Tsosie and Atwa Kee I can handle everything quite well."

Hernando smiled. Regardless of how hard he tried, he would never be able to speak the language as well as Carlin. "If Bah Tsosie will pack me some grub, I'll saddle up one of the horses and take off right after breakfast. I'll do some trading while I'm gone and drum up some more business."

It was settled. Hernando was grateful that the woman had come into their lives. Things might have been much more difficult for the traders if Bah Tsosie had not been there. He was also curious about his feelings toward her. Every day she seemed to become more attractive, and he was aware of a natural perfumelike odor which aroused him whenever he stood near her. He thought it was because he had been without a woman for so long. Regardless of the reason, it would be healthy for him to get away for a few days. He had no intentions of becoming involved with this beautiful Indian woman. He glanced at Carlin, wondering how the Scotsman felt about her.

They had only known her for a short time, but it seemed as if they had known her forever. The day she stood in the doorway of the kitchen, almost completely recovered from her illness, she made it quite clear to both Hernando and Carlin that she intended to stay at the post. Her hogan was *chindee*, and she explained carefully that she had no man to build her another. Her relatives would pick up the sheep, and she had no interest in getting them back. Both she and her son were warm and comfortable at the post and had never eaten so well.

She did not mention, however, that these were not her only reasons for staying at Po'Se'Da'. She stayed because she was sincerely grateful to Hernando and Carlin for saving her life and the life of her son. She believed the Spirits had willed it so because the traders needed her. It pleased her to be needed. She also enjoyed the position of importance living at the post provided for her with her clan.

Before Hernando saddled up for his journey, he arranged for Bah Tsosie to hire some young men to bring timber down from the high country. When he returned, the traders could work with the Indians and build another sleeping room, enlarge the cooking area to include a fireplace, build a strong, windowless room for the pawn, and because their handmade tiles were already beginning to crumble, put wooden floors down in all the rooms.

Hernando chose a lightweight army saddle and a strong bay mare, while Carlin and Bah Tsosie packed a week's supply of food, water, and trade goods on the back of one of the biggest mules.

He was on his way an hour after sunup. Sure that his decision had been a wise one, Hernando looked forward to exploring the north country. Carlin had adapted to the trader's way of life seemingly without a glance back at the past, but for Hernando it would always be like living in exile.

The morning air was cool, and the mare threw her head back at the prospect of a good ride. Hernando kept a tight rein in order to keep her from bolting. It was several hours later and miles from the post before his mount settled down to a slow even walk.

He was surprised at the intensity of the sun—it was ten to fifteen degrees hotter on the trail than it had been at the post. Hernando decided it might be wise to find a watering hole or hogan before noon, for neither he nor the beasts were in condition to travel in the heat of the day. It was a vast land and totally unfamiliar to him, yet he wasn't worried. He knew Navajo springs or wells were never further apart than a four- or five-hour ride. The key to their survival, however, was in finding them.

He could see miles in every direction, and in every direction there was nothing to be seen except a bare and desolate landscape. With the exception of scrub grass or an occasional porcupine cactus, there didn't seem to be a single living plant or creature. It was awesome. At times in the distance Hernando could see a dust devil weaving and whirling across the sand. There was no other movement. No life and no sound.

The sun was directly overhead now, and it surprised him that he had lost his sense of direction. He reined the mare to a halt, wiped the perspiration from his forehead, and dismounted in order to lead the horse and mule to conserve their strength. The sand was so hot he could feel the heat penetrating up through the leather of his boots. When he reached higher ground, he lengthened his spyglass and searched the area for a sign of a trail or water or a hogan. He could find nothing. He still felt no need to worry; he had plenty of supplies and water, and was certain he would spot some kind of shelter soon. He turned down a dry wash and found a spot where he and the animals could rest.

After a few minutes he unsaddled the mare and unpacked the mule, then rubbed them with sand to cool them down. He reasoned that in an hour or so the sun would be in a position where the high walls of the wash would provide shade, and until then they should expend as little energy as possible. His mouth and throat were dry, but he wanted to wait as long as possible before drinking in order to conserve the water—just in case. When he became dizzy and felt pain in his legs, he recognized the symptoms of dehydration, and only then did he allow himself a few swallows of water from his canteen. He watered the animals from the barrel, using his hat as a pail. When he put his Stetson on again, the wet felt cooled him for a few moments, but too soon it was dry again. They still weren't in any serious danger, although he realized that their circumstances were not the best. When they had rested, he would move to higher ground in order to find some signs of life.

Finally it seemed cool enough to move on. At dusk he found himself in one of the most spectacularly beautiful valleys he had ever seen. The land had been sculpted by water, wind, ice and snow into a stone forest of huge pinnacles and majestic canyons. In the sunset the colors were magnificent, even to Hernando, who usually failed to appreciate nature's beauty. He decided to camp at the foot of a towering column of eroded lava. There were giant logs everywhere, but the wood was petrified. To Hernando's surprise, there wasn't even enough brush around to build a fire. For dinner he ate cold beans and chewed on some beef jerky.

It was a land of violent contrasts and the contrast of temperatures between day and night was to be expected. A few hours after the sun had set the desert air was freezing cold. Even Hernando's bedroll seemed little protection. And still there was no sound—not the murmur of the wind nor the call of a bird nor the howl of a coyote! It was as if he were the only person on earth left alive. For the first time in his life Hernando felt unsure of himself.

Shaking with the cold, he awakened from a dreamless sleep. The first light of dawn did nothing to warm his body. He saddled the mare, packed the mule, and chewed on some more jerky in order to renew his strength, then rode off in the direction of the sunrise. He knew the mountains were to the east of him, and there would be water in the mountains. Once again, when the sun was high, Hernando lost his sense of direction. There were no shadows and he wasn't sure whether he was traveling east or west or north or south! He would have missed the spring completely if the mule hadn't smelled the water and bolted. He reared his head up, snapped the lead rope, and with ears and tail raised high, galloped into the rocks. Hernando, cursing the mule, spurred the mare and followed. He was ready to beat the animal to death when he noticed other animal tracks. He followed slowly now, afraid the signs might mislead him; then suddenly, hidden in the midst of high red sandstone rocks, pouring into a natural limestone basin, he saw the bubbling spring! Cool, sweet, fresh water! Never in his entire life had Hernando tasted anything so delicious.

When he had refreshed himself and the animals, he explored the area. There were signs of sheep everywhere, and he knew it was a well-used Navajo spring. He climbed to the top of the rocky crag to see if he could get his bearings or find some indication of where the hogan might be. Damned contrary Indians, he thought bitterly, any intelligent humans would build their homes close to the water—especially in this God-forsaken wasteland! But not the Navajo! They were sociable enough when they wanted to be, but they cherished their privacy. Hogans were built in secluded areas, often miles from the nearest water supply or neighbors. Even in family groups, where there were several hogans in one area, the dwellings were well separated. From his vantage point, Hernando could see no sign of life. He realized that there was a hogan out there somewhere within a few miles, but the Navajo's home was built to blend in with the desert terrain. A stranger might pass within yards of the hogan and never see it. He climbed down the rocks and had a lunch of more cold beans and dry bread. He would wait, he decided, until a shepherd came in the evening to water his flock.

He didn't worry about hobbling the horse or the mule; they wouldn't stray far from the water. He found a protected place high in the rocks, checked the area for snakes, and lay down to rest with his hat shading his face. He had second thoughts about pursuing the prospectors. Too much time had gone by, and it would be too difficult to try to prove his theory. Wouldn't help old Ben much anyhow now. What if the men were prospecting on the Indian land! It wouldn't be any of his business—let the Army take care of it. Fatigue set in and jumbled his thoughts. He fell asleep grumbling out loud to himself.

He could hear the mariachis playing in the streets and could feel the hot water in Felicia's tub licking his limbs. Across the room he recognized Felicia smiling at him. She seemed to be floating and beckoned seductively for him to join her on the bed. He felt her passionate kisses on his neck and chest. They were just about to make love when he heard a dog barking at him. What in hell was a dog doing in Felicia's room? Why did he feel he was still soaking in her tub?

Hernando awakened to find himself facing the late afternoon sun. His clothes were soaked with perspiration. A small black-and-white sheep dog stood on the rocks above him barking furiously. Next to the dog, staring curiously at him, stood a young Navajo girl. Hernando stared back at the child. She couldn't have been more than seven or eight years old, but the seriousness of her expression gave her the look of an old woman. Hernando laughed and spoke to her, using what words of her language he could remember. "I'm a trader—and I'm lost. Will you take me to your hogan?"

The child didn't answer. She stared at him for a few moments longer, then scurried down the rocks to where her flock was watering. Hernando rose quickly and followed her, trying desperately to remember the proper Navajo words to make himself understood. "I have gifts for your family and some *dulce* for you!" For the life of him he couldn't recall the proper word for candy so he substituted the Spanish word for "sweet" hoping the child would respond.

If she understood, she gave no sign. When the sheep had drunk their fill, she and the dog began herding them down onto the flat. Her manner was leisurely. Hernando saddled the horse, tied the gear on the mule, and trailed the herd at a respectful distance, so's not to disturb them. He shook his head with the attitude of the little girl. She never once glanced back to see if he were following. Half an hour later they arrived at their destination.

Several other children, all younger than the Navajo shepherd and painfully thin, watched as Hernando rode in. Dinner was already prepared, and the older Indians graciously motioned for Hernando to share their meager meal. He hesitated, realizing that there was barely enough food for the family and that they were frightfully poor. Finally, knowing they would be offended if he refused, he sat down cross-legged next to the fire and accepted their hospitality.

It was a remote area, and Hernando was able to understand eventually that he was the first white man they had ever seen. It seemed good to him for a change to be the first at something! The family accepted his gifts of food shyly, although they seemed pleased. None of the Navajos had ever tasted candy, and he had to show them that it was something to eat.

The old grandfather tried the first piece. The rest of the family watched anxiously. He was very solemn as he moved the hard, sweet morsel around in his mouth. Then he smiled approvingly and allowed the rest of his kin to try the strange sweet rocks. Hernando looked from one face to another as they savored the sweets, amazed at his own feeling of pleasure.

Breakfast the next morning consisted of weak root tea and thin gruel. Hernando brought out his iron skillet, cut some thick pieces of bacon from his slab, and fried it over the small flame. The Navajos watched curiously as he ate a piece, then passed the pan around to each member of the family. Once again they all waited while the grandfather sampled the strange food—and once again with his approval they tasted the fatty strips. They chewed the meat slowly, enjoying the salty taste and grunting with pleasure. They now regarded the trader with added respect.

When his belly was appeased, Hernando became restless. His confidence returned, and he was anxious to be on his way. But where was he going and in what direction?

"This land is unfamiliar to me. What do you call this place?" he asked in halting Navajo and sign language.

The old grandfather grinned and moved his arms proudly to encompass the area. *"T'eiya bikáá goō na'nishkaad. Diné a'doo na'nishkaad bidziilii át'e."*

Hernando looked intently at the old man, then around at the endless, desolate desert that the Navajo had referred to proudly as "the land of the people—Wonderful Valley!" The only thing that Hernando would consider wonderful about it would be to be delivered from it. "Is Wonderful Valley far from the mountains?"

"No, not far," the old man answered, "two, maybe three days."

"Is there water along the way?"

The old man drew a map in the sand with his finger, indicating that there were only two springs.

Hernando was thoughtful. He had filled his canteens and the water barrel at the Navajo spring. As long as he was sure he was headed in the right direction, the water should last until he reached the mountains. Once in the Lukachukais he could head south, and in no time at all make his way back to Po'Se'Da'. He slit open one of the leather pouches that carried supplies and using his knife, and with the help of the grandfather, made a crude map, careful to indicate the approximate location of the water holes.

He left his iron skillet, the slab of bacon, coffee beans, and candy with the grateful family and bid his farewell. Assuming that it had been a slight siege of panic that had caused him to lose his sense of direction, Hernando vowed to himself to remain calm regardless of any circumstances. If he made his way in an easterly direction, the mountains should become visible sometime the following day.

In order to get maximum energy with minimum effort, Hernando began pacing himself and the animals with rigid self-control. He was careful now to note and mark on his map every significant monument and gulley. When he came to an arroyo that was impassable and was forced to change direction, he patiently noted the approximate distance he had traveled, then after he had found a crossing, retraced his steps until he could once more face the sun. No short cuts. It had become quite clear to him that this was no longer an adventure but rather a test of survival.

He found himself traveling into dead-end washes and having to backtrack a maddening number of times. Each miscalculation took up precious time and energy. Hernando had never been known for his patience, but now he summoned control he never knew he possessed. At noon when the sun was white-hot in the sky and the shadows had once again vanished, he realized that it would be wise to return to a large cave he had passed more than an hour before in order to seek shade. He would make up the time lost in late afternoon when the sun would be at his back. No panic now, just good judgment.

He entered the cave cautiously, realizing that other creatures would also be seeking the coolness. When he was sure the area was safe, he loosened the cinch on the horse and relieved the mule of the pack. Satisfied that he was behaving with some degree of sanity, he sat down to wait until the weather would be comfortable enough to continue. The mule whinnied nervously and became skittish. Hernando watched the animal with interest but was too tired to investigate. Instead, he pulled his Stetson down over his eyes in order to rest.

On a ledge in the back of the cave a den of large grayish-brown snakes with a series of dark diamond-shaped blotches on their backs began to writhe in the dust. They were angered at having been disturbed by the intruders. The serpents were western diamondback rattlesnakes, some more than five feet long, with a series of white buttons on the ends of their tails. One exceptionally aggressive member of the venomous clan moved instinctively from his resting place to confront his enemies.

The mare bolted out of the cave as soon as she heard the warning rattle; the mule began kicking his rear legs at the deadly reptile. Before Hernando could get his wits about him, the mule had smashed the water barrel and had taken off out of the cave after the mare. Cursing, Hernando drew his pistol, took careful aim, and killed the creature just as it began to strike. The noise of the bullet echoed throughout the cave, setting off the other rattlers in staccato unison. The sounds came from every direction. Hernando fired his remaining shells into the darkness as he retreated from the cave, too unnerved to even try to recover what was left of the supplies. "Mother of God, deliver me," he murmured as the bright sunlight brought him back to reality. He noticed his hand was shaking and reholstered his gun to try to steady himself. The animals had vanished. Visions of his mother, father, Phoebe, Shell Woman, and Carlin flashed in his mind for a moment, then he took a deep breath. He had been lucky to get out of the cave alive. He still had the water in his canteen, but he knew that without the supplies and his mount he would have to start thinking like an Indian in order to survive. He reckoned it would be wiser to continue on toward the mountains than to try to return to the hogan—and he would still have to wait until it was cooler before he began to travel. Even then there would be several hours of daylight before he settled down to make some sort of camp.

At the end of the second day all but a few drops of water was gone, and Hernando began to wonder whether or not he had been traveling in circles. In every direction the landscape looked familiar—towering orange monoliths, banded vermillion cliffs, mazes of waterless washes, and outcrops of brick-red rock dikes. Although he used his bandana to shield his face, his lips were blistered and his throat was parched. His stomach cramped with hunger, and the pain in his legs was excruciating. He became dizzy, lost his footing, and slid down a precipitous drop into a ravine. For a time he was unable to move, then, determined not to die in a gulley, he summoned the last of his strength to crawl back up the sharp wall and make his way to the top of one of the dunes. Hernando drained the last of the water from his canteen, squared his Stetson, and buttoned his shirt. Perhaps if he rested for a moment, he would be able to think more clearly. He was sure of one thing. He was a survivor! Death would have to fight for his soul.

Just before he closed his eyes he thought he saw the

faint blue silhouette of the Lukachukias in the distance—lofty, majestic, and cool—but he knew he was beginning to hallucinate and easily convinced himself it was just an illusion. Staring up at the sky, he began to laugh—a mad, uncontrollable cackle that sobered him immediately. "I have to fight this madness! I have to regain control!" he whispered aloud. "I can't die here in this godforsaken wilderness. If I do they will never find my body!" He fought off the exhaustion with every ounce of his being, but dehydration had already begun to affect his mind, and he sank into unconsciousness.

The girl saw the vultures circling and wanted to herd the sheep in the opposite direction, but the boy was curious. He was afraid of ghosts, but he wanted to see what had attracted the birds. It couldn't hurt anything if he didn't get too close.

He didn't see the body until he was almost on top of it. It scared him half out of his wits, but before he could run he heard Hernando's laughter. His heart pounding, the young Navajo crawled slowly and cautiously toward the man. He had never seen a "crazy one"—but he had heard about them. He bent low over the prostrate body and whispered in his own language, "Are you crazy?"

Hernando, believing the soft voice to be a figment of his imagination, replied, "Yes!" He replied in Navajo. It was comforting to talk with someone even if that someone was yourself. He was truly mad.

"I've never seen a crazy one before," the boy murmured.

Hernando stopped laughing. "Is someone there?"

188

The boy didn't understand English. He yelled for his sister to come see the specter.

Hernando struggled to recall the proper Navajo words. "Is someone there?" he repeated, still unwilling to believe he might be saved.

"I'm here. Can't you see me?"

Hernando opened his eyes and stared up in the direction of the small voice. His eyes burned and felt as if they were filled with sand. All he could see were bright yellow spots. He was sun blind! "Where are you?" he screamed feebly.

The boy became frightened and started to run away. Hernando could hear his agitated breathing and his footsteps in the sand. "Stop! Don't run away—help me!" he pleaded. Then he repeated his entreaty in broken Navajo.

The boy stopped and walked haltingly back to where Hernando was now trying to stand. Summoning all of his courage, he touched the man's arm. "Bring me some water," he called to his sister. "Then run home and get our father. The crazy one needs help!"

Hernando had no idea of how long he had been unconscious. When he awakened his eyes were bandaged, and from the smell of coals and the sheepskins, he realized he must be inside a hogan. He heard the low, melodic sound of voices somewhere in the distance and called out. The voices stopped and he was aware of someone entering the shelter. He felt himself being helped to a sitting position, then someone put a crude cup of bitter liquid to his lips and urged him to drink. In spite of his blindness he felt comforted and safe. "Thank you," he mumbled in English. Then, remembering where he was and remembering that there were no Navajo words for thank you, he said, "I'm grateful that you found me!"

Several Indians spoke at once. "He speaks the tongue of The People! Who is he? Where did he come from?"

A strong masculine voice commanded, "Be still. Let him rest. We will question him tomorrow when he is feeling better."

After the bitter tea, a woman spoon-fed him some broth, then allowed him to lay his head down on the soft sheepskins. He was too weak to speak again or to wonder any more about where he was. He knew he was not going to die. For the time being, at least, that was enough. For the first time in his life Hernando had experienced hunger and thirst. He had been to hell and returned. He shuddered uncontrollably as he thought about his nightmarish experience. Just before he fell asleep he remembered that starvation killed hundreds of Navajos each year. It was an accepted way of life! "God!" he vowed aloud in English. "I swear on the life of my mother, I will *never* allow a Navajo to die of hunger if it's within my power to prevent it!"

CHAPTER TWELVE

Carlin worked like a man possessed, taxing his mental as well as his physical faculties to the limit. It was as if he was racing to meet some mysterious deadline to complete his destiny! And although Phoebe was always in the back of his mind, he had also become painfully aware of how attractive Bah Tsosie was—a thought that somehow troubled him.

The post was crowded from midmorning till midafternoon, yet few goods were actually traded at Po'Se'Da'. Carlin accepted the fact that the Indians came from their isolated dwellings several miles away more because they were curious or suspicious of the blond, blue-eyed Scot than because they needed supplies. Every move he made, every sound he uttered was silently scrutinized; and while Hernando had been instantly accepted because of his father's reputation as a trader with the Navajos, Carlin knew that he would have to earn the Indians' trust and respect before he could truly call himself a trader!

A slight smile or brief frown from Bah Tsosie let him know immediately whether he had done well or had erred in a transaction. Pennies were called "reds," nickels were "yellows," and dimes were "blues." He learned quickly that Navajo etiquette was as rigid as that of the English royal court; and while they were a very patient people, any breach of their etiquette was offensive. Bah Tsosie cautioned him never to ask a Navajo his name but rather ask one of his friends or acquaintances. It was considered rude to look directly into the eyes of the speaker; one should instead watch the speaker's mouth. It was not polite to hand anything such as a match, cigarette, or stick of candy with the point directed toward the Navajo. And Navajos did not shake hands but rather clasped them together gently for a length of time, depending upon when they had last met. There were no Navajo words for either thank you or good-bye. If one did something for someone else, he did it for the pleasure of giving and that was gratitude enough as far as the Indians were concerned. Good-bye was just unnecessary to say.

It was difficult for Carlin to understand the Navajo's sense of morality! Bah Tsosie explained that they often practiced polygamy with a man marrying two sisters or a mother and her daughter by a previous marriage. Adultery was frowned upon; and if it could be proven that a married woman and a man had committed the act, the man was forced to pay the injured husband a certain amount of sheep or money. The guilty wife was often stripped in public by her husband, a punishment that to the usually modest Navajo woman was worse than death.

Everything he learned was mysterious and wonderful. And, after he'd had a chance to think about what he saw, he realized that it was usually very practical. Carlin rarely made the same mistake twice.

Hernando had been away from the post for more than a week, yet it never occurred to Carlin to be concerned. He knew his friend, his adopted brother, to be cool, self-reliant, and as capable a man as he'd ever known. Besides, he and Bah Tsosie had so much to do from sunrise to sunset that most of the time Carlin was too tired to even think about him. As it had aboard ship, Carlin's life depended on orderliness and routine. After breakfast he always helped Bah Tsosie with the dishes, then together they cleaned the post and prepared for the day's business. If there were no customers, Carlin worked repairing fences or planting his garden.

Bah Tsosie showed him how to build her loom; and when she wasn't cooking or dusting or sewing or waiting on customers, she worked on it. Carlin watched her with admiration as she dyed, carded, and spun the wool, then began making her unique designs for the rug. Bah Tsosie didn't work from a pattern, but rather from a diagram she envisioned in her mind. She worked quickly and deliberately with a natural instinct for beauty and symmetry that had been instilled in her genes for centuries.

There never seemed to be enough time for everything that had to be done, yet each day seemed to Carlin more rewarding than the last. Every evening when they finished their supper, Carlin went into the bull pen and turned up the lamp for reading. These were the only relaxing moments in the entire day, and Carlin would be eternally grateful to Isabella for packing the box of books.

It had become a nightly ritual. Bah Tsosie filled a pipe for Carlin, moved his favorite chair—one she had fashioned for him of willows and deerhide—next to the stove, and then she and Atwa Kee positioned themselves on the floor next to his feet. It was story time! Carlin would first read a sentence or two in English, then she would try to translate his words into Navajo. It was a fast and painless way for them both to become more proficient in the other's language.

Carlin chose this evening's story especially for the boy. It was Dickens's *Bleak House*. He read to the bottom of the first page, " 'Did the boy know the deceased?' asked the Coroner. Indeed, Jo had known him; it was his only friend who was dead.' " He interrupted as Bah Tsosie began the translation. "How many days has Hernando been away?"

She looked at him intently, trying to remember. "I think it is ten or eleven days."

Carlin was troubled. He closed the book. "He's been away too long. He said he'd be gone a week or so, but this is too long."

Bah Tsosie sat quietly while Carlin struggled to collect his thoughts. It would be ridiculous for him to try to search for Hernando; he had no idea where he might have traveled. He might be able to make his way back to Santa Fe, but would Bah Tsosie be safe alone at the post? He began pacing the floor. Perhaps he could locate Hernando if Bah Tsosie could put the Navajo telegraph to work.

She assured him that she would begin to make inquiries the next morning. It saddened her that Carlin was concerned over Hernando's extended absence. She was much more comfortable with the fair-haired man who always seemed gentle and reserved with her. While she was grateful to Hernando, there were times when the way he looked at her embarrassed her.

"If we haven't had any word from him by tomorrow evening," he told her, "I think we should organize some sort of search party. Would that be possible?"

"Yes. The Navajo trackers would look for him," she replied. "But I'm sure you have no need for concern. He will be welcomed in every hogan and every clan."

Perhaps he was being foolish—but something was not right. He could sense it. "We'll wait until tomorrow evening," Carlin decided, "but if he hasn't returned by then, I want your people to be prepared to start the search at sunup the next morning."

As Carlin had directed, Bah Tsosie began her inquiries with the first family that rode into the compound. Sensing the young trader's concern, the Indians gathered in small groups outside Po'Se'Da' as they arrived. They murmured softly among themselves and touched hands lightly as a form of greeting.

When they received no news of Hernando's whereabouts by late afternoon, the trackers were organized. "I will be packed and ready to go with you first thing in the morning," Carlin informed the men.

Kiilbáhí, or Greyboy, slid off his lean stallion and touched Carlin's hands gently. "These men are the greatest trackers in the world," he explained slowly. "We move very fast, like the wind! You are a good man, but you would not be able to keep up with us. You must stay here. We will find Chee Dundee Begay."

Carlin knew the Navajo was speaking the truth. It was a helpless feeling, but he nodded his agreement and entered the post with Bah Tsosie. No business had been transacted during the day, and he was grateful that the bull pen was empty. He was weary, both from the work and his concern over Hernando's safety.

"I will heat the rocks in the sweat lodge," Bah Tsosie suggested. "You will find the answers you seek when you are alone."

He glanced gratefully at the Navajo woman. So small, yet so wise. He did feel the need of solitude. Everything had seemed simple before. He'd been confident that at last he had found his place in the world. But had he? He learned the language of the people so quickly, it had seemed natural to him that he had convinced himself that the Chinese philosophy of predestination was correct. Now he wondered.

He sat cross-legged, Indian style, inside the small hoganlike structure, allowing the hot steam to swirl around his body and breathing it deeply into his lungs. Head back, eyes closed, he tried to keep from thinking, but it was impossible. Visions of craggy rocks and dank bogs in the Scottish highlands swam around in his mind like a whirlpool. He could almost smell the heather. He was not Chinese nor was he a Navajo—he was a Scotsman! A man of joy and laughter—a man of the sea! He couldn't remember the last time he had really laughed. Glasgow? London? Marseille? And now he sat alone in a Navajo sweat-lodge, hundreds of miles from any form of civilization. The word *alone* touched a sensitive nerve in his body and

196

he repeated the word aloud. "Alone!" He realized suddenly that he never felt truly alone because of Bah Tsosie and Atwa Kee. Somehow he had clung to the idea that the only time in his life he had really been happy was when he had been surrounded by his natural family—his mother, father, and dear Megan. Now he realized that he had been living a lie, clinging to memories just for the sake of convention. In retrospect he realized that he was experiencing real happiness now! In the present! Bah Tsosie, Atwa Kee, Hernando, and even his brief friendship with Isabella and Andrew Dundee had given him much pleasure. They had become his surrogate family. And Phoebe. Phoebe, or rather his dreams of her, had allowed him to experience love—the strange, illusive, emotional stimulation that enabled him to awaken each morning looking forward to the day!

But what about his growing attachment to the Navajo woman to whom he owed so much? It might be well for the Indians to enjoy the favors and companionship of more than one wife, but the Christian principle was too deeply ingrained in Carlin for him to consider such an arrangement. He would have to make a choice between the two women.

Carlin had not even been aware of the questions buried so deep in his heart; and yet, just as Bah Tsosie had predicted, they were there, and the answers he sought were provided. A surrogate family would not do; he needed his own family! He had never detected a look or a feeling from Bah Tsosie that might indicate she was attracted to him. But then neither had he had any encouragement from Phoebe. In an instant he rationalized that of the two women Phoebe needed him more; and so, when Hernando returned—and now there was no doubt in Carlin's mind that he would—it would be Carlin's turn to take a short vacation away from the post.

Carlin would return to the Hacienda de Villanova Dundee and make his feelings known to Phoebe. He would then ask her hand in marriage, and together they would return to Po'Se'Da'. The Scot's feelings for the Apache woman were so strong, so real, it never occurred to him even for a moment that she might refuse his offer. Carlin smiled. He would—with the help of the Gahns—provide Phoebe with half a dozen children to make up for her stillborn child.

Naked as the day he was born, Carlin dashed from the sweat lodge and plunged into the icy waters of the spring. He felt exhilarated, and his laughter brought Bah Tsosie running from the kitchen to see what was wrong. Without the slightest trace of embarrassment, Carlin climbed out of the water, dried himself off, and dressed in front of the woman. "I feel wonderful!" he bellowed at the top of his lungs. "Let's have dinner and I'll finish Atwa Kee's story tonight!"

Hands on hips, shaking her head with good humor, Bah Tsosie returned to the post. Seeing him that way without his clothes, so relaxed and happy, had not offended her. Indeed, it had seemed the most natural thing in the world. She kneaded her dough and dropped it into the hot grease. Atwa Kee climbed down from the counter on which he had been perched and moved next to his mother. "You are happy?" he asked. She knelt down and hugged him. "Yes. I am happy."

* * *

The bullpen seemed more cozy as Carlin settled into his chair. "Come sit on my lap," he motioned to the small boy, but Atwa Kee could not be coaxed away from his mother. Carlin would reach the child some time, he was sure, and he opened the book. Midway through a sentence there was a pounding on the trading post door. Carlin was curious—Navajos didn't like to travel at night. Bah Tsosie glanced at the Scotsman with concern; Atwa Kee remained stoic. "Perhaps someone needs help," Carlin said, turning up the lamp and unbolting the door.

The first thing he saw was an old army rifle pointed at his chest. Then he looked up into the snarling face of a drunken Navajo brave he had never seen before. It flashed through his mind that this might be one of the renegades who had murdered Ben Myers. He wondered whether he would live long enough to find out.

Bah Tsosie recognized the man, Handing Out War, as one of the hostiles who followed Hoskinini. The old renegade chief controlled a small band of Navajos in the north, and because of his great hatred for the white ones was rarely seen out of his domain. She called the brave by name, Hosteen Begay, but he ignored her.

"Whiskey!" he demanded, pushing Carlin into the room with the barrel of his rifle.

"We have no whiskey. There is no whiskey allowed on the reservation. We have coffee and we have tobacco," Carlin replied firmly.

"Whiskey!" the brave repeated, shoving Carlin roughly aside. He walked unsteadily behind the counter and began smashing the merchandise and throwing it on the floor. He fired several shots into barrels at the end of the counter, then aimed his rifle directly at Carlin.

Bah Tsosie stood frozen in the doorway to the kitchen. No one noticed Atwa Kee. He had crawled away from the stove, behind the wooden counter, and now sat on the floor at the renegade's feet. Suddenly he grabbed the brave's leg and sank his teeth into the man's calf. Hosteen Begay screamed with pain and dropped the rifle. Looking down into the darkness behind the counter, he couldn't see the small figure of Atwa Kee and recoiled in panic. Surely it was an evil spirit who had attacked him!

Within seconds Bah Tsosie leapt from the doorway, grabbed the coffee pot that had been steaming on the stove, and hurled it into the drunken Indian's face. Once again he screamed with pain, blinded by the boiling liquid. Carlin made a dive for the fallen gun and hit the brave a solid blow on the head, knocking him unconscious.

Outside the post the ghastly screams of their companion could be heard by two mounted Navajos, who had not had the courage to rob the post but who had accompanied Hosteen Begay to share in the spoils. Before Carlin could fire after them, they galloped away into the darkness.

Unable to understand what had caused the Navajo to panic in the first place, Carlin stepped behind the counter to investigate. He lowered the lamp to examine the Indian and saw the blood oozing from his leg. Upon closer examination he found that the wound had been caused, unmistakably, from a human bite!

He moved the lamp slightly to find Atwa Kee curled up behind one of the overturned boxes and realized immediately what must have happened.

Carlin set the lamp down, picked up the shaking child, and held him close. Atwa Kee hung onto him tightly, then the boy's face broke into an ear-to-ear grin. Carlin stood him up on the counter and began laughing—the boy began laughing, too. Bah Tsosie smiled, then she, too, began laughing. It had been a desperate moment, and Atwa Kee had saved them all!

After a few moments Bah Tsosie began to relax; then she became angry. At first she had been afraid, but now that the danger had passed, she was furious. She spat on the unconscious figure and began kicking him. Carlin, who had never seen Bah Tsosie lose her temper, swept her into his arms. "It's all right! We're safe now. Calm down."

"He is a coyote! No good! You ought to drag him outside and shoot him!"

Carlin released her and laughed, partly in relief and partly at seeing the little lamb turn into a tiger. "We don't have to shoot anyone. I'll tie him up and in the morning we'll send for the Navajo police. They'll take care of him. Now get me some pie and coffee while I find a rope. All right?"

Bah Tsosie was not so easily appeased. "I'll find the rope, and I'll tie him up good. You fix the pie and coffee."

It constantly amazed Carlin how different the Navajo women were from their white sisters. Raised in a matriarchal society, the Navajo women considered themselves equal to their men. The women had specific duties, but when it came to policies or politics, they demanded an equal voice. Carlin noticed from his first day as a trader that it was the women who had the final say on what was to be purchased or traded at the post; and while the man was the representative in the tribal dealing, it was not without first consulting with his woman. Bah Tsosie also explained to Carlin that a woman could divorce her husband—an unthinkable thing for a white woman to do—simply by placing his saddle and belongings outside of the hogan. The man was then obliged to ride off. Their property always belonged to the woman and her family. He wondered if Phoebe would behave so outrageously?

Carlin shook his head as Bah Tsosie proceeded with an inner strength to drag the Indian from behind the counter and bind him as if he were a dead calf. The young Scotsman turned on his heel to brew fresh coffee and cut the pie.

After a sleepless night, Carlin awoke to find Bah Tsosie already hard at work cleaning the bull pen. One of Hosteen Begay's shells had hit the pickle barrel and another the honey keg. Everything was sticky, and the smell was less than appetizing.

Trussed up like a turkey, the brave had regained consciousnes and moaned in pain. The ropes were too tight, the wound on his leg throbbed, and his head—combined with a knot the size of a hen's egg and an even larger hangover—ached with pain. To make matters worse, he was hungry! His pleas for food didn't soften Bah Tsosie's belligerent attitude.

During the excitement of the prior evening the Navajo, drunk and armed, had seemed like a giant, but in the morning light he presented to Carlin an entirely different picture. He was young—perhaps younger than Carlin—and painfully thin. When the trader had slipped into his pants and shirt, he loosened the ropes, led the pathetic Indian into the kitchen, and proceeded to make flapjacks for breakfast. Bah Tsosie ignored the entire scene. Still wary, Carlin decided to feed Hosteen Begay instead of untying his hands. The brave was hungry enough to accept the first few bites, then humiliated, spat the food out onto the floor. This enraged Bah Tsosie and Carlin had to hold her to keep her from beating the Indian with a mop.

"I want him out of here! Put bars on one of the sheds and let him rot in there. He offends my eyes!" she cried.

Carlin acknowledged that her idea was a good one and found a hammer, nails, and some two-by-fours in order to secure the prisoner. Hosteen Begay offered little resistance. He was relieved to be taken out of the post and away from the fury of Bah Tsosie's tongue.

Carlin had just set the last nail in place when he heard Hernando call from the top of the hill. It seemed like a miracle! Screaming with delight, Carlin ran to meet him; he stopped short when he saw the condition his friend was in. Hernando had been gone two weeks to the day, but from his appearance he looked as if he been in the wilderness for a month! His clothes were filthy, his growth of beard failed to hide his sunken cheeks, and his eyes were swollen and bloodshot.

"My God!" Carlin gasped. "What's happened to you?"

Hernando slipped slowly and painfully from the saddle and put his arms around Carlin. He hugged him affectionately, then held him at arm's length, unashamed of the tears streaming down his face. "I wasn't sure I'd ever see you again, my dear brother. I have a lot to tell you, but for now I just want some coffee and something to eat. Then I want to sleep for a week!"

"We've sent trackers after you! Where have you been?" Carlin persisted as he led the horse to the corral. "And where in hell did you get this Indian pony?"

"It's a long story. For now I can just tell you that I've been to Wonderful Valley!" Hernando stopped, noticing the forlorn face of Hosteen Begay peering at him from behind the wooden bars. "Who's he? And why's he locked up?"

"That's a long story, too. Come on, let's get you some food!"

Hernando's mood seemed sober as he kept glancing back at the Indian. "I hope there's a good reason. I don't like to see anything or anybody in a cage!"

The post was still in disarray when they entered, and Bah Tsosie, who was stacking goods on the shelves, smiled a shy greeting at Hernando's return.

"You don't seem to handle things too well when I'm away," Hernando commented as he surveyed the mess. "Were you attacked by a grizzly or did Peaches come back?"

"Not a grizzly exactly, but close," Carlin answered. "It was that renegade you saw out there in the shed."

Before he could continue, Atwa Kee, who had heard Hernando's voice, raced from the kitchen and threw himself into Hernando's arms. "I caught him! I caught him!" cried the no longer "Quiet Boy" in perfect English.

Hernando, Carlin, and even Bah Tsosie were stunned by the child's sudden flow of words and enthusiasm. "What's happened to my Atwa Kee? Are you sick or have you just decided to join the living?" Hernando asked as he gave the boy a sudden and loving hug.

With very little help, Carlin allowed Atwa Kee to tell Hernando the story of what had happened with Hosteen Begay as Bah Tsosie prepared his breakfast. The child remained in Hernando's lap as he ate, beaming with pleasure as he was praised for his heroic actions. Carlin felt a stab of jealousy as he watched Atwa Kee so animated with Hernando.

"The problem now is what do we do with the renegade?" Carlin passed more flapjacks to the amiable trader. "Do you think we ought to get word to the Navajo police, or do you think that one of us should deliver him to the stockade at Fort Defiance?"

Hernando put the boy down and stared patiently at Carlin. "One of us? Do you honestly feel that you could find your way across a hundred miles of wasteland and just drop in on the soldiers at the fort 'n say 'here's a bad Indian—lock 'im up'?" Hernando's shoulders sagged and his voice was weary. "I just barely survived out there in that damned inferno, 'n I sure as hell don't feel like makin' another trip!" He remained quiet for a few moments, embarrassed by his untimely brush with death. "Has he had anything to eat?"

"Why should we feed him?" exclaimed Bah Tsosie.

Hernando stared sadly at the woman. "Just because he might be hungry."

"I fed him all he would eat," Carlin interjected. "He's all right. But what are we going to do with him? Bah Tsosie says he's one of Hoskinini's men; he could be a murderer."

Hernando closed his eyes. A week before he would have felt disgust at the mention of the war chief's name. He would have regarded him as rogue and hostile, a mad renegade whose only purpose in life was to make life hell for any white man who trespassed in his domain. His thinking was different now. It had been Hoskinini's children who had found him, and Hoskinini himself who had supervised his care. He arose from the table and poured himself another cup of coffee. "I'd like to rest a bit now. We'll talk about the brave later. Just make sure he has plenty of food and water."

They didn't understand his attitude, but he had made his meaning very clear. Carlin knew that it had something to do with Hernando's experiences in the past weeks. Something to do with the way he had survived. Carlin too had experienced a battle of survival, yet somehow those experiences, as recent as they were, had crept into the recesses of his mind. Hernando's attitude caused the Scotsman to reexperience his own pain, and he felt ashamed at being so unforgiving of the brave.

Hernando opened his bedroll under the cottonwoods next to the spring. He drifted into a dreamless sleep and did not awaken until sunrise the next morning. Sometime during the night Atwa Kee had made his way from the post and crawled inside the bedroll to snuggle up with him. It gave Hernando a feeling of love he had never experienced before.

Hernando spent an hour in the sweat lodge, shaved, dressed in clean clothes Bah Tsosie had prepared for him, and sat down to enjoy his breakfast. It took more than an hour for him to explain what had happened to him in the north county, the Wonderful Valley. Bah Tsosie and Carlin listened attentively, careful not to interrupt his thoughts when he lapsed into silence. When he finally finished, he decided it was time to question their prisoner. So Hosteen Begay had wanted whiskey, but then most men wanted whiskey at some time or another. So he had threatened them and broken a few boxes and barrels. Perhaps he had good reason to act like an animal.

He and Carlin pried loose the bars, untied the young Indian, and marched him into the post. Hernando began the questioning. "Are you feeling better in the belly?" he asked.

The brave stared at him.

"Are you feeling better in the head?"

The brave did not respond.

"You not crazy in the head anymore?" Hernando pressed the issue in order to make his point. "Son of Red Dundee and Tall Man Who Likes Yellow Faces have great medicine. Big Spirits to protect them and Po'Se'Da'. Only a brave who is crazy in the head would wreck the trading post to get whiskey! Whiskey bad medicine! You savvy?"

Hosteen Begay lowered his head to indicate he understood.

Carlin and Atwa Kee sat quietly at the table as Hernando got up and walked slowly around the Indian. He looked into his eyes, examined his teeth, and felt his muscles.

"Good eyes like an eagle! Good teeth like a bear! And strong muscles—strong like a mountain lion. Good man!" Hernando pronounced. Then to Carlin he said in English, "He's skin and bone. Might have consumption."

In perfect English the Indian answered, "I am not sick. I'm hungry! Are you going to take me to jail?"

"You speak better English than I do Navajo," Hernando admitted sheepishly.

"I was born at Bos Redondo and spent the first five years of my life in that fenced place," Hosteen Begay replied sullenly. "They didn't allow children to speak the Navajo tongue. Remember? My mother and father died in that stinking hole, and I was taken by a white family to be raised. But I was not their son—I was their mule! Hoskinini raided their farm when I was thirteen years old. He returned me to the land of my people. Now send for the soldiers to take me to jail."

"We're not going to send for the soldiers. You're not going to jail," Hernando informed the brave as he removed the remaining ropes from the Indian's arms and legs and handed him a bowl of mutton stew and some fried bread. "But you're going to have to do something to pay for the damage you've done. Any suggestions?"

Hosteen Begay wolfed his food down before he answered. "I guess I could do some work for you," he grumbled, as he scraped the last morsel of food from the bowl, "for a while anyhow."

"That sounds fair," Hernando agreed. "But if you

run off or cause any more trouble, I'll tell everyone who comes to the post the story of the cowardly Hosteen Begay, who was bitten and captured by a child. All the Navajos will laugh at you."

Atwa Kee squirmed in his chair as the Indian glared at him.

"Why do you drink?" Carlin asked, wondering if Hernando hadn't been too easy on the Navajo. "You know that whiskey can only get you into trouble."

Hosteen Begay looked coldly from one man to the other. "I drink whiskey because it makes me forget! It makes me feel like a brave again!"

"You will work for us for two weeks," Hernando decided, ignoring the Indian's excuse. "If you do a good job, you will be free to leave at the end of that time."

Bah Tsosie had remained silently in the background during Hernando's interrogation. It had been many years since she had been reminded of Bos Redondo. Her grandparents on both sides of her family had died while they were interned there. She recalled her parents' bitterness against the whites and the injustice of the Navajos' long imprisonment. Carlin noticed the strange expression on her face as she left the room. Concerned, he followed her outside. "What's wrong?" he asked when he finally caught up to her.

A warm wind started a dust devil on the horizon. She turned to answer her friend. "I'm going for a walk. A long walk." She knew he had no way of understanding her words.

CHAPTER THIRTEEN

Twenty-three years earlier, in 1862, a brilliant, well-respected, and God-fearing man, General James H. Carlton, spoke with his friend Kit Carson about his dream. "The Navajos are the worst savages in the West! I'd like to see them all rounded up like the dogs they are and penned in until they can be taught to live like civilized human beings. If we could kill off all the old ones and start reeducating the children, maybe the race could be saved—but I doubt it!"

Carson agreed with the general. Thus the plans for the eventual annihilation of the Navajo Nation were set in motion.

Together, Carlton and Carson drew a rough map of the Arizona and New Mexico territories. It was Carson who chose the spot on the banks of the Rio Pecos in a remote area of east central New Mexico Territory. The internment camp would be forty miles square, completely fenced, and when Carson had finished, it would contain within its perimeter more than 9,000 Navajos.

By the winter of 1862 Carson had gathered together a detail of Utes, Piutes, Mexicans, and New Mexicans to ride with him on his "drive." Soldiers of the makeshift army were under orders to execute a precise military plan. They would systematically round up the Navajos, poison all springs and wells in the area, slaughter all sheep and cattle, and destroy all orchards and gardens.

This maneuver, Carson told his men, would prevent any of the human "herd" from bolting or escaping the roundup! After all, where would they have to go, and what would they have to eat? And so the tragic event that would for generations be called by the Navajos the "Long Walk" had begun.

Carson's tactics were successful beyond his wildest imagination, but Carlton's dream became a nightmare. Although the camp was called Fort Sumner, it became known by the Indians as the infamous Bos Redondo. It was a concentration camp where countless numbers of the once-proud Navajos died either of starvation or disease.

Hosteen Begay's mention of Bos Redondo, and Hernando's vivid description of his ordeal in Wonderful Valley, recalled memories of tragic stories Bah Tsosie had been told by her mother. She walked for several hours before the sorrow she carried in her heart began to subside, and she sat down to rest. Bah Tsosie knew it was important for her to remember every detail of those experiences about what her parents' lives had been like before and during the internment at Bos Redondo. It was part of their history, their heritage, and it must be kept alive with the telling of stories. She must repeat the words to Atwa Kee so that he could tell his children and his children's children. She put her hands on her knees and looked upward into the cloudless blue sky. Slowly, she forced herself to recall the details.

Her mother, whom Bah Tsosie remembered as being very beautiful, was called Háyoolkááł, Dawn Girl. Her grandmother's name was Aszdaan Tsee Báhi', Gray-haired Lady; her father was called Diné Nééz, Tall Navajo; and her grandfather was Jaa'tl'ool Ninéézii, Long Earrings. Aloud Bah Tsosie repeated the names of those long dead in her clan, speaking each name with great reverence. Then, in the wind—or was it out of the sky?—she seemed to hear her mother's voice.

"My sister, your dear aunt, came for a visit. It was early in the morning, and she decided to take your brother out to the cornfields to gather some fresh corn. I didn't see her again for seven months! And I never again saw your brother, my dearest only son. When finally my sister and I met again, we were in Bos Redondo. She told me then that when she and my boy reached the cornfield, she saw a group of riders ride out from behind some rocks about a half mile away. They must have seen your brother playing in the field, for they headed in that direction.

"My sister sensed the danger and ran to pick him up. They crawled beneath a large bush of greasewood. The riders came on, screaming and taunting and laughing. For a moment my sister thought they might pass by; but instead, four of them turned their horses and headed for the hiding place. They carried long rifles and scabbards tied to their saddles. They dismounted and tore your brother from my sister's arms, then they pulled her from beneath the bush. And that is how they were captured. Somehow they were separated. I never knew what happened to your brother!"

Bah Tsosie shuddered, remembering how her mother's voice trembled as she repeated stories of the atrocities at the camp—rapes and murders and beatings and starvation. "We planted corn and squash, but the Spirits were displeased. They sent worms to eat up the crop, and we were hungry. We didn't know why we were being punished. The soldiers didn't believe that the clans had no one great leader, that we ruled ourselves separately, one clan from another. They said we were being punished because of Navajo raids on the white ranchers. When we tried to tell them that those raiders were not of our clan and we were not to blame, they spat on us and hit us with their guns."

The Navajos' Long Walk, from their homeland to the death camp of Fort Sumner, was over 400 miles. They were interned from 1863 until 1865, and more than half of the 9,000 men, women, and children held there died of pneumonia, starvation, or broken hearts!

Bah Tsosie sat on the rock for several hours, and when there were no more memories to be recalled and no more tears to be shed, she returned to Po'Se'Da'. Tomorrow she would recount their history to Atwa Kee.

CHAPTER FOURTEEN

Bah Tsosie took her time about accepting Hosteen Begay into their family. She ordered him about unmercifully, always finding odd jobs for him to do that had to be done immediately. Floors had to be scrubbed, wood and kindling cut and stacked for the winter months, new shelves built, and fences and holding pens were always to be in need of repair. If he complained that some of the chores were "woman's" work, she stood on tiptoe and boxed his ears.

Hernando and Carlin watched with a combination of amusement and bewilderment as the tall, thin buck tried to placate the Navajo woman.

When he had finished his work sentence, much to the surprise of the traders, Hosteen Begay decided to stay around the post. His surly attitude gave way first to curiosity then admiration for the men. "You are the first whites I've ever known who treated me like a man instead of an animal—or worse—a child," he confessed to Carlin. "Now I would like to stay, and I would like you to teach me to read and write."

It was the beginning of a dream for Carlin; the possibility of building a school for the Navajos—adults and children. After all, when he and Phoebe had their family, their own children should have a proper school.

Instructions in arithmetic and reading began for Hosteen Begay that evening right after supper. "Story time" was temporarily discontinued, much to the delight of Hernando, who was bored by the routine, and much to the dismay of Atwa Kee, who had come to expect the ritual as a normal part of his life. In its place Hernando began teaching the boy to ride, saddle, and care for his horse. The trader and the young Navajo seemed inseparable. Carlin looked upon the relationship with mixed feelings. Bah Tsosie, although she said nothing, didn't approve. She knew that when the lambs were sold in the fall, Hernando would return to the outside world, and it would only be a matter of time before he forgot all about them. Atwa Kee would be brokenhearted. He had already lost one father, and there was no possible way he could keep the man he had chosen to idolize as a substitute.

The young Scotsman was different. He would stay at the post. She gazed fondly at Carlin, who was busy splitting logs for the new additions that were to be added to the post. This man, she thought dreamily, would make both a good father and a good husband.

With the help of Hosteen Begay and several of the younger trackers, improvements at Po'Se'Da' were finished in record time. Both Hernando and Carlin had their own sleeping rooms, a special pawn room with a floor-to-ceiling gate that could be padlocked, a large fireplace in the kitchen, pegged wooden floors in all the rooms, and guest hogans to accommodate Navajo families who had traveled too far to trade at the post to return to their homes in the same day. It had been an enormous undertaking, and now that it was finished, the traders were proud and pleased.

Hernando and Carlin climbed to the top of the bluff behind the post to have a complete view of their accomplishments.

"Looks like the beginnings of a damned city," Hernando complained as he rolled a smoke. "Next thing to put in is a whorehouse!" He knelt down and watched as the miniature figure of Bah Tsosie hung their newly washed clothes over the bushes below. "If I don't have a woman pretty soon, I might just as well become a monk."

Carlin knew that Hernando was only half joking and felt it might be a good time to discuss his plan to marry Phoebe. They had been at Po'Se'Da' more than two months, and there was no doubt in Carlin's mind that trading would become his life's work. "I need a woman, too," he said quietly.

Hernando glanced up at his friend, not sure he had heard him correctly. "Pardon?"

"I said that I need a woman." Carlin's complexion reddened. "Or perhaps I should say a 'wife.' I've decided to marry."

"Something goin' on between you 'n Bah Tsosie that I don't know about?"

"No. Nothing like that. I had someone else in mind."

Hernando inhaled deeply on his cigarette and stared quizzically at the Scot. "I can't for the life of me figure out when you've had enough time to get acquainted with any female—leastwise well enough to get married. What in the world are you talking about?"

"I'd like to take a few weeks, ride back to Santa Fe, and ask Phoebe to do me the honor of becoming my bride." Carlin spoke slowly and deliberately, making sure that Hernando understood him clearly.

"You must be mad!" Hernando gasped. "You don't even know the woman, and you're talking about spending the rest of your life with her!"

Carlin smiled patiently. "My father had never laid eyes on my mother before they were married. Everything was arranged by the marriage broker in Glasgow. My mother's father paid the fee, provided the dowry, and it was arranged. Couldn't have been a better match anywhere in the country." Carlin paused, then vowed, "I will make Phoebe a fine husband."

It seemed to Hernando that he was addressing a stranger, yet he realized that the young man was perfectly serious. "I think you're making a dreadful mistake, but I'm not your keeper. We could use more supplies, so I suppose the journey must be made one way or the other. Hosteen Begay can accompany you, just to make sure you don't get lost." He stood up and faced Carlin squarely. "I don't think she'll marry you, but perhaps you know something I don't know. Guess you can get ready to leave in the morning." He started down the trail, then glanced back. "Have you asked Bah Tsosie how she's goin' to feel about sharing her hogan with another woman?"

Carlin laughed. "Maybe I'll marry her, too!"

"Well, squaw man, don't stand there jawin' and dreamin' all day. Better get back and start checkin' the stock to see what we need."

217

* * *

Although the return journey to the Hacienda de Villanova Dundee had only taken seven days, to Carlin it seemed an eternity. The landmarks were now familiar to him, and he had no doubt that on the next trip he wouldn't need a guide. They stopped briefly at the warehouse to leave the list of supplies for the post. There Carlin had old Tom saddle him one of the Dundee horses and left Hosteen Begay to fend for himself, promising to meet the Navajo at the warehouse dock early on the morning of the third day.

He arrived at the hacienda just in time for dinner and was pleased when both Isabella and Andrew greeted him as if he were a second son. Carlin could scarcely believe the improvement in Andrew's condition. The old man was walking almost normally with just the aid of a cane, his color was good, and he was in a jovial mood. The elder Dundee hung on every word Carlin uttered, insisting he repeat the story of what had happened at the post several times before he seemed satisfied. Hernando's adventures into Hoskinini's domain seemed to please Andrew no end. "I knew he had it in 'im. He yelled 'n fought like a tiger when I insisted he learn the Navajo tongue, but it saved his life. Didn't it now? And the way you've picked it up. Astounding. If it weren't fer the fact that you's a Scot, I'd of said it was impossible." Andrew's eyes sparkled with pleasure. "Didn't I tell you, Mother, we've been divinely blessed with our son and this young man."

Isabella seemed as satisfied with the turn of events as her husband. "But you must be tired after your long journey. Would you like to retire?"

Carlin had been waiting for her words all evening. "Yes, thank you. But first I've brought Phoebe a gift. If you don't mind, I'll take it to her in the kitchen." It bothered him that he couldn't be completely honest with his gracious hosts, but after Hernando's reaction to his decision to marry the Apache, he felt it would be better to speak with Phoebe before he made his intentions known to the Dundees.

He felt his heart pounding at an abnormal pace as he excused himself and made his way through the dark hall to the rear of the hacienda. He hadn't even glanced at Phoebe, with the exception of a brief acknowledgment when he first arrived, for fear that something in his eyes or the tone of his voice would indicate his feelings toward her.

She was seated at the kitchen table talking with Rosa when he entered the room. Her warm smile made him slightly lightheaded for a moment and gave him the courage to ask Rosa to leave them alone for a few minutes. The Mexican woman looked at him curiously, then smiled broadly. "*Sí! Sí!* I understand!" Carlin flushed, wondering if she truly did.

His plan had seemed so natural when he first made his decision to propose to Phoebe several weeks before. Now, seated opposite the reserved Apache, hardly able to breathe, he wondered. "It's good to see you again," he said.

Phoebe smiled and nodded, avoiding his intense gaze.

"Would you walk with me in the garden? I have so much to say to you."

"I have work to do. I must clear the table and tend to the dishes," she replied.

"Please. I have so little time and so much to say."

She frowned quizzically but, sensing the urgency in his voice, assented. Slipping a shawl over her shoulders, she led the way out onto the patio. A gentle breeze stirred the perfume of lilac and evening primrose around them as they walked. Carlin longed to take her in his arms—to kiss her full lips and caress her smooth cheek—but he knew he dare not touch her.

After a time she seated herself on the adobe wall that surrounded the central fountain and waited for the young trader to speak.

"This is difficult for me to say, more difficult than I had imagined," he began.

"Perhaps if you sit down next to me the words will be easier," she suggested.

The invitation gave him courage. He told her first of his own life, his family, his boyhood in Scotland, and his dreams of adventure and finding a perfect spot on earth in which to settle. "Po'Se'Da' is as perfect a place as I've ever imagined. Have you been there?"

"No. As a child my tribe lived in the mountains. Although the Navajo are our cousins, I have never seen their land."

"You'd like it. It's clean and free. The sunrises and sunsets are as beautiful as any I've ever seen. It's not really a desert—there are wildflowers and springs. All sorts of animals come to the post for water. I've seen them early in the morning."

Phoebe smiled. "It must be very beautiful."

"It is," he answered enthusiastically. "There's just one thing missing—and then my life would be complete."

Phoebe remained silent.

"You're what's missing in my life. I want to marry you and take you back to Po'Se'Da'."

If she were shocked or surprised, she gave no sign. She sat gracefully, her hands on her lap, for what Carlin considered an endless length of time. He wondered if she had heard him—or if she had, if she understood what he was saying. "I'll devote my life to making you happy. We'll have a dozen children if you like—or none at all." He lapsed into silence. There was nothing else to be said.

When she finally turned to face him, he could see in the moonlight that her eyes were filled with tears. She reached out and touched him gently on his cheek, then smoothed the hair from his forehead. "I am deeply touched that you have chosen to honor me as your wife," she said softly. "I have known much tragedy and I have known much joy. But my joy is here. I have no wish to marry. I have no wish to leave Dona Isabella, nor Don Andrew. They are my family and my life. You are young, and you are a good man; but you must look elsewhere for a woman."

She arose, and without a backward glance, returned to the kitchen. Carlin sat quietly, listening to the rhythmic flow of the fountain—too numb with disappointment to follow her.

Carlin rode away from the Hacienda Villanova Dundee before sunup the next morning, leaving a note for Isabella and Andrew explaining that he was anxious to return to Po'Se'Da' and assuring them that he would see them again in a few months.

The streets of Santa Fe were beginning to come to

life with the warmth of the sun as he made his way to the small adobe house at the edge of the city. The room was much as he remembered it—dark, filled with the odor of stale whiskey and powdered flesh. There were fewer patrons than there had been when he first entered the whorehouse with Hernando. He made his way to the bar and ordered a scotch. "Is Lydia around?" he asked the sleepy bartender.

CHAPTER FIFTEEN

Hundreds of miles away from the isolated Indian trading post of Po'Se'Da', in the village of Santa Barbara, a tragedy occurred. Almost at the very hour Carlin returned to the post from his unsuccessful mission in New Mexico Territory, more than half the population of the pueblo of Santa Barbara crowded into the Cathedral of Santa Inés to pay their final respects to Dolores's mother, the widow Castiaga.

Kneeling before the exquisite statue of their patroness, Saint Agnes, dwarfed by the magnificence of the pink-and-green walls, Mama Ignacia's enormous frame shook uncontrollably as she tried unsuccessfully to stop crying. She wasn't crying over the sudden death of her friend, but rather because of the pain and loneliness she knew Dolores would suffer without her mother.

Perhaps some of the tears were for herself, for Mama Ignacia, too, had suffered from the same loneliness. She had been baptized Anita de la Ignacia fifty-nine years earlier, in 1826, at the mission San Francisco de Asis, the youngest of fourteen children of Miguel and Eulalia de la Ignacia. By the time she had reached her thirteenth birthday, Anita was considered to be one of the most beautiful young women in all of California Norte. In that respect, Mama Ignacia remembered sadly, she and Dolores Castiaga were very much alike. Eligible Spanish bachelors for hundreds of miles around came to court the tall beauty. Anita had been so slender in her youth a man could circle her waist with his two hands; her skin and features had been flawless—she had been carefree and witty and gay.

Pressured by her family to marry, Anita had just about decided upon her choice of a husband when a Russian trade ship entered the harbor with a handsome young Russian nobleman as the captain. The de la Ignacias, being the most prominent family in the area next to the governor and his wife, hosted the young man with great extravagance; and within a few hours of their meeting the beautiful Anita and the gallant Vladimir Cherikov fell in love. The Russian charmed the entire family with wondrous tales of the court life in St. Petersburg, and before he sailed at the end of the week, his engagement to Anita was announced. It would take time to petition the Pope for permission for Anita to marry outside of her faith, but neither of the young lovers doubted that it would be forthcoming and were content to wait until Vladimir could return the following year.

"I will deliver our supplies to the Russian colonies in the north, return to Russia to prepare for your arrival as my wife," Vladimir promised. "And when spring returns to California Norte, I too shall return."

Anita and her mother began plans for an elaborate wedding. Dresses had to be sewn, the dowry prepared. The time would pass quickly, and although Anita knew she would miss him terribly, she consoled herself by remembering they would have the rest of their lives together.

The following spring the Russian captain did not return. Nor did he return the next year, nor the next. There were no letters or messages. Anita waited—and pined—and withdrew. Her only words of comfort, her only companionship, came from her dear mother.

On her eighteenth birthday, already considered a spinster, Anita was giving serious thought to entering the convent at Monterey when her mother became ill. The frail lady died within a week and on her deathbed pleaded with her daughter. "Your father will be lost without me. All of your sisters and brothers have homes of their own. They have their own families and care nothing about what happens to your father. Stay home, Anita! Stay home and take care of your father."

There was no other choice. Anita bowed to her mother's final wish. She saw to the servants, the hacienda, and accompanied her father to his place of business, a bazaar, every day. It was considered scandalous to the community that a gentlewoman, especially a *spinster*, should learn a trade and enter the world of men; her father felt it far more important that she be able to care for herself after he had joined his wife in heaven.

Anita's mind was quick and within two years she was considered as shrewd in buying and selling goods as her father. She never mentioned Vladimir Cherikov's name, but the pain in her heart could be measured by the enormous amount of weight she gained.

She was nearly six feet tall and weighed more than 200 pounds.

The more proficient Anita grew in the world of trade, the more nervous her brothers became. They were intolerant and quarrelsome, and when Anita's father was finally laid to rest beside his beloved wife, it was decided that Anita should be sent away to open a bazaar in another area. She was an embarrassment to her remaining relatives. She chose the pueblo of Santa Barbara because it was so isolated.

Her business was successful immediately and she was invited everywhere, but most of the time she preferred at the end of her day to go home alone to her *casita* and sit and brood. One evening, however, the Castiaga family insisted that she attend a very formal dinner party at their hacienda that was being given to honor a Russian dignitary. Anita was seated next to the distinguished guest. He was much older than she was but quite taken with her intelligence and humor, and soon they were engaged in a lively conversation. When he discovered that she had been born in San Francisco, he recalled that his nephew had once sailed into that port and had fallen in love with a young Spanish beauty. "When he returned to St. Petersburg, he couldn't talk enough about the girl. We were all looking forward to the treat of meeting her."

Anita felt her heart racing and finally summoned the courage to ask, "And did you have the chance to meet her?"

"No. Unfortunately, my nephew was lost at sea in a storm off the coast of Alaska and never had the chance to claim his bride."

"And what was your nephew's name?"

"Vladimir Cherikov."

Anita felt the blood rush from her head. Tears welled up in her eyes like springs gushing forth from the earth. Somehow she managed to get to her feet and was helped from the room. Neither the Russian nor any of the townspeople ever knew why the bazaar was closed for a week, but when she had recovered enough to reopen her business, Anita was like another person. She became "Mama" Ignacia, the kindest, happiest woman in the pueblo.

Mama had been a bridesmaid more times than she cared to remember; she had mothered the poor, the orphaned, and the unloved of the town; and she nursed the sick and fed the hungry. She was able to give love because after her conversation with the Russian, she knew that Vladimir had truly loved her. Yet she was lonely! Everybody needed somebody—and this was as true for Dolores as it had been for Mama Ignacia. Dolores would never be known as a spinster. Not if Mama had anything to say about the matter!

The mourners stayed at the Hacienda de Castiaga just long enough to be respectful. Although the widow Castiaga had been highly regarded, Dolores had alienated most of the Santa Barbarans with her caustic wit and arrogance. Her seeming lack of grief at her mother's funeral was the final outrage, and a few of the neighbors found it difficult even to be civil to the young beauty. Now, sitting alone in the antechamber off the living room, out of sight of the few stragglers and the servants, Dolores abandoned her facade of indifference and allowed herself to weep.

She scarcely noticed as Mama Ignacia entered the small room and sat down next to her on the sofa. "Now, now . . ." Mama comforted her, pulling a large handkerchief from her purse. "Everyone begins the path toward death from the moment they are born. Your mother lived a full and active life and will find her reward in heaven."

"I'm not crying for my mother. I'm crying for myself! She never prepared me to be alone. I have no relatives—no husband—and no money." The girl sobbed, sinking her face into Mama's ample bosom. "I know nothing about business—keeping books or tending to the land or the cattle. I have been raised with servants. The only thing I'm suited for is giving parties—and who will come to my parties when I have no husband? And what is worse, I have no money for a dowry, so I will never have a husband!"

"You will have a dowry. I shall provide for that. The only question now is who will you marry?"

The question was rhetorical. Mama Ignacia and the widow Castiaga had discussed the matter many times before, and it was a foregone conclusion that Hernando Dundee was the perfect choice. Mama Ignacia rocked back and forth, imagining what beautiful children the young aristocrats would produce, then she scowled. "What a fool that young rascal is." The words were spoken under her breath and Dolores was unaware of her thoughts. Mama looked out over the garden and thought how much easier it would have been for everyone concerned if Hernando had married Dolores when she had reached the proper age of sixteen. Oh, well, he would come around. She turned back to the girl. "You must listen to me carefully and do exactly as I tell you to do. Men don't know what's good for them, and it is up to us women to show them the way."

Time was important. Both Dolores and Mama Ignacia were well aware that the widow Castiaga had sold off her estate piece by piece—and the sheep and cattle head by head—in order to maintain their gracious life-style. Even the magnificent hacienda was heavily mortgaged. Most of the parcels and mortgage had been purchased by one man, the "Yankui" banker Hedrick Edward Norton. It would only be a matter of time before he would recognize the grieving period was over and foreclose on his property. If the marriage between Dolores and Hernando could be expedited, there might be a slim chance that the Dundees could recover some of the Castiaga holdings and restore them to Dolores. The matter was in God's hands.

Mama Ignacia's letter to Isabella Dundee was carefully worded. She explained that the girl had been left destitute, and "since we have all been such close friends for so many years, I wondered if by chance you could find it in your heart to allow me to send the dear and unhappy child to Santa Fe for a few months until she is able to recover from her tragic loss and decide what she is to do with her life. Perhaps this sad turn of events will bring Hernando to his senses, and he will realize what an asset Dolores would be to his life."

Express riders carried the letter from Santa Barbara to San Diego, then to El Paso, up to Santa Fe, and finally on to the Hacienda de Villanova Dundee.

Mama Ignacia received Isabella's reply by telegraph: "You are quite correct in your thinking. We could not be more pleased to have Dolores stay with us for as long as it takes to bring Hernando around. Wire when we can expect her."

Dolores allowed Mama Ignacia to make her plans. She had no intentions of spending her life in Santa Fe, however. She would marry Hernando, and then by whatever means necessary, she would pursuade Hernando to return with her to Santa Barbara. And one day, she was convinced, she would find a way to regain control of her beloved home, the Hacienda de Castiaga.

Hedrick Norton glanced at his calendar again, noting that it was now exactly two weeks to the day of the funeral. He hadn't wanted to discuss the foreclosure too soon, but neither did he intend to wait too long. For years he had coveted the home and its lush surroundings, and now, after the legalities were taken care of, it would finally be his. What a shame he wasn't twenty years younger, he thought pensively, for he also coveted the girl. It was too much to hope for and a totally irrational thought. He would continue to find his feminine companionship at Felicia's. But, my God, how wonderful it would be to sleep with Dolores—and as his wife she would be an enormous asset. He stood in front of the full-length mirror and smoothed down his graying hair. Ridiculous!

"John," he called to his secretary, "call for the coachman, then deliver a note to the Senorita Castiaga and inform her that I shall call upon her at two tomorrow afternoon."

* * *

Norton arrived promptly at two and found Dolores awaiting him in the garden. He was surprised to find her dressed in an exceedingly low-cut gown, violet in color, which accentuated her full young breasts and fair skin. "I must apologize for not coming sooner to express my sympathy over your loss," he stammered.

"It's been a difficult time," Dolores answered, rising and locking her arm in his. "Why don't we go indoors where I can offer you some wine?"

The nearness of her, and the sweetness of her perfume, made him tremble.

"I'm grateful to you for not coming sooner," she continued, as they walked toward the hacienda.

"Why?"

"I'm well aware of your business with me. And it will pain me deeply to leave this home where I was born; however, I have no money, and I am nearly packed. You may expect to take possession within a few days."

The banker steadied himself and patted her hand. "Please believe me. I have no wish to deprive you of your residence. Take all the time you need."

"You're too kind," she cooed softly. "But plans have already been made for me."

"What plans?"

"I am to journey to Santa Fe. I have little choice in the matter, really. After all, I'm alone in the world, and there is no one here to care for me. In Santa Fe I will stay with dear friends of my family, Andrew Dundee and his wife Isabella." She breathed deeply and allowed a tear to fall from her eye. "After a proper time I will marry their son, Hernando—we have been betrothed since we were children—and his family is very, very rich!"

"That will be a grand thing for you . . ." Hedrick was surprised that his stomach churned with jealousy. "But I know Hernando and was not aware that he was engaged."

"It was arranged by our families. He will have to marry me."

Hedrick helped Dolores to be seated, then seated himself. "But isn't that a bit old-fashioned? I mean an arranged marriage. Do you love him?"

"Love had nothing to do with it, really. I look upon marriage as—how do you say it—a merger. The merging together of two fine families."

"I don't believe you should do anything hastily," the banker ventured as he poured himself a glass of wine. "You are certainly in no position to think clearly at a time like this. Why don't you stay here in your own home for a bit longer and see if we can't find another solution? I don't believe you really love Hernando Dundee. He's quite a ladies' man, you know, and I think you deserve better."

Dolores could hardly believe her ears. Did she detect an invitation? "There is no time. I do what I must do."—She touched her handkerchief to her eyes—"You are so kind, may I ask just one favor?"

"Anything!"

"If and when I am ever in a position to repay you, would you allow me to buy my home back? I've spent so many happy hours here with my mother. I know I shall die if I'm not able to live out my days here."

For the first time in his life Norton found himself

speechless. It suddenly became very clear to him that Dolores would do almost anything to regain possession of the hacienda. It was possible that she might even enter into a loveless marriage to accomplish her ends. "I will give the matter some thought," he assured her, "if you will promise me something in return."

"Perhaps."

"Just promise me you will not marry in haste. I couldn't bear to think of you ruining your life simply because of a lack of money. Please consider me your friend—and allow me the privilege of being of assistance for your slightest need."

It was now Dolores's turn to be mute. She remained silent for several minutes, trying to digest his words and discover his true intent. Actually, she was not at all sure that she would be able to marry Hernando. Perhaps she might have another option—one she had never considered. She studied the banker's features with new interest. He was not unattractive. Old—and with a slight pouch—but tall and well dressed. His eyes were clear and shrewd, and he had a deep dimple in his chin. "I promise," she said finally. "Mama Ignacia has made arrangements for me to leave by railroad on Friday. Those arrangements cannot be changed. You may take possession of the hacienda then." She smiled sweetly and glanced around the room. "Think of me when you're here."

"I shall."

He thought it ironic when he remembered that it was he who had convinced his old friend Charles Crocker to add the Southern Pacific track north from

Los Angeles to Santa Barbara, even when Crocker's associates had felt it would be a bad investment. As he looked longingly at Dolores, he realized that the very railroad he had fought to bring into town would be carrying away a treasure far greater than any other he had ever wanted to possess. The tenderness and humility he felt surprised him. "Would it be too forward of me to ask if I might write to you?"

"Forward? I would be delighted!" Dolores replied sincerely. "You could tell me about your parties here, and what is happening at the hacienda!"

He finished his wine and placed the glass on the table. Everything that had to be said had been said. He needed time to plan his campaign to win the young woman. Only time would give him the key to winning her. He stood up abruptly, kissed her hand, and retreated to his carriage to be alone with his thoughts.

Dolores smiled as she watched him leave, then went slowly to her room to continue packing. The afternoon visit had proved to be extremely interesting.

When Norton told Felicia Montez of Dolores's proposed journey to Santa Fe and the possibility of her entering into an arranged marriage with Hernando, he was not surprised that the young madam was upset. He knew how deeply Felicia felt about the young Dundee and wondered if somehow they might form an alliance that would be beneficial to them both.

Although he knew Felicia to be a person who made her own decisions and tried to control her own destiny, she had allowed the banker to guide her in matters of finance. He was the only one who knew the extent of her success. He had made her independently wealthy.

As a ragged, barefoot child, Felicia had quickly concluded that the only difference between her and the so-called ladies of quality was money. And so that she might overcome that difference she chose the only profession open to her in order to earn the money that would negate that difference. She became a prostitute. She entered into the profession with such joy and confidence that soon her skills in providing pleasure were sought after by men who were both famous and infamous, rich and poor, from near and far.

Norton met her shortly after he arrived in Santa Barbara, when a few of his friends—leading citizens—took him on a grand tour of the pueblo. Their last stop was La Paloma Caida—the Fallen Dove—a notorious house of prostitution that was owned at that time by a slovenly madam named Consuela de la Nueva.

The madam weighed almost 300 pounds, believed in bathing once a year, and cleaned La Paloma Caida about as often as she bathed. She had first induced Felicia into the sisterhood, and what little the madam knew about personal hygiene she made up for in teaching her girls the skills of lovemaking!

At his friends' insistence, Norton chose to "go upstairs" with Felicia. The fiery young half-breed had never seen a man so elegantly dressed and was flattered by his choice of her. She was not flattered, however, when they arrived in her room and she began to undress.

ton was flattered by the girl's rapt attention. His tone became fatherly. "It is a rule of thumb that you should save ten cents out of every dollar you earn. When you have saved enough money, you can invest it and have something to look forward to when you're too old for this kind of work."

Felicia was thoughtful. "Could I ever be rich?"

"I don't think you'd ever be rich, but you could be independent. Always remember that there are two kinds of money: the kind you work for and the kind that works for you."

How brilliant, Felicia thought, *and how simple*. "What would happen if I saved ninety cents out of every dollar?"

Norton threw back his head and laughed heartily. It amused him that the child was concerned with such an impossibility. "Then, my dear, you would probably become *very* rich!" He handed her a twenty-dollar gold piece. "When you have saved your first hundred dollars, get word to me at the bank, and I will help you make some wise investments."

Norton never expected to hear from Felicia again, but in less than a month she sent word to him that she had saved five hundred dollars. He came 'round to see her at the close of business. She was freshly bathed and dressed in a simple black dress. "You learn quickly, Felicia. I think we might become friends."

That had been six years before; Felicia had been fourteen years old. Within a year Felicia was able to buy La Paloma Caida from Consuela, and under Norton's direction soon turned it into a showplace. The girls and rooms were immaculate, and men came from miles around to enjoy the wares. The banker never utilized Felicia's talent, preferring not to mix business with pleasure, but he was a regular and generous patron as well as a loyal friend.

Norton also encouraged Felicia to read and expand her mind, and under his tutelage she blossomed into an elegant as well as wealthy woman. In the first year as owner of La Paloma Caida she only serviced those men whose company she enjoyed; they became her regular customers and paid well for the privilege. Many men fell in love with her, but she could not return the emotion. She was sure she was immune to that illusive feeling until she met Hernando Dundee. From that moment on Felicia Montez never serviced another customer.

"In all the years I've known you, I've never seen you behave like this!" Norton scolded.

"Please, Hedrick, I'd rather not discuss it."

"But I thought you cared for this Hernando Dundee," he persisted.

Felicia turned to her friend, her face white with anxiety. "There is nothing I can do. Hernando has been gone for three months now—it's the longest time in five years that I haven't seen him, and now I know why. He loves Dolores. There is nothing more to be said. He will be a faithful husband."

"Ah, but does Dolores love him?" the banker asked slyly. "If you truly cared for the man you wouldn't allow him to enter into such a contract."

"But what could I do to prevent it?"

Norton had been waiting for the question. "Fight for him! Fight the same way you've fought for everything else. Go to Santa Fe and become a lady. You have the money for it. Let him see you as I see you—a lovely, beautiful, and wealthy woman."

"A filthy prostitute." Felicia fairly spat out the words. "Even if I could win him, his family would never accept me."

"No one would ever know. You can assume an entirely new identity. I can arrange that . . ."

"Hernando would know," she said simply.

"You're a clever woman, Felicia, you can accomplish anything you truly wish to accomplish. You've certainly proved that to me. You'll find a way if you want to."

Felicia studied Hedrick Norton's face. She had never seen him so determined. "Hedrick, my dear, I've known you as long as you've known me—and never once have I ever seen you do anything for anyone unless you, too, had something to gain. Just what interest do you have in this involvement?"

He looked almost boyish. "You are so young to be so wise." Then he smiled. "I intend to marry Dolores Castiaga myself."

CHAPTER SIXTEEN

Heavily veiled and almost suffocating in the July heat, Felicia, armed with documents proving that she was Chata San Vincente—the widow of Ernesto San Vincente of San Diego—managed to board the train just a few minutes before departure time without anyone recognizing her.

Norton negotiated the sale of La Paloma Caida without difficulty, then arranged for Felicia—Chata—to occupy one of the four private compartments on the Southern Pacific train that would take her as far as El Paso. Accommodations on the Atchison, Topeka & Santa Fe had been more difficult to manage but by bribery and influence from Charles Crocker he was able to reserve another private compartment from El Paso to her final destination. He was just as clever in arranging that no private compartments were available for Dolores when Mama Ignacia purchased her tickets.

Felicia waited until the train was several miles outside of Los Angeles before she summoned the conductor and asked him to deliver a note to the young lady who had boarded in Santa Barbara. Assured that he knew the woman of whom she spoke, she tipped him handsomely and waited.

The passenger car in which Dolores rode was overcrowded, overheated, and, in general, unbearable. Most of the passengers were unkempt, bearded men who carried revolvers in their belts and spit tobacco. The air in the car, which seemed at a minimum, was filled with the unpleasant smells of body odor, stale smoke, and foul breath. The language of the occupants was as foul as the odors, and Dolores held a handkerchief to her mouth to control her nausea.

She accepted the note suspiciously, opened it, and read: "I am a widow and would enjoy your company if you would prefer to join me in my private compartment." It was signed: "Senora Chata San Vincente."

Dolores nodded her acceptance to the waiting conductor and was so relieved at being rescued from her rude surroundings she fairly flew out of her seat. The intense summer heat had caused her to perspire profusely, and once inside the compartment she had to wipe her eyes in order to get a clear look at her benefactor. She was surprised that the widow was so young. Dolores guessed they were about the same age. She was also surprised at how attractive and well dressed the woman was.

"I am Dolores Castiaga and must thank you for your generous invitation."

"It is my pleasure," Felicia replied graciously. She had seen the Castiaga girl several times in Santa Barbara but always at a distance. This was the first opportunity she'd ever had to have a closer look, and she scrutinized Dolores as if she were examining a bug under a microscope. She noted immediately that her rival was proud as well as beautiful and understood how she had been able to capture the heart of Hedrick Norton. The way she stood, the angle of her chin, the coolness in her eyes portrayed an aristocrat. Yes, Felicia surmised, wherever Hedrick traveled in the world—if this woman were his wife—he would be considered nobility. She also took small comfort in knowing that she, rather than Dolores, was much more Hernando's type of woman.

This, of course, Felicia realized was her opinion and was highly colored by her jealousy. If she were to win out over her young adversary, she would have to study her well. Felicia unconsciously bit her lower lip. It would not be an easy victory. The girl was regal and appeared virginal. On the other hand, she reasoned, Dolores's regal quality could turn to arrogance—her virginal quality into ignorance—and her beauty into vanity. Before they reached Santa Fe, Felicia intended to know *everything* about Dolores Castiaga. She opened her traveling case and removed a silver flask. "I carry pink gin to help me over my sorrow. Would you care for a drink?"

Dolores had never tasted anything stronger than wine. It was not considered proper for a lady to indulge in stronger spirits, and she looked at Felicia quizzically.

"It will relieve the monotony," her hostess assured her.

Dolores bowed to Felicia's judgment and accepted a small silver cup of the liquid. The first sip numbed her lips and created a burning sensation in her mouth that sped down into her stomach and settled in her toes. Felicia smiled as she watched Dolores's eyes widen.

"The first drink is always the most difficult. Just sip it and you'll be fine," Felicia suggested. "Now tell me what a pretty young lady is doing traveling alone . . ."

The pink gin began to have its effect. Dolores felt light-headed and began to unbend. She leaned back in the leather cushions of her seat and let the breeze from the open window cool her damp brow. Then, slowly, she began to relate the events that had led her to make the journey. Even under the effects of the alcohol she was careful to preserve her image.

Although at times she seemed vain, and there was a certain hint of arrogance, Felicia was uncomfortably aware that this was not the prattle of a stupid young girl. Dolores was a foe to be reckoned with.

"But I've talked about myself for almost an hour. Please forgive me. Your note mentioned that you were a widow. Not too recently, I hope."

Felicia's eyes narrowed. It was obvious from the girl's tone of voice that the question had been asked out of politeness, and that Dolores had no interest in hearing about Chata's misfortune. "We will have days to become acquainted. Plenty of time for you to hear my story. Why don't we try to get a little rest?"

The drone of the engine, the rhythm of the iron wheels speeding along the iron tracks, and the effects of the pink gin were hypnotic. Dolores rested her head on the arm of the seat and within seconds was asleep. Felicia smiled thoughtfully. She wondered what price Hedrick would have to pay to possess this selfish woman. One thing she determined—she loved Hernando too much to allow him to fall into Dolores's web.

Isabella was beside herself with anticipation at the thought of having Dolores stay with them. She had given birth to two daughters—stillborn—and the emptiness she still felt in her heart at their loss might be lessened by the presence of this charming young girl. Isabella had not seen Dolores for years, but she remembered her as a beautiful, bright child, with a ready smile. And, as Mama Ignacia had anticipated, Isabella now determined that it was time for Hernando to marry and settle down. Both she and Andrew longed for grandchildren, and although her husband seemed to be recovering nicely, she worried about how much time they had left together. In her mind, Isabella was already planning the wedding and inviting the guests.

She set Carlos to polishing the surrey and currying the horses days before the arrival. Now she waited at the station as impatient as the horses for her first sight of the girl.

"Carlos, help me down!" she demanded. "And then you'd better dust these seats again."

He smiled condescendingly at his mistress. It was not like Dona Isabella to be this excited. The young senorita must be someone very special, Carlos thought, lifting the woman gently down from the high step of the surrey.

Felicia deliberately took her time leaving the compartment. She was not sure whether or not Hernando would be at the station to meet Dolores, and she had no intentions of letting him see her if he were. She watched from the window as Isabella embraced Dolores, trying to control the envy she felt. She immediately realized that the lovely, stately woman engaged in so animated a conversation with the Castiaga girl was Hernando's mother. The pride of Isabella's walk and the delicate bone structure was inborn, not cultivated. She was relieved to find that Hernando was nowhere in sight.

The porter busied himself with Felicia's luggage and helped her from the train. Felicia handed him a generous tip and opened her parasol in order to shade herself from the intense brightness of the mountain sun. She was about to look for a carriage when Dolores called out for her to join them.

"Chata! Chata, dear,"—Dolores clasped Felicia in a warm embrace—"I'd like you to meet Senora Isabella Dundee, my gracious hostess while I'm in Santa Fe!"

Felicia was stunned by Dolores's sudden transformation. Her attitude was so humble, so demure that Felicia was tempted to applaud her performance. The girl displayed such sweetness, such genuine affection that for a moment Felicia forgot about her own deception. Remembering, she flushed, wishing she had never heard of Hernando Dundee and his family.

"Dolores has told me how kind you've been and of the warm affection you've shown her." Isabella's dark eyes reflected her gratitude. "Are you being met by friends, Senora San Vincente?"

"No," Felicia replied softly. "After the death of my husband, I found that living in San Diego, surrounded by his friends and his memory, was too painful. I decided to live in Santa Fe only because I know no one here."

"How brave you young women are," Isabella commented, impressed by Felicia's apparent independence. "Why don't you stay with us at the hacienda until you're more acquainted with our village and know where you would like to settle?"

"You are most kind, but my banker has arranged lodgings for me at La Fonda."

"La Fonda is one of the loveliest inns in the entire West. I'm sure you'll be comfortable there. But I insist that we see you to your quarters." She took the girls arm in arm to the surrey and had Carlos arrange for another cart for the luggage. It was as if the three women had been friends for years.

Felicia sat in the ornate lobby of the La Fonda Inn, trying to accustom herself to her new role as a wealthy and respectable widow. She studied the endless fashion parade of wives as they greeted each other for lunch or browsed around the small exclusive shops in the mall, watching carefully how they carried their gloves, their parasols, and their beaded bags. She knew there was no difference between her and these refined women, yet inwardly, totally out of her own environment, Felicia shook with fear. She wondered how successfully she would be able to carry off the charade.

Isabella and Dolores had insisted that she visit the Hacienda de Villanova Dundee so that they could plan the party that would introduce her to Santa Fe society. After two weeks she could think of no more excuses to delay the affair. Fumbling nervously in her bag, Felicia withdrew the small musical French pocket watch Hedrick Norton had given her as a going-away gift and checked the time. She still had a few minutes before the ladies arrived. Filled with self-doubt she darted across the lobby and up the stairs to the safety of her room. Once inside she studied herself in the mirror. Did she have on too much rouge—was her dress conservative enough? She felt tears welling up in her eyes. What a fool she was, she thought, for ever leaving Santa Barbara! What if she were recognized? How could she face the humiliation? She patted her damp forehead with her handkerchief, added some more powder to her reddened nose, dried her eyes, straightened her shoulders, and retraced her steps to the lobby. Perhaps it would be worth the risk just to see Hernando one more time.

Isabella and Dolores were just entering the inn as Felicia reached the landing. Dolores ran forward like an eager child to greet her and exclaimed, "Chata, how beautiful you look!"

They embraced politely, then Felicia extended her hand to Isabella. "It's so kind of you to invite me to your home. As soon as I'm settled I hope I'll be able to repay your hospitality."

"We're counting on that; meanwhile, before we journey forth into the wilderness, I've arranged for us to lunch with a few of my friends. They can each be helpful to you in their own way." Isabella beamed and led the way into the dining room. The maître d' greeted them royally and ushered them across the crowded room with great flourish.

When they arrived at their table, Isabella introduced them to the three seated matrons. "Dolores Castiaga and Chata San Vincente, may I introduce my friend, Sarah Spiegelberg. Her husband Aaron runs the general store and imports goods from all over the world. And Esther Mendoza"—Isabella paused briefly and lowered her voice—"Esther, too, has recently been widowed. And last but not least my dear friend Lillie Taylor. Her husband owns the bank!"

When everyone was seated Isabella signaled their waiter to begin serving. Dolores was completely relaxed and began chatting immediately. Felicia, who had never particularly enjoyed the company of women, was more reserved.

"Isabella informs us that the first matter of business is to find you more suitable quarters in which to live," Esther said kindly, trying to bring Felicia into the conversation. "Now that my husband has passed on I have plenty of room in my home for the two of us."

The woman's generosity was unnerving. "That's very kind of you, but I think I would prefer to remain alone for a while," Felicia replied.

Esther was not at all offended. "I understand. But when and if you change your mind, I would be delighted for the company."

"I'm having a tea for the Ladies of Charity at my home next Thursday afternoon. You must join me! I simply won't take no for an answer," Sarah chimed in enthusiastically, "And on Friday we visit the poor with baskets of food. It's so rewarding to do our little bit."

Only Lillie Taylor remained cool. She seemed to be studying Felicia carefully, noting every movement and listening to every word. Once their eyes met, and

Felicia felt strangely uncomfortable under the woman's hostile gaze. When lunch was finished, Lillie excused herself.

Sarah seemed to be the only one to notice the peculiar byplay. "Lillie's acting very strangely, don't you think?"

"I think she's jealous," Esther volunteered. "Until now she's been the prettiest woman in town!"

The ladies laughed, then Isabella began to worry about the time. "Perhaps you should pack a bag and spend the night at the hacienda. It's a long ride in the carriage, and I don't want to tire you or worry about you returning after dinner. We want to take our time and make sure the party is properly planned."

She ignored Felicia's protests, and within an hour had helped her pack for the visit.

Andrew had almost fully recovered from his attack. Indeed, Dr. Vargas had begun to doubt that his diagnosis had been correct. On his last visit to see his patient, the doctor commented that he had never seen such a miraculous recovery. Andrew fingered the amulet around his neck and smiled at Isabella and Phoebe. The doctor's diagnosis had not been wrong— but they had had additional help from a source they preferred not to discuss.

Andrew waited on the terrace for the arrival of the women. He had not been as pleased as his wife with the prospect of having Dolores for his daughter-in-law. But that decision would ultimately have to be made by Hernando. Still, it surprised Andrew how Isabella had blinded herself to the fact that Dolores was intolerably spoiled and treated the servants harshly.

He had even been forced, at one point, to explain to the girl that it was much more proper to request something than to demand it. Isabella defended Dolores by explaining to Andrew that "she is young and still mourning her mother—she will grow accustomed to our ways!" Andrew wondered.

He arose to help them from the carriage. Isabella embraced her husband, then proudly introduced him to their overnight guest. "Andrew, may I present Senora San Vincente? Chata, this is my husband, Don Andrew."

Andrew grasped her hands warmly and stared at her. She was as attractive as his wife had described her. He looked directly into her blue-black eyes and noted the flawlessness of her ivory complexion. She wore her hair, as Hedrick had suggested, swept high off her neck, the curls held neatly in place with carved bone combs. "Chata?" Andrew repeated. "You don't look like a Chata!"

Felicia drew back, then realized he was joking.

"Let's go inside and have some tea. It's been quite some time since I've been blessed by such a bevy of beauties!"

Felicia felt herself pale and tried to avoid Andrew's piercing blue eyes—his expression was so like Hernando's. She felt wretched deceiving these warm and wonderful people and wished desperately that she had not agreed to spend the night. She prayed that she might find some excuse to leave early.

"I once knew a Rudolpho San Vincente in California. Was he related in some way to your late husband?" Andrew asked.

250

"No, no," Felicia answered, trying to retain her composure. "To my knowledge he had no relatives at all in California!"

"How sad," Isabella reflected. "And what about your own people?"

"I was orphaned when I was a small child and raised by a maiden aunt. She died shortly before I was married," Felicia lied in a shaking voice. The cup shook in her trembling hand. "It's been a long ride. Do you think I might rest a few moments?"

"Of course, dear. How cruel of us to pry! Dolores will show you upstairs." Isabella was concerned. "Are you sure you're feeling well?"

Felicia assured them that she would be fine after a short rest and allowed herself to be led away by Dolores. Carlos passed them in the hallway on his way to deliver a note to Andrew that had been given to him by Lillie Taylor. She had cautioned the servant to be discreet in its delivery. Carlos watched and waited until his mistress retired into the kitchen, then pressed the perfumed message into his master's hand.

Andrew stared curiously at the pale blue envelope then tore it open. The message read: "I must see you as soon as possible about a situation which might prove very embarrassing to you and your family. Say nothing about this message." It was signed: "Lillie."

Andrew read the note several times, then crumpled it up and slipped it into his pocket. "Saddle my horse," he directed the Indian servant. Then he found Isabella. "I think I'll go for a short ride."

"Andrew! What a ridiculous thought! You're not strong enough."

251

"As a matter of fact, Dr. Vargas has told me that it's a very fine thing to do. I must have some exercise, or I'll never gain my strength back. I'm going to ride into Santa Fe and see Aaron. Carlos can follow in the surrey. If I get tired, I'll tie my horse on behind."

Isabella knew it was impossible to argue with him. She touched his cheek gently. "Take care, Andrew. I love you very much."

He took her hands in his and brought them to his lips. "And I you!"

Lillie watched through the curtains as Andrew tied his horse to the hitching post and made his way up the shaded walk to the front door. Wondering if she had done the right thing, she waited for a few moments after she heard his rap. Then with sudden resolution she opened the door. "Andrew! How wonderful to see you looking so fit. I'd heard that your recovery has been nothing less than a miracle, and now I see that that is true. Let's go into the study and I'll get you a brandy."

"Your note sounded quite ominous, Lillie." Andrew spoke gruffly and directly to the point. He hadn't liked deceiving Isabella, and he hoped his journey was worth the lie.

Lillie motioned him to be seated and poured them both a snifter of brandy. She moved slowly and deliberately. When she was seated in the chair opposite the bearded man, she gazed around the room at the opulent furnishings. "I love my home, Andrew."

"I'm sure you do, Lillie. You've turned it into a showplace," Andrew replied impatiently.

"Please don't bother, young lady," Norton said as he pulled the blankets up over the soiled sheets. "I have no intention of utilizing your services."

Her face burned with humiliation. "Don't you think I'm pretty?" she asked.

"Oh, I imagine you'd be very pretty if you had a bath," he replied haughtily. "As a matter of fact I can't imagine for the life of me why a young girl as pretty as you would consider selling herself to any man who came along!"

Felicia leaned against the dresser and stared at the stranger. "Well, can you imagine being hungry?"

"I don't think that's much of an excuse. You could wash clothes or become a seamstress. There are any number of things you could do to earn money for food."

"Ah, yes! But I wouldn't earn enough to buy these pretty clothes." She rushed to her wardrobe and proudly opened the door.

Norton examined the gaudy finery. Most of the dresses were red-and-black silk brightly embroidered with sequined beads. He shook his head in disgust. "Your taste in clothes is no better than your taste in professions."

Felicia was dumbstruck. No one had ever talked to her the way this gringo had. She didn't know what to say.

He continued, "And what about the money you make? Have you saved any of it?"

"What for?"

Norton summoned the courage to sit down on the filthy bed. "Well, unless you want to look forward to a very sad old age, you'd better save your money." Nor-

The woman leaned forward in the chair and stared intently at the Scotsman. "Andrew—you, my husband, and a few dear and trusted friends are the only people in the Territory who know about my past."

Andrew was shocked at Lillie's statement. "That was long ago, and I thought we'd all agreed it was never to be mentioned."

"We have no other choice—now!"

Andrew recognized the agony in her voice. He waited for her to continue.

"You know, when I was living my 'other' life, I moved around quite a bit."

"Lillie, we don't have to go on with this conversation. You've proven yourself to be a reformed woman, and you've been a splendid wife to George. Why do you make yourself suffer so?"

"Because I must! Because now there's a possibility that everyone will know that I once was a prostitute." Lillie disolved into tears, sobbing as if her heart would break.

Andrew sat in shocked silence until the pathetic woman recovered sufficiently to go on with her story.

"The woman your wife is entertaining at your hacienda, the one who calls herself Senora Chata San Vincente is really Felicia Montez, the madam from La Paloma Caida in Santa Barbara."

"Impossible!" Andrew thundered. "How can you be sure?"

"Before I went to Montana—before I met George—I worked for her for almost two weeks. She didn't recognize me, it was years ago, but I recognized her." Lillie rose from her chair and began pacing the floor.

"You must force her to leave Santa Fe before she ruins my life and everyone else's!"

Andrew's first reaction was one of outrage, then disbelief. He had heard of the notorious Felicia Montez for years, and yet the woman his wife had introduced him to was so young and so refined. It seemed impossible that they were the same woman. "First I must be sure. If what you say is true, Lillie, you can rest assured that I will deal with the situation."

For the most part Andrew remained silent at the dinner table, listening as the women formulated their plans for the festive party. He spoke only when a question was directed to him personally. When they retired to the living room to finish their coffee, he focused his attention on Felicia. "I used to dine at a very elegant restaurant in San Diego. What was the name of that place? Ah . . . I remember! It was La Paloma. Do you know the place? Is it still in business?"

"Yes, I believe it is. I've never been there, of course, but I do remember my husband mentioning how extravagant it was." Felicia smiled, trying to control the knot in her stomach.

"Yes. It was indeed extravagant. And the Stockman's—did you ever dine there?"

"No. I don't recall ever dining at the Stockman's. After we married my husband preferred dining at home."

Andrew laughed. "He was probably very jealous! Didn't want anyone else enjoying his wife's beauty. I'm sure you know you're a very beautiful woman."

Isabella glanced sharply at her husband. His conversation was so unlike him, she could scarcely believe her ears. "Andrew, you'll embarrass our guest!"

"Nonsense! I'm just being honest. And speaking of honesty, I still can't imagine you being called Chata. If you had been my daughter, I would have found you a far more befitting name. Angelica—Eugenia—Felicia!"

Felicia felt the blood rush from her head. She gripped the arms of her chair in order to steady herself. She was trembling so violently she could hardly rise to her feet. "Excuse me, please," she gasped, "I'm not feeling well. I think I'll retire."

Andrew watched as Isabella and Dolores helped the fragile woman from the room. There was no longer any doubt in his mind that Lillie was correct. The woman was the notorious madam. But she certainly had charm!

Felicia insisted she was too ill to remain for breakfast and pleaded with Isabella to allow her to return to her lodgings in Santa Fe. Andrew agreed that the young woman was exceedingly pale. "I think it might be wise if I accompanied her and had Dr. Vargas examine her. I doubt that it's anything serious, but since she's alone in the world, I think we should make sure there's nothing wrong."

"You're entirely right, Andrew, but do you feel up to the trip? I could go with her," Isabella insisted.

"You have your day planned. I want to drop in at the warehouse anyway. I've been on vacation long enough. Time to get back to work."

Felicia moaned in agony. There was no doubt in her mind that somehow Andrew had discovered her identity. How could he be so cruel? Why couldn't he just let her be on her way? The elder Dundee helped her into the carriage, then sat up in front with Carlos.

When they arrived at the inn, he helped her down and had Carlos follow them to her room with her bag. He had a firm grip on her arm, but said nothing until they reached her door. "I'll see you inside."

"That really won't be necessary. I feel much better now."

"I insist. Do you have your key?"

It took her a moment to find the large wooden ring to which the room key was attached. She looked away as he unlocked the door and dismissed his servant. Andrew closed the door and marched her to the bed, then he seated himself across the room from her in a large overstuffed chair. She stared down at the floor, looking more like a frightened child than a soiled woman. She wore no make-up and her hair hung loosely around her shoulders.

"Don't be frightened, Felicia. I mean you no harm. I just want to know what you're doing here."

"It isn't important. I can assure you I'll be leaving for Santa Barbara as soon as I can make the arrangements."

She looked so fragile, so desolate, that Andrew's manner softened. "If you're short of funds, I could let you have some cash."

"That won't be necessary, Senor Dundee, I have sufficient money of my own. I'd appreciate it if you'd just leave me alone so that I can pack."

Andrew was about to leave the room when he noticed the silver-framed picture on the vanity. He frowned as he studied the faded tintype. "This is a picture of my son, Hernando! Where did you get it?" he demanded.

"He gave it to me," Felicia replied.

"You mean he was a customer of yours?"

His insinuation angered her. "He was never a customer! I love Hernando. Now please go!"

Andrew, still holding the picture, sat back down in his chair. "I don't intend to move from this room until we've talked a bit more. As Hernando's father, I think I'm entitled to know exactly what you're talking about."

Felicia turned her head away in order to hide her tears. She didn't care anymore that she had been found out—her only concern was not to embarrass these fine people any more than she had. It seemed of great importance to her to assure Andrew that she meant them no harm. The fact that there was no hope of ever becoming a part of Hernando's life was secondary. Summoning all of her remaining strength, she admitted to Andrew that she had ventured into his domain to try to prevent Hernando's marriage to Dolores Castiaga. "She is a selfish and spoiled child—and Hernando deserves more!"

"And you feel a prostitute could give him more?"

"I chose my way of life, and I'll make no excuses for it. However, I do sincerely believe that given the opportunity I would have made your son a wonderful wife. I love him." She lowered her eyes and sighed. "That is a very presumptuous statement, but it is true."

Andrew folded his hands on his lap and stared at the floor. Loving someone was never presumptuous.

Painful, perhaps, but very difficult to control. He remembered how, when he first saw Isabella, so fine, so regal; he had felt rather presumptuous, too. But his love had been sincere, and their marriage had been ideal. This woman, regardless of her past, had quality, and he determined to know more about her.

Andrew questioned her at great length about her past life and her future ambitions. For some reason he knew she was telling him the truth and was particularly impressed by her admission that she had not allowed another man in her bed since she had fallen in love with his son—but he wanted to know more.

If he had been her priest, Felicia could not have confessed her sins more fully than she did to Andrew Dundee. She omitted nothing. They had been together for several hours before she finished her story.

Andrew was thoughtful for a time. "I understand you had lunch with some of the leading women in Santa Fe yesterday. Let's see, Isabella mentioned that she had introduced you to Esther Mendoza and Sarah Spiegelberg and Lillie Taylor. Is that right?"

Felicia was sobbing quietly and could not answer. She nodded her head.

"I'm going to tell you something, in confidence of course, about those wonderful ladies." He hesitated for a moment, then, sure his judgment of Felicia was correct, he continued. "Esther Mendoza has a face like a horse—and a heart as big as all get out! She was a thirty-two-year-old school teacher. An ugly spinster. Then she answered an ad in the St. Louis newspaper for a mail-order bride. She didn't lie to Ernie—when she wrote back she told him how old she was and that she was ugly as sin. But she promised in that letter that if he married her, she would make him the best wife in the Territory!"

Andrew stopped to make sure that Felicia had heard every word of his story. "Ernie was no Beau Brummel himself. He wanted a woman who was strong, honest, 'n who'd take care of him. He sent for Esther. And he never regretted it for an instant! When he died, after fifteen years of marriage, he left her one of the wealthiest women in the Territory. I was there with them at the end. His last words were that he'd be waitin' for her in heaven—but she didn't have to hurry up there to meet him.

" 'N then there's Sarah. Sarah's parents were Spanish Jews. They wandered all over Europe 'n nobody wanted them. Sarah was only thirteen when they died, and a cousin shipped her sight unseen to America to marry Aaron Spiegelberg's brother Ben. Ben told his friends in Europe that he'd be willing to pay $5,000 for an Orthodox Jewish girl—there weren't none around here in the West. But when he saw Sarah he didn't want her. Said she was too scrawny. Aaron was older than Ben, 'n he fell in love with the little waif the first time he saw her. They've been married more than twenty years 'n I've never seen a happier couple—lest it be Isabella 'n me!"

Andrew had Felicia's full attention. Her eyes were as big as saucers.

"Know how I ended up with Isabella? A beauty who could have married anyone in the Territory?" Andrew didn't wait for Felicia to guess. "I won her in a poker game. That's right! She was the stakes I won from her father. 'Course I courted her for a year before I married her."

Felicia shook her head in amazement. It had never occurred to her that women other than herself had once been considered unmarriageable material.

"Now let's get to Lillie Taylor. How did she act when you met her?"

Felicia tried to remember how the woman had behaved. It had been less than twenty-four hours earlier, but it seemed like years. "I think she was rather distant. I know she left the luncheon early."

"Lillie's the one who told me who you were," Andrew stated simply.

Felicia gasped. "But how could she know?"

Andrew laughed and said, "Lillie used to work for you over in Santa Barbara. That was before she worked for Chicago Joe up in Montana. George Taylor made a big loan to a cattleman and had to go up there to collect the money. While he was there he met Lillie. Came back and couldn't get her off his mind. Finally, we talked about it—'n he went back up there after her. Married her 'bout a week after he got back. It would be hard for me to judge which one o' those women is the best wife—outside of Isabella."

"I don't understand why you've told me all this." Felicia dried her eyes and looked questioningly at Andrew.

"I'm not sure myself. I only know that although I don't go to church much—I do read the good Book. 'N I don't have no right to judge no one but myself. If you want to start out in a new life, who am I to tell you you're wrong? I don't have any right to tell you whether or not you should stay here in Santa Fe or move on to another spot, either. That's a decision you're goin' to have to make on your own. I've known a lot o' women who were called 'good women,' and I wouldn't give you a plug-nickel for the lot o' 'em! They weren't good for *nothin' else*. For a man to love a woman just because she's a good woman is the same to me as marryin' a woman for her money. It's worth of character 'n how you get along together that's important. There's nothing in this world that can make one person love another—it just happens—'n if you're lucky enough to marry that person, you'll have a good marriage."

"But I've been a prostitute. Are you telling me that I could still have a good marriage? That you would allow me to stay in Santa Fe and see Hernando?"

"I wouldn't think too much about Hernando if I were you. And I wouldn't worry too much about him marrying Dolores. Thing is, I really doubt that he'll marry anybody. For the time bein' anyhow. I don't try to outguess him—but he's wild and unruly. Probably time he settled down, and he could probably do worse for a wife than you."

Felicia stared at Andrew, not believing what she had heard him say.

"He's going to need a special kind o' woman. Someone who can stand up to him and tame the land." Andrew stood up and walked to the door. "You'd better get some rest. Isabella has her heart set on givin' you that party—'n I'd hate to see her disappointed!"

* * *

On the way home to his hacienda, Andrew wondered what in the world had ever caused him to say the things he had said. Lillie was going to be mad as a hornet. And, of course—and this was the most difficult thing for him to face—he would have to tell Isabella.

He felt tired and decided to take a short nap. His only comfort came in the realization that he had always been an exceptionally good judge of character. He prayed that his assessment of Felicia wouldn't prove an exception.

CHAPTER SEVENTEEN

Felicia's first instinct, when she was finally alone, was to pack and run. However, something Andrew said, or perhaps it was the way he had said it, made her reconsider. Hernando, if he did marry, would need a *special kind of woman*. A woman who would stand up to him and tame the land. Felicia knew, with the greatest certainty, that she was that special woman. Andrew had given her a real second chance in life—and she intended to grasp it with every ounce of strength she possessed.

She sat down at the small maple desk in the corner of her room next to the window and wrote a detailed letter of everything that had happened to Hedrick Norton. When she had sealed the note and posted it in the lobby, she returned to her room to rest. She laid down on the bed and closed her eyes. Although she had never attended services at the cathedral in Santa Barbara, inwardly she considered herself quite religious. Now in the solitude of her room at La Fonda, she thanked God that Hedrick Norton had come into her life. Then she gave thanks for being allowed to love Hernando—and then for Andrew's generous understanding. She determined that the following Sunday she would attend her first mass.

Of all the women she had ever met, Felicia soon realized that the horse-faced Esther Mendoza and the birdlike Sarah Spiegelberg were truly unique. Everything Andrew had told her about their kindness, warmth, generosity, and loyalty was true. And, in spite of their physical appearances, it was obvious that they were strong women!

They called on Felicia almost daily—each vying for her attention—each anxious for her well-being. Lillie Taylor, for obvious reasons, remained aloof. One day, Felicia vowed, regardless of what happened, she would be able to assure the woman that she had nothing to fear. Perhaps, Felicia hoped, they would have a chance to talk before the party.

As fate or circumstance would have it, the party had to be postponed. Just a few days before the scheduled gala, Phoebe was awakened from a sound sleep, shortly before dawn, by an unearthly scream! She sat bolt upright, wide awake, trying to determine whether or not she had experienced a nightmare. She strained to hear any sound, but there was nothing to interrupt the stillness of the night. Sleep would not return so she lighted her candle and turned on her side to stare at the statue of the Virgin. In the flickering light of the flame she thought, for a moment, she saw tears rolling down the cheeks of the alabaster figure. Upon closer examination she assured herself it had been an illusion. Still she felt troubled and restless and decided to dress and begin the day early at the hacienda.

Under other circumstances she would have enjoyed

the quiet time just before dawn, when she was alone in the kitchen with the smell of fresh coffee and sweet biscuits filling the room. This morning seemed different from other mornings. The coffee tasted bitter, the biscuits didn't rise properly, and the room seemed to stay cold in spite of the fire.

The first delicate fingers of color began to light up the eastern horizon when she heard the hoof beats of horses. She moved silently to the front of the house and watched as Andrew, who had been awakened by the commotion, tightened his robe around him and stomped down the stairs, pistol in hand, to confront the intruders. She waited as her master unbolted the door, then breathed a sigh of relief when he recognized the riders.

"Jee-ru-su-lem, Ben! What the hell are you doin' here so early in the mornin'?" she heard him ask.

"Just ridin' through, Andrew 'n decided to drop in fer breakfast!" the leader of the group replied. Phoebe recognized the voice of Ben Bush, sheriff of Santa Fe. "Got a friend with me," he continued. "Rode all the way in from Oklahoma. Jest wanted to say 'howdy!'"

Andrew stepped outside to get a better look at the men. "My Gawd! Marshal Thompson! If you ain't a sight for sore eyes! Take the horses over to the stables, 'n then get yer asses in here for some grub!" When Andrew reentered the house, he noticed Phoebe standing in the shadows. "Glad you're up, girl. Looks like we got a parcel o' company for breakfast. Better get Rosa to help you. I'm goin' up to get dressed."

By the time Andrew reappeared, Phoebe had already served the men coffee and was busy in the kitchen preparing their food. He surveyed the room.

Some of the men he recognized, others were strangers. Some of the twenty or more men wore silver stars indicating they were official lawmen.

"Pretty fair-sized posse, I'd say," Andrew observed as he shook hands with his old friend from Oklahoma. "Haven't seen you in quite a spell, Marshal. What brings you down to this territory?"

"Mornin', Andrew," Thompson's cool, low-pitched voice suited his steel-blue eyes and square jaw. "We're after a band of Comancheros. Killed seven of 'em already. Still got three or four to go."

Andrew raised his bushy eyebrows. The word *Comanchero* sent chills down his spine. The men who called themselves Comancheros were the scum of the earth. They weren't Indians, although their name had been bastardized from the Comanche Indians because of their vicious cruelty. Even rustlers and outlaws stayed clear of the Comancheros. These degenerates were composed of half-breeds and outcasts who delighted in torture, rape, murder, and slave-running. Wherever they banded together they spread a reign of terror—and when they were captured, they never lived to make it to court. It was an accepted practice to shoot or hang a Comanchero on the spot.

"Pretty far west for those varmits, ain't it?" Andrew asked.

"Yeah. We tracked 'em into the canyons just back o' your spread, Andrew. Sorry to say we lost 'em."

Phoebe began serving the breakfast and Andrew motioned the men to be seated. "Well, ain't that just dandy! I'll give you some of my men to ride with you. They know the area like the back o' their hands."

One of the strangers nodded his head toward Phoebe. "Is she Comanch' or Apach'?"

"She's Apache, 'n she's been with our family for quite a spell!"

"No offense meant," he apologized, hastily, "but I couldn't help thinkin' that if she was Comanch' she might jest be willin' to help the damned Camancheros!"

At the mention of the word Comanchero, Phoebe almost dropped her tray. She finished serving, then whispered to Andrew to join her in the kitchen. "Why are those men here?" she asked. "And what do they mean when they talk of the Comancheros?"

Andrew knew she was frightened and tried to reassure her. "They're trackin' three of 'em. Lost 'em last night in the canyons. Don't worry about it. I'm goin' to send Carlos and some of the other men with them. The Comancheros will be dead before sundown."

Phoebe was a woman who had learned to control her emotions since birth, and it surprised Andrew when he noticed she was trembling. "What is it, child? What's the matter?"

"I had a dream last night. An omen. The Virgin Mother cried, and deep in my heart I knew that my mother's spirit had traveled to the other side."

The picture became quite clear to Andrew at once. The renegades were trapped in the canyons to the rear of the hacienda, the same canyons in which Shell Woman's "secret place" was located. He took Phoebe gently in his arms. "I'll ride with the men. Chances are they would never find your mother's cave. And remember, Shell Woman has great power—the Gahns will protect her!"

* * *

The Comancheros were tired, hungry, and thirsty. They hadn't seen the entrance to the cave right away, but rather had stumbled upon it by accident when one of the band smelled smoke. Silent as cats, guns and knives drawn, they slipped inside prepared to dispatch the occupant quickly and skillfully. Shell Woman slept peacefully beneath her rabbit skin robe next to the fire pit with Andrew's bright red plaid scarf tied around her head for extra warmth.

The three desperados stared down at the sleeping figure, no larger than a child, and without a second thought slit her throat. They dragged the crippled, mutilated body to the rear of the cave, then sat down to gorge themselves on what food they could find, and threw more wood on the smoking embers. The cave filled with light from the flames, and for the first time they were able to get a good look at their surroundings. On one wall there were paintings of were-animals—a wolf, coyote, desert fox, and an owl. In front of the men, next to the fire pit, were a collection of clay pots, each containing various shades of ash, pollen, and dust. In another section of the cave they became aware of animal skins, bones, and feathers.

The oldest of the three men recoiled in horror. "We are in the cave of a witch!" he shrieked, making the sign of the cross. "We've killed a witch and we're cursed! We will never escape!"

The tallest man in the group stood up and laughed. "You stupid son-of-a-bitch! You stinking half-breed! You think one more killin' is goin' to make things worse fer us? It's jest as bad as it kin git right now.

None of us is goin' to make it, do you understand? We're all goin' to end up in hell 'n killin' a witch ain't goin' to make the fire any hotter. You jest make sure we take as many lawmen with us when we go as we can. Understand?"

"Shut up 'n kill that fire. If it led us here it kin lead the posse here, too. I want to git a little shut-eye 'fore the shootin' starts."

"We will die slowly," the older man moaned, holding his head and rocking back and forth, "and the flesh will rot from our bones."

"Everybody's got to go sometime! Now shut that yowlin' so's I kin git some rest, er I'll speed yer passin' right now!"

Andrew made sure the men had fresh mounts, then led the way as the posse zigzagged across the rugged terrain of the Sangre de Cristo foothills. The sun had broken free of the high, jagged east rim, bathing the area in white sunlight and revealing clearly the tracks of the outlaws. Carlos found the first horse, dead of exhaustion, just a few miles up the canyon.

"Won't be long now," one of the cowboys commented. "That horse ain't been dead more than a few hours, 'n they cain't get far ridin' double in this country."

Andrew agreed, but he scowled because the tracks led in the direction of Shell Woman's cave, and he feared that Phoebe's dream might prove valid. He nudged his horse on. They found the second and third horses a short time later. Carlos examined the area, then spoke quietly to his master. "Looks as if the horse that was carryin' the two men stumbled 'n broke his leg. The Comancheros who fell killed their horse, then shot the third horse out of spite."

Andrew spit on the ground. "Yep. Looks that way," he replied without emotion.

They lost the tracks for a short while in the rocks of the high country and fanned out in order to pick them up again. It wasn't difficult. The renegades had been too tired to try to cover the deep impressions their high-heeled boots left in the soft earth that had been moistened by the melting snow. Andrew directed Carlos to run ahead on foot, leaving signs along the way where he felt the posse should dismount. "They'll be waiting for us, wherever they are—so be careful," he instructed the Indian. "I've got a gut feeling that we'll find them in the Wind cave."

"The cave of the witch?" Carlos asked.

"Yes. The cave of the witch," Andrew answered sadly.

Carlos nodded that he understood and sped out of sight.

Within an hour Carlos rejoined the posse. "You were right, Don Andrew, their tracks lead right into the cave, and there is no sign that they came out again. It would be wise to tether the horses here and go in silently. They will not hear us approach."

Andrew informed Marshal Thompson of Carlos's discovery, and the iron-jawed lawman from Oklahoma ordered his men to dismount and spread out, in order to allow Carlos to lead them to their destination. When they were in sight of the entrance to the cave, Thompson positioned his men in a half-circle—an arm's reach from one another—and with guns drawn called for the Comancheros to come out.

Inside the cave the desperados checked their pistols to make sure they were fully loaded, then crawling on their bellies Indian-style made their way to the entrance to confront their attackers.

The Comancheros fired the first shots, and on Thompson's command the posse returned fire. More than twenty men fired round after round of ammunition into the mouth of the cave. Rifle reports, combined with the high-pitched zinging of ricocheting bullets, were deafening. The gunfire lasted for several moments, and then the air was still. Thompson signaled for several of the men to check the cave while he and the rest of the men covered them. "I'm pretty sure they're dead—but let's make sure."

Carlos was the first on the scene. Each of the Comancheros had been hit a dozen or more times. The cave stank with the smell of their blood. The men let up a lusty cheer! Not one of the posse had sustained the slightest wound. It was a job well done.

"Should we bury 'em?" one of the men asked the marshal.

"Hell, no. Let the buzzards eat 'em," Thompson replied as he holstered his gun. "Nice job, Andrew, I thank you. Guess we kin git on back down to the ranch now."

"I need a few minutes, Marshal. I have to look for someone who lived in this cave."

Marshal Thompson gave his friend a questioning look.

"An old Indian woman," Andrew explained.

"From the look on yer face, I'd say she was someone special."

"Yes, she was."

"I'll go with you—give you a hand."

"I'd appreciate that, Marshal."

It only took a few moments to find Shell Woman's frail body. Andrew and Thompson wrapped her gently in the rabbit skin robe and carried her down the hill to where the horses were waiting. A few of the strangers from Oklahoma couldn't understand why there was such concern over an "ole In'jun squaw," but the attitude of Andrew's cowboys silenced their comments.

They buried the Apache witch Indian style in the forest. Andrew and Carlos lingered for a while after the others had left in order to say their private farewell. Then they mounted up and returned to the hacienda to break the news to Phoebe and Isabella.

Phoebe's face remained expressionless as Andrew explained what had happened. Then she quietly wrapped her shawl around her and retired to her *casita*. She did not feel it proper to inflict her sorrow on the living.

Isabella was less contained. In addition to being upset over Shell Woman's senseless murder, she was concerned for Phoebe. "I think we should get word to Dr. Vargas to come look in on her!" she instructed Andrew, as he helped her to her room. "And perhaps you could ask Dolores if she'd mind terribly if we postponed the party for a few weeks. I'm just not feeling up to it."

Andrew agreed that the party should be postponed. He, too, had been more affected by the tragedy than he cared to admit. "I'll send Rosa up to look in on you, then I'll send Carlos to fetch Vargas."

The last of the posse disappeared after lunch and Andrew retired to the library to be alone. He knew how deeply Phoebe loved her mother and was concerned for the young woman's health. After all their years together Andrew realized that he had come to look upon Phoebe as a daughter rather than a servant. And now he felt her pain.

Dolores entered his sanctuary without knocking. "I'd really like to talk with you, Don Andrew!"

He could see that the young woman was upset, but it annoyed him to be disturbed. "What is it, Dolores?" he asked gruffly.

"I'd like to know why the death of some old Indian woman is so important that we have to postpone our party. I don't think it's fair to me or to Chata!"

"Oh, really?"

"Yes! And another thing—I want to know when Hernando is coming home. I think it's very unkind of you to keep us apart. He must be miserable up on that reservation."

Andrew contained his anger. "I don't feel like discussing it with you now. However, I have been thinking of riding up to Po'Se'Da' and visiting with Hernando. If he decides he wishes to return with me, I will allow him to do that. The decision will be his." He escorted Dolores to the door. "Now if you don't mind, I'd like to be alone."

Actually, before Dolores's intrusion, Andrew had never considered visiting the post. But now that the idea had been voiced, it seemed like a good one. It might restore his outlook if he got away from the hacienda for a few weeks. After a time he went upstairs to inform Isabella of his plans. "I think Hernando should know what's happened. And I really feel the need to get away for a while."

Isabella said nothing to dissuade him. She recognized his restlessness from the tone of his voice. It had been quite a while since Andrew had felt the need to move on, and while she was loathe to see him leave, she also realized it was a sign that he was probably completely recovered. She pulled him down on the bed next to her and kissed him. "I understand. But be careful, Andrew, and come back to me as soon as you can."

Andrew rode in the carriage with Dolores, his horse tied to the back until they reached Santa Fe. He could see that she was as restless as he was and wondered if she would still be at the hacienda when he and Hernando returned. Then he thought of Felicia. He wouldn't mention her to his son, but he was curious to know whether or not the prostitute's love was shared by Hernando. Time would tell.

Andrew found Jake at the office and instructed him to stay at the hacienda until his return. "I might be gone for a while. If I feel up to it I'll make the lamb drive with the boys. I've been cooped up in that house for so long I'm beginning to feel like an old man. Take good care of Isabella—'n make sure that Vargas does everything he can for Phoebe."

"I'll do my best," Jake assured his friend. "Jest one more thing, Andrew . . ."

"What's that?"

"We're both gettin' old. So take care!"

* * *

Felicia cared nothing about the party being canceled but was prepared to accompany Dolores back to the hacienda immediately if she could be of any assistance to Isabella or Phoebe. She was also curious about Andrew's decision to join his son at the trading post. "Will he be away long?" she asked.

"From what he said on the way into town, I imagine he'll be gone for at least a few weeks. Hernando will probably come home with him."

Felicia forced herself to smile and said, "That will be very nice for you."

"Awhile back I would have been excited about seeing him. Now I'm not so sure."

"I don't believe I understand," Felicia replied soberly.

Dolores fell down on Felicia's bed and pulled off her gloves. "I'm so bored! This town—even the hacienda—is so dreary!" She sat up and cupped her head in her hands. "Chata, you're the only friend I have, the only person in the world that I can confide in— and I must tell someone or I will die!"

"What are you talking about?"

"I have a secret suitor. He lives in Santa Barbara and is very wealthy. He's written me almost every day since I arrived—and he's positively mad about me. I've been telling Isabella that he was a very dear friend of my mother's and writes only to keep me informed on what is happening to my home, which in a way is true!"

"But don't you love Hernando?" Felicia asked, scarcely able to believe her ears.

"Oh, he's good-looking enough—much better-looking than Hedrick—but could you imagine spending the rest of your life in Santa Fe?" Dolores seemed as excited as a schoolgirl. "I want to travel. To see Paris and Rome. And give elegant parties. From what I've seen of life with the Dundees, although I do adore them, I would be bored to death."

Felicia sank back in her chair and stared at the beautiful Spanish noblewoman. Talking about Hedrick Norton, Dolores was as warm and animated as Felicia had ever seen her. That sly fox of a banker, she thought, was due more credit than she would ever have believed. Would she do as well at winning Hernando?

"Come, Dolores, we must tell Esther and Sarah that the party has been canceled. They can help us notify everyone else."

"Why don't you come back to the hacienda with me tonight? I know Isabella would be delighted with your company."

Felicia stood by the window and stared out at the imposing tower of the Cathedral of St. Francis. "Yes, I'd love to—but first I'd like to visit with Father Vieja for a short time!"

She had Hedrick's encouragement to find her new life; and she had Andrew Dundee's blessings. Would God somehow forgive her for her past and allow her to pursue her dream? Perhaps Father Vieja could set her on the proper path to find out.

CHAPTER EIGHTEEN

After five days in the saddle, sleeping out under the stars, Andrew knew he made the right decision to journey to the post. He felt stronger than he had before the attack, and the tragic memories of the past week seemed to fade from his mind. He felt young and vigorous! When he saw the new additions to Po'Se'Da' sprawling across the clearing, and the daisies and geraniums planted in front of the main building, he wondered if he were at the right trading post.

Carlin, who'd been working with Hosteen Begay in the orchard, recognized the towering figure on horseback and ran to greet him. "Mr. Dundee," he exclaimed with pleasure, "you're the last person in the world I expected to see!"

"Carlin?" Andrew asked, staring at the tanned, healthy-looking young man he'd seen just a few weeks before. "You've filled out considerably since we last met. Looks like this life agrees with you. Where's Hernando?"

"He's somewhere out on the reservation, spreading goodwill and promoting trade. Should be in tomorrow sometime," Carlin replied. "Let me take your horse and we'll get you some food."

Andrew dismounted and nodded at Hosteen Begay. The Indian extended his hand, white-man style, and spoke in perfect English. "I am Hosteen Begay, Chee Dundee, and am proud to know you."

Andrew raised his eyebrows. In Navajo Andrew replied, "It pleases me to know Hosteen Begay. Join me for some tobacco." He shook the dust from his hat and followed Carlin and the brave into the bull pen. He wondered what other surprises were in store for him. He wasn't disappointed. "I wouldn't have believed it if I hadn't seen it with my own eyes," Andrew announced as he examined the two new rooms and a counter. He fingered the shelves, surprised at the lack of dust, then ogled the pawn room and wooden floors. "You've turned Po'Se'Da' into the best-looking trading post in the territory. How's business?" Andrew couldn't hide his amazement at the transformation he saw all around him.

"Couldn't be better!" Carlin said, with a proud grin.

After Carlin introduced him to Bah Tsosie and Atwa Kee, and allowed him to enjoy a supper of corn-bread and mutton stew, they spent more than an hour going over the books. Andrew beamed with pleasure over how meticulously they had been kept. "We're due to make a hell of a profit," he admitted. "And you'll get your fair share!"

When they finished, Carlin escorted Andrew outside to show him the small schoolhouse he and Hosteen Begay had built. This, too, pleased Andrew; he had wanted to start some sort of school for the Navajos years before but had never found anyone who could put the plan into practice. "Seems to me you've been able to work some kind of miracle out here."

"Speaking of miracles, you don't look much like a man who's had a heart attack. You look wonderfully fit."

They returned to the kitchen and Bah Tsosie poured them some fresh coffee and joined them at the table.

The memory of his illness reminded Andrew of how Shell Woman had cured him, and he had no doubt that it was her magic that had done the job. The thoughts made him bitter as he recalled her brutal murder. Damned Comancheros! If it had been up to him, he would have let them die an agonizing death. The bullets were too swift.

Carlin noticed the old man's mood change. "Is everything all right at the hacienda? How is Mrs. Dundee?"

"Fine. Just fine." Andrew didn't sound sure.

"And Phoebe?"

Andrew turned his head away from his young friend. He considered it a sign of weakness when he felt his eyes cloud over with tears. His throat tightened. "She's not well."

Carlin felt as if his heart had stopped beating. "What happened?"

In a husky voice Andrew told Carlin the details of the Comancheros' attack on the old Apache woman and how Phoebe was grieving. He was too absorbed in his own sadness to notice how the trader paled.

Bah Tsosie noticed. Carlin excused himself from the table and went slowly out of the room, and after a few minutes Bah Tsosie followed him. He made his way over to the corral and leaned heavily against the railing. He felt as if he were suffocating. There had not been a day, nor hardly an hour, since he had been rejected by Phoebe that he had not thought about her. He regretted his experience with the prostitute, Lydia, for although he had been satisfied physically, emotionally he had felt empty. Everything had been so cut and dried! There had been no tenderness, no love in her caress. He had returned to the post determined never again to visit a whore. He would wait until Phoebe changed her mind, or he would remain celibate.

He envisioned the torture and agony Phoebe must have experienced over the loss of her mother—then he broke down completely and began to sob.

Bah Tsosie stood silently next to him, unable to speak out or comfort him. She had heard the traders speak of this woman, Phoebe, on more than one occasion. Now she understood why Carlin treated her like a sister rather than a woman. His heart belonged to this bereaved Apache. She understood his grief; her own grief over the loss of her husband was still inside of her. She hoped that time would heal the wounds for both of them. And it saddened her that Carlin wasn't even aware of her presence. She turned and walked quickly back to the post in order to prepare the evening meal.

After Hernando returned and had recovered from the shock of the news, he found a compatibility with his father that he had never thought was possible. The old man listened to his son for hours, never tiring of Hernando's suggestions for improving the life of the Navajo. For the first time since he could remember,

Hernando's father praised his attitude and offered sage advice rather than making demands.

"What's brought about this change in your attitude toward the Navajo?" Andrew asked.

Hernando needed time to think. He wasn't sure himself. He pulled his bag of tobacco from his pocket and rolled a smoke. "Perhaps it happened when I was in the north country, the first time I explored the area. I was so damned sure I had all the answers." He inhaled on the tapered cigarette. "You know, you've always given me everything I wanted. I never had to do without anything. Never was hungry—always had plenty to eat and drink. Then the damned mule smashed the water barrel, 'n there were more snakes crawlin' over them supplies than flies in a honey comb." He hesitated then looked directly at his father. "I was scared half to death. First time in my life I really knew what it meant to be afraid. After about three days with no food, the water in my canteen ran out, too. I knew I was a goner, 'n I remembered what you'd told me about how many Indians die of starvation now that we got 'em civilized. Guess that old saying, 'you can't judge another man 'til you've walked in his moccasins for thirty days,' is true."

Recalling his own youth as a mountain man in the Rockies, Andrew remained silent. He had known the great equalizers—hunger and thirst—many times. Perhaps that was why he had spoiled Hernando so and that had been his mistake all along.

"The first person I saw when I got my sight back was Hoskinini. He was sitting next to me in his hogan when his number-two wife removed the bandages.

God, what a fine-looking man"—Hernando's eyes sparkled with enthusiasm—"and smart as hell!"

Andrew laughed. "And do you still miss the women and whiskey?"

"I'll admit I've changed. But I didn't say I'd become a saint! Right now, if I could, I'd go on a five-day drunk and sleep with a different woman each night."

Andrew shook his head and patted Hernando on the shoulder. He couldn't help thinking of Felicia. Too bad, he thought, then his humor returned. "Plenty of time to think of settling down after you're married."

"That'll be a cold day in hell. I don't think there's a woman alive who could put up with me."

"Then you don't think you're a suitable husband for Senorita Castiaga?"

Hernando howled at the prospect. "I'd rather spend the rest of my life with a whore!"

The old man glanced sharply at his son. Without thinking, he snapped, "There could be worse things, you know." Then he caught himself and smiled. "I mean, Lillie's made old George a pretty fair wife—not important—forget it. We'd better turn in. Still work to do. We'll be able to start the drive in another month or so. The nights are gettin' cold already."

CHAPTER NINETEEN

Near the end of September, when the leaves of the cottonwood trees had begun to turn gold, Mulie Turner reappeared. Leading his pack train with their silver bells jingling merrily, he rode into the post on his mule and greeted the traders as if they had been his long lost sons. He embraced Andrew and danced a jig to celebrate their reunion after so many years and handed out gifts for everyone. He even had a special gift for Hernando.

"Traded for it with an In'jun who came all the way down from Montanee." the pixielike little man boasted. "It's a gen-u-ine Sioux concha belt. Belonged to a very rich chief. Had to do a damned sight of good tradin' to get it."

Hernando examined the heavy leather girdle. It was six feet long and adorned with twenty-two hand-fashioned brass conchas. Each concha was four inches wide, highly polished, and the entire belt weighed more than twenty pounds.

"Takes a pretty big man to wear this," Hernando exclaimed, obviously very impressed.

Hosteen Begay fingered the conchas and felt the

heft of the ornate article. "A man would be very proud to wear a belt like this!"

The traders agreed, and then Mulie continued, "Rumor has it that yer gettin' along mighty fine with my people. I'm mighty proud o' you both. Guess by now you know the Navees has changed yer names agin?"

Without waiting for an answer, he continued. "Naveehos has a smart way o' namin' folks. They names 'em according to what they look like or how they act or how they think about 'em. All they thought 'bout Hernando when he first come was thet he was the son o' old Andy." Then he turned to Carlin. "'N you was jest some kin' a furriner who liked some kin' a folk with yeller faces. But yah both got new names now." Mulie puffed up with pride. "Hernando is the Man Who Honors Justice 'n Carlin is Wise Teacher."

Hernando, hands on hips, flashed his friend a quick grin at the thought of becoming his own man rather than a shadow of his father. Carlin was more subdued. He was still concerned over Phoebe's health and was impatient to begin the lamb drive so that he could take some time off to visit her.

Mulie was wound up like a player piano. "You boys ever see a lamb drive?" he asked. Then once again not waiting for an answer, he went on. "It's a sight to behold! Thousands o' sheep at a time. The Navees bring 'em in from every part o' the reservation. They load up the whole fam'ly in wagons 'n bring 'em on in, too. Really a celebration! When they git paid 'n reclaim their pawn, they have dancin' 'n singin' 'n feastin' the likes o' which you'll never see agin anywhar." He paused for a moment to catch his breath. "Then they'll stock up on grub fer the winter months, 'n you won't see some o' 'em fer another six months." He danced over to where Hernando was standing. "By the by, yah got any idee who yer herdsmen are goin' to be?"

"I have a pretty fair idea—think ten men will be enough?"

Andrew interrupted. "Hell, I've seen ten good men herd more than two or three thousand animals. And all you got to travel is seventy miles. Me and a half dozen men should be plenty!"

"Father," Hernando said firmly, "Carlin and I are in charge of the drive. We'll decide who goes and who stays. Besides, don't you suppose you ought to think about getting back to Mother?"

Andrew began to bristle. It was the first time since he'd arrived that there had been a hint of an argument. The boy had proven himself a man, and Andrew regretted cutting into his thunder at this late date. He felt deflated. "You're right, son, it's time I was getting on home." He suddenly felt tired. "I think I'll rest awhile. I want to get an early start in the morning."

Hernando had not meant for his father's visit to end on a sour note, but there was nothing more to be said. He turned his attention back to Mulie. "We got the herders!"

Mulie had missed the tense interchange between the Dundees. "Got yer scales leaded?"

Hernando and Carlin looked at the gnomelike trader as if they had not heard him correctly.

"What do you mean 'leaded'?" they asked in unison.

Delighted that he knew something the young men didn't know, Mulie explained, "Wall, it's sorta like a game, yah see. When the Navees bring in them sheep, they'll keep 'em dry for a couple of days first. Then just before they bring 'em in to the post, they'll drive 'em to a waterhole and let 'em soak up an extra ten or twenty pounds of water. Then they'll want ya to weigh 'em right away, don't ya see? Then after they're weighed 'n in the holding pens, them sheep'll practically flood ya out." Mulie was doubled up with laughter. "They'll drop them ten or twenty pounds real fast. Ya got to lead the scales accordingly or it'll cost ya a ton o' money!"

"But why couldn't we weight them after they've been in the pens a few days?" Carlin protested. "The other way is dishonest."

"T'ain't dishonest at all! Like a said—it's a game. And the way I tol' ya is the way it has got to be played. Otherwise, yer sayin' that the Navees has set out to cheat ya. And that is not the case. They're jest bein' shrewd, and they expect you to be smart enough to protect yerselves." The conversation was over. "Ah'm goin' to bed," Muley yelled back at them as he stormed out of the room.

After a time Hosteen Begay and Bah Tsosie were able to explain the Navajo logic to the traders, and they decided to lead the scales in the morning.

Andrew packed his gear early the next day, and when they finished their breakfast, he prepared to be on his way. Hernando was right—the drive was a job for younger men. He was also beginning to feel guilty about being away from Isabella for so long. In the past it never would have bothered him. He was away from home months at a time in the early days of their marriage. Isabella had learned to expect him when she saw him. Bless her! She never complained. When he returned she always ran to greet him and chattered on as if he had just come in from town after running an errand. Perhaps that was why he loved her so; she was never quarrelsome or possessive. She knew when she married Andrew that he was a mountain man and used to his freedom. Isabella always waited until he volunteered to tell her about his adventures and never questioned him about whether or not he had been with another woman.

Andrew smiled thinking about the memories. He was sure that was one of the reasons he had never been unfaithful to her. It was time to go home.

He clasped his son to his breast, shook hands with Carlin, grasped Hosteen Begay's hands Indian style, gave Bah Tsosie and Atwa Kee a fatherly hug, and pounded Mulie Turner on the back. "Good-bye all," he said, with great emotion. "I'll see you in Santa Fe in a few weeks. Good luck with the drive." Then he threw his leg over the saddle and rode away.

Hernando watched the tall, shaggy old man sitting so straight and tall on his horse and uttered a silent prayer for his father's safe journey. He was suddenly proud to be the son of Red Dundee and hoped that one day he would be the same kind of man.

CHAPTER TWENTY

The Navajos began coming into the compound the second week of October. Both Carlin and Hernando were able to understand Mulie's enthusiastic description; he had been correct. It was a spectacular sight. Everyone was dressed in their best finery—the women and children in purples and reds and golds; the men, handsome and tall, with their traditional black felt hats set square upon their heads. Most everyone sported priceless silver-and-turquoise jewelry—necklaces, belts, bracelets, bowguards, and hatbands. Some rode majestically on horseback, others drove wagons, and a few walked barefoot, careful to save their moccasins from the mud of the recent rains.

Some of the older men wore their trousers with the seats cut out and deerskin flaps hung down to hide the opening. The women dressed in the white women's style of the 1870s—beautiful and feminine in their bright, flowing, multilayered velveteen skirts. Indian style, most of them wore colorful, intricately woven belts that encircled their tiny waists twice; and instead of using pockets or purses many of their prized possessions were tied to the fringes of their belts. Every family displayed colorful handwoven or Pendleton blankets draped gracefully over their shoulders to protect them from the autumn chill.

If they were accompanied by a drum and bugle corps, Carlin thought with delight, the steady procession would make a grand parade. He studied each face in wonderment. These Navajos were truly the most handsome race of people he had ever seen, and had they been dressed in brilliant blue cotton coolie pants and shirts, with wide reed hats perched on their heads, he doubted he could tell them apart from his Chinese friends.

Hernando was more interested in the animals. Most of the lambs and sheep were fine specimens, fat and healthy. He, Carlin, Hosteen Begay, and Mulie set to weighing the beasts immediately, then herding them into the holding pens. Hernando was amazed at the number of animals and knew it would be an exceptionally fine year financially for the family Dundee as well as for Carlin and the Navajos.

In the late afternoon of the third day, Hernando straightened up his tired body to find himself facing Hoskinini, the great war chief of the Navajo. They stared at one another, Hernando hardly able to believe his eyes. The stately warrior extended his hands to exchange greetings.

"I have journeyed far from the land of the Wonderful Valley in order to help my friend," he stated simply.

It was a splendid gesture of faith and friendship and Hernando was deeply moved. The war chief continued. "When you were in the north country, you spoke of two men—men who looked for the yellow rock. You wondered then if they were not the evil men who murdered our good friend Myers. You were correct—but concern yourself no more. The coyote and the bear feed upon their rotten flesh!"

Hernando was alarmed. "But if they're discovered, the Army will send troops in to find out what happened."

Hoskinini smiled and said, "I have brought their animals and belongings to you. You will take them to the fort and tell the soldiers that only 'good men' will be safe in my domain!"

Hernando knew that as soon as the drive was over, he would have to report the incident to the Indian agent, Galen Eastman, at Fort Defiance. Eastman didn't have a good reputation for dealing with the Indians and somehow Hernando would have to protect Hoskinini. It was his part of the sacred trust as an Indian trader.

Hoskinini helped the traders choose six of the best Navajo stockmen to assist as herdsmen on the drive to Holbrook. Some of the men had their own horses and others would walk the seventy miles. Hernando, Carlin, and Hosteen Begay would fill out the company.

Those who didn't have their own rifles were loaned guns from the post. It was not uncommon during the time of the drives to have to fight off marauding Apaches, renegades, or rustlers who began to appear in the region like locusts to prey on unprepared herdsmen. The weighing-in period was not a time to worry about the dangers of the trail—that would come later. Now was a time of celebration and feasting.

The women visited together during the day and played games. In the evenings they prepared fire pits for cooking. Men gossiped about their adventures of the past six months, and here and there a few groups gathered together to gamble. The compound was filled with gaiety and laughter. Trading went on hour after hour until Bah Tsosie and the men thought they would collapse from fatigue. The women were shrewd bargainers for provisions and domestic supplies; the men less formidable in their dealings for farm equipment, saddles, and hardware. Both Hernando and Carlin agreed that Mulie's help was indispensable.

Recovered pawn was worn proudly for all to see. And at the close of business, when the food had been prepared, the steady, musical beat of drums began, and the area vibrated with singing and dancing.

The activities continued for almost a week, then the Indians and their families who would not participate in the drive began to pack up their belongings and slowly move out. Within twenty-four hours Po'Se'Da' seemed deserted. Everyone felt the letdown, but Bah Tsosie was pleased to find time to be alone with her men. Although Carlin hadn't noticed, Bah Tsosie found herself very disquieted when the young, single Navajo girls congregated around the bachelor like butterflies around a flower.

Early on Saturday morning Bah Tsosie began supervising the loading of the chuck wagon. After some discussion it was decided that Carlin would drive the wagon, and Mulie would stay behind at the post to help Bah Tsosie. With Mulie in charge of running the business, Hernando and Carlin would be able to stop at the fort to confer with Eastman and then spend a few days in Santa Fe without worrying.

There seemed to be an uncommon number of delays, and it was the middle of the afternoon before they were finally on their way. As Hernando was about to mount his horse, Atwa Kee ran out from behind his mother's skirts and threw himself into Hernando's arms. "Take me with you!" the boy pleaded.

"Not this time, son,"—Hernando hugged him closely—"next time maybe." He put the boy down and swung up onto his horse.

"Will you come home soon?" the boy asked.

Hernando had to ignore the question. He had already decided that Carlin was capable of running Po'Se'Da' without him. It would be quite some time before he would return to the post—if ever. He had done the job he had set out to do, and now he was anxious to get on with his life. Hernando looked out over the herd and noticed the animals seemed nervous. Although there was not a cloud in the sky and the sun was shining, a strong wind had begun to blow from the north and the air was cold.

"I don't like it a bit," Mulie complained. "It's too early fer this kind o' cold. Feels like snow, 'n we ain't suppose' to have snow fer another month."

The traders scanned the blue sky and decided Mulie's concern was due to old age. "Don't worry about it, old-timer," Hernando called to him as he positioned the drive. "We'll be able to handle the weather."

Two other wagons would accompany the chuck wagon: one for bedrolls and gear; and one for Navajo blankets, rugs, and hand-crafted jewelry the traders were to sell for the Indians in Holbrook. Hernando made a final check of his rifle, sat straight in his saddle, and signaled for the men to start the wagons and animals moving. "Should be able to make ten miles or more before we set up camp!" he proclaimed to Carlin as he rode past the wagon to tighten up the herd.

It was a thrilling sight for Carlin—thousands of sheep spread out like an enormous white carpet against the horizon and the black-hatted Navajo, on foot and on horseback, directing their dogs with grunts and hand signals. He gloried in being alive and privileged to be a part of it. The scene was vaguely familiar, and he almost expected to hear the wail of Scottish bagpipes. He waved to Bah Tsosie and Atwa Kee. "See you soon," he yelled.

At sunrise the next morning Hernando wondered whether or not Mulie might have been right. The sky was slate-gray and threatening. There could be no doubt in anyone's mind that there was going to be a storm. Temperatures had been in the sixties the morning before; now gauging from the ice that had formed on top of the water in the barrels, Hernando guessed it to be in the high twenties. "Shouldn't amount to nothin' this time of year," Hernando told Carlin. He was as anxious to convince himself as he was his companion.

As they broke camp Hosteen Begay rode over in order to travel close to Hernando. "Think all that In'jun singin' and dancin' brought on this weather?" he said jokingly.

Hernando laughed. Strange, he thought, how much a part of their lives the young Navajo had become, and how much they enjoyed his company. His intelligence and sense of humor were always a surprise, and Hernando and he had become fierce competitors. If they weren't challenging one another to Indian wrestling or foot races, they tried to outdo one another at poker. Hernando glanced at the Indian at his side and realized, suddenly, that outside of Carlin, he preferred Hosteen Begay's company to any other man he knew. No doubt about it, Hosteen Begay had turned out to be a hell of a man—and a good friend. He would miss him!

Driving sheep across the monotonous desert gave a man time to think, and Hernando found himself examining his life. He remembered the women and whiskey, but there had to be more. How did a man judge his time on earth, he wondered. When his grandfather Villanova had died, he had still been consumed by resentment. The only one who had mourned his passing, it seemed to Hernando, was himself. Shell Woman's time on earth had been cursed with violent tragedy. It was as if her vicious murder had been planned since the day of her birth. How would his own end come, he wondered? And when it came, would he have a family and friends to mourn him? And what would he leave behind?

He thought of his parents, of Phoebe, of Bah Tsosie and Atwa Kee, of Carlin and Hosteen Begay. And of Felicia. Perhaps, he reasoned, a man should judge his life according to those who loved him, his good and loyal friends, how well he met a challenge and how capable he was of surviving in a hostile world.

The bitter cold wind on the back of his neck brought Hernando out of his melancholy. He realized that the weather was deteriorating rapidly.

Snow started to fall after they had been on the trail just a few hours. None of the men gave any outward sign of worry, but they all knew that if the storm continued it would mean trouble. Even if it were a light storm, the trail would become muddy and the sheep would burn up weight and fat trying to keep their footing. It would also mean that they would be on the trail for days longer—and every day meant money. The greatest danger, however, would be that if the freak storm continued and temperatures dropped even lower, grass and feed would be covered with snow, and the lambs might freeze to death.

The herdsmen kept the flock moving until it was too dark to travel any further. Continuous snowfall built up on the plateau, and in several places they found the drifts were several feet high. The men were cold and tired and hungry; the animals bleated in despair. Carlin was finally able to get a large campfire started with kindling Bah Tsosie had put in his wagon at the last minute.

Toward morning the men's worst fears were realized when the temperatures dropped way below zero. Hernando and Carlin routed the men from their bedrolls, and they all worked frantically most of the morning searching for lambs buried beneath the snow. Each animal found was carried immediately to the campfire in order to try to save it. To make matters worse, the snow had covered the brush, and there was no browse for the hungry sheep.

It was Hosteen Begay who came up with the solution. He ripped the side boards from one of the wagons and tied them to the rider's saddles to be used as "drags." The men and horses worked furiously, moving back and forth in front of the flock, clearing a trail and exposing the feed. Both men and animals were near exhaustion by late afternoon when the sky began to clear.

As the warmth of the sun began to penetrate, trying valiantly to thaw man and earth, the mood changed. Hopelessness passed, and even the bleating of the sheep was less despairing. But as the snow melted, the turf turned to mud. What next, the traders wondered.

That night, while the men huddled around the campfire, trying unsuccessfully to dry out and keep warm, one of the Navajo herdsmen, whose name was Dinet-Tsosi, called Hernando, Carlin, and Hosteen Begay aside. When he was sure they were out of sight of the others, he opened his blanket and revealed two bottles of wine. "I was saving these until we finish the drive," Dinet-Tsosi whispered in a harsh voice. "But I think we drink it now. Good med'cine for bad trouble!"

The traders and Hosteen Begay agreed, and that night at least a few of the miserable men slept like babes in the woods.

Carlin was the only one of the group who wasn't suffering from a hangover the next morning. He passed out sugared coffee and whistled as he mixed up the dough for biscuits. The wine had been mellow, the trail was beginning to dry out, and all seemed right with the world for the Scotsman. It had been clear to Carlin that he had acted instinctively during the trouble on the drive. No one had had to tell him what to do; and he had passed a severe test of his courage, faith, and determination.

The mood was catching. All the men had been tested by nature's wrath and had survived with the flock intact. They smiled broadly at one another—each giving the other a silent congratulation. The weather caused them to be three days later than they had first anticipated, but they would still make Holbrook in time to load the sheep on the railroad train.

The Navajos' excitement was contagious. None of the Indians had ever before seen an iron horse. They had heard tales of how it ate coal and belched out black smoke, and even steamed like the rocks in the sweat lodges. And how the howl of the whistle was loud enough, and strong enough, to frighten the Gahns. Now at last they would have a chance to see it with their own eyes.

The Southern Pacific route, from California to New Orleans and other points east and north, had been in operation since 1880, but the Atchison, Topeka & Santa Fe rail system that would link Santa Fe west to California hadn't been completed until mid-September. That particular section, which ran just south of the reservation border, enabled ranchers and farmers for miles around to load their animals at Holbrook for the journey east to the slaughterhouses in Chicago, thus saving in some cases hundreds of extra miles of herding. The railroad had even scheduled additional freight cars for the historic occasion—it was the first time freight trains had stopped in the heart of Arizona Territory to pick up sheep and cattle.

CHAPTER TWENTY-ONE

If Carlin Napier had thought he had witnessed bigotry in the heart of Captain Jonathan Waldren aboard the *Vesteen*, it was nothing to the hatred and intolerance he and Hernando experienced when they rode into Holbrook with their Navajo herdsmen. Even Hernando, who had been raised in an atmosphere with friends and relatives equally divided as to whether or not they despised or respected the Indians, was agitated by their reception.

No whiskey was allowed or sold on the reservation, but no one paid attention to the Federal law in Holbrook, which was located just a few miles south of the Navajo reservation border. In ordinary times some Navajos, who were known by the local residents to be "good" Indians if they were willing to pay double or triple the regular price, could buy all the wine or whiskey they wanted. The only condition exacted from these privileged few, by the merchants and local lawmen, was that the alcohol be consumed outside the city limits. Once outside of town it was the custom for the Indians to drink the contents of their bottles at one sitting and pass out cold.

Occasionally one of the braves would go on the warpath, firing off his gun or galloping his horse through town. But the commotion was tolerated and never lasted too long. No one ever reported an unconscious or drunken Indian because no one really cared.

The change in attitude came almost overnight to the sleepy little town of Holbrook, when the population suddenly quadrupled in size in anticipation of the coming of the railroad. Strangers crowded the streets, tents were set up as shops and saloons, and much to the dismay of the local citizens, Holbrook was turned into a sprawling, bawdy boom town. Rooming accommodations were at a minimum and were auctioned off to the highest bidders. Whiskey, women, and gambling were available to anyone who had the price. Indians, however, were no longer welcome by the outsiders under any circumstances, and if they did venture into town, they were arrested if they weren't off the streets by sundown.

The herd and drivers from Po'Se'Da' were late arrivals and Hernando was forced to camp and hold the sheep in check on the flatlands outside of town until holding pens could be located and the animals weighed in and loaded onto the waiting cars.

"I want you squaw men in 'n out o' here pronto!" the sheep buyer told Hernando and Carlin when they met at the scales after the final weigh-in.

Hernando had to restrain Carlin to keep him from punching the loathsome bigot. "Suits me. Just give us the money and we're long gone," Hernando forced a smile as the buyer reluctantly peeled off and counted the currency.

"Now let's divvy up with the men and head fer

town." Hernando was practically shoving Carlin ahead of him. "Ferget that bastard! We got some celebratin' to catch up on!"

A warm camaraderie had been established between the traders and the herdsmen on the drive. Without exception the Navajos had met every hardship and challenge with good humor and dependability. There was never a doubt about their mutual respect and admiration for one another. They were friends and equals.

Hernando added an unexpected bonus to the Navajos' wages and promised to replace Dinet-Tsosi's wine. "Better still, come on into town with us and I'll buy you some real whiskey!"

The gray-haired old Navajo nodded his approval and mounted up behind Hosteen Begay.

"I'm not sure this is a good idea from the reception we've gotten the past few days," Carlin confided to Hernando.

"Hell, there are four of us. 'Sides, if we run into any trouble we can't handle ourselves, the sheriff's a good friend of mine!"

There were armed guards at the entrances to all the saloons in the tent city. The traders felt the hostility in the glares of the men. "This looks like a pretty good waterin' hole," Hernando decided, stopping in front of a large tent with a temporary wooden front. They dismounted and tied their horses to the pegs pounded into a large log which served as a hitching post.

"No damned In'jun or In'jun-lovers allowed on the premises!" growled the guard as they started to enter the saloon. "If I was you I'd head out o' town. None o' the likes o' you is wanted here!" He lowered his rifle so that it was even with Hernando's belly.

"Take it easy with that gun, my friend," Hernando answered, taking care to control his temper. "We'll just mosey on down the street 'n find another place that appreciates the color of our money."

After several such receptions, it was Carlin who had to restrain Hernando. Both Hosteen Begay and Dinet-Tsosi were used to the senseless discrimination; and although they were angered, they were determined not to let their presence cause any more trouble for the traders. "Just bring some good whiskey when you come back to camp," Dinet-Tsosi instructed Hernando in Navajo.

The trader was not willing to give in so easily, but Hosteen Begay insisted. "We're tired. I want to get drunk tonight, but I couldn't have a good time with so many white coyotes. I'd rather be with my own people. 'Sides, I noticed some pretty squaws strutting around down by the camp. Maybe I'll find me a woman tonight," he winked at Carlin.

The four men touched hands in farewell, and the traders watched as the Navajos mounted their horses and galloped out of town.

"Shit! It ain't fair!" Hernando spat on the ground at the feet of one of the guards, then followed Carlin through the flap of the tent. A red-faced piano player pounded out the strains of "Swanee River" on an out-of-tune upright, but the melody could hardly be heard over the din of the crowd. The traders elbowed their way through the throng to the makeshift bar. The air was stifling and the smell of human stench was almost overpowering. "My Gawd! I forgot what white men smelled like," Hernando joked as the bartender put

301

two glasses and a bottle down before them. "Guess I've been out in the fresh air too long."

He poured himself and Carlin a full glass of whiskey and the two men raised their glasses for a toast. "Here's to city life!" Hernando proposed.

"Here's to savage life!" Carlin replied.

The raw whiskey burned all the way down and brought tears to Carlin's eyes. Even Hernando, who had drunk his share of rot-gut whiskey, gasped for breath. "Got any water?" he called to the bartender.

The man stared back at him in disgust. "If yah cain't drink it straight, get the hell out. We don't serve mixed drinks in here!"

Hernando and Carlin doubled up with laughter. They knew they were really in a frontier town when whiskey and water was called a "mixed" drink. Hernando filled their glasses again, and in less than an hour the bottle was finished. Carlin looked at his friend and grinned, then his legs gave out and he slipped slowly but gracefully to the floor. He was vaguely aware of Hernando lifting him up and throwing him over his shoulder—then everything went blank.

The sound of someone snoring loudly in bed next to him finally awakened Carlin. He assumed it was Hernando and gave the body a sound kick to silence the noise. Whatever his foot came in contact with under the covers, it didn't feel like a man. Carlin, his head pounding with excruciating pain, raised himself up on one elbow and looked. The body next to him was that of a woman! Her make-up was streaked, and the charcoal she had used to darken her lashes was smeared under her eyes, giving her face the appearance of a carved pumpkin. Her mouth was open and she continued to snore loudly. "Oh, my Gawd," Carlin moaned, "I need a drink!"

Across the small room in a second bed, Hernando sat propped up on his pillows, grinning like a Cheshire cat. " 'Bout time you woke up. How're you feelin'?"

"Never felt worse in my life," the Scot admitted. He noticed that Hernando had a bedmate, too.

"Well, let me assure you that you had one hell of a good time. I can vouch for that," Hernando informed him as he swung up out of bed and began putting on his trousers and boots. "And Carlin, you ain't a virgin anymore!"

Carlin lowered his head and stared up at the ceiling. He had never mentioned his rendezvous with Lydia to Hernando. "I been meaning to talk to you about that, but I think I'll wait until I feel a little better."

"Hope you enjoyed it as much as I did, 'cause it cost me a lot of money. Come on, shag out o' that bed; we got some more partying to do 'fore we head out o' here."

"You do the partying. I'm going to have some breakfast and head out to the camp and see how the men are doing."

"We'll compromise. Have a drink with me first, then we'll have breakfast together, and I'll ride out there with you."

For a twenty-dollar gold piece they were served steak, two eggs, biscuits, and coffee. The steaks were so tough they could hardly chew them, the eggs were greasy and undercooked, the biscuits were burned, and the coffee was weak. Carlin was thoroughly miserable, but Hernando didn't seem to notice. "There's a poker game goin' on in the bar. Think you could find yer way out to camp by yerself? I'd like to try my luck for a spell."

"I think I can navigate," Carlin replied sarcastically. "When can we expect to see you? I'd like to get on to Santa Fe before winter sets in."

"I'll meet you back at the camp tonight," Hernando promised. "We can leave for the fort and Santa Fe first thing in the morning."

Even from a distance Carlin could see their camp was deserted. The only thing moving were the mules as they grazed around the chuck wagon. When he was closer he noticed Dinet-Tsosi's horse tied to the rear of the wagon, but there was no sign of the old Navajo. Nor was there any sign of Hosteen Begay or his horse. Carlin wasn't too alarmed. He assumed that Hosteen Begay had found his woman, and that the other Navajos, once they had been paid, had decided to return to their homes.

He dismounted, unsaddled his horse, and tied it next to the Indian pony. As he reached inside of the chuck wagon to get his bedroll, he was stunned to see Dinet-Tsosi huddled up inside. The Indian stared at him through swollen and bloodshot eyes. For a moment Carlin thought the man's condition was from the effects of too much alcohol, but upon closer examination he realized the old man had been badly beaten.

"What happened?" Carlin demanded, as he proceeded to wash the painful gashes with lye soap and water.

Slowly, in a voice that at times was so low Carlin had to strain to hear the words, Dinet-Tsosie related the events of the evening before.

"Although he tried not to show it, Hosteen Begay was angered when we first left you. He say a man is a man and red or white should be treated equally. We ride on without speaking until we reach camp. Our brothers tell us that our cousins, the Apache, are in an arroyo—one hour's ride. They tell us our cousins have plenty of whiskey and that there are women with them, too!"

Tears forced the old man to pause and turn away. Carlin waited until he could continue.

"I did not want to go, but I was afraid for Hosteen Begay. When we found our cousins they were plenty drunk. They had some cattle they had stolen from a white man, and they cooked one in the fire. Women drunk, too! We thought they were Women Who Stand by Side of House. Our cousins say have whiskey! Have beef! Have woman! We no have beef, but we have plenty whiskey! Hosteen Begay see woman and take her, but this woman is not Woman Who Stand by Side of House She Apache brave's squaw!"

Carlin felt his heart quicken. "What happened to Hosteen Begay?" he asked anxiously.

The old man closed his eyes. "Big fight! I try to help but too many cousins. They beat me and leave me for dead. When I wake up, the Apaches are gone. Only Hosteen Begay is there. He is dead."

Carlin sat quietly, numbed by the thought of never seeing his friend alive again. He could almost hear the young brave's quick laughter and remembered how proud he had been when Hosteen Begay had first learned to write his name and add up a column of numbers. Violent death seemed to be a part of the life in the vast, untamed New World. "Are you well enough to ride?"

Dinet-Tsosi nodded that he was.

"We must pick up the body and take Hosteen Begay home for a proper burial." He found a canvas tarp and tied it on to one of the mules, then saddled his horse. He knew that the old Navajo suffered agony from the beating he had sustained, but there was nothing else to do. They would both have to ride to the arroyo. He would never find the Apache camp alone.

By the time they finished their mission it was late afternoon. Carlin rode into Holbrook alone to find Hernando and tell him what happened.

It was a big game and Hernando was on a winning streak. "Have a couple of drinks. I just want to play a few more hands."

"Now, Hernando. It's important."

The other players grumbled as Hernando threw in his cards. "Be back later, fellows, 'n give you a chance to win back yer money." Then he stomped out of the saloon after his friend. "Now tell me what in hell's so important!"

There was no emotion in Carlin's voice as he related the news of Hosteen Begay's murder. He had already used up every ounce of emotion he had when he wrapped the young Navajo's mutilated body in the canvas tarp and returned it to the sheep camp.

Hernando's face contorted in anguish. Without a word he tightened the cinch on his horse, leapt onto

306

the saddle, and spurred the animal to a full gallop. Carlin understood his pain and followed his dust out of town. Hernando would need time to be alone. By the time Carlin reached the camp, Hernando, who had ridden his beast to the point of exhaustion, was finally able to express his feelings. "He should have been with us. He had no business in a damned Apache camp! Those bastards in Holbrook—they're the ones who really killed him!"

Carlin couldn't argue his point. "I thought it would be better to postpone the trip to Santa Fe. Thought we might take his body back to Po'Se'Da' and bury him up on the hill."

Hernando agreed and they loaded the remains of the handsome young Navajo into the chuck wagon. Dinet-Tsosi sat on the seat next to Carlin, his horse tied on behind. Hernando rode on ahead; the sun was rapidly sinking below the horizon over his left shoulder. He welcomed the darkness which hid the harsh land from his view, relaxed his reins, and allowed the horse to guide them northward.

The sad procession arrived at the trading post at sundown on the third day. Early the following morning Hernando, Carlin, and Mulie carried their burden up the hill, and according to Navajo ritual, dug the grave. Hernando unwrapped a package he had picked up earlier at the post and threw the contents into the hole. It was the Sioux chief's concha belt, the one that Hosteen Begay had admired so much. "Sorry, Mulie," he tried to explain, "but he's the only man I know who's big enough to wear a belt like that!"

307

The old trader needed no explanation. He understood the love and friendship of the trader for the Navajo. When they had filled in the grave, Hernando broke the shovel handles and laid them down next to the mound. The three men were silent for a moment, then began the long descent down the hill to Po'Se'Da'.

Dinet-Tsosi stayed at the post until he was well enough to make the long journey back to his family in the Wonderful Valley. "Come back to the land of Hoskinini," he said fondly to Hernando, "and we will drink wine together and you will forget."

"No, my friend, I have to return to Santa Fe. As you miss your family, I too miss mine. But perhaps we will meet again," Hernando promised.

The old Navajo touched his hand. "We need you in Wonderful Valley. Many people hungry. Better you come soon."

The traders watched as the Navajo rode off. " 'Bout time we were thinkin' about gettin' on the trail, too," Hernando suggested to Carlin.

"How would you feel about going over to Santa Fe by yourself?" Carlin asked.

"What do you mean?"

Carlin knelt on his haunches and began to draw in the sand. "Well, tomorrow is November 28, 1885! I'll be twenty-one years old," Carlin explained. "I've been more than halfway 'round the world. I've seen the Mediterranean, sailed along the coast of Africa, spent time in India and China, and now I can never return to my home in Scotland again. I will never again see my mother, my father, or my sister. Lord knows, your family has made me welcome. It's just that I don't feel I belong in that world out there! I don't like the ways of the civilized white society. I'm happy here." He stood up and gazed around the compound. "I have no need to go into Santa Fe. Everything I ever dreamed I wanted is right here at Po'Se'Da'. It will do me no good to see Phoebe again. She made her wishes clear to me the last time we met. It would only bring more pain if I saw her again."

Bah Tsosie came out of the post to summon the men to dinner. She smiled as she walked toward them. The late afternoon sun shone on her face, and Carlin and Hernando glanced at one another, knowing they were both admiring her beauty.

"She moves as if she were carried on the wings of doves," Hernando said impulsively. He was about to say more when he noticed the look in Bah Tsosie's eyes as she gazed at Carlin. "But it seems her heart might belong to another," he murmured to himself.

Hernando became painfully aware that he had seen the same expression in another woman's eyes. Felicia's! At the time he had not truly recognized it for what it was, or perhaps he had known that she loved him and preferred to ignore her feelings. The adoration that filled Bah Tsosie's eyes when she looked at the young Scot was impossible to ignore, yet he realized that Carlin was totally and honestly unaware of the Navajo woman's feelings for him. He felt uncomfortable, as if he had come upon a secret that he had no right to share. "I think Bah Tsosie should prepare a special dinner for your birthday tomorrow, then I'll head on home."

Hernando had mixed emotions as he rode away from Po'Se'Da' the next day on the first leg of his journey to Fort Defiance and the hacienda. He had never before admitted to himself that he, too, felt the need to belong somewhere. In some ways he envied Carlin; at least the Scotsman seemed to have found his proper place. And in time Carlin would probably accept Bah Tsosie's warm bed. He wondered whether or not they would marry. It suddenly occurred to Hernando that he had need of the same kind of warmth and affection as Bah Tsosie would give to Carlin. Well, he supposed, those emotions were available to him from any number of women if he sincerely chose to pursue them.

He turned the collar up on his mackinaw. Mulie had warned him, once again, that there was a storm coming. This time Hernando knew it would be prudent to listen to what Mulie had to say about the weather.

The coldness with which Indian agent Galen Eastman greeted him made Hernando even more determined to protect his Navajo friends. "I've come many miles out of my way through rotten weather, I might add, to make an official report to you that the remains of two prospectors, one Billie Denver and one Charley Garren, were found in the northeastern section of the reservation, and what was left of their belongings were brought to Po'Se'Da', so that I could bring them here to the fort!"

Eastman examined the meager contents of the sack. Two billfolds, one pocket watch, one rabbit's foot on a silver chain, and a few letters comprised the extent of the dead men's possessions. "Nothing more?"

310

"Two horses and two pack mules. They're outside."

"The northeastern section of the reservation, you say? That's Hoskinini's territory. Why would that savage bother to return anything? And why would he trust you, Mr. Dundee?"

Hernando clenched his fists and gritted his teeth. "Why don't you ask him personally? I can only tell you that he did what was right and proper."

Eastman laughed sarcastically. "None of those misfits have the slightest knowledge of what is 'right and proper!'" He leaned forward and spoke with such contempt that Hernando was agitated. "I intend to check out the murder of these honorable men fully! I have no intentions of taking the word of a savage or of a squaw-man that all the facts have been brought to my attention."

"You'd better watch yourself, Eastman."

"No, Dundee. You'd better watch yourself. Now, get out before I have you thrown out."

Hernando was shaking with rage. Only the immediate intervention of two soldiers kept him from attacking the agent. General Boyd was more sympathetic. "Don't worry about it, Mr. Dundee. Your father has an excellent reputation in Washington; perhaps a letter from him to the right people could help us remove Eastman. He's totally unsuited for his position and has caused nothing but trouble since he arrived." The general poured them each a drink. "Nothing could be gained by sending the soldiers up to the north country now anyhow. The weather's too bad. By spring, when the thaw starts—with any luck and with your father's help—Mr. Eastman will no longer be with us."

Encouraged by General Boyd's understanding, Hernando decided to continue on to Santa Fe. There seemed no need to warn Carlin or Hoskinini of the madman's threats.

CHAPTER TWENTY-TWO

The introduction of Chata San Vincente—Felicia Montez—to the ladies, Esther Mendoza and Sarah Spiegelberg, was like opening a window and allowing fresh air to enter to the room. Upon Andrew's discovery of Felicia's true identity and the purpose of her masquerade, he had immediately discussed the situation with Isabella, leaving the final disposition of Felicia's future in Santa Fe with his wife.

It was not a time in the history of the Southwest when women had a choice of professions. If one were not fortunate enough to be born wealthy or to be protected by a loving husband or family, one's opportunities were severely limited. Because of this the more sensitive and intelligent women chose to accept feminine friends and neighbors on the basis of what they could contribute to a friendship, rather than what their backgrounds might be.

Isabella's reaction to Andrew's discovery had been swift and positive. "The poor creature! How brave of her to want to begin her life anew. And she's so bright and attractive! Andrew, we must do everything possible to help her and make sure she never has to return to a life of degradation." Isabella's mind began working so fast Andrew was sure he could hear the wheels turning. "Of course I don't agree with her for one moment about Dolores. But when she knows the child better, I'm sure she'll change her mind. Now I must tell Esther and Sarah; they'll adore having a new project!"

Isabella's assessment of her friends' reaction to the news of Felicia's courage had been accurate. And had it not been for the tragic incident with Shell Woman and the Comancheros, Isabella would have devoted her full time, with the other ladies, to insuring that Felicia was properly guided along the road to salvation.

She needn't have worried. Felicia, herself, was determined to find a way to insure her own salvation. She found time each morning to visit her new friend, Father Ricardo Vieja.

"Now show me where that is written," she insisted as he repeated the story of Ruth from the Old Testament.

"Right here," he assured her, pointing out the passage.

Felicia read the verses aloud, and when she reached verse sixteen her voice began to quiver. "'And Ruth said, Entreat me not to leave thee, or to return from following after thee: for whither thou goest, I will go; and where thou lodgest, I will lodge. Thy people shall be my people, thy God my God.'" She closed the book and wept silently. "It's so beautiful. And truly, if I can be forgiven, I would do anything in the world for Dona Isabella. Do you think I will ever be worthy?"

Father Vieja patted her hand. He had become very

fond of Felicia and had no doubt of her sincerity. "It is not up to me to give you that answer—only the Lord can guide you and judge you. You must look into your heart. And when you find yourself worthy, I feel that we can be reasonably assured that it is a sign from God."

Toward the end of October Esther and Sarah found a suitable home for Felicia to buy and hired servants who, in addition to doing their regular work, were sufficiently religious and respected to act as companions and chaperons. The adobe structure was located off the plaza and just a short distance from Esther's palatial mansion. Though it was large enough for Felicia to entertain properly, it was not ostentatious. Under the directions of her motherly friends, Felicia had the spacious rooms white-washed, the floors and windows scrubbed, and appropriate furniture chosen. Even in the early winter the grounds were well tended. By November 28, at the same time Carlin was celebrating his birthday at Po'Se'Da', the home was ready to be occupied and the women prepared a house-warming party.

What knowledge Felicia lacked pertaining to the social graces she made up for in genuine enthusiasm. Each new discovery in etiquette or homemaking was as big a thrill to Esther and Sarah as it was to Felicia. More important for the three unlikely companions was that they laughed a lot—which Sarah assured them "was good for the soul!"

Her party was given exactly four months to the day after Felicia arrived in Santa Fe, and she played the roll of hostess as graciously as if she had been born to the genteel life. She chatted easily with the women, inquiring about their families, and was genuinely interested in their conversation. When the party was over, it was obvious everyone had enjoyed themselves as much as the hostess. Felicia was exhilarated.

Esther, Sarah, Isabella and Dolores stayed behind to congratulate themselves as well as Felicia on the success of the debut.

"I know this is rather short notice," Isabella informed the women, "but I have decided that *my* party for Chata and Dolores shall be given on December 14. Phoebe is almost completely well—and I see no need to delay the affair any longer."

"But that's only two weeks away!" Esther and Sarah exclaimed. "How in the world can you make all the arrangements so soon?"

"It's the only weekend before Christmas that we haven't been asked to another party!" Isabella explained. "I assume that it's an open weekend for all of us, unless there's something going on that you haven't told me about or a party that I've not been invited to!"

The women laughed and assured her that this was not the case. "All right, then, I shall attend to the invitations tomorrow and have Carlos and the vaqueros deliver them by hand."

Dolores's eyes brightened at the thought of another party and especially one given in her honor. "I hope Hernando will be home in time!"

"Where is that young man?" Sarah demanded. "Andrew's been home more than a month. Surely the lamb drive is over by now."

Isabella smiled patiently. "After all these years I've

learned to accept the fact that Hernando is just like his father. I expect him when I see him come through the door."

Felicia watched Dolores closely. Although the young woman had assured her that she intended only to use Hernando to force a commitment from Norton, Felicia could not believe in her wildest imagination that when the actual time came for Dolores to choose between the two men, she would accept the gray-haired, middle-aged banker over the handsome and virile Hernando.

"I don't think it's proper behavior at all!" The girl was obviously agitated by Isabella's statement. "A woman should know where her husband is, whom he's with, and when he will return!"

"I'm sure you'll train your husband properly," Isabella replied, "but I've always found you have more control over a stallion if you give him a loose rein. Now we must be going. It's a long ride back to the hacienda, and we should go over the guest list this evening."

After Isabella and the penitent Dolores left, Sarah and Esther collapsed onto the sofa. "I don't know where she gets her energy," Sarah complained. "It would take me at least a month to prepare for a ball. Isabella could do it in two days!"

"And it will be the most glamorous event of the year. Everyone will be there, and the food and music will be divine," Esther added, then she sat bolt upright. "But what are we going to wear?"

"Esther, you have more gowns than any other woman in the territory, and yet you always worry about *what you're going to wear*. If you had a figure like mine, then you should worry!" Sarah chided.

"Stay here! Both of you! I must run home for a minute and I'll be right back!" Esther, as large as she was, scurried from the room like a gazelle. The two women stared after her. Within a few minutes she returned carrying a large package. Felicia and Sarah watched curiously as she unwrapped it with great care.

"My late husband was such a dreamer," she explained. "He was a dear but crazy man. On his last trip to New York he saw this gown in the window of a shop and brought it home to me." She shook the gown gently and held it up for her friends to admire. "In his mind he was sure it would fit me perfectly—such a devoted fool—it's a size eight, and I wear a size sixteen."

The gown was exquisite and made of white waterlined taffeta trimmed with ermine tails and seed pearls. The sleeves were long and fitted, the bodice cut low.

"It's the loveliest gown I've ever seen," gasped Felicia.

Sarah understood Esther's intent immediately. "And it will just fit Chata!"

The older women bubbled with joy. Felicia was speechless.

"Try it on," the women demanded in unison.

Felicia protested, but the women marched her upstairs and dressed her as if she were a doll. Then they stood back to admire their handiwork. The effect of the dress on Felicia was stunning! It was a perfect fit.

"She looks like a princess out of a fairy tale," Sarah gushed.

318

"Not a princess," Esther corrected, "a queen! A queen from the Spanish court!"

Felicia caught a glimpse of her reflection in the full-length mirror. In the rosy glow of the soft lamplight it was as if she were looking at a stranger. It surprised her how beautiful that stranger was! And then her confidence left her. She was sure that Hernando would be home in time for his mother's gala affair. Until now she had been living in a fantasy world. Norton's weekly letters had bolstered her courage until she felt she could honestly carry off the charade; but now the truth of her position weighed heavily on her conscience. These two generous ladies had accepted her into their hearts so easily, without question, without demands, that she flushed with shame. She wondered suddenly how she could possibly have imagined that she would be a better wife for Hernando than Dolores. Even if she were accepted into the church as a nun, she knew that Hernando would never be able to forgive her for her deception.

"Dear Esther—dear Sarah," she said quietly. "Please help me off with this lovely gown. Then let's go downstairs and have another cup of tea. I have something that I must tell you!"

The two matrons sat wide-eyed, sipping their tea, as a tearful Felicia confessed her true identity. "But my dear," Sarah finally interrupted, "we thought that you knew!"

"Knew what?" Felicia sobbed, blowing her nose into the fine lace handkerchief Esther had shoved into her hand.

"We thought that you knew—that *we* knew! We've

known all along, for months now, that your real name is Felicia Montez."

"Enough of that caterwauling, child! The only thing you're to concern yourself with now is who your escort will be for the ball!" Esther cut herself another large slice of cake. She always felt hungry when faced with a new challenge.

CHAPTER TWENTY-THREE

The Hacienda de la Villanova Dundee buzzed with frantic activity. With Dolores's help, Isabella managed to write over 100 invitations. More than 200 of the Territory's most prominent citizens were expected to attend the fiesta. Isabella checked and rechecked her guest list, deleting a name here and adding a name there. When they had finished, Carlos and a half dozen cowboys were dispatched in the cold gray afternoon to deliver the invitations.

Other men were sent into Santa Fe to hire musicians—both mariachi players and Anglo entertainers who were able to play the latest waltzes. Steers and turkeys were chosen to be slaughtered for the feast, and women were sent to the cellars to find the choicest wines and preserved fruits and vegetables. Poinsettias were repotted in the gardens to be brought indoors; and holly boughs and mistletoe were found in the foothills and carried back to the hacienda to be hung. Tallow candles were carefully placed inside of paper Chinese lanterns, which would line the road to the entrance of the hacienda for almost a half mile. Additional fire pits were constructed out-of-doors so that the meat and fowl could be properly smoked.

Dolores was ready to drop from exhaustion, but Isabella seemed to have an unlimited source of energy that renewed itself with each demand. She checked the silver and crystal to be sure that each piece was polished and shined to perfection and examined every nook and cranny checking for dust. Finally, after days of preparation, Isabella, too, began to feel the strain. She wrapped herself warmly in an Apache shawl and went to the chapel to rest and meditate. In the stillness of the muraled walls she bowed her head in order to say prayers for her mother and her stillborn children. As was her custom, she forced herself to add a few words to the Lord for her father. Then she sat back and looked sadly at the carved statue of her Lord Jesus and wondered if it would be sacrilegious to ask God's lamb to intercede for Shell Woman.

As if they had been connected together through some unique psychical power, Phoebe suddenly appeared and sat down next to her mistress. "I wondered if I might pray for my mother? Do you think it would be all right?"

"My dear friend, I'm sure it will be. We'll pray together, then let's take a walk. I've missed you so!"

The women strode arm in arm through the garden and into the orchard. "Are you sure you're feeling better?" Isabella asked.

Phoebe nodded that she was, and the women continued their walk. They were so close that words seemed unnecessary. After a time, Phoebe broke the silence. "I've been thinking of returning to my people. I'm still of marriageable age. And now that my mother is gone I feel a terrible loneliness."

Isabella was shaken by the woman's words. They

had been together so long that the thought of being without her seemed unbearable.

"Do you think you would be happy? You've been with us for almost half your life. Do you think you could adjust to becoming an Apache again?"

"I'm not sure. I will never know unless I make the effort."

Isabella took hold of her hands and looked searchingly into Phoebe's face. "Will you stay with us until after Christmas?"

"I feel as if I should go quickly."

Isabella felt the warm tears stream down her face. "Of course. Just know that this is your home. You will be welcome to return anytime you wish."

Isabella was scarcely aware of the savory smells as she walked through the kitchen. She smiled bravely at Andrew, who was in the living room busily directing the proper placement of flowers and candles throughout the area. She rushed up the stairs, desperately tired and distraught over Phoebe's pronouncement. As she opened the door to her room, she became aware of someone crying in the room down the hall. Pulling her emotions together and drying her tears, she rapped gently on Dolores's door and entered the room. There were a dozen ball gowns strewn on the bed and floor and in the midst of them sat the sobbing girl.

"Good heavens, dear. What's wrong? Are you ill?"

"No, I'm not ill, but I have absolutely nothing to wear." The girl gasped between sobs, "I wish my mama was here! I wish I were back home! I'm so cold and lonely!"

There was that word again. Isabella took a deep breath and draped her shawl over Dolores's shoulders, "How thoughtless of me. Of course you shall have a new dress for the party. We will ride into town first thing in the morning and buy you the finest gown in Santa Fe!"

She took the girl in her arms and rocked her back and forth until her crying subsided. "I'm sure Hernando will be home soon," she whispered, "and then you won't be lonely anymore!"

Andrew didn't like the look of the threatening sky when he awoke the next morning and decided it would be wise to accompany the women into town. Horses could bolt in bad weather, and although he had confidence in Carlos's ability to handle the animals, he felt more secure about his own ability in case of an emergency.

When he realized it would take Dolores quite some time to make a decision about what dress she was going to buy, he winked at Aaron Spiegelberg and informed his wife that when they were ready to return to the hacienda, he could be found at Father Vieja's.

"These gowns seem so old-fashioned," Dolores pouted.

Aaron found it difficult to keep his patience with the young woman. His wife, Sarah, had helped him select the merchandise, and he was sure they were of the latest style. "And look at the stitching," he insisted. "This is the finest quality of workmanship in the Territory. And probably in New York—or Paris!"

"You're so attractive none of the men will notice what you're wearing anyhow," Isabella assured her.

It took Dolores almost an hour before she decided

on an aqua-colored velveteen gown, trimmed with lace. She wasn't completely satisfied with her choice, but it was the most expensive gown in Mr. Spiegelberg's store.

"We'd better find Andrew and be on our way. It looks as if it's already begun to snow," Isabella commented, as she signed the sales ticket and hurried Dolores toward the door. "See you and Sarah at the party, Aaron," she reminded the frazzled shopkeeper.

Once outside, both women shivered with the cold, in spite of the fact they both wore fur capes and hats.

"How in the world will anyone be able to get to the party if this weather keeps up?" Dolores asked.

"We're used to the winters in the Territory. We just don't pay any attention to them. If you let the weather keep you from doing what has to be done or going where you want to go, you'd find yourself accomplishing very little and staying home most of the time," Isabella explained. But she wasn't thinking of the inconvenience the weather might pose for her guests. She was wondering whether Phoebe would be able to survive the cruel snows in the land of the Apaches.

Hernando rode ahead of the storm on most of his journey home from Fort Defiance, but twenty miles south of Santa Fe it overcame him with a vengeance. The distance, which under normal circumstances would have taken him only a few hours to cover, took him more than eight hours. And when he arrived at his destination, he was half frozen and exhausted. He rode immediately to Antonio's for a drink and a hot bath. My Gawd, he thought, it's good to be home!

He was surprised when he entered the facility and

didn't recognize anyone at the bar. "Where's Lopez?" he asked the stranger who served him his drink.

"Dead," the bartender answered.

Hernando shook his head. "Where's Antonio?"

"Went down to Mexico to spend the winter."

"What's your name?"

"Eduardo—I'm Antonio's cousin."

"I'm Hernando Dundee." The trader extended his hand. "Can I get a hot bath?"

The barman acknowledged that he could indeed. And, proud to finally meet the man he had heard so much about, he offered the trader a drink on the house.

"I suppose you've come home for your mother's Fiesta de Navidad? Everybody is talking about it!"

"My mother's giving a party?" Hernando asked and sipped the second drink more slowly.

"I hear it's the biggest one ever given in the Territory," Eduardo replied enthusiastically.

"I don't care much for parties. Better give me a double, and I'll head for my bath." Hernando listened with amusement as Eduardo caught him up on the local gossip.

The third drink began to warm him, but as a precaution he took a bottle of brandy into the tub with him. After a short nap in the hot water, Hernando awakened feeling much better. He found clean clothes in his locker, dressed, paid his bill, and decided it was time to pay a visit to Maria's establishment. He didn't feel like having a woman, but some female company would be welcome. The whorehouse would provide a refuge for a day or so, anyway, or at least until his mother's party was over.

By the time he left Antonio's it was after midnight and the streets of Santa Fe were deserted. The storm had calmed down, leaving the barren trees dressed in a mantle of snow. Ice crystals reflected the dim light of the street lamps creating the illusion of a thousand stars decorating the trees. Only the sound of Hernando's horse's hooves on the frozen cobblestones penetrated the silence. Hernando was aware that just a few months earlier he never would have noticed the beauty of the scene. It seemed, at that moment, he had been away for years rather than months. Everything appeared to be different. He wondered whether it was the town that had changed—or the man.

He rode past the plaza and wound his way through the narrow streets until he could see the familiar red light shining in the distance.

It took Maria a few minutes to open the door. Business had been slow because of the weather, and it was late for customers. Most of the girls had already retired for the night and Maria had been sipping coffee at the bar by herself. She turned up the lamp and forced herself to smile before she unlatched the heavy door; paying customers must always be greeted with a smile. She stared at Hernando as if he were a ghost then threw her arms around him. "*Querido!*" she screamed, pulling him in out of the cold. "Welcome home!"

She placed a bottle of whiskey on the bar and rang a bell summoning the girls to come downstairs. Hernando looked around at the tired faces, bought everybody a drink, then turned to the madam. "Send them to bed, Maria, I'm too tired to be of any use to anyone tonight. I just feel like talking."

Maria had never seen Hernando in such a sober mood. She dismissed the girls and led the trader into the kitchen. "Let me fix you something to eat, then we can talk all night if you feel like it. Tomorrow you can spend the entire day in bed. I have a wonderful new girl in from New Orleans, a Creole girl."

Hernando laughed. At least Maria hadn't changed. To the feisty madam, any and all problems could be solved with sex. Perhaps she was right. At least he had always been able to talk to her and part of her success as a madam was her ability to listen. Tonight the words wouldn't come. She didn't press him; instead, when he had finished his breakfast, she led him upstairs to her bedroom. "Sleep here tonight. I'll sleep with one of the girls. You'll feel better tomorrow."

Hernando was grateful for her understanding. Too tired to undress, he just pulled off his boots and collapsed under the the feather comforter.

The next day Maria instructed the Creole girl to take Hernando his coffee. Heavy draperies kept the room in total darkness, and she had to light the lamp next to the bed in order to see. Then she awakened him gently.

His eyes became accustomed to the light, and he wondered for a moment where he was, then he stared up at the girl. Her coffee-colored skin and dark eyes reminded him of Bah Tsosie. "Good morning," he said.

"It's not morning." Her soft voice held just a trace of an accent. "It's almost four o'clock in the afternoon."

"What day is this?"

"It's Saturday, December 14," she replied.

Hernando sipped his coffee and appraised the girl. "What's your name?"

"Noel."

"Well, Noel, looks like you're going to be my Christmas present." He set down his cup and began to undress. "Why don't you just slip under the covers so's you and I can get better acquainted!"

Hernando's lovemaking was furious and animallike, then gentle and tender. It was as if he exploded his tension and anger into the girl. When he was finally relaxed, his hostility to the world lessened, yet he still felt unfulfilled. Hernando dressed quickly and tossed the girl a gold coin.

"I have not pleased you?"

"Don't worry about it. You were fine. Maybe we'll get together later."

He made his way downstairs to the bar and was surprised to find the room crowded with customers. One of the men had brought a large Christmas tree inside, and the girls were busy decorating it. Maria welcomed him back to the world of the living and ordered the maid to bring Hernando steak and eggs. "You look a little lean; we'd better fatten you up." She looked on with pleasure as he ate. "I suppose you'll be going to your mother's fiesta tonight. Everyone's talking about it. The governor will be there, and I've heard that guests are coming from as far away as El Paso!"

"Mother gives fine parties," Hernando conceded.

"I understand that there's a very special guest of honor, a beautiful young aristocrat from Santa Barbara, and that there may be wedding bells ringing in the chapel of the Hacienda de la Villanova Dundee! Is that true?"

Hernando laughed, remembering his last encounter with the petulant Dolores Castiaga. "She is truly a rare beauty—but spoiled beyond belief. No, Maria. If the wedding bells were planned for me, they will never ring. I have no need for a wife."

"And what about your handsome young blond friend, Senor Napier? Lydia tells me that with some practice he might make a very good husband!" Maria cackled with glee; the prostitutes always categorized their clients marvelous, good, fair, or dreadful—lover, husband, or hopeless! "Good husband" immediately conjured up the physical as well as the mental attitude of the customer.

Hernando roared! It was the first really hearty laugh he'd had in weeks, and until now he had been completely unaware that Carlin had visited Lydia!

Maria left out no small detail of the young Scotsman's adventure and the loss of his virginity. "Where is our young friend?" she finally asked.

"He stayed out on the reservation. He'll make his life as a trader now." Hernando grew melancholic, then said, "I think I should have stayed out there, too."

Maria looked stricken. "I've been meaning to talk to you about that," she said. "How could you have stood it so long out there with those stinking, stupid savages? When I first heard about it, I couldn't believe your father would do such a terrible thing to his only son!"

Hernando had forgotten Maria's attitude toward the Indians was the same as his grandfather Villanova's. There was a common feeling of hatred among the residents of the New Mexico Territory, for many of them had experienced Indian attacks. A few months earlier Hernando would have dismissed the remarks or even agreed with them. Now he stared at Maria as if she were a stranger. Her hatred contorted her painted face, and her features seemed to melt together as if they had been made of wax. Hernando remained silent and shocked as he watched her superficial beauty distort into ugliness. He glanced around the room crowded with masses of sweating human flesh, made more repulsive because of its containment within the four walls. Maria's shrill voice became the voice of his grandfather and of Eastman, the Navajo agent. He caught phrases—"filthy, drunken, savages—string 'em all up!" Stale smoke, the acrid smell of whiskey, combined with the aroma of cheap perfume, seemed to suffocate him. In various stages of undress Maria's girls looked pale and bloated.

Hernando was surprised at his own revulsion. Suddenly he longed for the smell of the fresh clean air on the high plateau of Navajoland and the perfume of Bah Tsosie's raw wool as she carded it into skeins for her rugs. He longed to see the smiling face of Atwa Kee and be challenged once again to a foot race by Hosteen Begay. Had he once been bored by Carlin's reading of the classics after dinner?

"I'd better be getting on home, Maria," Hernando announced, not bothering to finish his drink. "See you around."

He pulled his wool scarf up over his nose and mouth to protect his face against the icy wind and started for the hacienda. It was a sad feeling to realize that another chapter of his life had come to an end, yet he knew that he had no more need of Maria's brothel. He was not anxious to attend his mother's party, but it would be good to see his family again, and he was anxious to discuss his conversation with General Boyd regarding Eastman with his father. The faster a new agent was found for the reservation the better it would be for everyone concerned.

For some reason the long, cold ride home reminded him of the lamb drive. He realized, in retrospect, that the drive had been a great experience for him in spite of its tragic ending. The companionship of the herders and the winning spirit of the men had given him a sense of worth he had not thought possible. For the first time there was no doubt in Hernando's mind that he would return to Po'Se'Da'. And one of the things he would do when he returned would be to change Atwa Kee's name from Quiet Boy to Happy Boy! The thought delighted him and he spurred his horse into a slow lope.

Hernando could see the lights of the hacienda and hear the sounds of the music and merrymaking from the far end of the valley. He couldn't remember when he'd seen more carriages and decided it would be prudent for him to enter the hacienda through the kitchen. When he reached the patio, he decided to check Phoebe's cottage first, just on the chance that she might be there; but the room was dark, so he continued on through the garden to the back door of his home. He hugged the ample frame of Rosa, the cook. "Not a word to anyone that I'm home!" he made the astonished senora promise. Then he vanished up the back stairway to his room in order to change into more formal attire.

It had been more than a year since he had been so elegantly dressed, and he was surprised that his coat and trousers hung so loosely on his lean frame. He had trouble with his cravat, and out of habit started toward his door to call Phoebe to help him. He wondered for a moment where she was, then, assuming she was probably serving in the main room, forced himself to do a proper job with his tie. When he was finally dressed, he appraised himself in the mirror and scowled. Who was this tall, thin gentleman? Hernando Dundee, the rich young womanizer and two-fisted drinker—or the sober Indian trader whom the Navajos called the Man Who Honors Justice? He recalled Maria's reference to the savages and questioned who the real savages were. Carlin Napier had influenced him greatly! He took a deep breath and left the room.

From the balcony he could look down into the transformed ballroom. He smiled when he noticed his father dancing with his mother. It pleased him that they were still so much in love after all these years.

Hedrick Norton knew nothing of the plans for Isabella's lavish Christmas party; he knew simply that he had been separated from Dolores long enough. When Felicia returned from her visit with Dolores and Isabella on the first of December, she found a letter from Norton dated November 13, 1885. It read:

> From what you say and from the letters I have received from Dolores, I feel that I will be neither embarrassed nor humiliated if I propose marriage. Of course, I could be disappointed, but I feel that I must journey to Santa Fe to see for

myself. And so, dear Felicia, I have secured my reservations, and you may expect to see me on the morning of December 14. I would rather you say nothing to my senorita, as I am rather anxious to see what kind of a reception I receive from her. I have done wonderful things restoring the Hacienda de Castiaga, but in truth the restoration will mean nothing unless I am able to return to Santa Barbara with Dolores and see her sweet face light up with pleasure when she sees what has been done. Perhaps I sound like a schoolboy, but she means the world to me. Do you understand?

Fondly, Hedrick.

Felicia read the letter several times, surprised by and impressed with its tender sentiment. Yes, she did understand. After careful consideration she decided to discuss the matter with Esther. The horse-faced woman was delighted. "We've been wondering about a proper escort for you," the widow commented. "Seems as if Divine Providence has intervened and provided the man. And if the Senorita Castiaga decides she isn't interested, remind Mr. Norton that I'm a widow and *very* available!" Esther roared at her own joke.

When the morning of the fourteenth finally arrived, Felicia hardly recognized Hedrick as he stepped from the train. The banker had lost twenty pounds, tinted his gray hair, and was attired in the latest gentlemen's fashions tailored expressly for him in San Francisco. He was equally astounded over her appearance.

"What have you done to yourself? There is such a gentle look about you," he exclaimed, peering into her face.

"Perhaps it's because I'm living a 'gentle' life," she explained, delighted at his astuteness. "I've booked rooms for you at the inn and made arrangements for us to ride with Esther Mendoza in her carriage. It will be more proper if we are well chaperoned."

"Is this the same Felica Montez who took my suggestion to save ten cents out of every dollar?" Norton asked mischievously.

"No, my dear friend," she replied, taking his hands in hers. "That poor child disappeared quite some time ago!"

Dolores Castiaga was at the punch bowl surrounded by admiring bachelors when the doorman announced the arrival of Senora Mendoza, Senora San Vincente, and Senor Norton. She moved to the entrance slowly, wondering if she had heard the name correctly. She was speechless for a moment when she saw Hedrick helping Felicia with her wrap, then rushed forward into the foyer to greet them. She felt her cheeks flush as she pecked Felicia on the cheek, then turned to glare at Norton. "What a pleasant surprise to see you so far from home. I had no idea you were acquainted with my friend, Senora San Vincente. How did you meet?"

Ignoring her question, Norton held Dolores at arm's length in order to fully admire her beauty. It was difficult to disguise his pleasure at seeing her again.

Isabella and Andrew had also heard the announcement and were just a few steps behind Dolores. Isabella wondered who the tall Anglo stranger might be and waited impatiently to be introduced.

"Hedrick, may I introduce our host and hostess, Andrew and Isabella Dundee? Isabella, Andrew, this is my dear friend Hedrick Norton from Santa Barbara. Hedrick is my banker, and by the strangest coincidence he was a dear friend of Dolores's mother."

The introduction seemed to placate both Dolores and Isabella, but it was still an awkward moment. Andrew broke the tension. "Let me escort you into the ballroom." Without further ado he proudly extended his arm first to his wife, then to Felicia. Hedrick followed suit with the stunned Dolores and Esther.

A little while later Hernando descended the stairs to the landing. He recognized almost everyone but was puzzled when he spotted Dolores waltzing gracefully in the arms of an older man who looked vaguely familiar. She looked more content than he had ever seen her, and her partner seemed oblivious to anyone else in the room. Then he turned his gaze to scan the other guests, and in an instant he became aware of the most beautiful woman he'd ever seen. She was dressed in white, her dark curls held high off her neck with a diamond tiara. Her expression was that of a Madonna, and she moved so gracefully she seemed to float in her partner's arms.

Isabella glanced toward the landing and caught her breath. "Hernando!" she cried with joy. "You're home! You're really home!"

Andrew followed his wife through the crowd and grasped his son's hands. "Merry Christmas, Hernando! Welcome home!"

Hernando found himself surrounded by friends and well-wishers that he hadn't seen for almost a year. The bartender at Antonio's had been correct. Everybody who was anybody in the Territory honored Isabella with their presence. After exchanging vague pleasantries with the guests who pressed around him, Hernando turned to his mother and bowed. "May I have the pleasure of this waltz?" he asked.

Felicia became instinctively aware of Hernando's presence almost immediately and began to tremble in her partner's arms. "Are you all right?" he asked, noticing the beads of perspiration that formed on her brow. "Would you like to sit down—or may I get you some punch?"

"I do feel a little faint," she murmured. "Would you mind terribly if I excused myself for a few minutes?"

The young man escorted her from the floor. "Perhaps you would like some fresh air?"

"No," she tried to assure him, "I think I'll just rest in the library for a few moments." She took her leave graciously, then fled into the library and closed the heavy doors behind her. Her heart pounded so hard she felt as if she might faint, and her legs quivered. "Oh, Lord," she prayed, "deliver me!" She made her way across the room to Andrew's large leather chair in front of the fireplace and collapsed into the cushions. "He will be furious when he sees me. He will never give me a chance to explain." She spoke aloud, wishing she could disappear into thin air.

Hernando caught sight of the vision of loveliness just as Felicia vanished into the library. He waltzed his mother into the waiting arms of his father, made his way through the chattering throng of people, and slipped into the room that held the mysterious beauty.

It took his eyes a moment to adjust to the darkness; the room was illuminated by a single candelabrum and the flickering glow of the fire. "Good evening," he said softly, "I hope I'm not intruding."

Felicia, paralyzed with guilt, couldn't answer.

"I'm Hernando Dundee—I don't believe we've met," he volunteered as he walked to the walnut cabinet that served as a small bar. "May I get you a glass of wine?"

"That would be very nice," Felicia replied in a throaty voice.

Hernando poured two glasses of sherry. The odors of the room were familiar and sensual to him—walnut paneling waxed to perfection with palm oil and lemon, the pungent smell of the fine leather-bound books that lined the walls from floor to ceiling, and the sweet, smokeless aroma of well-dried mesquite and oak emanating from the fireplace. He handed the woman the wine, then positioned himself in the chair opposite from her. There was something else familiar—the faint odor of perfume. She was leaning far back in the chair, her face partially hidden in the shadows, and he couldn't see her features clearly. "Am I being rude—have we met before?"

Felicia rose gracefully and stood in front of the fire, her back to Hernando. "Perhaps, a long time ago."

He could see the gentle curve of her neck, the silhouette of her magnificent figure, and once again became aware of the slight fragrance of her perfume. Lilac. Surely he could not have forgotten meeting such a woman. He placed his glass on the side table and stood next to her, taking her shoulders gently and turning her to face him. She was more beautiful than he first suspected. Her skin was pale and flawless, her lips full and moist; the low cut of her gown hinted at the fullness of her breasts—and, he noted with satisfaction, she was breathing as passionately as he. Her face was familiar, as was her scent, but he couldn't for the life of him place where or when they had met before. She remained like a statue, neither drinking nor speaking.

His awareness of who she was came slowly. He stepped away from her, staring, first in wonder, then in total disbelief. "Felicia?"

She remained silent and lowered her eyes.

He reached out with one hand and removed the tiara and pins that held her hair in place. When her thick black curls fell in a cascade over her shoulders, he was sure of her identity. His gaze became cold, but his anger was controlled. "What kind of charade is this? What are you doing here?"

"It's not a charade—Hernando . . ."

He recalled the familiar figure dancing with Dolores and interrupted her. "You're here with Norton!" he accused. "And that gown must have cost him a pretty penny! You may look like a great lady, but I think you have forgotten your place!"

"What place is that?" Felicia cried, indignant that he would think Norton had purchased her gown. "Listen to me, please . . ."

"No! You listen to me. I don't appreciate your masquerade in my mother's house!" His realization that he wanted to take her in his arms, to kiss and caress her, made him more furious. "How dare you!" He paled and grabbed her by her shoulders, unable to contain himself. "I should thrash you to within an inch of your life!"

Andrew entered the room, shocked to see Hernando shaking Felicia as if she were a rag doll. "What are you doing? Stop that immediately!" he demanded, rushing to shield the woman from his son's wrath.

"You don't understand, Father. This woman is not who she pretends to be!" he responded, his features unrelentingly stiffened. "Do you know who she really is?"

"Yes, Hernando. Both your mother and I know who she really is—and we know what she once was!"

Hernando was jolted by his father's reply. "I don't understand."

"Understanding never was one of your strong points. Now apologize to Senora San Vincente immediately!" Andrew's tone was threatening. "You might have behaved like a swine to Senorita Montez, but that unfortunate creature has been dead for almost six months!"

Hernando clenched his fists. "I will never apologize to this woman!"

"Felicia, my dear, allow me a few minutes alone with my son,"—Andrew accompanied the quivering woman to the library door—"and dry those tears! It would upset Isabella no end if she were to see you in this condition." He kissed her forehead and closed the doors behind her.

"How could you allow this?" Hernando was outraged. "A whore in the same room with my mother!"

"Lillie Taylor's been welcome here for years. Why shouldn't Felicia be welcome?"

Hernando was too exasperated to answer. Andrew poured them both a glass of bourbon and continued. "In the West, where there are a hundred men to every woman, it's usually been the whore who's given love and comfort to lonely men. In San Francisco the mothers and grandmothers of the most prominent families were all whores!" Andrew smiled patiently.

> The miners came in '49
> The whores in '51
> And when they got together
> They made the native son!

"Without whores the men never would have stayed! And if they hadn't stayed, the West wouldn't be civilized like it is today. Think about it. Your mother knows that I speak the truth."

Hernando stared at his father, unable to believe the words he was hearing.

"Most of those women made very fine wives. You know, Hernando, women get married in order to find someone to take care of them. That's why Esther Mendoza married her husband, and that's why Sarah married Aaron. In most cases, especially out here, *love* has nothing to do with marriage. It's just a matter of convenience. And if it works out, the love comes later. But the fact is that a wife gets paid by one man to take care of his needs, and a whore gets paid by a number of men. That's the only difference."

"You can't mean that!" Hernando was incredulous.

"I do mean it. Some wives are ladies and some ain't. Some are kind and loving—some ain't. Some are clean and some are dirty. And it's the same with whores.

341

Felicia is one hell of a lady 'n got plenty of guts. A man could look around for quite some time and never find a woman who'd make as good a wife as she would." Andrew poured them both another drink and then sat quietly staring into the fire. He had never expressed his thoughts on the subject before, and now that he had verbalized them, he was sure he was correct. There were exceptions, of course, like Isabella. But those exceptions, where there was real love and respect *before* the marriage, were rare.

Hernando tried to make sense out of what his father had said. He recalled the Navajo name for whores—Woman Who Stands by the Side of the House. There was no stigma attached to prostitution by the Navajos. But he was not so easily convinced. He felt that Felicia had somehow made a fool of him, and he was not in a forgiving mood.

Felicia was in the powder room weeping uncontrollably when Esther found her. "Oh, Esther, please find Mr. Norton. I must go home."

"I'll find him right away and I'll go with you. I don't want you to be alone in this condition. Do you want me to get the doctor?"

"No. I'll be all right. I just want to go home."

Esther had never seen anyone look more miserable. She couldn't imagine what had happened to render Felicia into such a state, but she was determined to find out. Norton was nowhere to be found, so she summoned Sarah and Isabella and told them of Felicia's distress. The three women joined Felicia at once to try to be of comfort.

"I wouldn't think of allowing you to travel so far in this condition," Isabella informed her. "I'm going to put you to bed upstairs and fetch Dr. Vargas to examine you."

Felicia was too distraught to argue. She allowed herself to be led upstairs and put to bed. Dr. Vargas assured the ladies that she was not feverish and gave her an opiate to calm her nerves. Esther decided to stay with her until she fell asleep.

Hedrick Norton turned up the collar of Dolores's coat and put his arm around her to shield her from the cold. Being alone with her at last was almost more pleasurable than he could bear. "Are you sure you're warm enough?"

"Yes, I'm just fine. Tell me more about Santa Barbara," she asked, adoring the attention he was showering on her.

"I think I've told you everything there is to tell— except for one thing."

"And what is that?" she asked coyly.

"I've completely restored the hacienda. I've purchased back all the original land and have stocked it the way it was before your father died. It's once again one of the most beautiful showplaces in California."

Dolores stared at the older man. Strange, she thought, she had never before noticed how attractive he really was. "That's thrilling news! You must be very proud."

"Only one thing would make me more proud." His voice was husky and he looked away, afraid she might see the love he felt for her in his eyes and mock him.

"When I return to the Hacienda de la Castiaga—I would like you to be at my side—as my wife."

She took his face in her hands and turned it toward her. Then she kissed him lovingly on the lips. He couldn't believe the softness of her kiss. "I love you, Dolores," he whispered.

"I know. And I love you. And I accept your offer with gratitude."

He held her tightly, afraid that if he let go, she might vanish, or that he would waken and find that it had all been a dream. They were still locked in their embrace when Isabella found them.

"I'm sorry to interrupt," she stammered, not quite understanding what was happening.

Dolores broke from Norton and ran to Isabella. She had never been happier and her face was radiant. "Oh, dear Isabella, Hedrick and I are to be married! And then I will be going home. Isn't it wonderful?"

The news was so sudden and so shocking it took Isabella a moment to recover. She had planned on Dolores marrying Hernando for so long, she couldn't believe what she was hearing. Isabella looked searchingly at the young woman. In spite of her own feelings she realized that Dolores looked happier than Isabella had ever seen her. Then she stared at Hedrick. He seemed to have become suddenly young. Isabella moved forward to embrace them both. "I couldn't be more pleased for you. We shall have the wedding here at the hacienda, and I shall see to it personally that it is performed by the archbishop!" She decided it would be more prudent not to mention Felicia's illness. "Now let's go in and join the other guests—I'll have Andrew make the announcement."

* * *

The sumptuous feast was served at one o'clock in the morning. Colorfully dressed mariachi players strolled through the rooms serenading the guests while they enjoyed the food and wine. Hernando didn't join them, preferring instead to stay in the library and finish a full bottle of bourbon. Andrew helped his wife tend to the guests' needs before they sat down to dine in a quiet corner by themselves.

Dolores's decision to marry the banker delighted him. Well, he thought with pleasure, that was one stepping-stone out of the way. Now if he could find a way of overcoming Hernando's prejudice and Felicia's guilt, there might be a double ceremony.

At the first light of dawn the guests began leaving. Isabella made sure their drivers had been well fed and had plenty of coffee to keep them awake on their journeys home. By seven thirty all the guests had departed, and she began directing the massive cleanup. She could never rest comfortably until the house had some semblance of order.

Isabella checked the library and found Hernando asleep on the sofa, an empty bottle on the floor beside him. "Hernando," she whispered, "wake up, dear. You'll be more comfortable in your room!"

When he finally opened his eyes, he couldn't remember for a moment where he was—a habit he seemed to be falling into more and more lately. His vision was blurred and his head throbbed. He looked around the room and finally focused on his mother's face. She looked so lovely he thought for a fleeting second it was Felicia!

"Go upstairs, son. You'll be more comfortable."

After Hernando was maneuvered into his room, she checked on Felicia. Dr. Vargas's opiate had been very powerful, and the young woman was still asleep. Esther was asleep in the chair next to the bed and snoring loudly. Isabella found a blanket, covered her, put another log on the fire, then retired to her own room. She undressed quietly so she wouldn't disturb Andrew, but when she crawled into bed next to him, he turned over and put his arm around her. She snuggled close to him, knowing she was protected from all the pain and problems of the world—and fell asleep pleased that her Fiesta de Navidad had been a success.

Felicia and Esther Mendoza returned by carriage to Santa Fe before the Dundee family awakened. Only Dolores, still unaware of what had happened the night before, bid them farewell—and then only after she had exacted Felicia's promise to be matron of honor at the wedding.

When they were in the privacy of Felicia's home, she was finally able to tell Esther of her encounter with Hernando. "I don't know what I expected, but I suppose I got what I deserved. It was wicked of me to think that he might love me."

Esther didn't know what to say. She had never been aware of Felicia's feelings for the handsome Hernando. "What will you do now?"

"I'm not sure. I'd like to speak to Hedrick first—he's always been so wise. He certainly knew exactly how to get what he wanted! And have you ever seen Dolores so happy? I would have thought it was impossible, but now I really think they'll be quite compatible together."

"You must promise me you won't do anything in haste. You won't run away or go back to . . ." Esther rolled her eyes, unable to continue.

"No. I promise I will never go back to that." Felicia smiled at Esther's concern. "But I can't promise that I will remain in Santa Fe."

It was midafternoon before the Dundees, Dolores, and Hedrick Norton gathered together at the dining room table. Hernando was astounded to learn that Norton had come to Santa Fe to propose to Dolores. He hadn't even been aware that they were acquainted. It bothered him, too, that he'd probably been wrong in his attack on Felicia. But his pride was strong and he refused to think about it.

"I couldn't be more pleased for you," he told Dolores sincerely, "and I'd like to offer my services as best man—if your fiancé has no one else in mind."

"That would make the most perfect wedding. You can be best man and Chata will be matron of honor. Come to think of it, you and she would make a splendid couple."

"And who is Chata? I don't believe I know the name."

Andrew set down his knife and fork and folded his hands. "Senora Chata San Vincente. Some of her friends call her Felicia."

Hernando bristled at the mention of her name. He stared from one face to another, not for the life of him understanding how Felicia could have inspired such enthusiasm in his family and friends in such a short while. He wiped his mouth on his linen napkin. "Excuse me. Father, when you've finished, I'd like to discuss the business of Po'Se'Da', and a problem I'm having with Galen Eastman. I'll be at the stables with the men. On second thought perhaps I'll take a ride. See you later this evening."

Hernando left the table and stormed into the kitchen. The kitchen only served to remind him of what his mother had told him earlier. Phoebe had returned to her people! He brushed past Rosa and slammed the door, then he stomped over to the stable area and saddled his horse. He could always think more clearly when he was riding. The day was crisp and bright and the frozen ground crackled beneath his horse's hooves. He rode up the trail in back of the hacienda until he was high enough on the mountain to have a clear view of the valley below. Then he paused to rest. Most of his anger was gone, and he tried to recollect his feelings of the night before. In some ways his father had been correct. He had never been concerned or felt uncomfortable when Lillie Taylor was a guest in their home with her husband, but then he had never been to bed with Lillie Taylor. Nor had he known her when she was still practicing her profession. It was asking too much for his father to expect him to accept Felicia on the same terms he had accepted Lillie. Hernando knew there was more to his anger. When he had first seen her and was standing so close to her in the library, he had been dazzled by her poise and beauty. No woman had ever affected him like that before. Had she not been Felicia, he had no doubt that he would have taken her in his arms and never let her go! "Lord—Lord," he said. "What's happening to me?"

Below him he could see the hacienda buzzing with activity. The cowboys and cattle looked like toys from Hernando's vantage point. He suddenly felt very much alone. His home no longer seemed like his home, and his town no longer seemed like his town. He didn't seem to belong there anymore.

He and his father had much to discuss. It had recently occurred to him that there was need of a trading post in Wonderful Valley. When they finished their business, Hernando decided he would return immediately to Po'Se'Da'. It would not be the first Christmas he had spent away from home; and although he knew his mother would be saddened, he had no desire to risk another meeting with Felicia.

CHAPTER TWENTY-FOUR

With Hernando's departure from the trading post and the senseless murders of Hosteen Begay and Shell Woman, Carlin found himself in an extended period of depression. If it hadn't been for Bay Tsosie's gentle understanding and Mulie's decision to stay at the post for the winter, he might not have survived. Violent winds and gales prevented most of the Navajos from coming to the post to trade or sending their children to Carlin's small, informal classes. There were long periods of time when the trader had nothing to do.

Bah Tsosie took over the task of reading the evening stories, and during the day Mulie badgered Carlin into getting the chores done. They had laid in a good supply of wood during the summer and fall months, so the extent of their daily work—once the inventory had been taken—was minimal. Their greatest concern was keeping the spring from freezing over and emptying the ashes from the iron stove and fireplace.

Bah Tsosie had another concern. She was perplexed as to why Atwa Kee had become so attached to Hernando and was shy and reserved with Carlin. She looked up from her sewing one afternoon and watched the boy as he nuzzled the old sheep dog who was trying to sleep next to the fireplace. "Atwa Kee," she smiled and said, "you are very fond of Dog, aren't you?"

The boy nodded. Bah Tsosie continued, "And you are very fond of Man Who Honors Justice?" Once again the boy nodded. "Are you fond of Wise Teacher?"

Atwa Kee thought about his mother's question before he answered. "I don't like him as much as I like Man Who Honors Justice."

"Why not?"

Atwa Kee hugged his dog and then sat up to address his mother properly. "He is not one of us," he said firmly.

Bah Tsosie put her sewing aside and motioned for the boy to come sit on her lap. "I don't understand. You mean he is not one of the Diné?"

The boy acknowledged that that was what he meant. Bah Tsosie was puzzled. "But Man Who Honors Justice is not one of the Diné either."

"But his hair is the same color as ours, and his eyes are the same color as ours! Wise Teacher has hair the color of corn silk and his eyes are like the sky!" the boy exclaimed.

Bah Tsosie smiled and began to rock the boy. It took her a few minutes before she could think of a proper answer. Then she called the dog over to them and lifted his head. "Haven't you ever noticed that Dog has one blue eye and one brown eye?"

Atwa Kee sat up in his mother's lap and studied his dog's eyes. It was true. He had never thought of it before. His mother continued, "Utes have black hair and black eyes, and yet they are our enemies! And the raven and the eagle are not the same, but they are both birds."

Atwa Kee looked into his mother's face. He remained silent, weighing what she said and waiting for her to continue. "Wise Teacher can only be judged by his heart, and his heart is of the Diné. And his light hair and light eyes make him very special—just like Dog." It was something for Atwa Kee to think about.

They were interrupted as the men came into the kitchen from the bull pen. Mulie was chattering like a nervous magpie.

"Now lookee heyar, boy," Mulie informed Carlin in an exasperated tone of voice, "Ahm sick 'n tired o' yah sittin' 'round 'n mopin' day in 'n day out. Thar's nothin yah kin do fer those who's passed on to the happy huntin' ground. Yah gotta think o' the livin'—'n you 'n me's goin' out thar 'n find the biggest Christmas tree in the canyon!"

"But it's snowing," Carlin complained.

"So what? Yah ain't made o' clay—yer made o' flesh 'n blood—'n that wet weather ain't goin' to melt yah! Jest bundle up some, 'n the snow won't hurt yah none. Now I'll go saddle up the horses, 'n I'll give yah five minutes to find an ax 'n git yer ass out that door to meet me!"

Carlin knew it was useless to argue with the old man, so he found the ax, put on Hernando's long Mackintosh, and headed for the corral. Just as they mounted their horses, Bah Tsosie and Atwa Kee came running out of the post. "I go, too!" the boy screamed.

It was the most enthusiastic Carlin had seen the

child in the two weeks since Hernando had been gone, and he reached down and pulled the boy onto the front of his saddle. Bah Tsosie laughed and warned them not to stay out too long, then returned to the warmth of the post.

The snow floated down from the gray sky in large wet flakes, and Carlin was grateful there was no wind. They rode in silence for several miles before Mulie spotted a tree that seemed to suit him. It was a medium-sized palo verde tree, whose roots clung to a craggy ledge.

"That one ought ta do nicely," he called to Carlin. "Do yah like that one, Atwa Kee?"

The boy had no idea what the old trader had in mind, but, caught up in the spirit of things, he readily agreed. They dismounted and Carlin lifted the boy from the saddle. As he turned around, Mulie hit him full in the face with a sloshy snowball. At first he was shocked, then Atwa Kee squealed with laughter, and the free-for-all was on. They frolicked in the snow as if they were all children, and, after they were thoroughly soaked, decided it was time to cut down the tree and head back home. Mulie had the palo verde down and attached by rope to his saddle horn in record time.

The outing was like a tonic for Carlin. It had been years since he had enjoyed himself so much. He hugged the boy and began thinking about the future. Mulie was right—there was nothing he could do to bring back Hosteen Begay, and Phoebe had made it clear that there was no place in her life for the trader. He would have to put his sorrow behind him, and start making plans for the future of Po'Se'Da'. He missed Hernando's happy-go-lucky conversations and wondered how long he would be away.

It was almost dark before they returned to the post, and they were shivering with the cold. Bah Tsosie scolded them for being so late, but her anger didn't last long. After they had changed into dry clothing and eaten their fill of her supper, she picked up her book and prepared to continue their latest story.

"Not tonight," Mulie said with a twinkle in his eye. "Tonight we're goin' to decorate the tree. Ah ain't had a proper Christmas in more years than I care to remember, 'n this year I'm goin' to make sure we all have a proper Christmas."

Bah Tsosie had never decorated a Christmas tree, and thought the idea of having the palo verde *inside* the post was completely mad! However, Mulie soon had everybody popping and stringing Indian corn, turning the red berries from the Christmas cholla into garlands, and stringing pieces of colored paper and sleigh bells for decorations. Before long even Bah Tsosie was caught up in the holiday spirit. When they were finally finished, Atwa Kee stood back and stared, wide-eyed, at the miracle. It was the most beautiful sight he had ever seen.

"Now—tonight *I'm* goin' to tell the story!" Mulie informed them. He ignored Bah Tsosie's concern that it was too late and that they should all go to bed, and sat Atwa Kee down on his lap. His brow wrinkled as he tried to remember how the story began, but it came back to him after more than thirty years, for that was how long he had been a fugitive and had last seen his wives and children. He began, "Once upon a time, way fur across the sea, there wuz three wise men . . ."

It took him more than an hour to tell the story of the small babe in the manger, and when he finished, both Atwa Kee and Bah Tsosie were fast asleep. Carlin was about to doze off when they heard the sounds of horses. It was after ten o'clock, and Carlin was alarmed. Remembering his experience with Hosteen Begay, he loaded his rifle and had it ready as he unbolted the door. Mulie stood next to him, pistol in hand. Bah Tsosie stood near the kitchen, holding her sleeping son.

The light shining through the open door revealed a small detail of soldiers. Two Navajo police stood with them. "Mr. Napier?" the young officer asked.

"Yes, I'm Napier," Carlin replied, lowering his gun.

"I'm Lieutenant McCrea. Here on Army business."

"You and your men better come in and get warm, Lieutenant." Carlin made room for the men to enter.

Mulie reholstered his gun and sank down into one of the chairs. His shoulders sagged and his eyes clouded over with tears. He knew what was coming, and he knew there was nothing he could do about it.

The Lieutenant withdrew some official-looking papers from his leather pouch and directed his attention to the older man. "Mr. Turner?"

Mulie looked up into the face of the young officer. His eyes had the anguished look of a caged animal. "Yeah, I'm Turner."

"I have a warrant for your arrest, sir, for the murders of Eli Fancher, Robert Kimball, Jedidiah James, and Roland Mapes." He instructed his sergeant to manacle the prisoner.

Carlin was stunned. "There must be some mistake!"

"I'm afraid not, sir. We're here with the permission of the Navajo police at the direction of Galen Eastman, reservation agent." McCrea removed his hat and gloves and moved over to the fire. "It's my understanding that Mr. Turner has been a fugitive since the fall of 1855! Until now he's never stayed in one place long enough for the Army to catch up with him. There are names on the original warrant of men who actually witnessed the crime. They swore that this man killed the victims in cold blood."

Carlin turned to Mulie, expecting some defense or denial of the accusation. Mulie remained silent. His small frame seemed to shrink even smaller. "Wall, I gis ah ain't goin' to have sech a good Christmas after all."

"If you don't mind putting us up for the night, we'll be heading back for the fort in the morning. The authorities from Utah will pick him up there," the Lieutenant informed Carlin.

The next morning, as the soldiers prepared to move out, Carlin tried to comfort his friend. "I don't believe a word of it! There must be something we can do . . ."

Mulie seemed very old and very tired. "What he tol' yah wuz the Lord's truth! I wisht it warnt. I wuz a good Mormon in them days—cap'ain o' my militia. Would 'ave gone to hell 'n back fer Brigham! Those men I kilt wuz bastards! Insultin' our womenfolk—'n makin' fun o' our kids. Then they hurt my little girl. I jest couldn't stand it no more!" There were tears in the trader's eyes as he recalled the event of so many years before. "Some us got together 'n decided to put a stop to it once 'n fer all. We kilt ev'ry last one o' em!"

Carlin remained silent. There was nothing to say. In the short time he had known the old man he had never seen anyone so kind and gentle. The Navajos held him in highest regard, and even Andrew Dundee told stories of Mulie's bravery when they had traveled together in the wilderness many years before. The old Mormon had suffered an attack of madness just one time in his life and Carlin was sure it was justified. Now, after all these years, he would probably have to pay the supreme penalty.

Bah Tsosie, who usually showed so little emotion openly, wept as the soldiers took Mulie away.

"Take good care o' my mules, Carlin," the old trader called back. Then Carlin, too, wept.

The post seemed unnaturally quiet, and even the brightly decorated Christmas tree did little to lighten their spirits. Atwa Kee couldn't understand what had happened to his friend, and neither his mother nor Carlin could find the words to explain it to him. They weren't able to eat much dinner, and Carlin decided it might be well if they all retired early. Bah Tsosie agreed. She and Atwa Kee finished the dishes and left Carlin alone with his thoughts. He was deeply saddened because he knew the reason Mulie had been captured after all these years was because of his decision to remain at Po'Se'Da'. He realized it had been Mulie's hunger for companionship that had kept him at the post. Every man needed companionship and every man needed a family. He imagined his family in Scotland would be decorating their tree soon—it wouldn't be a palo verde—but a tall Scots pine. Holly and heather would be tied with tartan ribbons, and mugs of hot eggnog served to their guests. Before dawn on Christmas morning his father would gather the presents that had been hidden throughout the house and lay them, with great care, beneath the tree.

Then he recalled Mulie's words: "Nothing you can do for those who have passed on. You have to think of the living!" Carlin would miss the old-timer, but what he had said was true. There was nothing he could do for Mulie; he had to think of Bah Tsosie and Atwa Kee. They needed him. And he needed them. He needed their love and companionship!

He found a big log, one he was sure would burn until morning, put it on top of the hot embers, then went to his own quarters. Hard as he tried, sleep would not come. Finally he gave up and made his way to Bah Tsosie's room. He rapped softly on the door, thinking perhaps she might still be awake, and they could talk. He was about to retrace his steps when she opened the door. She was wearing a long, white flannel nightgown, and her thick dark hair fell loosely over her shoulders. She looked longingly up at him, and untied the ribbon at her throat, allowing her gown to slip to the floor. Carlin appraised her slender and feminine body, swept her up into his arms, and carried her to his bed. Perhaps he was not a virgin, but when he made love to Bah Tsosie, it was as if he were making love for the first time! Their bodies fit together as if they had been made for each other— their kisses were gentle, but filled with fire. He felt her join him in his climax, and it was as if he suddenly knew the meaning of life! She was his woman! The fulfillment of his destiny!

"We'll be married in the spring," he informed her.

"In the Navajo custom?"

"Yes," he agreed, "in the Navajo custom."

Then, wrapped in each other's arms, they fell asleep.

CHAPTER TWENTY-FIVE

Hernando was riding past Spiegelberg's store on his way out of town when he remembered that it was Christmastime. He didn't want to return to the post without something special for Atwa Kee, Bah Tsosie, and Carlin, so he decided to go to the Spiegelbergs' home to see if he could convince Aaron to open the store for him.

Sarah had always been fond of Hernando, and although he hadn't been a guest in their home often, she welcomed him warmly and insisted he come inside for a bowl of hot chicken soup. It was impossible for anybody to refuse to eat when they visited Sarah and Aaron Spiegelberg, and before he knew what he was about, Hernando found himself seated at their dining-room table. After his second bowl of soup his mood improved considerably and he was able to explain to Aaron why he had come.

"You're going back to Po'Se'Da' so soon? Well, of course I'll open the store for you, Hernando, but only if you agree to spend the night with us. It's much too late to be starting out for the reservation. We'll go down and pick out what you want, and you get a nice start early in the morning!"

Sarah was just as determined as Aaron, and Hernando found himself accepting their kind offer.

The Spiegelbergs had six children, ranging in age from six to eighteen. Three girls and three boys. Sarah insisted each child learn to play a musical instrument, and after dinner each night, she and Aaron were entertained with a family concert. Tonight was no exception. The older boys, Herbert and Leonard, played violin and guitar; Rebecca and Hannah played piano and viola; and the younger children, Jeremiah and Ruth, played mandolin and tambourine. Hernando found himself enchanted with the talented family. The children were all exceptionally good-looking, and not the least bit shy when it came to displaying their talent.

"Uncle Hernando," Rebecca asked, "do you have a favorite song?"

Hernando thought for a moment, then replied, "Yes, Rebecca, my favorite song is 'Streets of Laredo'!"

Rebecca tapped her foot for the proper beat and began to play. Herbert put down his violin and stood next to the piano; in a clear tenor he began to sing:

> As I walked out in the streets of Laredo,
> As I walked out in Laredo one day,
> I spied a young cowboy wrapped up
>   in white linen,
> Wrapped up in white linen, and cold
>   as the clay . . .

The other children joined in the chorus.

> So beat the drum slowly and play
>   the fife lowly . . .

Hernando thought of young Hosteen Begay as they sang. An Indian cowboy who had died too soon. And he thought of Felicia. "Streets of Laredo" had been her favorite song, too. He sighed. Somehow he felt as if she had betrayed him, but he wasn't sure how. Did she love him as his father had said? Had he ever loved her? Could he ever love anyone? He had no answers to his questions.

When the song was finished he applauded the children and asked to be excused. "I have tough days in the saddle ahead of me—and this will probably be the last good night's sleep I'll have for a week!"

Sarah led him to the guest room and gave him a motherly peck on the cheek. "Sleep well. I'm sure things will look brighter in the morning."

Aaron wakened him before sunrise and the men had a quiet cup of coffee together before the rest of the family stirred. Hernando was curious as to whether or not Aaron knew Felicia.

"Well, Sarah's very fond of her," Aaron answered in a noncommittal voice when Hernando questioned him about the widow San Vincente. Then he was thoughtful. "And she's a very beautiful woman. I like beautiful women, but I wouldn't want to marry one!"

Hernando laughed. "But do you know anything about her background?"

"What's to know? If my wife likes her, you can believe that she is a very fine person. My wife never makes a mistake about people. Why do you ask, Hernando?"

"I'm not sure myself, Aaron. But I do know I must be on my way."

Hernando stopped by the warehouse to pick up some pack mules and supplies. At Aaron's store he had chosen a complete western outfit for Atwa Kee, including cowboy boots and broad-brimmed hat as well as a toy holster and gun. He decided on a bolt of pale-blue velveteen and some ivory combs for Bah Tsosie, and a fringed buckskin jacket and some books for Carlin.

If it hadn't been for the smoke rising from the great stone chimney, Hernando would have thought that Po'Se'Da' was deserted. The cottonwoods were bare, the corrals looked deserted, and with the exception of an oversized jack rabbit that scurried into the hay shed, there was no sign of life. He unsaddled his horse, loosened the cinches on the pack mules, threw the large sack of gifts over his shoulder, and proceeded into the post.

The bull pen was deserted. "Anybody home?" he called from the door.

His voice brought Atwa Kee and Carlin running from the kitchen to greet him. He dropped his sack and hugged them both. "Good to be home!"

"We didn't expect you so soon! I was sure you'd spend the holiday with your family!" Carlin exclaimed.

"That's what I'm doin'! This *is* my family." Hernando laughed at the surprised expression on Carlin's face, then spotted the palo verde tree. "Never thought

I'd live to see the day when we'd have a Christmas tree in Po'Se'Da'—looks great. Now help me put the gifts around it and we'll be in business!" Hernando grabbed the delighted child and threw him up onto his shoulders. "Where's your ma?"

"I'm here," Bah Tsosie answered, standing serenely in the doorway of the kitchen. "Welcome back."

"Hope you got a pot of stew on the fire. I haven't had a good meal in a week—'n after I've had somethin' to eat," he instructed Carlin, "you n' me better get out to the corral 'n unload some mules. And speaking of mules, where in the hell are the animals?"

"Mulie built a new corral and shed over on the south side of the hill—thought the animals would be better sheltered for the winter."

"Mulie still around?"

Carlin finished emptying the sack before he replied. "Let's get you some stew and coffee, then I'll tell you about it."

Hernando recognized the uneasiness in Carlin's voice and with Atwa Kee still on his shoulders followed the trader into the kitchen. For some reason it was not the homecoming that Hernando imagined. Atwa Kee climbed down from his perch and seated himself comfortably on Carlin's lap. Bah Tsosie was pleasant yet reserved. But it was Carlin's attitude that puzzled him the most. The young Scot had always been enthusiastic, ready to forge ahead, and filled with a boyishness and naiveté that Hernando had not found in other men. Carlin seemed more somber now—more deliberate in his speech and actions. Hernando was concerned. "What's the problem—what happened to Mulie?"

Carlin related the story of how the soldiers had come to the post accompanied by the Navajo police, and how the arrest had been authorized by Galen Eastman.

"When did all this happen?"

"Almost a week ago."

Hernando was thoughtful. "Where did they take him?"

"Fort Defiance. The authorities were to pick him up there and return him to Utah Territory to face trial."

Hernando turned to Bah Tsosie. "Any chance of getting the Navajo telegraph in action so's we could see what's going on? If I could get word to Hoskinini, maybe he could break him out." Even as he spoke, Hernando knew that it would be impossible to save the renegade Mormon, but it saddened him to think that perhaps if he had been there something might have been done. Eastman was a bastard, but his father had promised to write to some of his powerful friends in Washington and start the wheels in action for the agent's removal.

At dinner it finally became apparent to Hernando why he felt uncomfortable. He was sure Carlin and Bah Tsosie had become lovers while he had been away. He could sense it in their glances, and the way Carlin's hand lingered on Bah Tsosie's hand when something was passed across the table. Even something in the tone of their voices as they spoke to each other seemed to exclude him from their midst. Once again Hernando felt an overwhelming sense of loss, the same feeling he had experienced high on the mountain above his hacienda. A feeling that a period of life was over.

Later, when he crawled into his bedroll, he tried to analyze his feelings. He was sure he wasn't jealous. Although he had been physically attracted to the Navajo woman, he had not wanted to compromise her. Sometime, he wasn't sure just when, the physical attraction he had originally felt for Bah Tsosie had turned to fondness, and he began to appreciate her special qualities.

Aware that Carlin, too, was having difficulty sleeping, Hernando whispered, "Do you love her?"

"Yes."

"That's nice. I'm happy for you both." Hernando stared into the darkness and knew he was no longer needed at Po'Se'Da'. Carlin could handle the trading quite well without him. Nor did his adopted brother need his companionship—he had Bah Tsosie's love. Hernando closed his eyes and wondered if there was any place in this great land where he was wanted or needed.

After the gifts were opened Christmas morning, Hernando reached a decision about what he must do. It was time to travel on to the north country. To Wonderful Valley. Carlin and Bah Tsosie helped him pack up Mulie Turner's pack train, bells and all, and included two bottle of forbidden wine for Dinet-Tsosi and Hoskinini.

"Wish you'd reconsider and stay with us until spring. I'm going to be worried about you out wandering around all through the winter," Carlin told him.

"Nothin' could get to a tough old bachelor like me," Hernando assured him, fingering his new compass with admiration. " 'Sides, with a gift like this—and the new moccasins yer gal made me, I feel like a pretty lucky fellow. I'll be droppin' in from time to time, but now that Mulie's gone there are quite a few families scattered around out there who never make it to a trading post, 'n they'll be plenty happy to see me." He reached down and pulled Atwa Kee up onto his saddle. "You be a good boy 'n take care o' things around here 'til I get back. Help your ma and mind what Carlin tells you. Okay?"

The boy pressed his tear-stained cheek against Hernando's and promised he would do as he was told. The trader then handed him into Carlin's waiting arms, squared his Stetson, and rode out of the compound leading the bell-laden pack train. It was good to be free.

During the next few months Hernando Dundee learned the true meaning of what it meant to be an Indian trader. On more than one occasion he recalled his father's words. "We must establish *commerce* with the Indians and at all costs prevent their *conquest!* If the Indian cultures die, the traders die; and if that happens there is no hope for mankind. If the Indians prosper, we will prosper; and they can only prosper if they are treated equally and with dignity!"

In addition to trading Hernando found himself acting as financial advisor, banker, marriage counselor, teacher, confidant, mortician, and diplomat. He found that it wasn't renegades but ignorance and the natural elements that were to be feared. He rode the length and breadth of the reservation and at times found archaeological sites he knew had never before been seen by any white man. It didn't take long for him to realize that if these sites were to remain sacred and unspoiled, it was best not to mention them to any other of the Anglos whose paths crossed his on occasion.

He visited other posts, some of which were managed by good traders and a few that were run by men who were outright thieves who exploited the Indians to the breaking point. He knew that it would only be a matter of time before these coyotes were driven out of business—by death or accident or bankruptcy.

He camped during blizzards where the wind was so fierce drifts were piled more than twenty feet high; and he passed through country so sparsely settled that he never saw or spoke to another human being for weeks at a time. There were days, as winter thawed and spring was near, when he thought the solitude would drive him mad. It was at times like this that he spoke aloud to his horse or to the mules or to a curious wild creature who, still unused to man, had no fear and stood its ground as he passed by. When the desert began to color with wildflowers, Hernando decided it was time to return to Po'Se'Da'; he had need of a good chess game with Carlin and some of Bah Tsosie's strong coffee. From the post he planned to return to Santa Fe and make the arrangements with his father to try to secure another trading permit so they could build a new post in Wonderful Valley.

This post, if they were able to secure the license, would be *his*! It would be built according to his specifications on the exact spot where Hoskinini's children had found him dying. He would call it *Há jishzhiis*—

Where He Came Out Dancing. Hernando smiled as he rode southward, planning what he would say to Carlin and Bah Tsosie, how he would greet his father, and what they would say to each other. There was something else he would do when he got to Santa Fe; that is, if she was still there. He would make a bargain with Felicia. If she would live with him at *Há jish-zhíis* for one year—and the Navajos accepted her—and if she still thought she loved him at the end of that time, he would take her as his wife.

CHAPTER TWENTY-SIX

Dolores Castiaga became the bride of Hedrick Edward Norton in an elaborate ceremony performed, as Isabella had promised, by Archbishop Lamy. Andrew acted as father of the bride, and Felicia, her head held high, was maid—not matron—of honor. When the couple said their good-byes, and the holidays were over, Felicia put her social calendar aside in order to try to get a true perspective on her life.

Her confrontation with Hernando had left her shattered, and although it wasn't apparent to those who didn't know her well, the scars were slow to heal. She forced herself to help Sarah with charitable works, enjoyed an occasional dinner with Isabella and Andrew, but, with the exception of visiting with Esther, preferred to remain alone most of the time.

"You can't go on like this, you know," Esther commented one day as they sat sipping tea. "You've been moping around like a wounded lizard too long. Spring is here and you should be outside puttering in the garden or buying bright new dresses and meeting gay young bachelors."

"I know you mean well, Esther, but I'm just not up to it. Perhaps in a few weeks."

"A few weeks might be too late."

"I don't understand . . ." Felicia looked at her friend in surprise.

"You are suffering from a severe case of self-pity, and a total lack of self-confidence. Those are two diseases of the soul that can totally destroy a person. I know. They almost destroyed me once long ago." Esther put her cup aside and continued. "Mr. Mendoza was not my first love."

Felicia watched quietly as Esther rose and walked slowly to the window.

"My first love, my real love, was a handsome, arrogant Irishman who hired me as a tutor for his children. He was a young widower, and it was my first position," Esther confided. She sighed, pained at the recollection, then forced herself to continue. "There was never anything improper between us, but I worshipped the ground he walked on. I would have done anything in the world for him. To make a long story short I was in his employ for fourteen years. Raised and educated his three children as if they were my own—loved them as if they were my own—and when the youngest, Ian, reached his eighteenth birthday and was married, Michael called me into his study and handed me an envelope." The older woman turned to face Felicia, her voice soft and resigned. "It contained twenty dollars severance pay."

Felicia gasped. Esther motioned her to be silent. "I really haven't been totally honest," her voice was barely audible. "I said there was nothing between us— and that is not true. I shared his bed for twelve of those fourteen years."

"And he dismissed you with twenty dollars severance pay?" Felicia was aghast. "What did you do?"

"I took the envelope, went to my room and packed, then hired a carriage to drive to St. Louis. I found a room in a boardinghouse and a job teaching in a small school. But there was only one problem: I lost my appetite and couldn't eat. One day I woke up and found myself in a hospital room, too weak to move. I didn't care. I just turned to the wall and decided to die."

Felicia rushed to her friend's side and embraced her. "How horrible!" she cried. "You are one of the dearest, kindest women I've ever known. I can't bear to think you've suffered so."

Esther hugged Felicia compassionately, then they sat down. "I was saved by a salty old nurse who simply refused to let me die! She forced me to eat, to speak, to smell the flowers, and praise the Lord. She forced me to look in a mirror—and every time I wailed about how ugly I was she'd slap me. 'How dare you say that?' she'd scream. 'You were created in the image of God and God is not ugly.' She finally got me to a point where I was actually laughing! Then she read the notice Mr. Mendoza had placed in the paper, advertising for a wife. I answered the ad and the rest is history."

Felicia was flabbergasted by her friend's story. After a time she asked, "What do you think I should do?"

"First of all, I think you should begin building a better opinion of yourself. Everything else will fall into place. Why don't you start by talking to Father Vieja?"

Felicia nodded and lowered her head. "Of course,

you're right. I shall call on him first thing in the morning."

The next day was the first of many meetings with the Father. Felicia and he would read passages from the Bible, passages Father Vieja thought applied to Felicia's position, and then they would talk.

"I think you should look closely at this verse, child," the priest instructed her one day. "Chapter seven, verse forty-seven. We discussed it some time ago, but I fear you have forgotten it."

Felicia took the Bible and read aloud in Spanish: " 'Wherefore I say unto thee, Her sins, which are many, are forgiven; for she loved much: but to whom little is forgiven, the same loveth little.' "

"Go on, Felicia. Read the next verse."

" 'And he said unto her, Thy sins are forgiven.' " Felicia closed the book slowly, and stared wide-eyed at her priest. "I remember now, but does that mean that *I'm* forgiven?"

"I am quite certain that our Lord has looked into your heart and found it pure. The great question now, Felicia, is have you forgiven yourself?"

CHAPTER TWENTY-SEVEN

Carlin sat in the sweat lodge preparing himself for his wedding ceremony. He breathed deeply, drawing the purifying steam into the recesses of his lungs. There was a clarity to his thinking that he had never experienced before, as if the light of truth had suddenly illuminated his brain. He felt certain that he had not been the master of his fate nor the captain of his destiny. Instead, it seemed that a divine power had maneuvered him into a position that was his right and perfect place in the universe.

This power had taken him halfway around the world to an alien land—he was still not sure for what purpose his presence was intended—but he felt, somehow, that he would be ready when that purpose was revealed. It seemed that all his training for a life at sea had really been preparing him for life in the uncharted desert. His knowledge of navigation enabled him to map the desolate reservation lands as easily as he had steered a course across the ocean.

His education under the iron fist of Captain Jonathan Waldren instilled in him rigid self-discipline and had given him a true picture of right and wrong—and good and evil. Even his brief encounter with the

Chinese and their philosophy had been of help in preparing him for his life among the Navajo.

He intended to expand his school and one day build a hospital for his adopted people. All of his energy would be devoted to bringing pride and independence to the Navajos.

His vision expanded and he knew with great certainty that one day he would be able to see his family in Scotland. There was no doubt in his mind that it would only be for a short visit. This land, the land of the Navajo, would from this day forward always be his true home.

Carlin and the important tribal leaders agreed that some of the marriage customs would be fulfilled and others set aside. Because Bah Tsosie had very few living relatives, her maternal uncle was chosen to give the necessary consent for the marriage and set the date. According to the law the wedding was planned for an odd number of days after the betrothal agreement and would take place in a hogan built especially for the ceremony. Her uncle graciously accepted the traditional gift of ten horses and predicted a long and fruitful union.

Carlin was not allowed to see Bah Tsosie for twenty-four hours prior to the ritual, and now as he dressed he realized how much he missed her in just that short period of time.

Navajos who traded at the post regularly provided the prospective bridegroom with traditional gifts of turquoise-and-silver jewelry to ensure he would be well dressed for the occasion and proudly sport a splendid showing of wealth.

Late in the afternoon of the chosen day Bah Tsosie's

uncle and her few remaining aunts and cousins rode up to Po'Se'Da', parked their wagons, and, impressively dressed in their finest apparel, made their way to the wedding hogan. Carlin, well coached, solemnly entered the bowllike structure and proceeded around to his left until he reached a place opposite the doorway where purified blankets had been placed. He sat down, cross-legged, and waited. Within moments Bah Tsosie's uncle entered the hogan carrying a container of water, a ladle, and a small buckskin pouch filled with corn pollen. After what seemed to Carlin an eternity, Bah Tsosie entered holding her wedding basket, which contained specially prepared cornmeal mush. Carlin's heart almost stopped as he glimpsed her beauty. She walked slowly and proudly around to the same side of the hogan where her betrothed was seated and set the basket down before him. When she had taken her place on the blanket next to Carlin, her uncle sat down beside them and the ritual was begun.

First he handed Bah Tsosie the ladle and directed her to pour water over her bridegroom's hands as he washed them. To Carlin the intent was clear. It was a symbolic act of entering into the marriage with clean hands. Then her uncle adjusted the wedding basket so that its open edge pointed to the east. With a pinch of pollen from his medicine bag he drew a line from east to west across the mush, then from south to north, and finished by encircling the mush near the edge of the basket with a thin line of pollen.

Carlin then took a pinch of the mush at the point where the lines met at the eastern edge of the basket and ate it; Bah Tsosie followed suit. In like manner the bride and groom took pinches of the cornmeal from the south, the west, the north, and the center. After this the basket was passed to relatives sitting nearby, who finished eating the mush.

When the contents of the wedding basket had been completely devoured, Carlin listened attentively as Bah Tsosie's uncle instructed them on what their exact duties to one another would be. His sage advice was followed by additional sermons from the rest of her clan—and then at last the service was complete.

Bah Tsosie's aunts and other women of her clan spent days preparing the feast for the ceremony, and Navajos from as far as a hundred miles around had ridden horseback or driven their wagons into the compound for the happy event. A dozen different kinds of breads and cakes, squash, beans, mutton stews, and strong sweet coffee were served. The celebration lasted for several days.

Atwa Kee, as young as he was, took everything in stride, but complained loudly to his new father when the post was closed down for several hours. "No good for business! I run post. Okay?"

Carlin gazed fondly at the child. "You run post—okay!" He put his arm around the lovely Navajo woman who had become his wife. "Andrew Dundee would be proud of our son. He shows a good head for business!"

Shortly after the wedding celebration, when things began to return to normal, Hernando Dundee rode into the compound. He was heavily bearded and wore his hair Indian style in two braids. If it hadn't been for his pack train, Carlin might not have recognized him.

They clung to each other, unashamed of their open affection. "Thank God, you're safe!" Carlin told him in a choked voice.

Hernando stayed only long enough to congratulate the couple and tell them of his adventures and news of the outlying districts of the Navajo land. "Eastman didn't wait for the authorities from Utah. He conducted the trial for Mulie himself and hung him the same day he arrived!" he told them sadly. "I'm anxious to get on to Santa Fe and find out if my father has made any progress in having that madman replaced." He said nothing of his plans for the new trading post or of Felicia. He allowed Bah Tsosie to trim his hair but insisted on maintaining his beard. Then, when he was thoroughly rested, he took his leave.

For the first time in his adult life Hernando made no stops in Santa Fe before reaching his home. His attitude was subdued and respectful as he kissed his mother and shook hands with his father.

"It's been a long time!" Andrew said, reluctant to release the handshake. "You're thin. First have something to eat, then why don't you go upstairs and rest? We'll have plenty of time to talk after that."

"Just one thing," Hernando hesitated. "Has there been any word of Phoebe?"

Andrew and Isabella exchanged glances. "No. We haven't heard a word from her since she left," Andrew replied sadly.

"I pray for her every day," Isabella added. "I dream at times that there is a rap at the door—I open it—and there stands Phoebe with a small babe in her arms. I know in my heart that she is safe, and when she is ready, she will come home."

Hernando put his arm around his mother's shoulder. "I believe she will, too."

Hernando slept the clock around, then met with his father. It was as if he were visiting a dear friend, and they talked as they had never talked before. Andrew thoroughly approved of applying for a new permit to establish a trading post in Wonderful Valley. "As for your relationship with Felicia, it will be up to her to decide. She's been living a very quiet life since you left. I've seen her a few times since Dolores's wedding; your mother sees her more often. I don't pry into what they talk about." He poured Hernando a brandy. "I do have some good news, though. Let me find that letter."

He rummaged through the papers on his desk until he found what he had been searching for, then seated himself down in the large leather chair opposite his son and read:

Your recommendation for the removal of Galen Eastman as government agent for the Navajo people was strong enough to move us to begin an immediate investigation. We had had many complaints, Andrew, but yours was the first we considered valid. Your claims regarding his attitude and actions have been substantiated to a point of being shocking, and for that reason, you may rest assured that by the time you receive this letter, he will already have been recalled. In the interim, General Thomas Boyd will be acting agent.

We would greatly appreciate any recommendation from you as to whom we might appoint to that position permanently. The man should be of strong moral fiber, intelligent, have a working knowledge of the Indian way of life and their culture, and it would be helpful if he spoke, or understood, the Navajo language.

With greatest respect,
Your devoted friend,
Edward Hatch
Brevet Major General
Commander, Headquarters District
of New Mexico Territory.

Hernando smiled, pleased at the fact that his father had taken such immediate action. "And have you made any recommendations?"

Andrew grinned, his eyes sparkling. "Yes, I have," he said. "I've recommended Carlin Napier for the post of Indian Agent to the Navajo Nation!"

Hernando leaned back and shook his head approvingly. It was a splendid choice. "And who will take his place at Po'Se'Da'?"

"You can, if you like. If not, now that things are running so smoothly, I'm sure I'll find someone who can do a proper job. I'd like a married man, of course. Now that there are proper facilities for a woman."

Hernando was thoughtful. "I'd like to take a few days before I give you my answer."

Andrew rose and walked to the door. "Take all the time you need, son. Whatever you decide will be fine with me."

* * *

Hernando, his beard trimmed and his clothes freshly pressed, stood in the foyer of Felicia's home, waiting for the servant girl to announce his arrival. He fingered his beaver hat nervously as he grudgingly admired the decor.

"The senorita will see you now, senor," the girl announced, motioning him to follow her into another part of the house.

He found Felicia seated in a bright, sun-filled room with large windows that faced a well-tended garden. She was embroidering and glanced up briefly from her work as he entered.

"It's nice to see you again, Hernando," she said politely.

He was surprised to find Esther Mendoza seated in another corner of the room. Embarrassed, he hesitated for a moment, then crossed the room to kiss the hand of the elder woman. "Aunt Esther, how well you're looking."

"I think you're looking well, too, Hernando. Although I must admit I can hardly see your face with that beard." She studied him closely. "It's rather attractive, I suppose, but it does make you look older."

"May I offer you some tea? Or some sherry?" Felicia ventured.

"That would be very nice. The sherry would be fine." Hernando flushed, remembering the last time they had drunk sherry together in his father's library. Once again he was sharply aware of her fragile beauty. It seemed impossible that this lovely creature sitting so graciously opposite him was the same passionate, irreverent toy whom he had used so badly.

Felicia rang a small bell to summon her maid and asked that the sherry and one glass be brought for her guest. Hernando watched her closely, relieved to find that his attraction for her had not lessened.

He and Esther chatted about his new role as a trader and the changes that had taken place in his life. After a time, noticing how restless he was becoming, Esther excused herself.

"Must you go?" Felicia asked in a pleading voice. "I had hoped that we would lunch together."

"If you have no better offer, we surely will," Esther replied, giving Hernando a brief but meaningful glance. "But for the present I have a thousand things that need my attention."

"Let me show you to the door," Felicia insisted, dreading her time alone with the man she loved.

"I can find my own way quite well."

Hernando and Felicia sat in awkward silence for several minutes after the widow departed. Finally Hernando summoned the courage to apologize for his past unseemly behavior and to inform her of the conditions for their future relationship.

As she listened her fingers worked rapidly pushing her needle back and forth through the hoop. She didn't look at him as he spoke. When she was sure he had finished, she laid the sewing aside and stared out into the garden. At last she turned to him. "Let me be sure I understand you correctly, Hernando. If I agree to accompany you back to the reservation for one year as your mistress, and at the end of that time you are satisfied with my performance, *and* the Navajos accept me, you will agree to marry me. Is that correct?"

Hernando suddenly felt uncomfortable and squirmed in his chair. He was at a loss to understand why his words, which just moments before had seemed so proper and generous, now had a hollow ring. "Yes, that is what I propose."

She looked directly into his eyes and smiled sadly. "I'm sorry, but I must refuse your offer." Her voice was soft, yet the tone was determined. "It isn't because I don't love you. I do. Very deeply. But I have also learned to love myself." She leaned slightly forward. "I made some very unfortunate decisions when I was younger about what I wanted out of life. Those same decisions, as wrong as they were, enabled me to meet you and to acquire the life-style I now enjoy here in Santa Fe. I cannot change the past, as sordid as it was, but I can be grateful for what has emerged from the ashes. Hernando, my dearest, I would accompany you, willingly and happily, anywhere in the world. But *not* as your mistress. Only as your wife. We have known each other for more than five years, and if you feel you must still test me, you do not love me. Knowing that, I wouldn't walk across the street with you."

Hernando couldn't believe his ears. He was angered by the divination of what she was saying, for it was in direct contrast to the dialogue he had envisioned. He placed his glass on the sideboard, bowed, and left the room without a word or backward glance.

The crisp spring air soothed his pounding head as he stormed from the house. His first inclination was to mount his horse and ride as far and as fast away from Santa Fe as he could—but instead he decided to walk.

"How dare she make demands," he said, talking to himself. "Wife indeed!" And yet he knew in his heart that Felicia was the only woman in the world for him.

An hour later he returned to her home and entered without knocking or waiting to be announced. He found her where he had left her and could tell she had been crying. "If I could, I would promise you that you would never cry again," he whispered as he took her into his arms. He kissed her swollen eyes and tear-stained cheeks. "I love you, Felicia, and I've just come from the Archbishop's. He will perform the ceremony next Sunday in the Cathedral."

She nestled in his arms, safe and sure. She felt as if she were a very special woman—and with her man by her side, she would help "tame the land!"